CU00842991

SURVIVAL

Invasion of the Dead
Book 2

OWEN BAILLIE

ISBN: 1500709964
ISBN-13: 978-1500709969

Edited by Monique Happy Editorial Services
Copyeditor Monique Happy
www.indiebookauthors.com

Cover design by Clarissa Yeo
www.yocladesigns.com

ACKNOWLEDGMENTS

Thank you to Vinnie Orlando and Michiko Malcolm for their continued thirst for the story and ongoing excellent feedback. To newbies Joe Barker and DeLinda Jiles, your observations were simply outstanding, and far beyond my expectations.

To a fabulous team of first time beta readers–Shannon Sharpe, Wendy Johnson, Karen Dziegiel, George Velos, Erica Hill Strauss, Alana Sullivan, Rob Stevens, and Lisa Hillman–thank you for your time and generous comments. You all helped to improve the story, and I'm so grateful for you were part of the process.

A big thank you to Monique Lewis Happy, my editor at MHES, who did a super job under challenging circumstances. Her ongoing support is tremendous, and without her, I'd receive a ton of reviews and e-mails about poor grammar and bad word choice.

Thank you to my wife, Donna, for her endless support and encouragement, and for always doing the dishes (amongst a million other things). To my three daughters, sorry my writing time sometimes meant I couldn't spend time with you, but I am making it up.

Last but not least, thank you to all the readers who purchased Book One, who left a review or sent messages on Facebook or via e-mail. Never underestimate your generous words and encouragement. You are helping my dream come true.

WARNING: Adults only. This book contain high-level violence and coarse language.

PREVIOUSLY

Survival is the second volume of a much longer series called Invasion of the Dead, a post-apocalyptic zombie tale set in the south-eastern states of Australia.

The first volume, Aftermath, tells briefly of a high-ranking army official and a government scientist in an underground defense department facility in Canberra. As the final survivors, they consider their options to counteract the virus that has killed millions across the globe.

Nearby, five friends in their late twenties return from a camping trip in the Snowy Mountains to their hometown of Albury. Callan is trying to bridge the gap with his girlfriend of two years, Sherry, a self-centered and tactless beauty. Kristy, Callan's sister and a doctor, grows closer to her old friend, Dylan (who was somewhat of a nemesis to Callan in high school), and Greg (a beer drinking country boy, also Callan's best friend) who has fancied Kristy since they were children.

At a remote gas station, Kristy finds an old newspaper that reports a virus has killed millions of people along the east coast of Australia. Concern grows when they discover the old couple who own the place have committed suicide.

An encounter with a sick, elderly man on the roadside leads to a conflict, where he snatches a gun from Callan and shoots himself dead. At a toilet stop on a back country road, Greg asks Kristy if she has feelings for him, but she explains she thinks of him as a brother. They find another abandoned store along the dirt road, where Sherry tells Dylan she slept with Callan's best mate, Johnny.

Back on the main highway, they find an army roadblock and an infected soldier eating through a pile of bodies. The soldier attacks Kristy as they try to escape. Greg saves her, and Kristy is lucky not to have been scratched or bitten.

Reaching Albury, they suffer a flat tire and must change it. Seeing a house with a faint light on inside, they request help, but are denied. They bungle through the tire change, and as they escape in the car, a horde of zombies wanders down the road towards them.

In the town center, they discover another mob of undead, and the pathway towards Callan's parents' house is thwarted. A dog taunts the zombies, then runs off into the night. They alter course towards Dylan's parents' house.

After reaching the property, Dylan is attacked by several zombies as he opens the gate. Greg saves the day. They enter the house in darkness and find it deserted, although it is clear that Dylan's parents were there recently. Unloading supplies from the Jeep, Greg goes missing, and Callan rushes out to find him. A tap on the window draws Dylan and the girls; his mother looks in with the twisted face of a zombie.

Looking for Greg, Callan kills a zombie and saves Greg, who is fighting off another inside the shed. Greg is wounded though. Dylan confronts his mother, but fails to kill her, and she attacks him. Callan arrives and finishes her. Kristy stitches up Greg's wound. Dylan and Callan start the generator, electrifying the fences, and Callan helps Dylan dig a grave for his mother. Kristy discovers Sherry is pregnant.

The next day, Callan wakes to find Sherry throwing up, and happily learns of her condition. Greg's injuries find him confined to the couch, where he drinks heavily. Concerned, Callan and Greg have a heart to heart where Greg reveals his worries.

Callan and Dylan check the other houses and gather supplies. Sherry's parents are gone, and so are Callan's, but at the latter house, surrounded by zombies, they must fight their way back to the Jeep. They reach the car, but Dylan is attacked and Callan saves him; then Callan is attacked, and Dylan repays the favor. They abandon the swarmed Jeep and run through the streets as a posse of undead give chase.

Sherry and Kristy prep the house, but a type two zombie approaches up the driveway. Kristy fires a rifle but misses and the zombie attacks. Greg appears, takes the gun and kills it. He is ill though; the girls soon discover Greg collapsed on the lounge room floor.

Callan and Dylan reach the town center. They find Kevlar motorbike gear and are forced to hide from a mob of zombies at a gas station. They replace their lost Jeep and see an identical one driving by on Main Street, but don't acknowledge it. Kristy investigates a noise, and Sherry is attacked by a zombie. Kristy stabs it through the eye, saving Sherry.

At Greg's grandparents' house, they find a loving note, and the old couple wandering the yard, infected. Callan shoots them both, and orders Dylan not to tell Greg what happened. Last stop for the boys is the supermarket. They collect groceries, but are attacked and separated. Both are lucky to survive, and Dylan is saved by an anonymous man in army gear. They escape as dozens of zombies chase after them.

They reunite at the house, where they decide to leave the next day. After dark, the lights of a vehicle slow past the property. Callan and Sherry make love, and Callan sleeps with a smile on his face for the first time in a while.

The next morning, Sherry is ill, while Greg's fever has spiked. The boys decide to return to the town center to obtain antibiotics for Greg. They debate whether they should all leave, but Sherry has severe morning sickness.

As they drive away, Dylan kills the several zombies lined up at the fence, but sees more in neighboring properties. They break into the hunting store and load up on guns and ammunition. Zombies attack and they flee. Callan is saved by the dog they saw earlier.

As they reach the drugstore, they encounter the identical Jeep. Two dodgy men they knew from Albury talk to them. Their presence and actions leave Callan and Dylan unnerved. In the drugstore, Dylan finds his father's N.Y. hat.

Back at the property, a long line of wandering zombies stretches down the road, and more zombies appear at the fence. Kristy shoots several, but others cross into the neighbor's property and she decides it's time to wake Greg.

Dylan and Callan drive around looking for his father. They discover signs of the other men heading in the direction of the property and suspect they have gone there. Heading back, they find Dylan's father and another man chased by a pack of zombies. Callan keeps driving, desperate to get back to the others.

Feeders overwhelm the property boundaries as the girls run inside. Three other cars appear and smash down the front gate, and the occupants begin firing randomly. Kristy sends Sherry to the BMW in the garage while she fetches Greg. He wakes, still ill as more zombies swarm the property. Kristy helps him towards the garage, but Johnny, Callan and Greg's friend, bursts through the front door and tells them to run.

Dylan yanks on the steering wheel and pulls the car off the road. Dylan's father makes it to the Jeep, but the other man dies. The dog that helped them at the gun store also appears and they take it with them, learning that Dylan's father, Bob, knows the dog, which he calls Blue Boy. Dylan realizes something is not right with his dad.

Kristy saves Johnny, and they race up the stairs as other zombies pour in. Johnny saves Greg as they reach a back bedroom with a window leading to the garage roof. Johnny escapes first, Kristy second, leaving Greg to follow with the zombies closing in.

In the Jeep, Bob confirms he has been bitten. Callan wants him out, but Dylan persuades him otherwise. As they reach Silvan Road, they find the property overrun with zombies and men fighting.

Kristy saves Greg using the tomahawk. Steve Palmer fires at them as they stand on the garage roof. Callan and Bob creep inside to find Sherry. Dylan helps Kristy down and puts her into the Jeep. Greg joins Dylan as Steve and his cronies appear. The numbers are three against two.

Callan heads to the back of the house, and Bob goes upstairs. Callan finds a feeding type one zombie, but has run out of ammo. It attacks. He runs, but is caught and faces certain death until Blue Boy distracts it and Bob kills the zombie.

Outside, Steve Palmer and his boys prepare to kill Dylan and Greg, who can barely stand. Johnny appears at the final moment, evening the numbers for a tense confrontation. Steve and his group agree to depart. Smoke appears from the house.

Finding Sherry dead in the garage, Callan is attacked by the type three that killed her. Bob arrives and kills it, but Callan must face Sherry's death. Bob reveals he is not going with them. Zombies bang on the door outside. They realize the house is on fire and a large explosion occurs.

Dylan goes inside the house. He finds zombies attacking Callan and his father, and shoots two. Callan departs in tears. Dylan and his father hug, then Dylan flees, the house now completely on fire.

They leave the property as several type threes wait at the bottom of the driveway. They drive through them as they attack the Jeep. As they drive down Silvan Road, another explosion shakes the ground, sending a second plume of smoke into the sky. Kristy lifts her chin and drives on towards town, wondering if things could get any worse …

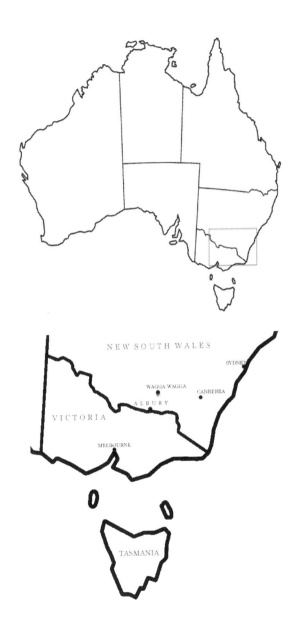

ONE

KLAUS WEINSTREM THREW THE glass beaker into the sink. It smashed into pieces, the sound splintering his ears in the silent confines of the laboratory. He went to the laptop on the bench and entered another set of failed data into a spreadsheet, punching his fingers down on the keyboard.

"Rubbish," he mumbled under his breath.

Each day brought more of the same frustration and failure. He wasn't accustomed to such challenges. The concept of not being able to solve a puzzle infuriated him. Solutions normally presented themselves easily, but not this time. He had deliberately told Major General Harris that it might take months to devise the vaccination, but in truth, that had been a lie. He had never expected it to take long. Under promise and over deliver, a genetics teacher at university had once taught him. That had always served Klaus well.

The plan had been to deliver a manufacturable vaccine in a week, two at the most, and knock the socks off Harris. Although it hadn't happened yet, Klaus felt he was close to a discovery. He had profiled the virus' behavior and introduced countless agents to pacify its effects. Most had done nothing, but some caused a slowing of the virus' replication, only to accelerate shortly after. He had pushed aside the notion that someone had tampered with it to cause the more aggressive subjects, instead focusing on a tangible solution.

After preparing for the next lot of tests, Klaus keyed his code into the security pad and the triple-thick glass door slid back. He stepped into an air-locked room where jets of a powerful sanitizing agent sprayed over his impenetrable suit. When the voice-over stated that he was sterile, another door opened. Klaus walked into the preparation room and removed his suit.

Each time he left the security of his laboratory, Klaus felt the stirrings of worry. The prep room was still remarkably well-protected, but beyond the walls, outside the locked doors, they were roaming. There had been battle after battle inside the facility. Klaus was lucky, in a way, having the sanctuary of the lab and his important work on which to focus. The vaccine drove him; it was all he thought of, aside from his survival. He buried thoughts of his old friends deep, his parents, deeper, and Lana, his one and only love, in a place he could only find in the quiet time before sleep.

He kept on, infecting cultured cells with the virus, adding potential antivirals, and analyzing readings. Sometimes he felt the distance to discovery was greater than ever. It frustrated him more than any project before, but he refused to surrender. And he wouldn't. Couldn't. To every problem, he would find a solution. Klaus needed to know.

He emptied the coffee machine he had tucked in behind a series of expensive apparatus. Before the outbreak, he'd never have kept it in the room, but now there was nobody to police the rules. That part was good. He filled the hopper with fresh-smelling beans and readied it for his brew, thinking about other angles of approaching the problem. It should have been a simple fix–the government and various drug manufacturing companies should have been able to develop a vaccine fairly quickly. For reasons to which Klaus was not privy, they hadn't. Major General Harris, whom Klaus hadn't seen for a week, suspected the government's reaction was too slow, diverted by a number of major foreign political issues that had occurred just before the outbreak. Either way, the vaccine hadn't happened, and Klaus didn't know who was still alive to make what.

He'd been lucky that the installation had a small disease control section. They kept a range of pathogens, in addition to many of the components required to formulate antivirals and low-level vaccines. The government, in building the deeper levels of the facility, had taken into account a number of potential catastrophic events, including a pandemic. The one shortcoming Klaus now faced was the inability to produce a quantity of any vaccine or serum he might manage to formulate.

He had abandoned the idea of creating a vaccine though. Instead, he had diverted his attention to developing an antiviral drug. He had access to the components required for this and felt they offered the best hope of success. Viruses were smart, mistakenly incorporating antivirals into their genomes during cell replication, but with the right antiviral, the virus could be halted from developing any further.

The coffee machine beeped, and Klaus took the hot brew, sipping the frothed milk from the surface. His process has been simple, growing cultures of cells and infecting them with the zombie virus, then introducing the other antivirals that he thought might inhibit viral activity. He then had to observe whether the level of virus in the cultures rose or fell. He had tried Acyclovir, used for the herpes virus, and Lamivudine, for HIV, as well as a multitude of other antiviral drugs to target different stages of the virus' life cycle. None had worked though. The idea behind the antiviral was to identify parts of proteins within the virus that could be disabled. Klaus could then use existing drugs to prevent its replication. Before the outbreak, he'd have been able to design candidate drugs at the molecular level using powerful computers, but he was back to simple methods now. All he had left was to try a new class of protein called an interferon. The next tests would use these. He already felt an eagerness to return to the lab and start the process again.

The air door at the front of the room opened, and Admiral Gallagher staggered through the entrance holding an almost empty bottle of booze. Klaus felt himself bristle. Stubble covered the admiral's face; even Klaus had continued shaving to keep a semblance of normality. Not Gallagher, though.

"What is it?" Klaus asked abruptly.

Gallagher fell against the desk, the bottle clunking on the hard surface. He burped and chuckled. Klaus could find no humor in his actions. Here was a man with one of the highest ranks on the base, yet he had essentially abandoned his post and taken up with grog almost immediately after the outbreak had occurred.

"I don't have time for idle chat," Klaus said. He knew they were possibly the last people alive on the base, but he couldn't resist. The former Naval officer wasn't worth his time in conversation. He turned, placing his cup on the bench beside the coffee maker. "And are you stupid? Walking around out there. I'm surprised they haven't torn you apart." A thought struck him. "You're not bitten, are you?"

"French is dead." Gallagher's voice was thin and raspy. His cheeks and nose were red. Klaus had to force his mouth to stay closed. French. The public relations woman who had gone crazy and locked herself up in the food hall on level four. "Shot herself."

No surprise. "Is that all?" Klaus asked.

"You found a cure yet?" Gallagher hiccupped.

Klaus felt his upper lip quiver. "You're a disgrace. You're a drunken scumbag who doesn't deserve his rank. Get out of here."

Gallagher launched the bottle at him, but Klaus was too slow. He'd never been good at physical activity; his reflexes were sluggish and clumsy. He managed to raise his arm and the projectile struck his elbow, pain shooting through the bone. The bottle clattered off the wall and onto the floor.

Klaus screamed, "Asshole!"

Gallagher laughed. "Oh Klaus, you're not very good at getting angry. You can't even scream a good insult. You think you're the last hope for mankind. Big deal. Everybody clap for Klaus Weinstrem." He coughed, a deep, raking convulsion, his face red and intense. When he had himself under control, he said, "You're wasting your time. There'll be nobody left by the time you find a cure."

Klaus wanted to rush over and strike him, but he knew how that would end. Gallagher would chop him up with a flurry of punches. "Just leave. Let me do my work. You're no good to anyone anymore." Gallagher stared at him for a long moment, then turned away. Klaus remembered he was still good for at least one thing, and called after him, "Don't forget to check the holding cells." That was one job Klaus wouldn't do.

"Fuck you," Gallagher said. "And don't come running to me when you need help."

TWO

IT HAD BEEN A long, hot morning for Evelyn Burson and her son, Jake. They had packed their belongings into two backpacks at dawn and started off from her parents' place along the silent, deserted streets of Wagga Wagga, heading for the military base on the eastern side of town. Evelyn had estimated it would take two hours, but distractions and rests had turned that into more than three, even cutting through streets and backyards. The flies had been maddening. They had been unable to find a vehicle with fuel *and* keys, and while they hadn't seen any zombies up close, the threat of their existence felt close. They had become almost relaxed, the earlier tenseness dissipating, replaced by weariness and fatigue, and a constant perspiration. She regretted her abandoned gym membership, and suspected she would pay for the activity later. *Maybe now the weight will come off,* she thought. The water from front yard taps was still drinkable, and they had checked a number of houses looking for food, Evelyn not wanting to use the small amount they had in her pack. She felt immoral for taking, but felt the circumstances justified the actions.

Things heated up when they confronted the zombie stumbling out of a double-story weatherboard place on the corner of Graham and Johnson Street. She almost squealed, but caught her breath just in time and clamped a hand over Jake's mouth. He never looked like screaming though. In addition to his blue eyes and dark, messy hair, he had his father's calm, calculating nature. He pulled her hand away and walked backward, never taking his eyes off the thing.

"Want me to kill it, Mom?"

"Don't be silly, Jake." It staggered in a jerky motion along the street towards them. Evelyn did a take of their position. There was an escape path, but they would have to be quick, and as she led him sideways by the hand, she said, "Now," and they ran.

Why had they left the house again? Her father had recommended it, although those were the words of a dead man. Before his death, he had told her not to stay, that there would be others beyond the realms of their property that could help. Her cautious nature had argued though. Why couldn't they make a life for themselves in the underground shelter? It had been built in the forties during the Second World War, and he father had kept it in good condition. Nothing stays the same though. Jake had begun to get restless, begging her to let him outside to play on the swings and kick the ball around. He didn't understand the terror that lay beyond the mud brick walls. It had taken her two days once she had made the decision. The idea had been percolating in her mind for a week, but she had built the courage on an incessant case of reality. It was only when their supplies had depleted beyond survival that she felt the pressure of making the move.

The zombie ambled after them, eyes bulging, fingers pointing. Terror impeded her movement; not for herself, but for Jake. As if justifying those feelings, he tripped, knocking his knee on the curb enough to cause a cry.

"Get up," she hissed. "Move, Jake."

He did, hobbling away as the monster reached the gutter. She had taken one of the big carving knives from the wooden block in the kitchen, and thought about using it, but Jake was in no harm yet and they dashed away unimpeded.

After trying several without luck, they found a battered, stinking car on the next street. She saw the keys were still in the ignition through the driver's window, although there was a dead body in the seat. She touched a hand to Jake's head as she sat him in the back, wishing she had more food to help put some weight on his thin arms. She removed the stiff corpse from behind the wheel, asking Jake to turn away as she fought to drag it out. Swollen red eyes stared out the windscreen, and a line of dry blood trailed from the corner of its mouth. But it was the smell that forced breakfast up

15

her throat. She held her breath, twice abandoning the task to seek fresh air.

Evelyn turned on the engine and the fuel gauge lifted a hair above the red line. Her hands trembled as she drove off, forcing herself not to look at the body on the roadside.

During their trek across town, they had checked the homes of friends she had not spoken to or heard from in weeks, people with whom she had grown up, others that had become close through Jake's school. All the houses had been empty. The advantage of the underground shelter now proved a disadvantage. They had survived the initial period of chaos, but their isolation over the following weeks meant there was nobody left.

There were still a handful of places to visit. She sped through the nearby streets for fifteen minutes, parking at the stairs or beside the porch of each dwelling. She left the sedan running, threatening Jake with more than death if he left the vehicle. After banging on the door or ringing the bell, she waited fifteen seconds and tried again before abandoning the post. Nobody answered. She had expected it, but the confirmation saddened her.

At the final check, Evelyn noticed the fuel gauge had dropped below the red line. She needed a gas station. Panic washed over her when she realized what might happen if they lost the car. Her sore feet and aching back begged for luck.

She crept along at twenty-five, hoping to conserve fuel. What would Cameron have done? He would have been calm and controlled, and have planned well in advance. The ideas would have been plentiful. She had only realized after his death just how much she had relied on him for the simple elements of life. Evelyn had spent the last six months grieving, clinging to her parents to get through. Now they were gone too, and although she had Jake, Evelyn had to be the one to whom he could cling. Her time for grieving, for feeling sorry, was over.

She had earmarked the BP gas station on Rutherford Street, but ran into a multi-car crash less than a quarter of a mile from it. She edged the car in close, the tires cracking and popping over broken glass. Her heart began to hammer as she thought they were going to get trapped and Jake would be at risk again. He was all that mattered now. She had to find a place where he would be safe, where others, besides her, could look out for him. Although there were no zombies in view, she could feel them loitering in the shadows of the houses, waiting for the car to stop. It seemed hopeless, as though she would have to turn around, but she kept at it, nudging cars aside, driving them sideways and backward with the scrape of rubber and screech of metal. Eventually, they cleared the blockage and drove on.

At a roundabout on Carter Street, they saw a fresh body lying in the gutter that reminded Evelyn of her father: a mop of grey hair and a stomach built on beer and peanuts over many years. Though she had buried him in the first week of the plague, his memory remained strong, and she often sought his advice from past sermons. How she missed him.

The BP had been crawling with the infected, and the Shell gas station near the shopping centre had no bowsers. Someone had gotten creative. The engine spluttered and gasped before they reached the next fuel stop, and they ditched it near Fraser Avenue. They took a backpack each, but Evelyn could feel pain in her feet before taking a step.

They were still a mile or so from the army barracks, and at their slower pace it would take them until late afternoon. As the hot midday sun began to descend, they finished off the last of their food beneath the shade of a wide oak tree in a park, inspiring them for the next leg. She watched Jake with growing concern; his knee still hurt, and he'd complained about blisters on his feet. Despite that, she didn't want to sit for too long, knowing comfort would set in, making it harder to get moving again.

They started off through the long grass, past a set of swings, and a tall, yellow, spiral slide. Normally, Jake might have asked for five minutes to play, but now, he didn't even look at it. They reached the entrance of the park where a steel railing defined the boundary on the other side of the walking path. Ahead on their left, beyond the gated entrance, lay an overturned bus. The windows were colored by a dark stain obscuring the view inside. *Blood.*

"Go, Jake, quickly."

The cracked door began to move, folding in. Then it crashed open and she saw a gruesome hand reach out.

"RUN!"

THREE

KRISTY BLINKED BACK TEARS and tried to focus on the road. She couldn't decide the route by which to leave town, couldn't get her brain to make the connections. Her vision blurred, and she had to wipe her eyes with one clumsy palm. What had just happened? Was Sherry really dead? In the rear-view mirror, her brother Callan's silent, forlorn face peered out the window. There were no tears; she couldn't recall the last time he had cried. His jaw flexed as he grinded his teeth, a trait that usually precluded intense anger. They had to get out of Albury, get away from the zombies, and the death, and the reminders. While they stayed here, recent memories would hang around them like a chronic illness, undermining their happiness.

She wiped again, switching hands until her cheeks were dry. Movement through the back window, beyond the trailer, caught her attention: another car. The white Ford scooted along, growing larger in the mirror. "We've got a problem. I think those idiots are following us."

Dylan peered into the side mirror. "It's them. Steve and Chris."

Kristy closed her eyes. She just wanted it to be over. They had just lost Sherry—couldn't they get a little time to recover and recoup from that?

Callan unclipped his belt, leaned forward, and scooped up two of the Browning 9mm automatic pistols from a bag on the floor. He handed one to Dylan. "I'm gonna fucking kill those two."

Kristy tightened her hands around the wheel. They had just survived the most intense fight imaginable, and mentally she had nothing left. She wasn't ready for another battle. None of them were. "Wait, Callan, don't make it any worse."

"Any worse? They just tried to kill us!"

"Yeah, but they might be just trying to scare us now. Do we need anyone else to die today?"

Greg moaned, and said in a low, husky voice, "Don't … trust 'em."

Kristy looked to Dylan for support, but his lips were pressed into a thin line. She checked the mirror again and saw the muzzle of a shotgun poking up from Chris' hands.

The trailing vehicle sped up, all three men pointing and threatening, their horn blaring. Kristy maintained a consistent speed. Callan lowered the back window, and Dylan did the same.

"What are you doing?" Kristy asked.

"I'm not letting these fuckers get any closer," Callan said. "I can promise you that."

Kristy steered the car around a long, gentle left turn. Callan and Dylan used the roof to brace themselves.

The empty, broken shells of several cars blocked the way, and Kristy was forced to slow the Jeep. The car behind drew close enough for them to see their snarling faces. Kristy swerved in and out, trying not to drop below forty. She clipped the bent fender of an old Holden Torana, knocking them in their seats. "Sorry."

Gunfire sounded, like a car backfiring. Blue Boy had his face pressed against the rear window, barking. "Down," Callan said, reaching over to protect the dog. "The pricks are shooting at us." Kristy ducked, peering over the dashboard.

They approached one of the prettier streets in Albury, where trees lined the curb the entire length. Picking up speed, Kristy checked the mirror again. Callan leaned out one window, and Dylan stuck his arm out the other.

Multiple gunshots sounded. Bullets zipped and pinged off the roof of the Jeep. One hit the trailer chassis with a thunderous crack.

Callan returned fire, screaming obscenities. Kristy thought he might be going mad.

A bullet shattered the windscreen of the white Ford. It slowed, then skewed sideways and ran up the curb. It smashed head on into a tree with a thunderclap, the rear end bouncing. Glass showered the tree and road. Kristy slowed the Jeep.

The vehicle stopped in the middle of the road about fifty yards away. For a long moment, nobody moved. Blue Boy whimpered. Then Kristy unlocked her door and slipped out. She was still a doctor, and injured patients required her attention, even if they had only just endangered her life. In her opinion, the world hadn't quite descended into immorality yet.

"KRISTY!"

She stopped at the rear door. She had planned on retrieving her medical bag, but Callan's voice froze her.

He joined her, his face sharpened with anger. "What are you doing?"

"I was going to check on them."

His mouth made a big O. "No fucking way. Leave them. They just tried to kill us. Again."

"But—"

"Sherry might still be alive if it wasn't for them. Get back in the car. They're getting nothing from us."

A vein in his neck bulged. His cheeks and forehead burned red. She had never seen him so angry. There was no point arguing. "You're right."

"We help people who deserve it."

As she returned to the driver's seat, Kristy heard a faint hissing sound. Smoke wafted from underneath the Ford's hood. There was no sign of movement. Killing zombies was one thing, but the death of another human still unsettled her. Callan was right though. Without Steve and Chris' attack, Sherry might still be alive.

She drove away and didn't look back.

FOUR

CALLAN RAMMED THE BELT into the buckle. *Fuck 'em,* he thought. Why should he let Kristy help? They had turned into savages. Sherry was dead; they did not deserve to live. They were lucky Callan hadn't gone over to the car and shot them all. He'd fought the urge to do so, fought it with more self-control than he'd ever needed. He reached over the backseat for Blue Boy, scratching at the dog's ear. He was terrified he'd break down in front of the others and wouldn't be able to control himself. A well of tears waited behind his eyes ready to burst.

The dog's black ears pointed towards the roof, its face stiff, eyes alert, listening. It glanced at him, whimpered once, and licked its lips. It was clever, and had survived this long relying on its own resources for food and water. Surely, *they* could make a go of it.

Maybe Blue Boy was all he had now. Sadness filled his mind and heart with an unprecedented ache. He stopped scratching the dog and stared out his window, watching the passing houses; they were on Sackville Street, probably heading towards one of the hospitals to find some antibiotics for Greg. That was good; he couldn't sit there for too long, or he'd go mad. He needed to kill these fuckers, take out his anger on the bastards that had killed Sherry. The odd zombie poked about in a front garden, or stood before a window looking at its gruesome reflection. Part of him wanted to stop the car and kill every last one of them.

A deep sobbing welled in his chest. He held his breath, fighting it. He wanted to cup his hands over his face and let the tears come, wanted to purge the pain with screams and fists. Come on, where are you now? He wanted the zombies, needed to tear them apart. He thought of Sherry and his unborn baby. His lower lip quivered, and he had to bite down hard. His eyes filled, blurring his vision. His stomach and chest twisted. He balled his right hand into a fist and struck out, pulling it up short of the door. When was the last time he had really cried? He couldn't recall. Whenever it had been, whatever the reason, it paled in comparison to this.

Greg moaned, and it drew Callan's attention. His friend was in bad shape, eyes closed, his breathing short and shallow. Sweat glistened on his brow. How much longer would he last?

"Hey, mate. Hang in there," Callan said.

Greg moaned. "Got any water? I'm so bloody thirsty."

Callan reached over the back and found a bottle, opened the lid, and held it out for Greg. He sat up, took it in shaking hands, and sipped.

Callan had to hold the bottom and guide it to Greg's lips. "Shit, buddy, you're in a bad way." He could feel the heat off Greg like a warm kettle.

"I feel cold, though, man. Real cold."

The Jeep rolled along Sackville Street and turned left onto Poole. He knew where Kristy was going. They slowed to a stop in the middle of the road out front of the Mercy health building. It reflected the state of Albury as a whole—a battered, crumbling shell.

A tall, scruffy-haired male zombie stood in the window, leering at them between shards of glass. It wore a short-sleeved green uniform and might once have been an orderly. Bloated eyes and a mouth sullied by rotted flesh beckoned. It made a dry, hacking sound, as if it was trying to cough something up.

Pistol in hand, Callan opened his door and swung a foot out.

"Wait," Kristy said. Callan stopped. Others had appeared beside the zombie, stumbling to the window. A second, third, and fourth materialized out of the shadows. Suddenly there were ten, pushing at each other with slow desperation. Callan realised the ones in this state were mostly harmless, as long as you kept your distance. Killing them all would be easy. "Don't. This place is mostly for the elderly. There might not even be any antibiotics inside."

Callan didn't believe her. "I'll take a look."

"Suicide, man," Dylan said.

"You're just a pussy."

Dylan flinched. The zombies called for Callan. He needed them; needed to blow their heads off, to satisfy the pain. It would help. The more he killed, the better he would feel. Or maybe he was chasing Sherry. Maybe he wanted to die, and take as many out as could first. "I get it, man."

Callan read the shame on his mate's face, and that struck him, because Dylan had never acted in a shameful way. He wasn't a pussy, and he knew what Callan felt. Maybe more so. It knocked him back into reason. "Hey, I'm sorry. I didn't mean that." Dylan nodded. "Got any better ideas?"

"The main hospital on Borella Road."

A crease of Kristy's brow, and a pleading, earnest look in her eyes convinced Callan. He loved his sister immensely, and his admiration for her had grown over the last five weeks, particularly in the last few days. *You still have her. Don't give up on her yet.* He pulled his foot back inside and shut the door. The ache for killing would have to wait; there would be zombies elsewhere.

"Okay."

Kristy drove on, turning right onto Kiewa Street and left onto Guinea, where fewer zombies were visible. They weren't milling in the streets, or poking about in the houses or shop fronts. They'd moved out. Callan felt certain that once an area was cleared of food, they would seek new sources. The property damage though, was horrendous. Smashed windows, burnt-out shells, refuse spread across front lawns. He felt a deep sadness that Albury would never again be the same town in which he'd grown up. He loved the place, and would be sad to leave.

As they drove over the Hume Highway Bridge, Callan glanced in either direction along a motorway that was once one of the busiest in Australia. A scattering of vehicles parked in odd places and at irregular angles stretched as far as he could see. He wondered if their parents were lying in amongst those cars. On their arrival back into Albury, they had been the priority. Callan had argued about checking on his mother. It felt like a lifetime ago. He supposed now he'd accepted that they were dead. *Better we don't find out,* he thought.

As the first blue signage for the hospital appeared, Callan recalled the last time he had been there. They had been involved in a minor traffic accident; Callan had split his nose open on the wheel after an elderly man had hit the rear of his mother's car. On Sherry's insistence, he'd gone into the ER and had finally had it stitched up by a lovely nurse.

About two hundred yards from the hospital, Kristy slowed the car. "Do you guys see that?"

Zombies wandered along the street in a scattered trail, more than they had witnessed since leaving Dylan's parents' property. Callan felt the urge to kill wash over him. He would cut them all down like tall weeds in an overgrown garden. "Let me out," he said in a flat tone.

Kristy glanced back. "Wait. There. What is that?"

"What?" Johnny said, peering out the side window from the back seat.

Callan scanned the road ahead. At the intersection, an ambulance had driven up on the curb and tangled itself amongst a number of other smashed up cars. A group of zombies lingered around it.

"I think there are people in the ambulance," Kristy said. "It looks like … a man, in the front seat."

Callan felt the rush of anticipation. Still holding the Browning pistol, he snatched up the tomahawk, shoved the door open, and spilled out, floundering for balance.

"Callan?"

"Go," he said to Kristy through the closed window. She lowered it. "Get to the hospital. I'll meet you there." Kristy didn't move. "GO! GET OUT OF HERE!"

He ran off with the tomahawk primed. It was madness, he knew, but he wanted it; needed it. Even if the ambulance was empty, he would get his chance to kill.

Kristy's high-pitched voice screamed, "Callan! Come back!"

He waved them off, sticking the gun into his waist. The first attacker approached on his left. Callan turned to face it, lips drawn back in a snarl, and raised the tomahawk gripped tightly in his right hand. At the last moment, he spun the blade and put the thick end into the side of its rubbery head. It grunted and tottered off balance. He swung back the other way, and knocked it to the ground, then lifted the tomahawk high, blade down, and cut the thing's head off, spraying blood over the gutter.

The ambulance engine groaned and started moving away from the wreckage along the eastward street, tearing bits and pieces from the other cars like a scrap metal yard. Callan jogged after it as another zombie followed. The ambulance lurched right down another street, then picked up speed. There had to be somebody inside, and they needed his help. He sprinted as it opened a gap, but then it slowed to a short spurt and stopped suddenly.

Several zombies poking about in front gardens moved in, but they hadn't noticed him yet. They reached the ambulance and beat on the windows. As he closed in, Callan saw a man wrestling an attacker inside the cabin. *I know him*, Callan thought, but couldn't immediately place the man.

One of the feeders detected Callan and lumbered around the front of the vehicle towards him, its bleached, bony fingers pleading for his flesh.

"Come and fucking get it," he said through gritted teeth.

Callan launched the tomahawk at the zombie's emaciated frame. It cut through its flesh and struck the side of the ambulance with a metallic clunk. Blood sprayed over the white door and windows. The feeder collapsed to the bitumen, its head lolling sideways.

On the opposite side, the door slid open. Someone screamed. Callan scooped up the tomahawk and sprinted around the front just as two zombies clambered inside. From the cabin, the man's cries rose to a growl, and Callan felt goose bumps on his neck. Through the driver's window he saw the zombie biting into the man's arm.

Another scream sounded, and a young girl, perhaps eleven, or twelve, long blonde hair trailing, leapt from her hiding place in the back of the van. Sobbing, she crawled between one of the zombie's legs, clawing for the door and her freedom.

"Hey," Callan said. "Come here."

She tumbled out of the ambulance, grazing her knees, then sprung to her feet and ran at Callan. He lifted an arm to catch her, but she sped past and ran off down the street, the soles of her sneakers slapping the road. Two feeders heading toward the ambulance changed direction and started after her. Callan contemplated chasing them, but the man in the cabin needed his immediate help.

Two zombies stumbled from the van and attacked. Callan stepped to meet them, imagining what they had done to Sherry. He stuck the tomahawk into the side of one's skull. Blood jetted out, dousing the other across the face. It staggered, held up by the armament. Callan drew his weapon back and stuck a foot into the zombie's belly, then yanked on the blade. It collapsed and he stepped aside, preparing for the other. This time he swung the blade sideways, twisting his hips, and it struck the side of its head with a flat smack. The monster went sprawling onto the bitumen. It tried to stand, but Callan shoved it back to the ground under the sole of his boot. In a sickly, pale face, bulging eyes stared, and it opened its rotted mouth, revealing teeth the color of old pipes.

"This one's for Sherry." He lifted the tomahawk and dug deep, ploughing the blade into its neck up and down like a piston until the head rolled away through a wash of dark blood. He stood, panting, sucking air deep into his lungs. There was little satisfaction, and the pain of Sherry's loss still enclosed his heart in a dull ache.

More zombies arrived as Callan threw the door of the ambulance cabin open. He was too late. A screwdriver stuck out of the zombie's head, but a gaping chunk of flesh flapped from the man's bicep. He lay back, eyes closed, a grimace of anguish Callan couldn't imagine on his stubbled, lined face. Then it hit him; he remembered where he had seen those brooding brows and thick moustache.

It was the man from the house outside of which they had changed the trailer tire. He had been angry and unhelpful then. Now, as his eyes came open and he recognized Callan, terror stole his courage, and he wore a mask of helplessness to which Callan could relate.

Dark shadows had surrounded the ambulance. Hands beat against the rear and sides, and a rat-faced female zombie with dark, soulless eyes glared in through the driver's window.

"My daughter," he said, in that gravelly tone. "Where is she?"

"She … ran off."

"Help her … please."

Callan nodded. "I will."

The man closed his eyes, grimacing, and nodded. "I remember you. The flat tire. You asked for … I'm sorry. We had some … bad luck with … the same."

"Forget it."

"Help my—"

Fingers dug into Callan's shoulder. He swung around and met two zombies clawing at his arm, but he felt nothing through the Kevlar fabric. He drove them backward behind a strong kick and swung the tomahawk, striking the first one in the face. The second replaced his friend, and Callan booted it to the road.

Another zombie had wrenched the door open and attacked the man. "My daughter," he groaned, and then the zombie was upon him, devouring his neck like a hungry dog. He cried out, twisting around, and served blows onto his attacker.

Callan snatched the gun from his waistband, leaned into the cabin, and pressed the barrel into the zombie's head. The shot shrieked, spraying blood over a second offender, and the thing, which had once been a fireman, fell backward and hit the tarmac with a loud thud.

The man's glassy eyes stared out the windscreen towards a cloud-covered sun that would never beat down on him again. Callan shot the second zombie in the face and reversed out of the cabin.

Others were on him before he could shoot, scratching at his clothes, grabbing at his arms and legs. He almost overbalanced as one of them tried to bite into his thigh, but he clunked it on top of the head and it fell away.

Screaming, he struck out with the sharpened points of both elbows, the lean flats of his forearms crunching their faces and heads, and they went down one after the other, the pain in his bones comforting. Beyond them, a dozen more hurried towards him. *Run. Get out of here.*

First, he had to get the girl.

FIVE

UNTIL CALLAN'S DEPARTURE, DYLAN had been contemplating the group's losses. He wondered whether they had been lucky to last so long without a fatality amongst the original members. He, or Callan, should have died sooner, on one of their ventures into Albury, perhaps. They *had* been lucky. His father had been lucky too, having survived so long away from the refuge of the property. Dylan had accepted his death, and was grateful for their brief reunion, but now, having had the contact, the loss burned deeper and he wished for the time over again.

"Why the fuck did you drive away?" Johnny asked. He leaned forward, wearing a stiff, open-mouthed expression. Saliva flew from Blue Boy's mouth as he barked at the back window.

"Ease up, man," Dylan said. "Give her a break." Johnny sneered.

Johnny might have partially redeemed himself back at the house, but that didn't wash away years of ill feeling, and his betrayal of Callan was difficult to overlook. Dylan had wanted to ask him about it, but the opportunity had never presented itself. He decided that the moment he had the chance, he would quiz Johnny and give him the chance to tell Callan himself.

There was no point wasting time on understanding Callan's decisions. Dylan had tried and failed. He sensed Callan's anger, and maybe running off and killing zombies was a way to purge it, to release the suffering. Dylan wondered whether he should go after him, but the idea of leaving Kristy alone again was too risky. He thought Callan would probably have preferred him to stay and protect her.

"Are you serious?" Kristy asked. "You make him get back in the car."

"Can't stop Callan," Greg mumbled. "Don't waste your time." As if in agreement, Blue Boy ceased barking and lay down in the back.

The Albury base hospital appeared on their right, a low collection of brick buildings; dark and ominous windows beckoned. Dylan had only been there a few times in his life, but he remembered the throng of activity: people walking from one building to another; ambulances and emergency vehicles coming and going. Now, a silent cloak had been thrown over it.

"The main entrance is on the service road off East Street," Kristy said, turning the steering wheel to the right. The car rolled past an empty fire truck. A body wearing a black coat lined with yellow reflective bands lay beside it. "There's a pharmacy not far from there."

Long nature strips leading to flaking weatherboard houses made East Street seem wider than it was. Numerous untarnished vehicles sat parked on the street. A blue and red sign marked Albury Wodonga Health pointed towards the parking lot. The red section stated EMERGENCY DEPARTMENT.

The Jeep turned into the wide opening as the road snaked around, leading to a large, flat parking area surrounded on the left and rear sides by towering pine trees. On the right, a giant awning led into the main entrance. Dylan estimated about twenty-five cars were parked in the lot. Several ambulances sat in the emergency spaces, while another had been backed right up to the doors. Could there still be people alive inside? Kristy swung the car into a disabled parking space, and they all watched the silent, eerie scene. The first drops of welcome rain sprinkled the windscreen.

"It's not right," Kristy said. "A place like this, so quiet." But it wasn't silent for long. A team of zombies appeared from behind a stack of broken-up cars, drawn by their arrival. "There's a lot of them."

In the backseat, Greg struggled to sit up. "How many?"

"Maybe seven, or eight," Dylan said. He suddenly wished Callan was there, or that Greg wasn't so ill. They could drive away and avoid the confrontation, but that wouldn't help Greg. They were there for him, and if he didn't get the antibiotics, they might lose him. Dylan wouldn't let that happen.

He leaped out of the front passenger seat holding the Remington and levered the bolt. The first feeder hobbled toward him baring teeth, so he shot it through the mouth. The back of its head splattered over the road, and another took its place.

The zombies were coming from several places: a blue Ford Charger and a small Toyota hybrid that had both been smashed up, and a door that led into one of the buildings. Ten, maybe fifteen feeders staggered toward them in a zigzagging line.

Two of them reached the Jeep, and Johnny pushed his way out of the rear seat by shoving one of them backward using the door. It fell down. He leaped out screaming and shot it in the forehead.

The rain grew heavier, creating wisps of steam from the hot bitumen. Johnny was yelling and firing, taking feeders down under single shots of his Winchester rifle. He had worked his way around to Dylan's side, his black hair greasy with sweat, his face twisted into a mask of rage. When he saw Dylan though, he grinned like a madman.

But there were too many, and Dylan needed ammo. He told Johnny between gunfire, cursing the danger of it. Johnny shuffled towards the back of the Jeep as Dylan fired his last rounds, hitting one feeder in the neck and another in the shoulder. The firing stopped, and an unnatural peace filled its place around them. In the distance, shots sounded.

Blue Boy tried to push past the boys and leap out the rear window. Dylan put a shoulder to him, jostling him back. Greg reached over the seat to calm the dog, but it kept barking, desperate to get to the zombies.

As Dylan fumbled for more ammunition, a fresh wave of feeders staggered out of the open door of the hospital building. Johnny had found the ammunition for his Winchester .30-30, but Dylan couldn't find any rounds for the Remington.

"Dylan!" Kristy shouted from the driver's seat. "They're coming. Hurry."

He tossed the rifle into the back and felt around in one of the sports bags they had taken from the hunting store. His fingers touched cold metal, and he pulled out a Browning 9mm pistol like the one Callan had given him to shoot at Steve Palmer's car. He found the magazine release and dropped the mag into his other hand to confirm it was full.

Johnny had reloaded, but a skinny zombie in need of a feed reached him from the other side of the vehicle. Dylan slammed the back window shut and saw they were almost surrounded.

The driver's door swung open, and Kristy climbed out with the axe.

"No!" Dylan screamed. "Get back in."

Kristy called out, distracting the feeders from the boys, and they turned, smelling her desirable scent.

Johnny blasted his newest fan in the throat, the sound stinging Dylan's ears. He cocked the pistol and lifted it, then took aim at a zombie drawn to Kristy, conscious of his poor record with a pistol.

The first shot missed everything and blew out a window in the building directly behind them. Glass shattered onto the concrete. Swinging the axe, Kristy shuffled backward, drawing the zombies away. It created a space for Dylan. He followed, firing again, but he met his own expectations and missed again. He wanted the Remington back, and cursed himself for not finding ammo. Other zombies had noticed the altercation and lurched in Kristy's direction.

"Get back in the car, Kristy!"

She stopped, realizing her growing peril, and ran for the Jeep. A tall male in a green hospital gown tried to cut her off, but she pushed it aside. Others chased though, closing in as she approached the vehicle.

Dylan stood on the other side of the car, defending himself. Fingers clawed at his leather jacket. He swung his right elbow around and heard the crack of a jawbone. A wispy-haired blonde in a white hospital gown came at him, and he thrust his boot into her gut, knocking her backward. He put bullets into the heads of those that wouldn't move, but there were others, full of insatiable interest, with shaggy clothes and purple-red skin, their flesh withered, eyes sunk deep into over-sized sockets. They weren't fast, or intelligent, like the crazies, but they were tenacious, as though their existence depended on drawing the sustenance from their human prey.

Kristy made it to the passenger side door, but two zombies were close behind, grunting and drooling over their prize.

Blue Boy stood barking at the side window. He could help. "Open the door!" Dylan screamed.

She tried, but her fingers slipped off the handle. The feeders crowded around, and her back thudded against the window as she turned to fend them off. Kristy screamed, throwing her fists and elbows to keep them away.

Dylan ran past another zombie and rounded the hood of the Jeep. He felt the soles of his boots lose purchase on the slippery bitumen, and the world tilted suddenly. His arms pinwheeled, and pain flashed through his jaw as his cheek hit the rough surface. He shook his head to clear it, and then pushed onto one knee as lumbering footsteps arrived. Their cold, skeletal hands groped at his hair and neck, but he climbed to his feet and stumbled away, crashing into another attacker.

Where was Greg? The big man had always delivered when it counted, but Dylan realized that this time he was too sick to do anything except get bitten himself.

Kristy had fought her way free, although other feeders had closed in. A zombie missing half of its face reached out and hooked a hand around her thigh. Kristy stumbled, steadied herself, then lost her balance and fell to the ground, her palms scraping over the asphalt. They crawled over her, obscuring the blonde hair Dylan had fallen asleep smelling the night before. Screaming, she punched and kicked out at them, her fists and feet a blur.

Cold fear spread from his chest. He screamed. "KRISTY!"

The back door of the Jeep opened, and Greg tumbled out like a drunkard falling from bed. He landed on his elbows with his head down, looking like a man on the edge of death.

Others rushed him. Dylan pushed them away, tangling his arms in their lanky limbs, and giving himself enough space to shoot one in the right eye. A projectile of gore shot from the back of its head, covering the road, but he was still too far away, and another two closed on him. He was going to lose her.

Barking, Blue Boy leapt out over Greg and jumped onto the shoulders of the closest zombie crouching over Kristy. The zombie overbalanced and tumbled off. Others had pinned her though; one sat on Kristy's back and took her calf in both hands. Blue Boy darted back in, barking and growling, snapping his jaws and threatening to rip the zombie's face off. He repeated his earlier trick and jumped at the thing, pushing with his front paws and distracting it.

Dylan broke through and ran for Kristy. She had managed to kick her main assailant free, and as it reset for another attack, Dylan shot it in the head. It folded into a heap on the road. He kicked the other one in the face with a crack like the breaking of a stick. The thing fell back moaning. Blue Boy scampered about, barking and threatening, distracting the zombies momentarily. Dylan shot two more and then the immediate threat was over as Johnny dropped the last zombie on his trail of dead.

Dylan helped Kristy to her feet, and she clung tight enough to pinch the skin on his arm. "You're okay," he whispered between gasps for breath. Her hair no longer smelled as sweet as it had the night before, and when he pulled away, streaks of zombie gore clung to her leathers. "Did they get you?"

"No, I don't think so."

Johnny joined them, splashes of dark fluid covering his blue denim jacket and spots of blood on his neck. Dylan nodded as their eyes met. "Nice work. I don't know how we got out of that."

Greg lay back against the car, his face pinched with discomfort. "I'm sorry. I just couldn't get up."

Blue Boy ran in barking, pushing against Kristy's legs for a pat. She roughed his neck and his tongue lolled in glee. "If you hadn't let Blue out," Kristy said to Greg, "I might not have made it." She bent, scratching the dog harder, and she let him lick the side of her face. "Is everyone else okay?"

The Kevlar had saved Dylan, and probably Kristy too. He realised how close they'd come to losing her. How close he'd come. Dylan took her by the arms. "You gotta stop doing this. You should have stayed in the car. You're just as bad as Callan." She nodded and he pulled her tighter, feeling the rapid beat of his heart against her.

Not all the zombies were dead though. Several had crawled to their feet, and three new ones ambled towards them from the emergency doors.

"We gotta get out of here," Johnny said. "What about Cal? We'll have to go back for him soon."

Kristy sighed. "Greg needs antibiotics first. That's the most important thing." She and Dylan helped Greg back into the car. Dylan had never felt such heat coming off a body. Kristy went on. "Someone needs to go in and find them."

"We'll go," Dylan said, looking at Johnny, feeling as though a greater trust existed between them given what they'd just overcome.

"We'll circle back to where we left Callan and try to pick him up," Kristy said. "The pharmacy is just in through those emergency doors." She pointed to the area from which the main source of zombies had come. "But you might have to find another way in. It's not far. Get every single antibiotic you can find." She gave Dylan's hand a squeeze, looking into his eyes with a thin, terrified smile.

SIX

THE GIRL HAD OPENED up a good distance.

With the tomahawk in one hand and the pistol in the other, Callan ran along the road in long, fluent strides, following a thin trail of zombies who had fled the other scene in search of easier pickings—the girl—whose scent of flesh and blood they couldn't resist.

Callan reached the first lumbering soul from the rear and tripped it with a leg sweep he had learned as a Taekwondo junior. The female fell flat onto the bitumen with a slap and thud, her hands and knees breaking the fall. He jumped to her side and kicked her in the face with his boot. Her head snapped back, a stream of blood flying from her crusted mouth. She made no sound and her bulbous eyes viewed him with indifference. Callan poked the pistol muzzle in her face and pulled the trigger. Flesh exploded in a sickening mess. He jogged on as several others turned back with curiosity. He shot the first in the forehead, but then decided he'd better save bullets. He ran past the others, fighting the urge to beat them to death.

It was as though the difficulty and loss of the last week had built to this, a devastating, climactic explosion of his self-control. Anger surged through him, begging to be unleashed. Although he had abandoned the others, had he stayed, who knew what might have occurred.

On either side of the road, modest suburban houses stared down at him. A trail of abandoned vehicles littered the way. He thought about trying one, but decided he might lose valuable time attempting to start it. He slipped between their shiny fenders and even slid across the crumpled blue hood of one that had smashed into a parked SUV. Glass lay sprinkled on the road and the half-eaten body of a man in a brown suit caught his attention for a moment.

He slowed as he reached a gathering of zombies lingering around a black Holden Ute. It was the kind of gas-guzzling car Callan had driven in his early twenties, with a tray for work tools or a motorbike. Several had climbed into the tray, while others crawled beside the fender, swiping pale, ineffective hands underneath.

Callan circled, staying back from the zombies, and crouched to view beneath the vehicle. He saw one leg in a pair of red jeans attached to a dirty white sneaker. The girl had crawled right into the middle, as far from her attackers as possible. At the edge though, a big dirty zombie in an ambulance uniform lay on its stomach trying to reach her.

The girl screamed.

Callan dropped the magazine from the Browning and found five of the thirteen rounds remaining. He should have taken another mag, but there had been little time and even less thought. He wondered on how many occasions he had cursed characters in movies for not performing obvious actions.

The girl screamed again.

Squatting down, Callan yelled, "Hang on! I'll get you out in a minute. Don't let that ambulance zombie get you."

He glanced back along the road and saw a dozen or more feeders walking towards him. They would reach them before he could save the girl. He had to clean them up first.

Callan tucked the pistol into his belt and gripped the tomahawk handle in a tight fist. The girl screamed again as the ambulance zombie squirmed for her. Callan imagined Sherry getting attacked in the BMW, the scratches, and the bites, and the terror she must have felt. Rage swept over him. He had failed to protect her; failed to keep his unborn baby safe. It was unforgivable, and as much as Callan hated the zombies, he hated himself more.

He took the first with a one-handed swing, the blade splitting its face diagonally across the bridge of the nose and spraying blood in a shower. It crumpled, distracting the second feeder, but Callan's scent was too strong and it turned back, lunging at him with an awkward grope. He waited, then smashed the back of the blade down onto its skull, caving the cranium with brutal force. The blade scratched the road and sent up sparks. Others turned, shambling his way. He tried to number them again, but lost count after four or five when he realized the fat ambulance man had disappeared further underneath the van. One or two seemed satisfied with the two casualties and steered wide of him. A truck driver with a dark handlebar moustache, wearing a checked shirt and rolled up sleeves, decided he was going to put a stop to Callan's handiwork. He charged, red eyes bulging. Callan swung the tomahawk high and split the trucker's head in half like a watermelon. Blood gushed and the goggle-eyed zombie fell to the side, gore scattering over the bitumen the way an exploding water balloon had done when they were kids. It was the first time in days of killing he felt his stomach lurch. That set the remaining off, and they abandoned the challenging girl in favor of the troublemaker. He took two more with hefty swings, spreading blood and guts over the road, and providing the remaining an easy feed, which they took.

Callan dropped the weapon and took the fat man by the feet, attempting to drag him away from the undercarriage, but he wouldn't move. With a strained face and bulging cheeks, Callan took hold and leaned back, groaning as the zombie's loathsome body slid free. He walked rearwards until the thing was clear, its thick arms clawing above its head for the lost treasure. Time was growing short, so Callan removed the pistol and shot the zombie in the head.

After ensuring there was no more immediate threat, he squatted beside the van, arms and legs trembling, his burning lungs scratching for air. The girl was sobbing. "Come out, please." She groaned and mumbled something. With his palms pressed against the warm bitumen, Callan lowered himself until he could see her.

She was gangly, with long sandy hair and a narrow face turned towards him. She was sobbing and full of the sniffles. Her body seemed to be twitching, or convulsing, and Callan knew immediately that she'd been bitten.

40

He ground his jaw, thinking. It was a situation he suspected they might face more often. Fairness was not even a word anymore. It just didn't exist in this world. Whether he let her live, or shot her dead, it wasn't right. Standing, Callan pulled the pistol from his waistband, flexing his hand around the grip. In that moment, he hated life more than ever. His right hand struck out in a fist and thumped against the side of the vehicle. Pain spiked up his arm, and he savored it. Could he kill a young girl just bitten and probably not yet affected by the virus? The idea made him feel sick.

He bent down. "Hey? Can you hear me?" She groaned. "Are you bitten? Can you come out?" She mumbled something. "Huh? Talk louder."

But she didn't say anything else. Either she wasn't speaking, or could no longer do so. Something wasn't right.

Callan put the pistol down, dropped onto his belly, and crawled beneath the vehicle, scraping his back on the undercarriage. Her eyes were closed, body slack. The idea that she was faking, luring him into a trap so she could savage him in the tight spot flashed through his mind. But he couldn't leave her there. He had to establish if she'd been bitten.

Callan took one of her sneakers in hand. "I'm going to pull you out of here. It's safe now." But there was still no response. It took all his strength to move her, and he worried her head would be hurt dragging her over the road. He had no choice though; both their lives were at great risk. He expected at any moment to feel the rough grope of a feeder on his leg.

The girl was light though, and when he made the first pull, he shuffled backward on his elbows and repeated, holding his breath, imagining the zombies closing in.

The moment they were out, Callan sprang to his feet and scooped up the gun, ready to attack. But the zombies were all still face deep in entrails.

He pulled her out the rest of the way, and the moment Callan saw her, he knew something was wrong. Her forehead was slick with sweat, and her eyelids flickered.

"Let me come with you, Daddy," she said.

Callan examined her arms, then turned her on the side and checked her back. He scrutinized the rear of her neck, collarbone, and throat, pushing aside a dirty necklace with a silver locket. Apart from the grime of survival, her clothes were intact. He checked her legs and feet, but she was clear. No bite. Something was definitely wrong though. He felt a flash of guilt for thinking about killing her, coupled with relief.

"Hey, can you hear me?" he asked, shaking her gently. "Sweetie? What's wrong?"

She frowned, grimaced, and then groaned. "That's not right … he didn't … take it with us." Her eyes flew open, and she tried to sit up. Callan put a hand behind her back to support her.

"What is it? What's wrong?"

She had no capacity to answer though. He took one of her hands and felt it shaking. She closed her eyes and lay back down, but this time, they remained shut.

He needed Kristy.

Callan turned, hearing the sound of footsteps. Several of the zombies had finished eating and were shuffling towards them. They never stopped. They just kept eating. He picked up the tomahawk, stepped in front of the unconscious girl, and tightened his grip.

SEVEN

DYLAN STEPPED OFF THE road and onto the grass as Kristy steered the Jeep and trailer away from the curb. Leading Johnny towards the far end of the main hospital building, Dylan said, "You were great back there, man, and at the house, too, but I have to ask you something. I have to know if it's true." Johnny stopped, narrowing his eyes. "Did you sleep with Sherry?"

Johnny glared at Dylan. "It's none of your business."

"Yes it is. I need to know if the guy I'm going into battle with would do such a thing."

Johnny dropped the Winchester rifle and leaped at Dylan. It took Dylan a moment to realize what was happening. Johnny twisted the neck of his shirt, threw two left punches and a right, clipping Dylan on the chin. Dylan struck back with the same combination that his dad had taught him as a youngster, but it was wayward, and Johnny ducked easily out of the way. Johnny growled, pushed in close, and took Dylan in a strong headlock, dragging him to the ground.

They wrestled, rolling on the grass, both fighting to get a fistful of shirt or skin. "Are you fucking crazy?" Dylan asked in a muffled voice. Johnny swung a fist up and under, hitting the point of Dylan's nose. Tears filled his eyes, clouding his vision. All he could think to do was reach around and grab a chunk of Johnny's thick black hair, then yank his head back.

Johnny screamed. "Fucking girl! Don't pull hair!" He threw an elbow and struck Dylan in the ribs, knocking the breath from him. He fell back into the grass and Johnny pounced.

Dylan tried to roll away, but Johnny dug a knee into his stomach, pinning him to the ground. Another punch hit Dylan's nose. Pain exploded through his face. He stuck both forearms in front of him, deflecting the fists. The instant they stopped, he reached out and grabbed Johnny by the throat.

Dylan rolled again and this time dislodged Johnny, who was busy trying to break the grip. Johnny fell, thumping his head on the concrete walkway.

Dylan had a moment to strike, but fighting wasn't his intention; he just wanted to know the truth. He climbed to his feet and stepped back, readying himself for another attack.

"You're a fucking idiot," Dylan said. "We're on the same team." Johnny stood, staring back, breathing heavily. A dark mark had appeared on his cheek. Dylan felt wetness at his nose. He touched a finger to it and saw blood. "You haven't changed. I thought you had, but I was wrong."

Johnny glowered. "Don't mention it again."

"You should tell him, man. How can you live with yourself?"

"I'm not telling Callan. It's in the past. What good could it do him knowing that shit? What good would it do for the group?"

Dylan made a face of disbelief, but the last thing Johnny had said made some sense. Perhaps it wasn't the best thing for the group. Could Callan handle knowing the truth? He was the cornerstone of their band, the leader. Unconsciously, they all fed off his energy. What if he couldn't deal with it and the treachery brought them all undone?

"You might think it's the best thing, but you're wrong," Johnny said.

More zombies had drifted out of the emergency entrance. Several had noticed them, and wandered closer.

It was a hopeless conversation to have. "Whatever. We need to get this medicine. Can we manage that for now? You give a shit about Greg, don't you?"

Johnny nodded.

Dylan wiped sweat from his brow with the back of his arm. The rain had stopped, the clouds blowing eastward revealing a patchwork of sun, its heat biting, the humidity thick and heavy against their skin. He led them onto a paved pathway that ran alongside the building as zombies lumbered after them. He had spied a smaller entrance away from the main area, and decided they might draw less attention using that. A door greeted them that read: EMERGENCY EXIT ONLY – 24-HOUR ALARM.

He expected the door to be locked, but the dark strip jutted out an inch from the frame, and he pulled it open by the heavy steel handle. Johnny slipped through the doorway and Dylan followed, twisting his nose at the smell of decay. He pulled the door shut behind him.

Johnny turned his face away. "Oh, fuck, that's putrid."

A narrow, empty passageway led to the main hallway. Dylan followed Johnny along the slick white tiles, the familiar Remington bolt action rifle resting easy in his hands. He levered the bolt, snapping the round into the chamber, reminding himself to expect the unexpected. He felt more comfortable with the rifle than the pistol.

Johnny stopped at the end of the corridor and raised his hand. He appeared to have moved on past their fight as quickly as he had instigated it. Dylan edged forward and peered around the corner, listening for the sound of movement. Johnny stepped out into the corridor, turning the barrel of the rifle along the hallway. He peered both ways, then signaled for Dylan to join him.

"Where's the pharmacy?" Johnny asked.

"A hundred yards or so straight ahead."

It was a wider section of the hospital, with neat sofas stuck in the middle where people could sit and rest. On either side of the hallway sat rooms filled with desks, computers, and chairs.

They crept along in slow step, alert and cautious. Thoughts of Dylan's father kept resurfacing, and he had to fight to keep them away. *Kristy*, he remembered, and in that moment, Dylan made a pact with himself that he would do something in spite of the world ending: marry her. It filled him with a rare warm delight, and he couldn't help but smile. Suddenly his knees were lifting higher, and his step felt a little softer.

Johnny halted, raised a finger to his lips, and pointed ahead.

Dylan listened, pushing away the excitement of his idea for now. At first, there was only silence. Then, he heard it— a crunching sound, like cracking bones. He scanned the hallway and rooms around them without seeing anything obvious. "You hear that?"

Johnny nodded. "Yeah." He licked his cracked lips. Dylan's felt the same, too. When was the last time he'd taken water? Eaten? Even peed? It wouldn't come to him. *None of it mattered now, anyway*, he thought. They pressed on.

The hallway turned and then opened up into a circular intersection with stores on all corners: a gift shop, a cafeteria, and a florist. Here, the place resembled chaos; hospital trolleys lay on their sides, flowers had been smashed across the floor, petals and stems smeared into the white flooring. Medical instruments were scattered across the room along with poles with tubes, bags of saline, and numerous electronic devices. Several wheelchairs lay overturned, and it was here they saw the first of the bodies.

Strapped to one of the wheelchairs was a zombie. Its eyes were open, but its bloated, yellow face, streaked with the dead flesh of its victims, was still. Johnny approached, examining its features.

"You are one ugly motherfucker." The thing hissed like a cat, then snapped its jaws and jumped the wheelchair across the floor. "FUCK!" Johnny screamed, leaping back. He tripped on a saline stand and tumbled onto the tiles, the bang echoing down the hallway.

This wasn't one of the slow and stupid type one feeders, Dylan realized, but he didn't think it was one of the crazies, either. "Shit man, why would you do that?" he asked.

Johnny's face went as pale as bone. "I thought the fucker was dead."

"They're only dead if their heads have been shot."

Dylan fired a bullet into the zombie's head. Dark blood sprayed across the green carpet.

The sound of rustling floated from the gift shop. Both boys glanced in that direction, although no perpetrator was visible. "Let's keep moving," Dylan said. "We could waste all our ammo on finishing off this mess."

They picked their way around the scattered debris and moved down one of the hallways towards the pharmacy. On the right, a cafeteria beckoned, and Johnny headed towards the dark refrigerators and shadowy corners beyond the counter. Several bodies lay on the floor, but Dylan turned away from their stiff, lifeless faces.

"No," he said, and Johnny turned. "We gotta keep moving."

The hallways were too quiet. The floor was still messy: hospital carts, food trolleys, and the odd portable bed, along with rotten food and drinks were strewn about. There should have been zombies feeding on dead bodies, or at least more of them wandering around. A seed of worry put Dylan on edge. Perhaps most of the feeders had broken through the emergency doors and gone outside. He didn't buy it though; the hospitals had patients, and a huge number of staff.

Johnny strode towards a room on the left side of the hallway, beyond a set of elevators. Smoky glass obscured the top half, and the milling legs of a dozen zombies filled the bottom. The throng pushed gently against the doors. The handles had been roped together.

"Someone locked them in," Johnny said. "Brilliant."

Dylan glanced to his left and recoiled. Lying on the carpet behind a half-raised hospital bed was the body of a policeman, decked in full uniform: navy pants and a pale blue shirt. His eyes were open, and his police hat was askew. A pool of blood had seeped out onto the green carpet beneath him.

Johnny hopped over the body and squatted beside it. Dylan admired his guts to get so close. Johnny prodded the guy, and pushed him onto his back. "He's no zombie, and he hasn't been bitten." A coil of plastic-coated wire remained clasped in his hand, and a steel pipe protruded from his belly. He wore a timeless expression of surprise. The irony of this washed over Dylan. "Poor bugger. He probably did all the work locking up those zombies." Johnny reached out and closed the man's eyelids.

They saw the pharmacy thirty yards along the hall through a sea of more clutter. When they reached it, Dylan had a sinking feeling. The man who had locked the office full of zombies had also secured the pharmacy doors using the same cord, trapping another horde of feeders.

"That's why we haven't seen many wandering the hallway," Dylan said.

The dead pressed their faces against the doors and windows, tongues and fingers smearing gore over the glass. They were three or four deep, six wide, squashed in like a mosh pit, and growing irritated. A nurse, who Dylan was certain had once been pretty, gnawed on the frail arm of an elderly zombie dressed in pajamas. Another woman, topped with a bun of grey hair, leered at them through a set of glasses. Dylan marveled that they had remained unbroken.

Ahead, from another section of the building, a thunderous crash sounded and the ground shook.

Johnny's face dropped. "What the fuck was that?"

Dylan shook his head. "I don't know."

EIGHT

KRISTY STEERED THE JEEP around the corner towards the street where Callan had left them. She had a grim feeling. *You're going the wrong way*, her mind kept saying. She was, and on consideration, she couldn't help blaming Callan. Admittedly, he had gone to help the people in the van, but without thinking of their primary objective—getting meds for Greg. He clearly wasn't thinking straight; there was no other explanation. The image of Sherry running for the garage appeared in her mind, and she bit down on her emotions by holding her breath. Was it her fault? Maybe. She had directed Sherry toward the supposed safety of the BMW. That was their last contact, and would be the fading memory for the rest of her life.

Focus. The best thing she could do now was find Callan, then return to the hospital and pick up the boys.

Blue Boy peered out the rear window. He had barked several times on Callan's departure. It was his dog, no question. He had always garnered a strong loyalty from pets. They had owned a dog when they were kids—Aussie, another blue heeler—and he had slept on Callan's bed each night. If anybody threatened Callan, even playfully, Aussie would growl and bark. Now, Blue Boy had found that same strain of loyalty that Aussie had possessed for so long.

Greg lay slumped down in the seat again, his long legs tucked into the footwell. She felt a sick desperation to get him medicine. He was more than a patient; he was a close friend, and had saved all their lives more than once. He always perceived their need at the right time.

"Hang on, Greg. Won't be long. You still with us?"

Greg moaned. "Yeah."

What if there were no antibiotics? Worse, what if Dylan and Johnny were killed trying to get them? What if Callan was killed and all that was left were Greg, Blue Boy, and her.

Did she have enough time to find another hospital and then some medicine?

Stop. She would drive herself crazy.

The trailer tugged on the back of the Jeep as she dragged the wheel left, missing a sprinkling of broken glass from the rear window of an old Holden station wagon parked diagonally in the street. It would surely spell their demise if one of the tires went flat. She had a vague idea of the direction in which Callan had run, and guided the Jeep around the final corner and onto the street.

She had survived another onslaught; in those final moments she'd been certain her time was up. Such incidents were becoming common, although she didn't know how much more she could handle. If she let her ego run a moment, she had to admit she was pleased with her efforts. She was alive. With help, she had survived, again.

I've changed, she thought. They all had.

The Jeep rolled along the street, past a row of glaring houses, and huddles of abandoned cars. Callan had to be there somewhere. She guided the vehicle around a blue Toyota sedan that had crashed into a parked SUV. The tires crunched as they rolled over more glass, the half-eaten body of a man glaring up at them.

In the distance, she saw someone standing in front of a black Ute. It had to be Callan. Kristy sped on, then feathered the brakes on approach. It was Callan, standing with the tomahawk raised, a throng of zombies shuffling towards him.

A flood of anger washed over her. The zombies had stolen so much from her, so much from the world. Kristy might one day have had a niece or nephew, maybe even a father-in-law. But they had all been taken. She had accepted that both her parents had died, and probably most of her friends. These things that kept trying to kill them had caused it. They were people, she knew, but if she thought about that too much, her strength might waver. What they were now was not what they had been, and Kristy didn't think killing them would denigrate the spirit of their previous existence.

She aimed the Jeep at the long, broken line headed towards Callan, and ran over a body lying in the road. The car jumped as though hitting a speed hump. The trailer bounced, too, thumping back down with a metallic crunch.

Greg sat up, a painful expression on his face, but his eyes were wide, taking it all in.

"Sorry," Kristy said. "Hold on." In the rear, Blue Boy barked in anticipation.

Bodies scattered as the front of the Jeep struck the zombie line. Half a man in a grimy blue sweater rolled up the hood and hit the window. Kristy screamed, then flinched, pulling the vehicle off course, but she quickly straightened it. Others with their ogling eyes and rotten mouths didn't move, and she ran them down growling, her hands choking the steering wheel. She couldn't get them all though, and had to turn away in the end, or run Callan over. Several scattered, and she took them down, leaving the seat as the big wheels drove over their fallen bodies.

She stopped the Jeep and saw Greg looking out the rear window. Several zombies had made it through her barrage, but she had reduced their numbers, and Callan had engaged the remaining with the tomahawk. Lying on the road was the body of a girl, but they were too far away and Kristy needed to get the Jeep back around to them. She switched her foot to the gas pedal and took off with a jerk.

The path ahead was clear. She steered the car through a narrow section between more abandoned vehicles and turned in a wide circle, driving up onto the curb with a bump. She worked her way back around until she reached an open space near the girl. Callan was still busy trying to drive the zombies away from her. Four of them had closed in on him with searching hands and mouths. Three more lay on the road with their skulls and necks split.

Kristy swung the door open and leaped down from the seat, then ran to the rear of the Jeep. Inside, she pulled a

Remington .308 pump action from the edge of the compartment and checked the ammo. There were several rounds within. Blue leaped out of the back barking, then zipped away towards Callan. Kristy followed.

The zombies stood just outside of Callan's range with their limp arms and clumsy legs. Tattered, dirty clothes hung from their emaciated flesh, and their smell made her gag. As she walked forward, Kristy took aim at one of the zombies in line for Callan's blood, and fired.

A hole opened in the side of its stomach. Blood spurted out. She fired again and hit the same feeder in the head, and it fell back like a falling tree.

Callan yanked the tomahawk out of a neck. "Grab the girl. She isn't bitten, but she's sick."

Kristy ran to her as Callan dispatched another zombie, then drove the other two backward, giving her more space in which to work. She offered him the Remington, but he kept swinging the blade, bloodier than a meat cleaver in an abattoir.

Kristy checked the girl's airway. Clear. She lifted her hand and detected a slight tremor, then felt for her pulse with two fingers. The beat was rapid. Kristy put a hand to her forehead, finding hot, clammy skin.

Callan finished off the other two zombies and joined her.

"Was she unconscious when you found her?"

"No. I saw her running from the ambulance, but by the time I arrived, she was underneath the car and … mumbling."

"Mumbling?"

"Yeah. As if she was talking to someone."

"Hallucinating?"

"Maybe."

"Did she hit her head?"

"I don't know."

Kristy felt around her skull for any swelling. Nothing. *Think.* Shaking hands, hallucinations, sweating, and loss of conscious. Kristy perused the girl: her face, torso, arms, and legs. The t-shirt hung loose on her thin frame. The tattered jeans had been cut to three-quarters length, and the bright pink running shoes had half a flap hanging loose. She couldn't have been more than eleven or twelve. Kristy took her hand, contemplating asking Callan to carry the girl, when she noticed the ends of the girl's fingers, and it struck her like a static shock.

She examined the tips. The marks were fading, but still evident: tiny red dots of dried blood. Finger prick marks. She yanked up the girl's top and examined her lower abdomen.

"What are you doing?" Callan asked.

Kristy felt the wash of relief. That was it. She wasn't wearing any form of identification, but she felt certain. "She's a diabetic. And she's hypoglycaemic."

"What?"

"We have to get her a shot of glycogen, or she'll die soon. Very soon."

NINE

THE FIRST ZOMBIE CLIMBED out of the bus. Evelyn had not seen one so up close before. Its face resembled rotting pastry, its skin tight around sharp, angular bones.

Jake froze. "Mommy?"

At first, she couldn't move. Then she stepped in front of Jake. "Move back, honey."

A second withered specimen slithered out. It had a shock of fuzzy brown hair and big buggy eyes. A third, surprisingly fleshy, followed. The first one ushered towards them.

"Go, Jake. Run."

They sprinted for the fence, ducking to go underneath the top railing. Jake moved with the smoothness of a twelve-year-old. Evelyn had to stop, falling into a deep squat, feeling the bulk of her thighs protest. She clipped her head on a metal beam, wincing as pain flashed through her skull.

The zombies were surprisingly quick. Or was it that she was slow? Two more had joined the original three. The first closed in.

"Hurry, Mom!"

Evelyn pulled herself up using the rail and shuffled along the path after Jake. Exercise wasn't her favorite activity. She hadn't been able to shift the pregnancy weight after the loss of a child during the second trimester three years ago. Cameron had never mentioned the extra pounds, but Evelyn noticed every day. Now, she wondered if it might cause a premature end to her life.

Jake had pulled ahead. He even had time to turn around and tell her the zombies were still chasing. She had once been like him, light of foot, possessing the stamina of a pack horse. In school, she had won the cross-country two grades below the other kids without even training.

It took less than a minute for her breathing to grow short and her chest to tighten. *Oh, Jesus,* she thought, *I'm going to die*. The idea of leaving Jake alone provided a second wind, but by the time they reached the corner, it felt as though she had an object caught in her throat.

"Got to … stop," she wheezed, leaning over, hands on knees.

Jake spun, eyes wide, unable to believe it. "Don't stop! They're coming."

She shuffled, still bent, and saw two of them had maintained their pursuit.

Evelyn found strength, stumbling along the path, but the pain in her chest turned from an ache into a sharp stabbing sensation. Anger came in a sudden burst. Why hadn't Cameron pushed her more to use the gym membership? Her thighs burned, and a shroud of agony settled over her body. She imagined herself giving up. Jake could keep going. He'd have to find a way to survive.

The pack thumped against her back as she ran. Maybe she should ditch it. They would find more supplies. *Yes*. That would help. She slowed, her muscles and airways screaming with relief, but Jake had sensed her failing stamina. He reached out and took her hand, begging her to keep trying.

But she would need more. Her jelly legs stopped working. She tried to shake the bag free and wriggled the last bit off. It fell to the ground with a thump. Jake screamed.

She wasn't going to make it. A thought flashed across her mind. The kitchen knife. In the bag. She fumbled the zipper.

The first infected reached them, grabbing for her shirt. She was surprised they had been so close. Jake screamed again, beating his fists against the thing. Evelyn fought the urge to grab Jake's hand and run. She knew she wouldn't last. Instead, she rammed her shoulder forward, knocking the thing from their space, now grateful for her size.

She had placed the knife beneath the clothes, covered by a cardboard sleeve. In hindsight, such a move had been stupid. Hands digging between a pair of jeans and a t-shirt, Evelyn shoved other garments aside. Finally, her fingers touched cold metal. She curled the handle in her grip and wrenched it from the bag.

The long, shapely blade glinted in the sunlight. Screaming, Evelyn thrust it into the infected thing's eye, squirting reddish fluid across her shoulder. It stooped, and when she pulled the knife backward, it collapsed to the ground. The second thing reached for her and she did the same again, but she missed the eye socket and the weapon bounced back. She lunged again and caught it in the soft jelly, where it disappeared until the taper of the steel no longer fit.

She couldn't get the knife out and the thing fell back onto the concrete. Two more hitched towards them. Jake pulled her shirt and they ran.

They had reached the end of the street before Evelyn realized she had left her backpack. A zombie had begun rifling through it while the other marched on. All they had now were Jake's clothes in a small pack. Evelyn fought the urge to cry. Maybe she should give up. She had lost Cameron–thankfully, long before this–and now her parents. It would be easy to lie down and let them take her, except for the knowledge that Jake would never do the same, and then he'd be alone.

A sound drifted to them from the right, but Evelyn kept watching the zombie limping towards them. Jake said something, but she had tuned out. She kept imagining what it would feel like to die. Then her cheek stung, and she swung around, realizing he had slapped her.

"What—"

A dirty, beaten, brown Toyota Land Cruiser had pulled up beside them.

"Get in," the driver said. He was young, with sharp, pointed features. Greasy brown hair covered a face lined with dark stubble.

Jake nudged her. "Go, Mom."

She did, stumbling her way over the curb and to the vehicle. She swung the door open, helped Jake up, and fell into the seat. The tires chirped and they sped away, Evelyn still wondering how she had survived.

TEN

A THOUGHT OCCURRED TO Dylan as they stood outside the pharmacy, watching the zombies growing more agitated. Johnny could kill him. Nobody would know. His secret would remain safe, and Callan would never learn the truth. Perhaps it had been a mistake to venture into the hospital with Johnny. He should have come with Kristy, instead. She would have been at greater risk, but he could have protected her, and she'd have his back. He understood now why people insisted on trust in combat.

But there was no turning back now. They were there and needed those meds. The quicker they found them, the sooner he could return to Kristy.

Dylan had an idea. "The dead guy," he said, running a hand though his sweaty hair. "We use him as bait." Johnny's face was blank. "We need something to draw them away."

They negotiated their way back along the hallway through the mess, careful to avoid those rooms that sounded as if they had residents. Dylan selected an overturned bed, and once they had it upright, both boys cleared a path for it to be wheeled to where the dead man lay. Even at the gurney's lowest point, they grunted and strained, lifting him onto the trolley. Dylan marveled at the weight of the dead body.

With Dylan pushing, they guided the equipment back along the hallway until they reached the pharmacy. He kept glancing around, making sure he could still see Johnny.

"How's this gonna work?" Johnny asked.

"I guess we just open the doors and hope they follow us."

They cleared a path leading away from the pharmacy, and Dylan made mental note of where he might park the trolley once he had drawn them all out. It was going to be tight; if the feeders spread out in a wide line they might not be able to sneak back past. Dylan found several bags of blood underneath an overturned cart. When they had the gurney in place, both boys stood before the pharmacy, looking into the throng of killers.

"We just open the doors?" Johnny asked.

Dylan nodded. "And we stay close together so they don't spread out."

"Why don't we just shoot them?"

"I've only got half a dozen rounds. How many do you have?"

"'Bout the same."

"If we need to shoot, we can."

He couldn't think of anything else. There wasn't time to devise a better strategy. Once he opened those doors, the zombies would come piling out. He was scared. Perhaps his courage had finally run out. He was sick of facing off with them, sick of the blood and gore, and the risk to their lives. Hadn't he given up enough yet? And now his face ached where Johnny had slugged him. He just wanted to leave it all behind, to get away from it for a while. He'd earned that, hadn't he?

Don't. It was his father's voice, the one that had reminded him so many times as a child never to complain about the circumstances he was dealt.

Dylan remembered his grandmother's death when he was a boy. He had sat with his father on the faded yellow plastic swing set in the front yard before the funeral.

"It's not fair," Dylan had said.

"Nope."

"Aren't you angry?"

"Yep."

"What are you going to do about it?"

"Get on with living," his father had said. "It's sad, alright, and I miss Mom already, but life is tough, son. Bad things happen to good people. You gotta get on with it, keep their memory in here," he touched Dylan's chest where his heart beat, "and make the best of what they left behind. Make them proud. Honor their memory."

"So I can't be sad?"

"Of course you can be sad. You *must* be sad. But don't ever feel sorry for yourself. There's always somebody worse off."

Dylan thought of Greg, and the times he had saved each of them, throwing himself into danger without regard for his own life. Greg would never sulk. He'd just get on with what needed to be done. And now, Greg needed medication.

Dylan stepped up to the doors.

"I'll do it," Johnny said.

Dylan hesitated. "Thanks, but it's my idea."

Before Dylan had finished unwinding the cord from around the handles, the zombies were pushing their way out. He leaped away from the doors as they clanged open. "Back," he said, driving the gurney along the carpet.

The zombies were slow, and he was again thankful it was just the simple ones. He edged the gurney through the swamp, Johnny pushing and pulling the end where it required extra guidance. The pace was right on, keeping seven or eight yards ahead of the pack, but Dylan couldn't move any faster.

They reached the drop-off zone, then turned and waited for stragglers to catch up. The front feeders had almost reached the gurney. Dylan ripped open the bag of blood and tipped it over the dead man. The smell stung his nostrils, and he felt his stomach convulse.

He snatched up his rifle off the bed. He would now find out if Johnny had any plans for him.

They sprinted to the other wall, sidestepping and leaping over refuse. Hunkering low, they moved alongside a series of couches and upended cupboards until they reached the pharmacy doors. The last stragglers of the group were five yards away.

"In," Dylan said, pulling back one of the doors for Johnny to enter.

But a zombie, with its dark, hollow, eyes, lifted its nose to their scent, and turned just as Johnny reached the entryway. It started towards them.

Johnny was all instinct. His rifle was in position before the feeder had taken another step.

"No," Dylan said.

The thought struck him again; maybe this was Johnny's chance to create unnecessary confusion, increase the risks of Dylan getting hurt. The rifle exploded and the feeder fell back with a chunk of its head missing. Others turned. Their advantage had been lost. The zombies shambled towards them. Johnny lifted the rifle and fired again. Ribbons of gore flew from another zombie head. "IN!" Dylan screamed.

Johnny did, and Dylan followed, pulling on the handles until both doors met with a clang. He turned a small metal lever and the lock clicked into place.

"Fuck man, what'd you do that for?"

Johnny's chest heaved. His eyes were large, his nostrils flared, the excitement bursting to escape. Dylan realized then how similar Johnny and Callan were.

"Who cares? We'll have to kill them sooner or later."

Frustrated, Dylan turned away. Johnny wasn't as intelligent as Callan. It was pointless trying to explain the idea of stealth. Now the feeders would be waiting outside, and escaping was going to take luck, skill, or a combination of both.

As if to confirm his thinking, a slow thud beat against the glass doors. Dylan ignored it and scrounged through the medicine shelves.

They found various types of antibiotic tablets: Amoxicillin, Augmentin Duo Forte, and Erythromycin capsules. They had all been on Kristy's list. Dylan considered other general illnesses that might befall them and shoved items into the plastic basket: bandages, antiseptic, asthma medicine, even an anaphylactic EpiPen. Who knew if this would be their last chance to stock up on medical items?

Their shopping basket soon overflowed. Johnny found a rectangular-shaped plastic trolley with multiple layers used for carrying cleaning items, towels, and toilet paper. The top section had a narrow groove where he placed the medicines.

They filled it until items fell out the sides. *We might lose some of it on the run out*, Dylan thought, *but it will hold more than we can carry, and the cart will be useful as a blocking tool.* He rolled it to the door, feeling a biting, burning sensation in his upper abdomen.

"If Callan finds out what happened with Sherry, I'll have nobody left," Johnny said. "He'll kick me out of the group. I know it, and you know it."

The fist-throwing lunatic who had attacked Dylan earlier was gone. Before him stood a man with all the bravado and anger stripped away. Dylan sensed Johnny was asking for his help. In that moment, he felt a pang of sorrow for him.

"I don't think he will," Dylan said. "Callan is a changed man. Yeah, he'll be pissed, and probably belt you in the nose, but he won't kick you out." Johnny nodded, but his expression told Dylan he didn't believe him. "Anyway, we won't let him. What you did was foolish and wrong, but it was a mistake, not a death sentence." He let the thought sink in. "We ready?"

"Yeah." Johnny placed his fingers on the lock. "And thanks."

Dylan nodded. "Let's do it."

ELEVEN

HYPOGLYCAEMIC. CALLAN DIDN'T KNOW what it meant, but based on Kristy's reaction, and the girl's condition, he knew it was bad. "Where do we get the shot?"

"The hospital," Kristy said. More zombies staggered in their direction. "But we'll need more than that, Cal. We'll need needles and insulin, too. They were probably going to the hospital for more supplies. Without insulin, she'll die."

Callan took the girl beneath the armpits and lifted her up against his shoulder. She felt like a bag of clothes washing, far too light for her height. He carried her to the van and, after Kristy opened the door, laid her on the back seat.

Greg stirred. "She okay?"

Kristy slid into driver's seat. "She's diabetic. Her blood sugar has dropped too low. If she doesn't get sugar soon, she'll die."

"Drive," Callan said, falling into the passenger seat. The first zombie reached the Jeep, slapping a pair of bloody, pale hands against the window. Others were close behind, but Callan showed no interest.

Kristy accelerated, and within three minutes they were at the front of the hospital parking lot. A dozen or so zombies lingered about, close to the emergency entrance, feeding on the remnants of the earlier battle. Callan spied a door near the corner of the building.

"Drop me off over there and come back in fifteen minutes."

"What about you guys?"

"We'll find you. It's easier this way. You can't wait here, you'll be torn apart."

What else did he need? A face mask. He couldn't remember what had happened to that. His Kevlar clothes were in need of a wash, but still effective. Ammo. He still had some, but could do with another full magazine. They had taken a heap for the Browning from the gun store.

Callan had never seen a man look as ill as Greg. His cheeks were flushed, his eyes red and swollen. His chest rose and fell in jagged movements. It looked as though breathing was a chore, almost beyond him. Maybe it was the virus, and they had been fooled.

In a whisper, he said to Kristy, "You sure he doesn't have the virus?"

"I don't think so. There should have been signs by now, though I can't be certain."

Kristy stopped the Jeep beside the curb. "There will be a section in the pharmacy with diabetic supplies. Blood glucose monitors, insulin pens, and needles, that sort of thing. There might be a glucagon pen. If it's not there, it'll be with the prescription medicine." Callan nodded. "You have to find this, Cal. She'll die without it."

"Okay. I got it. Anything else?"

"Insulin. It'll be in flat rectangle boxes about the size of a slice of cheese, but much thicker. Get as much as you can. And don't forget the insulin pens—that's literally what they are: big, oversized pens. And if you can't find them, get some syringes."

Jesus, Callan thought. He wasn't good at remembering lists. His mother had been able to tell Kristy a range of items to buy at the supermarket, but for him, it had to be written down. That's just how your brain is wired, she had said. The thought of her, something he had not done for what seemed like weeks now, filled him with a soft, warm sadness.

Kristy brushed a strand of blond hair from her eyes. "Maybe I should go in."

"No." Callan opened the door. "I'll remember. You just get out of here and come back in fifteen minutes." He turned to the backseat. "Hey, buddy. Hang in there."

"Yeah," Greg croaked. "All good."

"Sure. You fucking look like it. Just stay here and don't be a hero." He contemplated taking Blue Boy. The dog had a keen sense of self preservation, but who knew what they were walking into. "Stay there, Blue." The dog whimpered, pleading with Callan to let him out. Was this his last goodbye to Kristy?

"Is this ever going to get easier?" she asked

Callan had wondered the same thing himself. "Maybe. But not today. And not tomorrow, either." He smiled, leaned forward, and kissed her cheek. "Stay safe. And don't leave us behind." He took another full magazine from the back, stuffing it into his pocket.

A handful of feeders approached the Jeep. Callan tapped on the roof, and Kristy took off.

It came easier now; he didn't have to think. Callan lifted the semi-automatic pistol and shot the first zombie in the head, emitting a spiral of blood from the back of its skull. The thing crumpled to the ground. One of its friends fell onto its knees and dug in as though it hadn't eaten in weeks. Callan fired on the other three, then jogged across the grass to the entrance near the corner of the building.

The handle wouldn't budge, though. He knocked on the door, feeling the weight of the metal under his knuckles, and tried it again without luck. He hugged the wall as he jogged towards the emergency exit, and had almost made it when a large, middle-aged nurse wearing full uniform lumbered out from behind one of the thick pylons underneath the awning. Her fat hands clutched for him, her red tongue and discolored mouth offering more. Callan stepped back, lifted the pistol and fired, but at the last minute, he pulled the shot left.

He knew the woman; she had stitched up his nose after the accident. A tumble of bleached blond hair sat atop her head. Her cheeks were miniature pillows, her ears large and protruding. He didn't need to read her name tag. She smiled at him, but this time there was no friendliness. She wanted to eat him alive.

Last time, they had waited for two hours before receiving any attention. The nurse, Angela, had discovered this, and promptly ushered them into a room.

"Are you Callan Davidson?"

65

"Yeah." He had tried to recall doing anything of ill recently. "Do I know you?"

She smiled. "No. Well, yes, but you won't remember me." She seemed proud to know him, standing straight, a beaming smile. "You'd be twenty-seven now. I was mid-wife when you were born. You were the first baby I ever delivered." Callan hadn't appreciated such a fact at the time, but such things meant more to him now.

Angela was the Director of Nursing, and had ordered a doctor and two other nurses to provide their immediate services. She had laughed and joked with him, making them feel comfortable, treating Callan like an old friend. He had charmed her, as he often did, and upon his discharge she had given him a peck on the cheek, wishing him a speedy recovery. Nurse Johnson. She had been lovely.

As a zombie, she was quick for her size, the jowls of her belly bouncing as she danced towards him in her plain white nurses' shoes. Rotted teeth beckoned, and the whites of her eyes had turned a putrid yellow.

Callan realized he couldn't kill her. It was idiotic, against everything he knew of sense and logic. He turned and sprinted away, drawing her out from underneath the awning, then ran in a circle back to the emergency doors, leaving her blundering after him.

Two other zombies stepped into his path. Callan shot them both with three bullets, landing one atop the other in a neat heap.

He jerked open one door, feeling a twinge in his shoulder, and pulled it closed behind him. He stood inside the emergency doors, reloading the chamber, his lungs chasing air. Where was the pharmacy? He tried to recall what Kristy had told him.

He took off in a jog down the middle of the hallway to a large round intersection with shops on all corners. The place had been hammered. He stepped over the lifeless, broken bodies of hospital equipment and myriad other items strewn about. He glanced at a zombie strapped to a wheelchair, and turned away.

Who would ever clean it up? Would there ever again be enough humans, without the stresses of daily survival, to bother? Or would it just be about raiding the hospital supplies for lifesaving medicines? And when they were gone? Would anybody ever come back? Callan ignored the useless questions and zigzagged his way along the hallway.

From behind, the crashing sound of closing doors came to him. He imagined Nurse Johnson scrambling in through the emergency entrance, drawn by his pulsing blood.

And then he heard something worse from ahead. A human voice, screaming, followed by the sound of gunfire.

TWELVE

JOHNNY SWUNG THE DOORS open and ran out firing as the zombies crowded in. Grateful for Johnny's courage, Dylan followed, pushing the cart with his rifle resting on the upper shelf. Johnny shot the closest one in the nose, and it fell onto the others, but they knocked it aside in their haste to get to him. They clawed at Dylan's arms but he shrugged them off, his skin tingling with terror. He held his breath at the closeness of their vile smells, cringed at the gore stuck to their faces and hanging from their mouths.

Despite the proximity, two of Johnny's shots went wide, blowing out the windows on the opposite side of the hallway. Dylan halted, swept up the rifle, and dropped one of the feeders with a messy shot through the ear. Johnny's gun boomed again and this time found its mark. The closest feeder collapsed at his feet with a broken, bloody face. Drawn by their insatiable desire to feed, others stopped, reducing the crowd just enough to clear a narrow path.

Dylan shrugged off more groping hands as he slammed the rifle down and drove the trolley forward, ramming their legs. Strong fingers dug into his shoulder, halting his progress. He let go of the cart and spun to face his attacker, fumbling for the rifle.

A pale, balding man in blue overalls, with pocked skin and bloated eyes, came at him. A dark, grizzly tongue rolled around its mouth. It must have outweighed him by sixty pounds. Dylan snatched at the rifle, but it was too far. As the thing closed, he threw out a left jab and struck its cheek. It blinked and staggered forward with its bony arms out.

He stepped backward, but his heels crashed into the cart and he almost overbalanced. He put out a hand and clutched onto one of the handles, preventing his fall. The zombie was on him though, skeletal fingers around the leathered neck of his jacket. He pulled at them, but it was like trying to bend steel bars, and he gagged, scratching for air. His weight shifted; the cart tipped, and he tumbled backward with the thing still latched on.

They hit the floor with a crash, the medicine and other supplies spilling onto the carpet with a tinkle of glass. Dylan tried to roll away. The moment he turned onto his knees, he realized it was a mistake. The zombie's knee fell onto his spine and he dropped, his chin hitting the carpet. *This is it.* Even if Johnny could save him, this was his chance to let his treachery against Callan die away as if it had never happened.

Dylan groped for its clothes. He had to drag it off. Where was Johnny? He tried to turn his head, but the zombie grabbed a chunk of his dark hair. Dylan reached back with his left hand, scratching at it, but it was too heavy, too strong, and his arm fell, fingers slapping the carpet. The gun, where was his gun? He tried to push up onto his elbows, but the pain in his knee kept him flat. He thought of Kristy, and what would happen to her when he was gone. Greg would take care of her. A strong hand tightened around his neck, cutting off his airways. Dylan gagged. Where the fuck was Johnny? *Probably laughing.*

Gunfire roared.

The weight released off Dylan's back, and the zombie toppled off. He sucked in air and scrambled to his knees, then onto his feet, wondering why he wasn't dead.

Johnny stood nearby holding the smoking Winchester .30-30. But it wasn't over yet. Numerous zombies were still in close vicinity, clamoring for their flesh. Johnny swung the rifle around towards Dylan, and as he dropped to the floor, it exploded, knocking a zombie onto its ass. Dylan spied his Remington and scrambled towards it. Ahead, another feeder had spotted him, and decided he looked nice enough to eat. It was a race to the gun, but Dylan wasn't going to make it. The zombie reached it first, and Dylan realized he was beaten. But then its head exploded and it slumped aside, leaving him to the weapon. As he swung around to thank his partner, a zombie latched onto Johnny.

Dylan screamed, "Look out!"

The thing bit down into the soft flesh of Johnny's upper arm. He turned to break free, and they crashed over another pile of refuse.

Dylan fired instinctively, but the shot went wide and blew out another office window. More zombies closed in, sensing a victim from whom they could all get a feed.

With Johnny in its grip, the zombie looked up, as if calling to its associates. Dylan saw fresh blood on its face, and a chunk of flesh in its mouth. Johnny thrashed about, screaming. "LET GO MOTHERFUCKER!" They were moving so much that Dylan couldn't get a clear shot.

A muffled voice called out, "Just shoot it!"

Two more zombies approached Dylan on his left, with listless arms, jerky movements, their bloody clothes hanging in tatters. He shot them both in the face, flinching at the explosion of blood and bone.

Snatching rounds from his pocket, Dylan held his position as he reloaded, poking them into the rifle until it was full again. In this time, Johnny had managed to crawl free, providing Dylan a foot of clear space with which to kill the fat feeder. It crawled after Johnny on stout arms and bulky legs, tongue hanging, flesh still in its mouth. Dylan jabbed the rifle muzzle into the side of the zombie's head and pulled the trigger. A jet of rose-colored matter shot over a pile of clean linen, and the thing fell onto its face.

Johnny lay back against a mound of plastic instruments, his face twisted in agony, one elbow cupped in the palm of his other hand. Dylan ran to him and fell on his knees at his side.

"I'm sorry, man. So sorry."

Johnny's furrowed brow begged for help. Dylan picked about the mess for some bandages. He found a roll and wound it around Johnny's arm.

Johnny froze as he stared straight ahead. "Oh shit, man."

One of the zombies had risen and picked up the Winchester .30-30. It turned the gun in its hands, the way it might a severed arm, or leg, and then lifted the weapon to its rotted nose.

"Did you load a round into it?"

"Yeah. I did, just before it got me."

With limited movement, Dylan tied off the bandage and laid Johnny's arm across his chest. Eyes on the zombie, Dylan reached out for his weapon and slid it back to his other hand.

A second and third zombie drifted from a smoky-glassed office nearby. One fell onto its knees and ripped off a piece of a brother's arm. The second stood beside the type two, who now had the gun pointed in its direction.

The gun exploded and both boys jumped. The zombie's neck caved in, blood and matter exploding across its chest, and it crumpled to the floor. The feeder holding the gun looked confused. Then it turned the gun and aimed it directly at Dylan.

THIRTEEN

CALLAN SPRINTED ALONG THE hospital hallway, leaping rubble, following a crisscross path through the mess. He repressed the urge to shoot feeding zombies as he sped past several; he didn't have the time, or ammo. His friends might be in trouble, and he wasn't prepared to let anyone else die.

Johnny had long been a good mate, someone for whom Callan would give his own life to save. Two months ago, he'd never have said the same about Dylan. They had begun the journey as distant associates through their high school days, and more recently, Kristy. They had never been friends though, and while Callan's liking for him had grown during the camping trip, it wasn't until the last few days, as they had shared such personal circumstances, that he'd classified Dylan as a mate.

Callan reached the long stretch of open hallway spread out like a bad scene in a movie. He slowed to a jog and took it all in: a zombie holding a gun, Dylan standing over Johnny, sitting on the carpet. Carnage littered the hallway: bodies slumped over fallen medical instruments, lying flat on the floor, even one lying against a hospital bed. Several zombies were devouring their own dead.

Callan squatted behind a pile of equipment and took aim. The zombie had the rifle pointed at Dylan, with a finger looped around the lever that chambered the round. For it to be handling a weapon, it had to be a type two. Surely it couldn't—

The zombie moved, and the rifle exploded. Callan jumped. Dylan threw himself onto the floor.

Callan fired but the shot went wide, and then he was up, screaming, running towards them, the gun drawn and pointed. The zombie turned the gun on him with the familiar, senseless expression. The passionate hatred exploded, and Callan ran directly at it, unafraid of the consequences, knowing only that he had to kill it.

The pistol thundered and the zombie's head rocked back. It fell onto one of its brothers. Callan kept moving from one feeder to the next, shooting them in the head, and the face, through the ear, and in the chest; waiting for the magazine to empty. None of them moved, too preoccupied with their lifeblood. He shot them all with a feverish intensity, and when he was done, he stood amongst the slaughterhouse, breathing hard, his eyes wild.

The smell of gun smoke hung like miniature clouds, and Callan sucked it in, enjoying the scent. It beat the rest of the shit. A noise echoed from further along the hallway.

"We're gonna have company soon," Dylan said.

Callan turned. "You fuckers need me to save your asses again? What have you been doing?" Dylan looked away. "What is it?"

Johnny touched a bandage in his arm. "Fucker got me." He pressed his lips tight, but still they trembled.

Callan felt the weight leave his body. "What? No." He stumbled towards them and fell onto his knees, fighting to keep control. "What'd you mean?" Neither of them could look him in the eye. "What the fuck happened?"

Dylan chiseled the words out. "Johnny got bitten. He saved me, but one of them got him from the side."

It was Sherry all over again, the moment of realization that he couldn't take back, that the damage had been done, and he was powerless to change it. "FUUUUCK!"

There was a series of heavy thuds, followed by the sound of large-scaled movement from further along the hallway. Glass crashed and Dylan said, "We gotta go. We don't have much ammo, and—"

"You guys go. I have to get some more medicine. We found a young girl, and she's a diabetic."

Dylan helped Johnny onto his feet. "We'll wait."

"No. Go. Get yourselves out of here."

Dylan nodded. He righted the fallen trolley and stuffed medicine and supplies back onto it. Callan replaced the empty magazine with a new one. He put a hand on Johnny's shoulder. "Don't worry, man. We'll work something out." But it felt like a lie.

He watched them shuffle away, wishing he could change the outcome. When they had disappeared around the corner, Callan went into the pharmacy.

He picked his way over the fallen stock and broken display cases. He slipped on an army of plastic bottles: shampoo, or some kind of hair treatment. While the feeders had damaged the bulk of the floor stock, the prescription medicines were untouched, and he was able to locate the insulin, and most importantly, the glucagon device. He couldn't find the insulin pens Kristy had referred to, though. He took a large polyester bag from one of the shelves and dumped all the supplies under the diabetic counter into it. He found boxes of small syringes and added those. He slung the bag over his shoulder and stood behind the doors listening for movement. Silence sent him out the door.

A pack of zombies wandered along the hallway ahead. Their soft footsteps hadn't quite reached the chaotic mess outside the pharmacy. He could make it. He pulled the straps of the bag tighter around his shoulders and ran in the direction the others had gone.

He'd only made it a short way when a tall male in bone-colored slacks and a green, bloody shirt stumbled out of an office. Callan stopped, took his stance, and shot it in the throat. It fell back onto a smashed scanning machine, grasping at its neck with blood gurgling from between its hands. He felt like a cop, the way he had shot it. The thought filled him with pride. He'd wanted to be a policeman as a boy.

The pack of undead had reached the pharmacy. Callan ran on through the mess and down the hallway towards the exit. He passed through the main intersection and turned into the wide corridor that led to the emergency area. A zombie staggered from one of the offices, followed by a second. He shot them both, but a bad feeling washed over him. Two more stumbled out of the next doorway, then another from a long passage with a toilet sign above.

A man resembling a zombie in all but the face shuffled towards him with his hands up. "Don't shoot, please," he said in a raspy voice. He stopped three yards away but kept his hands up.

"Jesus, fuck, I almost shot you," Callan said. The other two approached. He spun around and knocked them down. He hadn't missed a shot since the pharmacy. "Are you bitten?"

"No. No."

The look on his face was sincere, and strong. "Follow me. And keep up."

"Thank you."

Finding somebody alive was a win, a flash of hope, of goodness, amongst all the despair. The larger the troupe, the stronger they would be against the dead, and anything else that might oppose their existence.

He stopped at the emergency doors and peered outside. The zombies he had shot at the ambulance lay still, and there were no other signs of danger. But neither the jeep, nor the boys, were in sight. They had to go, though; they couldn't stay in the hospital any longer, and besides, three people needed his urgent attention.

"Stick close. What's your name?"

"Howard."

"We're going for a black Jeep with a trailer attached. I can't see it yet, but when you do, run for it."

Callan opened the door and stepped out, using his elbow to hold it open for Howard. He ran three paces and saw Angela, the nurse, rise to her feet from a dead body in a corner nook of the external wall. She wobbled for him, hunger and adoration in her dead eyes, and Callan cursed himself for not remembering her as she closed in.

FOURTEEN

KRISTY HAD TAKEN THE JEEP and trailer away from the curb as Callan headed towards the hospital. Blue Boy had barked at the side window until they were out of sight. Despite Callan's advice to move right away from the hospital, she didn't want to go too far, in case Dylan or Johnny reappeared in need of a quick getaway. He plan was to pull over just up the road, where she could still see them.

"I know it's bad timing," Greg said in a gravelly voice, "but I'd kill for water."

It was his first request in hours. Kristy checked it was safe to pull over, glancing into both side mirrors, before edging the Jeep back into the curb on the street. She cut the engine, double checking for zombies amongst the abandoned cars, shaggy trees, and weatherboard houses. Even though she couldn't see them, she could smell them on the wind, that fetid, deathly scent that had leeched into their clothes and skin.

She opened the door, repressing her fear, and walked to the trailer, where she unhooked the tarpaulin and searched around in the supply boxes for water.

Dylan and Johnny should have returned by now. Something had gone wrong. Concern spread, causing an icky feeling in her stomach, and she told herself not to think about it, that they had to be cautious, which took time.

She found a bottle of water and took it back to Greg. His hand shook as he clasped it and struggled getting it to his lips.

"How are you feeling?"

He closed his eyes. "Had a viral infection … when I was nine … spent six days in bed—ended up in the hospital. This is worse."

She touched a hand to his forehead and felt baking heat. He would get much sicker if they didn't administer strong antibiotics soon. "How's the ankle?"

"Throbbing. What … about her?"

It pained Kristy not to be able to provide medical attention to someone so ill. The girl needed glucose to raise her blood sugar level, but because she had passed out, the only way to administer it was through an injection. Under normal circumstances, they would need an ambulance. "If we don't get her what she needs soon, she'll die."

Greg lay back and shut his eyes. They sat in silence for a time, suffering in the humidity. A memory came upon her suddenly, and she touched a hand to her cheek. She had stood in almost that same spot, once before. Her face had been sore that night, bruised and swelling from the hand of her then-boyfriend, Karl. He had been driving her to the hospital on her insistence, only because she had promised not to tell them what he had done, but in the final stretch he had pulled over, panicky about others finding out.

"What are you doing?" Kristy asked.

"You're gonna tell them."

"No I'm not."

"Bullshit." He wore the same stiff, spiteful expression as when he had struck her.

"Karl, I promise I won't say anything."

He considered it, glancing at her with a tight jaw. In the end, he said, "Fine. But you can get out here."

"You're not going to drive me to the door?"

"I don't want them to see me. They'll fucking know."

It had been a fractured cheekbone, as she'd suspected. Kristy had falsified the incident, blaming a wet floor and a kitchen table. Later on, she would witness similar lies in the ER at Monash. She had broken up with Karl, but replaced him with a similar hothead, although not one that used his fists. She hoped Karl had found a long, painful death.

The dog had stopped barking. Kristy left Greg with the water and returned to the trailer for some pain relief medicine. Before she reached the supplies though, Blue Boy barked again, causing her to look up. Three zombies had wandered out of the parking lot onto the road.

Kristy hurried back to the vehicle. Blue Boy had his tongue out, face pressed against the back window, growling. She turned the jeep in a wide circle and headed back towards the hospital. It made no sense to her to leave the boys waiting for their ride. She wanted to be there when they came out. Circling the lot was her best option.

She passed the zombies and took the Jeep around the outside of the parking lot. One of the feeders popped out from behind a red van and caught the front right corner of the hood. The zombie went spinning into the side of another car with a heavy clunk. She flexed her fingers around the wheel and drove on.

They made three eventful laps, taking down four more zombies with deadly accuracy, before Dylan appeared from a door near where she had left them. He ran across the grass, pushing some sort of trolley full of supplies. Her heart skipped a beat, but she was instantly alert and terrified that one of the wandering zombies would catch him. Johnny appeared in the doorway holding his arm at an angle. Something had happened. He stepped out into daylight with several feeders in close pursuit. One secured a bony grip on his shirt, but Johnny shrugged it off and ran on.

Kristy pulled the car over to the curb. Blue Boy scratched at the window, barking furiously. Kristy took the Remington .308 pump action from the passenger side and slipped out of the driver's seat. She started towards the building, surprised at how good the weapon felt in her hands. It was protection, and with it she could defend herself, her friends, and loved ones.

She pumped a round and took aim. The rifle cracked, and the shot took the first zombie in the leg. As it tried to climb back onto its feet, she made a red hole in its forehead, laying it on the grass. The second glanced down, but drawn by human scents, staggered onward. She tightened her grip, concentrating on its demonic face. The gun barked, and the thing fell, motionless. The boys passed her, and she finished the third zombie off with a frontal shot to the top of its skull.

She stood back, taking deep breaths, her chest heaving. It had come over her like a drunken buzz. Dylan opened the rear door of the Jeep. Blue Boy leaped down from the back and raced towards the hospital emergency doors.

"Where's Callan?" Kristy asked, raising her voice above the shrill yaps.

"Still inside," Dylan said. "He had to get some more medicine, and …" His voice trailed off.

Kristy spotted the bandage on Johnny's arm. "What happened?" She saw defeat in Johnny's eyes. "Let me see." Johnny turned away. "Johnny?"

He shrugged her off. "*No*."

From the emergency entrance, Blue Boy howled. They all turned in that direction. Callan burst through the doorway with another man staggering behind him. At first, Kristy thought it was a zombie, but then the awkward gait ceased, and his legs took over, displaying too much control for one of them.

"He's found someone." Callan had his own problems, cut off by a larger woman dressed in a white nurse's uniform. "Dylan, get everyone in the Jeep, squash in if you have to." Kristy hurried across the grass towards her brother.

"Wait," Dylan said. "You're out of ammo."

She stopped and checked the chamber. He was right. From the back of the Jeep, Dylan took two handfuls of shells and met her halfway. Kristy planted a kiss on his cheek. "Thank you. Be ready to go."

Other zombies poured out of the emergency doors, clutching and clawing for Callan and the other man. Kristy stuck rounds into the chamber, wishing she were faster, and poked the remaining into the tight gaps of her pockets. Blue Boy ran towards the scene, barking at the feeders, then darted back as they swiped at him.

"Get back, Blue!" Kristy screamed.

The nurse caught hold of Callan and pulled him close to her massive breast, her open mouth searching for his throat. Callan stuck his hands up between them, trying to pry her loose, but her desperation overwhelmed him and they went down in a tangle.

Kristy ran, screaming Callan's name as she drew the back of the zombie into sight. "Push it away!"

Terror stole her breath. The thing was all over him, but its exposed back was tempting. Kristy stopped, looked through the rifle sight and squeezed the trigger. A chunk of flesh leaped up near the nurse's shoulder blade, and it withdrew momentarily. Callan squirmed, crawling out from beneath it. The other man dragged it off, allowing Callan's escape. Kristy pumped and fired again, scalping the nurse's head. It slumped forward and hit the ground with a splat.

Callan battled to his feet and stood over it, staring as though he had lost a good friend. A second string of zombies rushed at him from behind, and he stumbled away. Blue Boy intervened, snarling and snapping at their legs, deflecting their concentration. Kristy fired at them, splitting concrete off the wall with a puff of dust.

Callan cut a wide circle around the crowd of stragglers that had emerged through the emergency doors. The other man, who had avoided being caught, found two feeders closing in on him. Kristy took aim and fired again.

The first two shots missed, but the third dropped the closest zombie, and the man was able to break away, reaching Callan and Kristy.

"Quickly," Kristy said. "In the Jeep."

When they reached the vehicle, Callan helped the man into the backseat, then closed the door and gave a high-pitched whistle. Blue Boy's head perked and his ears stiffened. "Here boy," Callan said, hurrying towards the trailer.

Kristy ran to the driver's seat, wondering how they would all fit, but Dylan had leapt over into the rear compartment. As she slid in, she saw Callan call Blue Boy who jumped onto the trailer. She turned on the ignition and they rolled out of the hospital lot, battered, bruised, and bitten. A trail of feeders stretched from the hospital entrance, and all Kristy could think to do was drive.

FIFTEEN

"THANK … YOU," EVELYN SAID between breaths. "I thought … we were dead." Jake smiled at her from the back seat. His cheeks glowed red, but he wasn't panting. An unsettling queasiness sat in her gut at the thought of what might have been. "You okay, Jakey?" He nodded, but he had to fight for the smile. She reached back and squeezed his hand.

"You look like you had a bad time of it," the man said. He ran a hand through his dark hair, brushing it back from his forehead. He had a small nose and a narrow face. His green eyes and pearly smile gave her a feeling of comfort and ease.

"Yes." The air filling her lungs again felt good. "I don't know what would have happened without you."

He laughed. "People gotta stick together. We got enough problems. Where you headed?"

Evelyn shrugged. "We're looking for other people." She explained where they had been.

"Lady, this is your lucky day. There's a whole bunch of people staying at the Kapooka army barracks. We got all kinds of folks–families, singles, kids, grandparents. There's shelter, clothes, and plenty of food. Best of all, everybody is safe."

"That sounds … wonderful." The man, whose name Evelyn still hadn't caught, filled in more details. Most of the army personnel had been redeployed across the country once the outbreak took hold. None of the army people were still there, but many civilians had contributed to help make it the safest place in the region. People received food and shelter in exchange for tasks to keep the base functioning, and other jobs to support the men who did the work detail. The place was thriving. They had already engaged in getting the local power plant secured and functional.

As the vehicle drove through the town outskirts, Evelyn considered their luck. Without the man's help, she would have died. That much was certain. Now, they had a chance. If they were accepted into the barracks, she would do her utmost to show her gratitude.

"Name's Alex. Alex Sanders."

Evelyn returned the greeting. He had a friendly disposition, and again his smile set her at ease, but still the seed of caution flickered. Evelyn supposed part of it was what her father had said before his death: *Be careful.* As the thin ropes holding the country up had begun to break, he had told her that in a catastrophe, carefulness was critical, that she should suspend her natural belief in people until altruism was proven again. At this point though, she had little choice.

On the corner of Pearson Street and the Sturt Highway, a big blue Ford utility braked. A man stuck a hand out the driver's window and waved them over. Alex positioned the vehicle so the driver doors faced each other.

"How goes it, Roger?"

A brown, crinkled face regarded them. One wiry forearm covered in a faded green tattoo—almost illegible—leaned on the open window. Roger coughed once and spat a wad of phlegm onto the road. His eyes stopped on Evelyn. She felt uncomfortable and looked away.

"Alright, Al. We cleaned up the north side of town. The aquatic center and the civic theatre are clear of infected now. The boys are getting right into the swing of things. They're gonna wanna party tonight." He tipped his head. "Whatta ya got there?"

Alex glanced at Evelyn and Jake, then shifted in his seat. "They ran into some trouble over near Harris Park. Takin' 'em back to the base. Is that okay?"

Roger's eyes widened. "Sure. Great. We need all the help we can get."

The small talk continued, but Evelyn didn't feel comfortable again until the man had driven off. "Is he a friend of yours?"

Alex shook his head. "No way, but he's in charge of the work detail out in the town, and one of the original members of the base, so it pays to keep on his good side." His fingers clasped the wheel tight enough for Evelyn to notice. "Stay clear of him and his friends. He's not someone you want your son hanging around."

It wasn't until the car reached the barracks that Evelyn decided they were safe. The wide, metal gates opened for them, and Alex parked in a dedicated area alongside other vehicles, including several large army trucks. A number of men moved about the complex. Those who greeted Alex smiled at her and Jake.

He guided them through a form of induction, where they received blankets, a pillow, and a bed allocation from a shed containing supplies: tents, torches, ropes, and gas bottles.

By dark, Evelyn had begun to feel a little better. Although the confines were unfamiliar, they were with people now, and she didn't feel as exposed or as poorly equipped anymore. Following a meal of bread and beef stew, Evelyn and Jake took a stretcher near the back of the mess hall with some other newer arrivals. Alex came to check on them before lights out, and Evelyn was pleased to see him.

As they discussed the plan for work detail the following day, Roger, the man in the blue Ford, appeared. He was taller than Alex, with broad shoulders and cropped grey hair. He had tattoos on both forearms, and looked like a man suited to laborious work.

Alex stiffened and finished talking as he approached.

"Don't stop on my account," Roger said, grinning.

It seemed like a false smile to Evelyn. Something about the man made her uneasy. Even Jake looked worried. She wanted him gone.

"Anything I can do to help?"

"Alex has looked after us. We're fine now, thank you."

The smile faded. "Okay. Sure. If Alex is taking care of you, I'll leave it to him." He nodded, then turned and walked away.

Alex watched him leave. Evelyn thought he was going to say something about Roger, but then he smiled and said, "I'll leave you to it. See you tomorrow."

SIXTEEN

DYLAN PULLED HIS LEGS into his chest and held onto the back seat. The rear compartment was squashy, but they were full up, and those were the times. Dylan peered up over the back door towards the trailer. Kristy kept the speed low, taking corners in wide, cautious turns. Callan had the difficult job of holding on atop the trailer and keeping Blue Boy on. "Don't go too fast," he said to Kristy. "They're okay for now. See if you can pull over soon though, we need to turn this thing into a seven-seater."

They needed to get out of Albury. Perhaps they could find a small place to stay halfway between the big towns, where the population was low and the zombies minimal. From the backseat, he could hear Johnny fighting to keep his pain and anxiety quiet. Despite what they'd been through, their history and contrasting perspectives, Dylan felt for him. It couldn't end well for Johnny, and however it played out, his death would hurt the group even more.

Part of him was still buzzing about Kristy. She had taken over at the end, and shot them all to freedom. He had never seen her take over like that before, although she came from tough stock, like Callan. If she had been more aggressive in the beginning, Dylan might never have engaged her at all. Her calm, easy-going nature had allowed him to entertain the idea that a man like him and a girl like her might end up together. It had been an impressive effort though, and the change in her since the start of the trip—hell, even the end of the trip—was staggering. He supposed they were all altered, killing zombies, fighting for their lives, but Kristy had changed the most, and with it, his love for her had tightened its grip around his heart.

They had driven clear of the hospital and surrounding streets. There were no zombies in sight, and as if reading his thoughts, Kristy edged the Jeep and trailer over to the side of the road. Dylan supposed she could have just stopped; there was no traffic to block, but old habits prevailed.

The rear door opened and Dylan wriggled out. He stood, and Kristy wrapped him in a bear hug, pulling him to her with concern he had never felt.

"Oh sweet Jesus I'm glad you're okay," she whispered in his ear.

He closed his eyes. "Me too. And you … were amazing."

She kissed him softly on the lips. "I have to fix the others up."

"Can you do anything for Johnny?"

"What happened?" Callan asked in a low voice. Dylan explained. It had been a lack of concentration from them both, if only for a moment. Callan rubbed the bridge of his nose between thumb and forefinger. "I'm not giving up yet."

Kristy administered antibiotics to Greg and dosed the glucagon pen. The girl lay against the back seat, murmuring.

The old guy Callan had brought with him said, "Thank you. I might have died in there if I hadn't found Callan." Beneath dirty skin and a messy, unkempt appearance, a pair of bright, intelligent blue eyes inspected them.

They made their introductions, and Dylan asked, "How long have you been in the hospital, Howard?"

"Just over a week." He hesitated, considering his words carefully. "I was receiving chemotherapy–bone cancer—and wasn't handling the treatment well. It's my second bout."

A silence fell over the others. Dylan's lips pressed into a thin line. Howard's appearance confirmed this, though Dylan had thought the tight skin and sharp angles of Howard's face were caused by a lack of food. "I'm sorry to hear that. Is there … any hope?"

"There wasn't much hope then, and there sure isn't now." He put up a hand. "But that's fine. I'm comfortable with my own mortality. I've had a long time to deal with it." He smiled and looked them all in the eye, and in that moment Dylan saw a strength with which none of them could compete. "Imminent death is a strange thing. The older you get, the more you think about it. You know you're going to die one day, but until it looks you in the eye, it doesn't really mean anything."

"You're brave," Kristy said, placing hand on his arm. "I am—was—an ER doctor, and I've seen people on your situation before. I have great admiration for you."

His smile widened. "Thank you, young lady. My only advice would be a classic cliché— to appreciate what you have, while you have it." It cast a somber mood over them, but Howard wouldn't allow it. "Don't fret about me. Each day is a risk to us now. There are plenty of people I've outlived, I'm sure."

"What about family?" Callan asked.

Howard's hopeful expression softened. "I don't know. I'm divorced–I don't really care much for my ex-wife, to be honest. I have a son, a daughter in-law, and a granddaughter, who all live in Wollongong. I'd love to know they were all right, especially Bec. She's my angel."

"We don't know which way we're headed yet," Callan said, "but we'll keep it in mind. Speaking of that, we should get moving. How long before the girl comes good?"

Kristy checked her watch. "Ten, maybe fifteen minutes. I've never had to do this before."

Callan frowned "And what about Greg. Is there any chance he's got the virus?"

"I doubt it now. He should start to improve within a day. He's in a bad way, so the antibiotics should help the moment they take effect." They both looked at Greg, who sat on the edge of the front seat, elbows resting on his knees, head hanging between them.

"How you going?" Dylan asked.

When Greg spoke, his voice sounded like he'd been screaming for hours. "Better than Johnny." Dylan clapped a hand on his back. A small part of him still wondered whether Greg had the virus.

Johnny had remained in the back seat beside the little girl, his head lying against the rest. Dylan guessed he was battling the terms of his future. A man who had never taken life too seriously now faced a painful countdown towards the most horrible fate. Regardless of what Johnny had done, he didn't deserve such an ending.

Johnny climbed out and limped away from the Jeep. At first, Dylan thought he was going to the toilet, but there were no trees in that direction.

Callan, who had been rearranging the fold-down seat in the back compartment, called out. "Hey, stay close, man. We don't know what's around here."

Kristy piped up from tending to the little girl. "Johnny, I want to look at your arm." He kept walking.

"He isn't stopping," Dylan said.

Callan jogged after Johnny, Blue Boy at his heels. Dylan followed, feeling awash with fault for the situation Accidents were part of their lives now, but he couldn't help feeling some guilt. He was certain Johnny had saved him from getting bitten.

"Hey, man? Stop for a minute."

Johnny's limp became stiffer, his step slowing. "Leave it, Callan."

Callan reached out and grabbed Johnny's shoulder. "What the fuck—"

Johnny spun, swinging a clenched fist to break his friend's grip. "I'm fucking serious. It's better this way. Just leave me be."

They had wandered onto a vacant block of land between rows of weatherboard houses. Yellow grass crunched underfoot. Beyond the block was a park with a playground, swings hanging stiff in the thick, humid air. *No child will ever scream with laughter down that slide again*, Dylan thought. "Come on, let's just get out of here and talk about this later."

"Stay the fuck out of it," Johnny said. Bushy black brows protruded over narrowed eyes. "It's mostly your fault." Dylan glanced at Callan for help, but his frowning gaze hadn't left Johnny.

Dylan wondered whether Johnny was referring to their earlier conversation. He didn't want to get into a discussion about that. There was too much emotion and, regardless of Johnny's transgressions in the previous life, he shouldn't have to walk away to his death.

"You guys sort it out then. But don't be stupid, Johnny, none of us are gonna let you walk away like this." He turned his back before Johnny could respond, but thought he saw his expression soften. Their voices grew louder as Dylan walked back to the Jeep.

"What's wrong?" Kristy asked as he reached her.

Dylan waved a hand at them. "I think Johnny wants to leave."

Kristy pressed her lips into a thin line. "I can't say I blame him. He must be terrified. What happens if he turns into one of them?"

She was right. One of them would have to kill him. It was a horrible thought. "Is there anything you can think to do? Could we draw out the venom the way you sometimes can with a snake bite?"

"I was thinking about that. I don't know how the virus works, but it's worth a shot."

Dylan converted the rear section of the Jeep into seating and rearranged the evicted belongings into the trailer. Callan and Johnny walked slowly back towards the Jeep in light discussion. It appeared Callan had convinced Johnny not to leave. Kristy poked around in the trailer and came out with a first aid kit.

"Let me take a look, Johnny," she said as they reached the Jeep. Johnny's eyes were red, and Callan put a hand on his shoulder, directing him towards Kristy.

"There's nothing you can do. I'm done. I wish you'd just let me deal with it myself."

"I'm going to apply an ointment that's used to extract the venom from snakebites. It might draw out whatever poison is in you." Johnny watched her closely, and in the furrow of his brow and the lines around his eyes, Dylan saw a little hope. *Please, let him be okay*, he thought. He couldn't even say Johnny was a friend, but the group had suffered enough, and nobody deserved to die like that.

"Where do we go know?" Callan asked. "We should decide as a group." Greg climbed out of the car, and leaned back against the wheel. "North or south?"

"What are we looking for?" Dylan asked. "Government help? Safety? A vaccine?" He liked the idea of heading south to Tasmania, as his father had suggested, but he wouldn't offer it as an option unless the alternative was unacceptable. His sister had been in Melbourne, and the truth was, he wanted to find her.

"I don't care," Kristy said, "as long as we get out of Albury."

Callan turned. "Dylan?"

He raised his eyebrows. Three days ago, democracy was not a concept Callan had understood. It was a pleasing change. "My father thought Tasmania was a good option. I think we should head in that direction. I know—"

"It's a long way," Callan said

"I realize that, but if we think about our long term survival, it's a good option."

"We're closer to Sydney though. Imagine if we even made it all the way to Tasmania, and then found out Sydney had safety, and a vaccine?"

Dylan shrugged. Callan wasn't giving up on Sydney. "Wherever then. Just as long it's away from here."

"We're done here," Kristy said, closing up the first aid kit. Johnny rubbed the fresh bandage. "But we can't leave until the girl regains consciousness."

The boys packed the dislodged belongings into the trailer and sipped warm water from fresh bottles. The clouds continued to break up, and the sun cast a biting heat upon them. Dylan had expected zombies, but there were none, only the silent, brooding houses of a now abandoned world.

"Seating's gonna be tight for a bit," Callan said, splashing his face with bottled water, "but we should try and find another reliable vehicle and split up."

"Is that sensible?" Dylan asked. The thought of driving in separate vehicles concerned him.

"Yes and no. If something happens and we're all in the one car …"

The girl spoke for the first time. Kristy had her sip orange juice and eat some carbohydrates to sustain her blood sugar levels. Dylan marveled at Kristy's knowledge and skill. She was treating three of them now; knew exactly what to do for each, and when to administer the treatment. Had she not been with them, there would have been more than one casualty.

Callan took on the driving, while Johnny, Howard, and the little girl, whose name was Sarah, sat in the back. Dylan and Kristy squashed up in the rear, pointing their knees to the ceiling in the cramped space. *Still*, Dylan thought, *I've got my girl, and my life, for now.* He couldn't think about anything else; his mother and father, or the likelihood of his sister's passing. Even the loss of Sherry brought sadness. She had been one of them, good or bad, and the pain of her death was palpable in Callan's existence.

The car rolled away from the curb, and not for the first time, Dylan wondered where they would be when he lay down to sleep that night.

SEVENTEEN

AS THE AFTERNOON RODE into evening, the heat fell on the land like a heavy fist, sucking the last of the rain from the dry earth. It was summer, and aside from the occasional downpour, the grass remained yellow and the roadside gutters filled with crinkled leaves until mid-autumn.

They ran the Jeep's cooling system, but the fuel gauge seemed to fall faster, and Callan found himself glancing underneath his hand at the dashboard often. They passed a gas station that had been set alight, the charred remains of the shop telling a new story in the history of the world. Each bowser had been torn from its post, and two blackened car shells sat underneath a bent and twisted awning. The road was empty, although Callan thought a twinkle of light had glittered in the rear-view mirror several times, though it turned out to be nothing.

Callan's mind buzzed, his thoughts jumping and jiving from one to the other. There were a million things to consider: Johnny, the little girl, their parents, where they were going, Sherry ... the last thought made him feel sick. The closest person he had ever lost was his great-grandfather when Callan had been eighteen, and that had only stung a little. One set of his grandparents had died when he was young; the other had probably perished with his mom and dad, whose whereabouts remained unknown. But Sherry had been real. He'd held her in his arms, felt the cold, lifeless touch of her skin, and wished with every piece of his soul that he could swap places. Intensifying her death was that of his child, maybe a boy, or a sweet little girl that could have cared for him in old age. He would never love again; the pain of losing someone wasn't worth it. He would rather hold onto Sherry's memory, and remember that.

The Jeep had drifted toward the edge of the road. Callan jerked the wheel and realigned it. *Stop thinking about that shit, man.* He felt guilty for telling himself such a thing, but knew too much contemplation would make him crazy.

They finally found gas at a roadside diner. Callan went inside and turned the pumps on, not expecting much fuel. The fourth and final bowser flowed though, filling the Jeep and a second scratched-up army-green Jerry can. Sarah walked around, even talked a little, saved by the glycogen kit and revived by juice and food. Callan had known little about diabetes before, but suspected they were all going to understand it now. She staggered up to him, holding Kristy's hand as Callan poked the gun back into the bowser.

"This is Sarah," Kristy said. Callan smiled.

"Thank you for saving me," Sarah said in a sweet voice. She opened her arms and wrapped them around Callan. He stared at Kristy, unsure what to do. She nodded, and Callan rested his hands on her back, conscious not to squeeze her. Finally, she released him, looking a little uncomfortable.

Callan tried to smile. "You're welcome. Feeling better?" He raised his eyebrows at Kristy, wondering whether the girl knew about her father. Perceptive, as always, Kristy's mouth curled down, and she tipped her head, confirming Sarah did.

"I'm sorry … about your father. I lost someone very special to me today, too." She nodded, bottom lip curled over the top one, and her eyes became glassy. Poor kid. She sucked in a deep breath, trying to keep a straight face. She had some guts though.

Callan herded them all back into the vehicle as soon as the fuel refill was complete. He still felt strongly about trying the Holsworthy barracks in Sydney. Although there was potentially a larger population of zombies, he thought it was their best chance of finding help. The army base in Wagga was closer though, and they could investigate it on the way to Sydney. But they wouldn't arrive there until tomorrow. It would be dark within several hours, and they needed shelter for the night. They were about fifteen minutes out of Holbrook, and after that, it was either an hour to Wagga on shitty roads, or the same distance to Gundagai. Holbrook was the best option.

Callan steered the Jeep and trailer back onto the Hume Highway, with not another vehicle in site. They saw the truck soon after.

With his hawk-eyes, Dylan called it from the back as the road arced gently into a long, straight stretch. In the distance, the air shimmered above the bitumen like a magic window. Callan guessed the temperature had risen to over a hundred.

It sat at the horizon for a long time, onward in a straight line. A sense of anticipation bubbled through them. There had been no other vehicles on a road since Albury, although that hadn't been a successful meeting. As they drew closer, it was again Dylan who suggested something wasn't right.

"They're all over the place," he said, leaning forward "See that?" Callan kept silent, unable to confirm and a little frustrated by it.

The closer the truck grew, the more restless they became. The others sat forward in their seats, and while it had been quiet before, now nobody spoke. All of them watched the approach.

As it drew within a mile, two things became clear: it was swerving in and out of its lane, and driving slowly. Callan considered pulling over and letting it pass, but the roadside was narrow, leading into dense bush scrub, with no place to park.

"Be careful, Cal," Kristy said, as they pulled to within a quarter of a mile.

Callan tightened his hands around the wheel. The truck had straightened up, but he was prepared for it to change course at any moment, remembering that he was carrying a trailer, and sudden changes in direction might overbalance them.

And then it was there, right ahead, a big Bedford eight-ton truck used for hauling full-pallet freight. It moved in a straight line toward them, on its own side of the road, and out of direct harm. Callan thought for a split second that they might avoid it, that they'd be safe, that the driver had managed to keep control, but then it started to go wrong. The pale, dying face of the man with shaggy hair and a rough beard sat slumped forward with his mouth open.

The truck drifted to the right.

Kristy grabbed onto the seat. "Watch out."

Callan edged over toward the roadside, careful not to touch the loose rocks. In that moment, he had a flash of risky inspiration, touching the brake pedal down.

The truck jagged right, cutting in front of them. Callan floored the brake, and they were all thrust forward. He thought the trailer was going to jack-knife, but his earlier speed reduction had made the difference. The truck drove off the road and crashed into a wide gum tree.

The noise was like thunder. The ground reverberated up through the seat and into his back. Callan stopped the car. "Everyone alright?" They were.

He climbed out, and the others followed.

The truck had embedded itself around the tree. Steam rose in several columns, hissing like a pit of snakes. Callan approached, slow and watchful. The man driving had looked sick, and after what they had all witnessed, he wasn't taking any chances.

There was a metallic click, and the door of the cab creaked open. The driver held onto it with grim death. It swung outwards, and he toppled forward into a prickly bush.

Kristy reached Callan's side, but he was pleased she didn't rush forward as she would have three days ago. They glanced at each other, waiting, and after a moment, the man crawled out of the bush.

A deep echo sounded from inside the truck as something banged on the wall. Callan stepped back. Kristy stood her ground. "Move back, Kris."

"'S alright," the man replied in a wheezy voice. He made eye contact for the first time. The whites were bloodshot. He'd cleared the bush, but now stopped on all fours as a violent coughing fit engulfed him.

"He's got it," Callan said, putting out a hand to ward Kristy back. "He's infected."

The man nodded, coughing again, trying to suppress further spluttering. "Yes."

Dylan arrived with a Winchester .30-30 rifle. He drew it up to his line of sight, and again, Callan was reminded of their character evolution. Violent banging sounded from inside the truck again.

"And what's in there?" Callan asked.

"My family."

A painful moan sounded from within. *His family.* Callan could guess. He suspected it was a familiar story the world over. "They're sick too?"

The man climbed to his feet, tottered, then grabbed onto the shrub. The creases at his eyes and the grimace of his middle-aged face told of more horrors than one could dream. "Yes."

Callan rubbed his jaw, feeling a thicker beard than he had ever worn. He didn't know when that had happened; he hadn't looked in the mirror with any sense of understanding since before the camping trip. Even the two showers he'd taken at Dylan's house had been full of distraction, his reflection a long forgotten friend. The others were looking at him now though. Callan imagined himself in such a situation. It might well have been him, too.

"What happened?"

"We lived in Bonnells Bay, up on Lake Macquarie, past Sydney." He coughed, clearing his throat. "Too many of 'em 'round near where we lived. Had to get out."

"How long ago?"

He shrugged. "Two, three weeks. To be honest, I don't remember." Callan nodded. "Went south to Sydney." He glanced at the truck. "That place won't exist soon."

"Sydney?"

"It's getting worse by the day. If you're going there, you'd better hurry. Won't last much longer."

"What about the joint operations command center in Canberra?"

"I heard it was … still operational. But that was … weeks ago. Don't know now. We were heading to Melbourne. Got family down there."

This man's plight was tragic. He was infected, and his infected family, perhaps a wife and some kids, were locked in the back of the truck. He had backed himself to reach Melbourne, but he had been wrong, probably like so many. They should leave. There was probably nothing they could do for him or his family.

"Is there anything we can do for you?" Callan asked.

The man shook his head. "No. But thank you."

Callan turned to Dylan and tipped his head towards the gun. Dylan nodded, sticking it out towards the man. "We have more."

"No," he said, shuffling towards the truck. "You keep it."

Nobody looked back as they drove away in silence.

In the west, the tip of the sun poked its head over the horizon, casting a sweet pumpkin colour through the cloud-stained sky. It was a lovely sunset, and in another life, a person could have taken the time to appreciate it, snapping photos to remember the rarity.

Callan left his window down, kept the cooling off, and felt the warm air on his face. The wind barreled through the opening, creating his own little noisy world, and it helped shut out the bad thoughts. He wondered if, in the end, anything would stop them.

EIGHTEEN

KLAUS LAY BACK AGAINST the bench in the laboratory, closed his aching eyes, and let the tiredness draw him away from reality. He had no idea what time it was; hadn't slept properly since before his argument with Gallagher, and still was no further progressed in discovering any form of inhibitor against the virus.

While he tried the most popular interferons available to him, none so far had worked. This didn't surprise Klaus; he knew that some strains of the influenza virus were resistant to them. Interferons were another way of fighting viruses, stimulating the body's immune system to attack them, rather than targeting the virus itself, the way most other antivirals worked. They were now used as part of the standard treatment against multiple sclerosis, hepatitis B and C, and were high on the list of investigation against various other diseases. Klaus had used the limited range available, but now only had several fringe types left that were unlikely to work.

Where did he go from here? There were no other scientists to whom he could refer; no technical resources on the other side of the world to offer advice. Should he quit? Go back to his quarters and wait out the inevitable death? Without his difficult search for a medical answer, he had nothing, and quitting wasn't in his DNA.

As a boy growing up in the tough western suburbs of Sydney, Klaus had learned about unwavering commitment. The other boys had initially ostracized the kid with the 'funny' surname. He had watched from the sidelines as they had driven their billy karts down the streets, wishing he were part of the fun. Klaus would devise solutions for their engineering problems, but was too afraid to offer help. Things were exacerbated when three weeks into the second grade, his teacher had approached his mother and told her Klaus needed to skip two grades. Klaus had begged his mother not to allow it, but his pleading went unheard. She made him promise he would find new friends, and knowing she would never rescind her request, he did so.

Klaus found himself facing the wrath of his younger classmates, who excluded him for being too smart, and the older ones, who felt threatened. He suffered beating after beating in those early weeks: bloody noses, black eyes, even a fractured cheekbone. He fought back with feeble skills, and they laughed at him as he lay on the ground with tears on his cheeks and blood running from his nose. But he would not give up. He would not hide away from them like a coward. From his mother, Klaus had inherited an insurmountable determination. Once he had committed to a task, he couldn't concede until completed. Not only had he promised his mother he would make friends, but Klaus felt he was being treated unfairly, and he would stand his ground until they accepted him. The final tumultuous fight behind the bike shed left Klaus bleeding and wheezing on the ground. An older boy, who had only ever watched, stood over Klaus and laughed. *That's it*, Klaus had thought, waiting for the final punch that would kill him. *I'm going to die*. But it had never come. The big boy had laid out a hand and Klaus had almost cried as he was pulled to his feet.

"You're a stubborn son-of-a-bitch. Don't you know when to give up?" He turned to the crowd of dirty, disheveled boys and said, "Nobody touches him again. Understand?" None of the boys spoke, and neither did they ever touch him again. Klaus had realized then that anything was possible, as long as he never gave up. And forever after, that affirmation had served him well.

He was due a break, but worried that Gallagher might return if he left the laboratory. He hadn't seen the drunk since their altercation, and if he was honest, he didn't care what had become of him, other than the fact Klaus might be the last person alive on the base. That idea scared him, especially with the things in the cells downstairs. He didn't know why Major General Harris hadn't just terminated them. He understood that for the sake of science they might be useful for trialing medicines, but Klaus was a long way from having anything worth trialing on a subject in such a state of advancement. Had Gallagher been checking on them? Probably not. It was his job to ensure the facilities were secure, that the class threes were still locked away.

He decided to delay his coffee break, try the last few slides, and then get some sleep. He could return fresh again after a few hours. Time away from the lab provided greater clarity and the occasional surprise solution.

With his heavy-gloved hand, Klaus took the long-handled instrument and picked up one of the slides. He inserted it under the microscope and pressed the plastic face mask close to the eyepiece, holding his breath. Despite his suspected futility, he felt a thin slice of optimism with each inspection. It was like gambling in a way, although he knew luck played only a small part.

The cells on the slide were riddled with the virus.

Klaus suppressed the desire to toss it across the room. Instead, he took it out and laid it carefully in a tray with the other failures, to be incinerated before he left the room.

The next two followed the same result, and as he looked at the final slide, he considered destroying it without checking. The thought was fleeting though; such would be giving up, and he would never do that, no matter how desolate the situation appeared.

Klaus pushed the final slide underneath the microscope. He bent with his hand on the tongs, ready to toss it across the room upon failure.

The cell was clean. Klaus felt a jolt of hope. He pulled back from the microscope and slipped the tongs away from the slide. He placed them onto the bench with an unsteady hand and stepped away from the counter. *Jesus*, what had he just observed? The cell was clean. There was no sign of the virus degradation that he had witnessed in all previous samples. Klaus leaned forward and whacked the plastic mask against the eye of the microscope. He steadied himself and peered through the lens.

There it was. *Clean*. Klaus cried out, the sound muted by his air-tight helmet. There should have been rabid activity showing the virus attacking the cell. The cell contained a hazy appearance, which indicated the virus' presence, but it hadn't progressed. The interferons had worked. It had done its job in preventing the viral replication. He didn't know what sort of side effects it would bring, and he'd never be able to undergo the correct protocols for testing, but if anyone was ever bitten, or contracted the virus, based on what he had discovered the interferon should halt its development.

"Remarkable," he whispered, grinning. Sometimes Klaus even surprised himself.

But he still had to find a way to obtain a sizeable quantity. While he had access to all the well-known pathogens and viruses, their interferon stock was low. The best facilities for such were in Sydney or Melbourne, at the Commonwealth Serum Laboratories, where much of the country's influenza vaccinations were produced.

He had reached an important point of discovery, though. In the old world, he would have told his colleagues and made a dozen phone calls, but such behavior was no longer necessary. Klaus considered finding Gallagher and telling him. That could wait. At some point, the bastard would need him, and Klaus would have the last word.

For now, he had work to do.

NINETEEN

IN THE BACK OF the Jeep, Kristy closed her eyes, feeling the warmth of Dylan's body as she lay against his shoulder. It had become her most peaceful place in the world, a place where she felt safe and comfortable. She berated herself for having wasted so long apart from him. Perhaps, if they got through all of this, they could settle down and get a place together and live a somewhat normal existence. In another life, they might have even ended up married. Kristy had never imagined it for herself. Although she'd had her share of boyfriends, the concept of finding one man that fit all the requirements had always been a dream. Dylan was different though.

As late afternoon turned into early evening, sleep beckoned, but Kristy pushed it away, using the time to consider their unrelenting circumstances. As soon as they survived one episode, another awaited. Kristy had always struggled with the stresses of the ER, but this … in comparison; the ER was a holiday. It was safe, and protected, with the best equipment and conditions, and she was there to save the lives of others, not her own. She hadn't had the time to process it all, moving from one desperate moment to the other, but there was her parents, and the rest of her family to consider, too. They had all left relatives behind.

There would be a time to reflect on those things. Now, she ran through her mental to-do checklist. Greg had taken the first lot of tablets. The boys had found the strongest antibiotics, and by the morning, they would be working their magic and Greg would feel better, assuming he didn't have the virus. It had been close. Perhaps another day and his leg would have been under threat. That would have meant surgery, amputation, and a whole other world of mess. Greg would recuperate, and having him fit and fighting on their side made a big difference. Sarah had recovered, but her health issue would provide an ongoing challenge. Type one diabetics relied on insulin to survive. Without it, she would die, but even having it, the balance between eating, medication, and activity was a fine line. The hypoglycaemic episode she had experienced meant her blood sugar levels had dropped too low. Unconsciousness from low blood sugar was perilous, and if they hadn't found the treatment, she too, would have died. Kristy would have to monitor her closely. There was less optimism for Johnny. She had applied the snakebite cream, but in truth, Kristy lacked hope for him. The bite was deep, the damage severe. Based on Howard's comments, and Dylan's father's information, once the skin had been broken, time was short. The best they could do for Johnny was to make him comfortable. She wondered how it would end though, whether Callan could walk away from his friend, or whether Johnny would conclude matters himself. Although she was no longer in the ER, and probably never would be again, nothing much had changed. She was still thinking about patients.

They reached Holbrook at dusk, after getting off the Hume Highway exit ramp. The air remained thick with heat, and bugs milled around the headlamps in tiny puffs. Callan ran the windscreen wipers frequently to clean the splatters off the glass.

"My parents were friends with the owners of the Town Centre Motor Inn," Dylan said as they rolled down Albury Street. The headlights cut contrasting yellow beams through the darkness. "It's not far along this road, up on the left."

Kristy peered out into the blackness at shadowy houses and trees. It looked like a normal street in a normal town, but they knew better. She was reluctant to get out of the car. As soon as they left the Jeep, they were exposed, and there would be things out there trying to kill them. The reality though was that they couldn't drive forever, and they all needed a proper rest. Lying in bed beside Dylan was incentive, too.

The car stopped at a wide, two-story structure. Callan pulled into the curb behind a lime green Volvo station wagon. So far, the town appeared to have survived much better than Albury. The motor inn was dark and lifeless, like the other buildings in the vicinity, but they all knew that zombies didn't need light to exist. "Looks pretty good."

Dylan leaned on the seat in front, peering out each of the windows. "There's a central courtyard down the driveway that opens out in front of all the rooms. Maybe we should park in there, out of sight."

Callan guided the Jeep around the Volvo and into the entrance. The trailer hit the curb with a loud bump, sending a shudder through the vehicle. Kristy felt her heart jump.

"Sorry," Callan said.

With the lights on low, they drove along the gravel strip and into a square section surrounded by two-story units on half of the four sides. There was space for perhaps twenty-five cars, although they were all empty now. Callan circled the jeep and trailer, parking against the longest edge. "I guess we can have the pick of the rooms."

Those capable took weapons and led the way with torches. Kristy found herself beside Dylan and Callan. With Greg and Johnny ill and injured, they would rely on her to fight, if it came to that. The knowledge filled her with pride, and she realized how much mentally stronger she had gotten in only a few short days.

Her brother led them toward the ground level units, perusing all angles with the cone of light. Blue Boy ran at his heels, the way a heeler might herd cattle or sheep in the outback. They reached the building and Callan stood aside a door with the number eleven marked on it. Kristy and Callan fell in against the wall. It felt like they were part of some SWAT group ready to enter a bank or building.

Callan opened the door, and Dylan followed him in close behind, poking the beam into the room. Blue ran after them, not yet barking, which Kristy took as a good sign, but she held her breath, expecting there would be zombies and they would fight, guns blazing, for their lives. That's how it went now, and strangely, she accepted it.

Tall, menacing shadows danced on the walls, hiding deep corners and angled recesses. The yellow beam fell on a couch and a small television. Through an archway was the kitchenette, the sink and fridge neat and clean, as though the place was ready for the next lot of guests to arrive. The heat hung thick and heavy, pressing against Kristy's face and down her throat. The boys pushed forward into the kitchen, probing the light over the dirty walls and cracked roof. The dog skirted the perimeter, nose trailing the floor. Satisfied it was clear, they backed out and headed into the final two rooms, one containing a double bed with a neat green spread, the other a set of bunk beds.

The first unit was clear. Callan, Dylan, and Kristy checked the two units on either side of the first. Same result, with the exception of the end unit, where the covers had been stripped off one of the bunk beds in the second bedroom.

"You think it's strange they were all unlocked," Dylan asked as they returned to the central unit.

Callan shrugged. "Maybe. But what isn't in this world anymore?"

They carried supplies from the Jeep and trailer into the three rooms under low torchlight, careful not to make too much noise. In the center of the driveway beyond where they had parked, Blue Boy stood with his ears pricked and his tail stiff, looking up towards the roadway. Callan left him out there until they had finished, then called him in.

Sarah would sleep on a bunk bed in the unit on the right, with Kristy and Dylan, while Callan and Howard took the end room furthest from the Jeep. With their injuries and illness, Greg and Johnny took separate bedrooms in the middle apartment, where they set their ammunition, food, water, and other supplies they would need for the night. There was an internal door between each room, and although they were locked, Callan managed to break the latch with the tomahawk. It allowed movement without going outside. Once they had settled their gear, they locked the external doors, closed all the curtains, and lit candles, limiting them to one per room. Johnny went straight for a bunk bed and lay down, holding his arm. Greg had taken more pain relief medication, and although the antibiotics would not have begun working yet, his spirits seemed to have lifted, albeit his pale face and red eyes.

Howard surprised them by offering to create a meal despite the limited ingredients. He had worked as an apprentice chef for two years before throwing it in to become a schoolteacher. The stovetop ran on propane gas, so they were able to boil water and heat a large wok. Using a variety of tinned vegetables and various liquid ingredients, Howard managed a rice dish that drew them from their various locations to ask of its progress with the tantalizing smell of the orient. It was better than they had eaten in days, possibly weeks, for those who had gone to the lake.

They wandered in and ate at different times, each with a palpable sense of tiredness. Howard told them of his plans to travel the globe prior to finding out about the cancer, to visit the places of his ancestors in Scotland and England. After helping Howard clean up, Kristy found Dylan in their room changing out of his Kevlar motorbike gear. She crept up behind him and ran light fingers over his bare back, then kissed the trapezius muscle that ran from his neck across the top of his shoulder. Dylan closed his eyes. She wanted him badly now. They kissed, and this time there was no delicacy in it, but rather passion, tongues darting in and out, and Kristy could sense his need. She took the tip of his tongue between hers and sucked hard. He moaned, lost in the pleasure, and when she finally pulled away, his eyes remained closed for a long moment. When he opened them, she stared at him, smiling.

"Amazing," he said, and laughed.

"There's more where that came from." She winked playfully.

"Just let me wash up." He disappeared into the bathroom.

Kristy found Sarah standing by the kitchen table holding one of the 9mm semi-automatic pistols. "Oh no, honey, don't play with that," Kristy said, taking it from Sarah. It looked awkward in her small hands.

Sarah frowned. "But I need to learn. What if one of those things attacks me?"

"We'll protect you. You don't need to pick up a gun, sweetheart." Kristy tousled her hair, and smiled. "Now come over here, I want to go through something with you."

Kristy sat with Sarah and sorted through the medication Callan had collected from the pharmacy. Thankfully, the girl had a good understanding of her own requirements.

"Those two," Sarah said, pointing at two different types of insulin. One was used to offset the carbohydrate in her meals, the other acted slowly, and worked through the night to keep her blood sugar levels stable.

Callan had done an excellent job finding the medication and the consumables required to administer the injections. Kristy unpacked a syringe and drew insulin from one of the cartridges. It wasn't cold, and required refrigeration, but they didn't have a choice. Under normal circumstances, the cartridge required an injection pen, but for now, the syringe would suffice. She watched Sarah inject the slow-acting insulin with the practiced expertise of a person who has lived with the disease for years. There was probably not a lot Kristy could teach Sarah, other than to watch over her, and ensure she had eaten a sufficient amount.

"Alright," Kristy said. "Have you had enough dinner? Or do you need something else to eat?"

She shook her head. "No. Rice is easy to manage. I know the right amount of insulin to have with a bowlful."

"We need to get you eating a bit more. You could do with some weight."

"I have been hungry, but we haven't had much food. Dad gave most of it to me, anyway."

Kristy knew a discussion about her father was imminent. While she had explained the outcome, Sarah appeared to have accepted it easily. The shock and grief was coming though. "He looked after you, I bet."

Her mouth curled up, but there was pain in her expression. "He always did, even before this happened. I loved him so much. He kissed me goodnight every day, and told me how much he loved me. I don't even think he ate sometimes. Told me he did, but I knew he was lying." She smiled, and this time it was for a nice memory. "When he was alive, I felt like nothing could happen to me, you know?" Kristy nodded. "He also made me promise that if he died, I'd survive, that I'd never stop trying to live on, regardless of how bad things became. But I feel like with him gone, I'm alone."

"No, no, honey. You're not alone. You have us. And *I* promise I'll take good care of you, and I know Callan would do the same."

"I like Callan. He makes me feel safe."

"I know, me too. And he likes you. If it wasn't for him, you might have been in real trouble today." Sarah smiled, nodding. "See, there *is* someone looking out for you." Callan had a way of drawing people to him. He was a natural leader, and had always been so. In school he had been captain of the football and cricket teams, and kids had inherently followed him. He looked after people, Kristy realized, and he had been doing so for the entire trip, organizing and leading them from day one.

"Thank you," Sarah said. "It's my fault he died though. We were going to the hospital for me, to get more supplies."

"Don't say that." What did she say to a child who had just lost her father? Sarah gave a weak smile, then burst into tears. Kristy took her shoulder and pulled her forward. They embraced, Kristy squeezing her gently and rubbing her back. "Shh. Shh."

After a moment, Sarah pulled away, wiping at her wet eyes with clumsy fingers. "I don't know why I'm crying."

She sniffed. "Dad told me it might happen. He made me promise I wouldn't cry too much." She took a glass of water from the table with shaking hands, and sipped.

Kristy thought she was handling the day's events remarkably well for a pre-teen. She helped Sarah to the lower bunk and tucked her under a light sheet, the soft orange glow of flame on the bedside table revealing fresh wetness on her cheeks. Kristy crouched by the bed and put one hand over Sarah's, and with the other stroked her hair. "I'm so sorry, Sarah. Life is just so unfair at the moment." Sarah lay down and twisted the sheet up under her chin. "We'll look after you now." Kristy wished she had something more comforting to say. She'd never been an orator of powerful or inspirational sermons. Instead, she continued the action her mother had done to her in times of distress, drawing her fingertips through Sarah's hair. The girl calmed, closing her eyes, tears running down the flawless skin of her cheeks. "I'll leave the candle on. We'll just be in the next room."

Kristy sat for a few more minutes, watching her. A spill of dark golden locks covered the pillow. Sarah had a thin, slightly upturned nose and small lips. Callan had saved her, but Kristy would care for her. That's what she did, and regardless of how deep the spiral of the world descended, she would continue doing so. But as she sat there comforting the girl, she decided that Sarah needed a focus, a purpose in the world besides survival. Kristy would teach her first aid, and then more, about the workings of medicines, and the treatment of illness and injury. She understood the mechanisms of her own illness already, and they needed a backup, because who knew what tomorrow would bring for any of them.

TWENTY

DYLAN SAT IN THE darkness of the first apartment, full of regret and guilt at what had happened to Johnny. It was true, there had been hate between them in the past, but Dylan had buried that now. Johnny faced a death sentence, and there was nothing any of them could do about it. Dylan decided he would apologize, at least for their altercation before Johnny was bitten, whether he needed to or not.

He checked on Kristy, sitting in with Sarah, and then entered the central unit through the internal door. A pile of bags sat in the middle of the room, and a candle burned on one of the bedside tables. He stopped at the first door when he saw Greg lying on the bed with his eyes closed. He considered chatting, but didn't want to wake him. Dylan was part of Greg's problem, too.

He found Johnny in the next room, lying on the bottom bunk bed, his bitten arm resting above his head. More candlelight glowed on a small table. The air was stifling, hot.

Johnny looked up. "If you've come to give me another lesson in morals, then fuck off."

Dylan stopped. "I—"

"Save it, man, you win. I'm a dead man walking. You're alive, you get the girl, and you win."

"Johnny, hold the phone, man. I'm not here to ride you about today. I came to say I'm sorry. I shouldn't have …" What exactly shouldn't he have done? Johnny was the one who had betrayed his best friend. It shouldn't have required Dylan to call him on it. A guilty conscience will always prevail though. "It's just fucked up. The whole thing. I'm sorry it's gotten to this."

There was movement at the door. Callan stepped into the room, hands on his hips. "What's going on?"

Dylan glanced at Johnny. His face was impassive, unreadable. This was it. Dylan had his chance. The conversation was setup. He could tell Callan he thought

Johnny had something to say, then walk out and leave the two of them to it. Johnny had once filled Dylan's school locker with rotten prawn heads and fixed the door shut. Dylan had no idea how he had done so, but it was the kind of inventiveness for which Johnny was known. He owed him a payback more times over than this, but he couldn't do it.

"Nothing. Just shootin' the shit."

Callan asked, "What'd you want to apologize for?"

"Nothing."

Callan stepped into the room. "I know, I know, you hate Johnny. Always have. But this," he waved an arm around. "This is bullshit, man. Leave the guy alone. He's on his death bed, and you're riding his ass again?"

Dylan felt the sting of Callan's erroneous words. Given all they had been through, he thought that Callan wouldn't have been so quick to judge him. Maybe Dylan had been wrong about just how close they had become. He felt his own response leap up, but he bit it down with a clearing of his throat.

"Hold on, Cal," Johnny said.

Callan put a hand up. "Don't defend him, man. He's—"

"No mate." Johnny slid off the bottom bunk. "It's not his fault."

The situation was about to explode. Callan was not the kind of person to let something like this go once he'd sensed a problem. He would need every detail, whether extracted from Johnny, or Dylan himself.

"Relax, Johnny," Callan said, helping him up. "I just wanna know what the fuck's going on with you two."

Dylan decided it was time for him to leave. He didn't want to be around for Callan's reaction if Johnny had grown the courage to tell him about the infraction.

"Don't run away," Callan said. "You can't cause trouble and then piss off."

Dylan threw his arms in the air. "For fuck's sake, man, I didn't—"

Johnny stepped forward. "It's my fault, Callan. Not Dylan. I fucked up."

Oh, shit, Dylan thought. Callan frowned. Suddenly, Dylan wanted to run. Callan would go crazy. He'd just lost his girl, and now he'd learn that one of his best mates had done the dirty on him.

Johnny forced himself to look at Callan. "I … slept with Sherry." The words hung in the air like poisoned gas. "I swung past your place one night to see you, and she was a bit depressed. You were stuck at some work function. I had a beer and she had one and then two and we got pretty wasted. I'd just broken up with Gloria." He gritted his teeth and shook his head. "Fucking stupid. I've done some dumb things in my time, but that's the dumbest. Sherry too." Callan's gaze tightened at the mention of her name, but the rest of his expression remained impassive. "She cried for weeks afterwards. Gave me a disgusted look every time she saw me, which wasn't often." He finally looked away. Tears ran down his cheeks and the thin line that was his lips trembled. "I fucking deserve this," he said, holding out his wounded arm. "As soon as it happened, I knew it was payback. Karma. I've always believed in that shit."

Dylan couldn't move. Now that it had happened, he wasn't so pleased. Watching their pain brought him no satisfaction. But it might get worse. If Callan lost control, nobody would stop him. It could impact the group; they might fracture, and things would never be the same again. In hindsight, perhaps it had been a mistake to ever question Johnny.

Callan stepped towards Johnny, his mouth a grim line, his breathing deep and controlled. Johnny didn't move. Dylan admired his courage not to run. Johnny's eyes were large and round, his face full of terrified anticipation.

Callan lifted a fist, poised to strike. *That was it*, Dylan thought. Johnny would have a busted face. He supposed it was fair penance.

Callan shook his fist. "You stupid *prick*." Johnny glanced down at the hand he had cheered for rearranging the faces of numerous drunken foes in a past life. Callan turned to Dylan and shook his head. *Keep calm.* He saw the anger in Callan's expression, the rage of betrayal, both from his girl and his mate. What could possibly appease such treachery? Nothing. That was the answer Dylan saw in his eyes.

Callan's appearance faltered. He turned back to his old friend, lowered his fist, and rubbed the bridge of his nose with both hands. "Arghhh." He dropped his hands and let out a big sigh. "You're lucky. If you weren't bitten, I'd kill you." There would be no beating. Here was a changed man. Had Callan discovered the treachery out camping, Johnny would have suffered. Tears of gratitude fell from Johnny's red eyes. "You should have told me, man. We could have sorted it out back then."

Don't tell him I know anything, Dylan thought. Johnny narrowed his eyes, and for a second, Dylan thought Johnny was going to tell him to fuck off. Then he turned back to Callan and said, "I'm sorry, man. I fucked up. I know you'll never forgive me, but I'm so sorry."

"Yeah. Well, it's in the past, now." Callan lingered a moment, then turned and walked out with his head down.

Johnny wiped his eyes, and Dylan followed Callan from the room.

TWENTY-ONE

ERIC NORMAN STOOD AT the front window of his modest home watching the darkness. Thirty minutes ago, he'd caught two sets of headlights moving past along Main Street. He felt a mix of both excitement and fear. They hadn't seen anybody for days now. He'd thought that everyone in the town had either died, or fled. Every night he'd pulled back the drapes and looked out at the sunset, looking for movement until well after darkness, hoping to see an army truck or a friendly vehicle. Until now, it had been black, lifeless. The arrival of people might be the start of something good, or bad, he supposed.

"What is it?"

Julie, Eric's wife, stood by candlelight in the entranceway to the kitchen, her grey hair dark in the shadows. She wore an apron, and had her hair tied up in a voluminous bun. Julie wasn't handling the circumstances well. She was jumpy; scared of anything that made a loud noise, suspicious of the outside world, although that was probably not unusual. She had taken the death of the children like any loving mother would; blaming herself, spending days looking at photos and video footage. He wondered whether she would ever recover. Eric hadn't brought it up again after a heavy bout of crying, and subsequently, her invariable pessimism for death had cloaked them in an even darker cloud. Eric couldn't think about his children. The place where such thoughts were considered had gone numb, never to be mended again.

"Other cars," Eric said.

"Close the blind. They'll see you."

"It was half an hour ago. I was thinking of going outside to—"

She started forward, waving a knife at him. "No. You're not."

Eric raised both hands. "Calm down, honey. I won't go far. I need to find out who they are and what they're up to."

115

She lowered the knife. "No you don't. You don't have to see anything. You can stay right here, and we'll be just fine, thank you very much."

"Julie—"

"Don't." She backed through the entrance into the kitchen, her eyes becoming glassy. "We're not doing this, Eric. I've told you before, I'm not going anywhere." She laid the knife on the table and began to sob. "I can't keep going. When will it end?"

He took her in his arms and gave a gentle squeeze. "We can't stay cooped up in here for the rest of our lives, can we? You'll get sick of me at some point and need the company."

"If anything happens to you, Eric, I won't survive."

"Shhh. Nothing's going to happen to me."

"You don't know that."

"I need you to be strong. We both have to toughen up if we're to have a chance at surviving this thing."

"I'm not strong."

"You are, for God's sake. I saw you labor through three births. No man I know could have done that."

"It's different."

"It's not. You had to be brave then. You had to do something you'd never done before, not knowing how it would turn out. And you did. You were bloody brave, and I need you to do the same now."

She finally hugged him, but didn't say another word.

Eric stuck a revolver into the back of his pants, feeling like a cop in some crime movie, and for light, took the mobile phone his oldest daughter Michelle had given him last Christmas.

"It'll be alright," Eric said.

"You don't know that."

As much as he loved her, he was losing patience with her pessimism. She had always been inclined that way, but with the events of late, it had darkened her spirit considerably. "You're going to have to trust me, darling. The same way you have for the last three decades."

As he went out the door, Julie watched through the dark crack. Eric thought sadly that at the moment, she might not survive without him. Her frail nature had relied on him since they had first become a couple all those years ago. It was also imperative that they find others as a contingency should anything befall either of them. He wondered how he would fare without his beloved wife. The thought was too painful for consideration.

The street was dark. Eric stood at the edge of his scruffy lawn, a victim of the incessant heat and lack of attention over the last weeks. In the old days, he'd stood out on his lawn on a summer evening, sweeping a spray of water over the grass. Kids rode their bikes. Eric waved back. He wished for them again with a deep, painful regret.

North, along Main Street, was black and silent. He stepped out onto the footpath, glancing around into the shadows, his pulse slowly climbing. He'd done little adventuring after sunset, but this demanded a look. Besides, there had been a drop off in zombies of late, as if they'd all gone elsewhere to search for food.

He reached the driveway of the motor inn and saw the shape of a large vehicle and a trailer parked in the courtyard, parallel to the rooms. The travelers were resting for the night, which meant they would probably leave the following day. He needed to find out if it was worth making contact.

As he started off down the gravel track, the door to one of the units opened. A large figure rushed out, slamming the door behind. Eric felt a stab of panic at their hostility. If he was to meet anyone, he wasn't sure this was the person.

He darted backward to the street and scurried into the bushes of the house next door, pulling the branches of a spindly bush in front of his face.

He waited.

A man arrived at the edge of the curb, talking to himself in low tones. He put his hands on his face, and Eric felt something different, a touch of empathy. Something was wrong.

Perhaps the man needed help. Eric considered all that had gone on, all that he'd seen

And so, as he always done, Eric, pulled the branch aside and stepped forward.

TWENTY-TWO

GRAVEL CRUNCHED UNDERFOOT AS Callan strode down the driveway of the parking area. The heat pressed against his skin, smothering his face and nose, and he felt like he couldn't breathe. For the moment, he had control of his anger, burying it under the mess of the last few days, but he couldn't be sure for how long.

He reached the street and stood on the curb, looking in either direction. Darkness blacked out the world, but he could perceive the vague outline of rooftops under a thin slice of moon. In the distance, the grunts and groans of the feeders floated to him. Nothing close by, but a part of him welcomed it. He had taken one of the pistols from the table top in the center unit and tucked it into his waistband, just in case.

Where did they go from here? Johnny and Sherry's treachery had stolen a part of him. How could he ever trust another person? His initial response had been to beat the shit out of his old mate, but Johnny was a dead man, and Callan couldn't hit a man in such a position. Such control had surprised Callan. Part of him felt it was a weak response, that he needed to break bones and draw blood, but another part, the newer, stronger part, understood it would not help.

It was not Johnny so much; sure they had been mates a long time, but Callan accepted his personality. Johnny had betrayed most of the people close to him; maybe Callan had been expecting it. But Sherry? That had struck his core, and he would feel a burning pain forever. In that moment, when he had realized, it all made sense. He'd been trying to make something work that wasn't supposed to work. Sherry had given him signs all along, and more so of late. He had just hadn't recognized them.

"Nice night for a walk," a deep, raspy voice said from beside him.

Callan jumped. "Ha?" His hand clutched the pistol, removing it from his pants.

"Sorry, son, I just didn't want you to shoot me."

"You're bloody lucky I didn't. Jesus, man, you move like a ninja."

The man pressed a button, and a thin white light appeared in the top pocket of his shirt. He was older, perhaps sixty or seventy, with thinning hair brushed backward. The skin of his face sagged in places, covered in short white stubble. He wore dark pants and a shirt, with the sleeves rolled up.

"Where'd you come from?" Callan asked, slipping the gun back into his waistband.

The man turned and pointed down the road. "Not far. My wife and I saw you drive in."

"Your wife?"

"Yeah. She's back at the house. Won't come out."

"You've been here, in Holbrook, all along?"

"Lived here all my life." The man pulled a packet of cigarettes from his other pocket and slipped one into his mouth. He offered the pack to Callan, who put up a hand. "Quit for seven years," the man said. "Figured it didn't matter anymore. I'll probably be dead soon anyway, so why not enjoy my nicotine fix for the last bit?" He tucked the cigarettes away, lit the smoke, then stuck out his hand. "Eric Norman." Callan shook it, feeling the strong grip of an old country boy. "Where you lot come from?"

"Albury."

"Trouble there, I expect."

"Albury is gone."

He drew long on the cigarette and let the smoke filter out his nose. "There might not be much left anywhere."

"How is it here?"

Eric tipped his head from side to side. "Liveable. Just. Most of the town folk are dead or turned. There were a couple of people scattered about, but we haven't seen them lately. We keep our heads down."

"You have family here?"

"Did. Two daughters and a son." He turned to Callan while inhaling, and shook his head.

"I'm sorry."

"We've all lost someone, right?"

Callan nodded. They had. Aside from Sherry, he and Kristy had lost their whole family. Callan hadn't thought about his poor mother or father for what felt like days. They were dead, no question. "Yeah." His thoughts drifted back to Johnny, and Sherry. "It's strange, you know? One moment you're talking to a person, alive, breathing. Then they're dead. There's no more after that."

"Nope. That's it."

"I've seen a lot of dead people in the last few days. But when people that you know die, that you've lived with and talked to … it's hard to comprehend."

Eric finished his cigarette, dropped the butt on the ground, stomped it out, then picked it up and slipped it into his pocket. "Life is precious. If it's one thing we've seen with this plague, it's that things can change in a second. But do we hide away and not *live*? Is that how we go on from here?"

"That's the question."

"My wife is paranoid about doing anything. She won't leave the house. She's a wonderful woman, a real ripper, don't get me wrong, I don't know what I'd do without her. We've been married forever."

Callan thought he'd had a wonderful woman, too, but he'd been wrong. "Yeah, I hear you. I had one of them too. Or thought I did. I lost my girl today. I figured we'd end up like you and your wife."

"I'm real sorry to hear that. I can't imagine what you're going through."

Callan felt the words building, and he didn't know how to stop them. Maybe he needed to tell somebody about it, and this man, who instinct told him was a good person, familiar, in some ways, was the one to hear it. "It gets worse though. I

OWEN BAILLIE

found out she'd cheated on me." Eric grunted. "Not only that, but with one of my good mates."

"Ah, my friend, I'm sorry. That's a tough gig."

"But he's here, now, with us. And he's been bitten." A long silence filled the gap. Callan waited for Eric to say something. Suddenly the importance of this man's words weighed heavily.

"I can't tell you how to handle that," Eric said. "It's a sad situation you find yourself in, and I pity you, especially the way the world has gone. All I can do is tell you about a circumstance I found myself in many years ago—similar, but not exactly the same. I held onto resentment for many years. I couldn't forgive a betrayal, and it ate away at me. It made my life and the lives of those around me difficult. I wouldn't acknowledge certain things, and I couldn't see past the treachery of it. Took me a long time, but in the end, though, I was able to forgive, and it's the best thing I ever did."

"So you reckon I should forgive him, and her?"

Eric shook his head. "I'm not saying that. I'm saying that I held onto my anger and resentment for many years and it almost killed me. When I finally did let it go, it saved my life."

Is that what Callan would do? Carry his anger around until it killed him? Maybe that was better. Maybe the world was better off without him. "Thanks for sharing it with me."

"No problem. But I should be gettin' back now. Julie will be getting worried, as she does. How about we meet up in the morning? You all set for the night? Need anything?"

"No, thanks. We're good."

"Okay." Eric smiled then, and Callan felt comfortable with him. "It was enjoyable seeing a normal pair of eyes and a set of teeth that don't wanna take a chunk of flesh from you."

Callan laughed. "Yeah. Too right."

Eric walked away with the practiced silence of a man who has almost died making too much noise, his feet floating over the ground.

Callan returned to his immediate problem. Johnny had committed treachery of the unforgivable kind. Callan didn't have to forgive him, but he wouldn't let Johnny die without a fight. They probably had a day, or two. They could drive to Wagga Wagga, or Sydney, in search of a vaccine. They had to try. As for Sherry, he just didn't understand. Maybe Kristy could shed some light on it. Callan turned and headed back inside, mindful of Eric's silent footsteps.

The candles were out in Johnny's and Greg's rooms. Callan didn't feel like talking. They had decided to keep the internal doors open, and a faint glow broke the shadows from his sister's apartment. Callan bumbled his way through his unit until he reached his own room. He lit the bedside candle and lay back against the wall with his hands clasped behind his head, two hard pillows for support. He closed his eyes and felt a warmth pervade his body. Sleep pulled at him, and for once, he welcomed it, seeking the temporary respite from the mess that his life had become.

The floor creaked outside the door. Callan sat up, peering into the shadows beyond the door. Blue Boy appeared with his ears flattened back, tail wagging.

Callan let out his breath, then patted the bed. "You scared me, fella."

The dog leaped up onto the sheet and collapsed on the end of the bed. Callan lay back down and the dog crawled up beside him.

"You won't cheat on me, will you, boy?" The dog smiled, tongue hanging out. He pressed his ears back and wagged his tail again. Callan scratched right in behind his ear, and the dog groaned in delight.

He'd had another heeler when he was a boy, just like Blue. Arriving home from school one day, his father had surprised him. Callan had named him Aussie. Wholly unoriginal, but Aussie had been a wonderful companion for a boy: protective, playful, and he had slept at the foot of Callan's bed every night. He had wished on every birthday that Aussie would live forever, but in the end, the dog had succumbed to death, as they all did. *Don't get too attached to this one*, he told himself.

With that thought, Callan undressed, tossed one of the pillows aside, and lay on the stiff bed. It was too hot for blankets, and even in the stuffy heat, it didn't take long for sleep to come.

He dozed, but woke sweating and sobbing sometime later, the remnants of a nightmare washing over him in cold terror. Whimpering, Blue Boy pushed closer. Callan reached out for the comfort.

Sherry had been alive, fighting off zombies, begging him for help. He had clawed his way there, and this time, he had saved her, but suffered a bite himself. It had been Sherry begging *him* not to die, demanding that he take more care and not throw his life away.

He lay back against the bedhead, thinking about the day. He had been reckless. Did he want to die? "Does it matter if I get killed, Blue?" The dog whined. Callan scratched the soft fur on top of his head. "Maybe Sherry was right."

This time when he slept, there were no dreams.

TWENTY-THREE

A STRIP OF BRIGHT sunlight lay across Kristy's face. She blinked and came awake with a start. Her last memory had been lying beside Dylan, watching him sleep, her promise to make love with him lost again. They had been talking, but he had struggled to keep his eyes open and had drifted off. She hadn't the heart to wake him. She hoped they'd get another chance, whatever the day brought.

Dylan had told her of the incident between Johnny and Callan. While it had shocked her, in reflection, it had been no surprise. Sherry had never quite convinced Kristy of her commitment to the relationship, and the pregnancy seemed to have been false hope for a bad situation. *Poor Callan*, she thought. Her brother had suffered emotionally more than anyone else.

Kristy slipped out of bed and walked into the bathroom. Staring back at her in the mirror was the unfamiliar look of an exhausted woman. While the ER had brought its stresses, she was always able to refresh after a day or two. Now, there was no respite. Dark bags cupped her eyes. Her complexion was pale, washed out. She had broken out in pimples on her chin, probably from the stress, and her blond hair, withered and dry from the sun, needed a wash. On cue, she reached up to scratch her itchy head. She closed her eyes, and when she opened them, Kristy saw her mother peering back.

Where were her parents? Dead? Turned into zombies? They would probably never know, and maybe that was better. She held onto the slim chance that they had escaped, left town early with the Keanes, and driven with them to their holiday house in Merimbula. In reality, though, they were likely dead, and she had to believe this for her own sake, otherwise she might never move on with her life.

She washed up, decided to leave Dylan asleep, and crept past Sarah, who lay sprawled on the couch with the covers pulled over her head. She wanted to check on Greg, and if his condition had improved, talk about her and Dylan again. It was a difficult conversation to have, but she wanted to know Greg had accepted the situation and offer him the chance to speak his mind.

A faint light came from his room, and she found him sprawled out on the double bed. A bottle of Johnny Walker sat on the bedside table. Kristy tapped on the timber door frame.

"Hi."

Greg sat up, grimacing.

"How are you feeling?"

He groaned. "Still average, but a little better."

"The antibiotics will start to work soon. You'll feel better later today." He reached out for the Scotch. "That's not such a good idea with the pills."

He looked at the bottle and put it back. "The rate I'm going, it'll never be a good time." Kristy sat on the end of the bed. Greg looked back with his eyebrows raised.

"I just wanted to see how you were. You know, with the whole Dylan and me situation."

He didn't look away, but his expression softened, and the edges of his mouth turned down. "You can't love someone for twenty-eight years and just stop. That's impossible. Could you do it?"

Kristy felt heat in her cheeks. She would have preferred he yell at her. How would she have felt in his position? Worse, he had saved her life on more than one occasion. Dylan's, too, and he had done so sick up to his eyeballs.

"I … don't … know …"

He frowned. "That's right. You don't know how this feels."

She didn't, and there was no comfort in her words. Greg bore a lifelong infatuation, but Kristy felt only a brotherly kind of love. Perhaps it had been defined when they were children. She wished she could do something to make him feel better.

Kristy pushed off the bed. Coming to see him had been a bad idea. "Don't forget to take your tablets. They won't work unless you finish them all." She turned away, fighting within herself to attempt reconciliation. She knew Greg though, knew his moods, and in his current state, he would continue to argue.

From the third apartment, Kristy saw light and headed towards it. Callan stood by the window, peering out through a crack in the curtains. Blue Boy lay curled up on the bed.

"Morning. Anything?" Kristy asked.

"No. Streets are empty. For now"

They went into the kitchen, where a plate of crackers sat on the Laminex bench top beside a tub of margarine and a jar of Vegemite. Kristy took a plain cracker and bit off a corner. Chewing, she said, "How do you feel? You have a bad dream last night?" Callan raised his eyebrows. "I heard screaming."

"Yeah. It was bad. But I feel better now. I think it helped me." He rubbed a bristly chin. "Yesterday I just felt like I didn't know what to do, didn't know where to go, or how to act. I knew I was being reckless running off after that ambulance, but I didn't care. I just felt like I wanted to kill them all."

"And today?"

"I don't have the anger I felt yesterday. It's almost as if finding out about Sherry and Johnny washed it all away." Callan described meeting Eric the previous night. "I think the conversation might have had something to do with it, too. Dylan told you what happened?" Kristy nodded. Callan scoffed. "I'm an idiot, aren't I? Infatuated all that time."

"No, you're not an idiot. You did what any person in a relationship should do. You committed to it, one hundred percent, with trust, and loyalty."

"And look where it got me."

"She wasn't the one for you. I know you loved her, but it wasn't meant to be."

"You're a hard woman sometimes."

127

She smiled. "I've been there too, remember. Maybe I wasn't as deep in a relationship as you and Sherry, but I know how you feel."

Callan nodded and stepped towards her. "Give me a hug."

It was a rare moment of affection from a man hardened by a truck-driving father, and a group of friends that frowned upon physical warmth. She wrapped her small arms around his muscly back and squeezed with all the love a sister could give. She felt the warm sensation of tears at the back of her eyes. He deserved better. Girls had thrown their phone numbers at him during his relationship with Sherry, and he had ignored every one.

They parted, smiling. Kristy said, "What's the plan for the day?"

"Before Johnny got bitten, we were heading for one of the army bases."

"Wagga?"

"What about Holsworthy? Or the joint operations command centre in Canberra? That man said it was still operational."

"But that was weeks ago."

"Who knows if any of them are even worth visiting? Are you sure there's nothing we can do for Johnny?"

"Wait. See if he gets sick. Other than that …"

Slowly, the others woke, and with the exception of Johnny, they congregated in the kitchen area. Howard's gratitude was obvious as he explained to them some of what he'd endured over the past week or so stuck in the hospital. He had survived by eating vending machine food and hiding in broom closets whenever he saw zombies. He had smeared himself in a deodorizer from one of the chemical cupboards to prevent them catching his scent.

Kristy suspected his survival was not by accident, and that his wily skills would be useful to them at some point. Greg hobbled out to the kitchenette, his ankle sore but his fever down. He even managed to smile, although he didn't converse with Kristy. They ate crackers and ageing fruit that would spoil in another day or two, and drank water from plastic bottles.

"So," Dylan said, after everybody had eaten. "Where to from here?"

"We have a couple of choices," Callan said. "Kapooka military base is in Wagga Wagga."

"That's where they do all the basic training for new recruits," Howard said. "What are we looking for?"

Callan's eyes widened. "Help. A place to stay. A vaccine."

"I know I've said it before, but I still think Tasmania is the best place to go."

"That's smart," Howard said. "I can see how you might be able to control things on an island like that."

"We could go through Melbourne; check out the vaccine manufacturer the truck driver was talking about."

Kristy liked the idea of Tasmania, but the immediate practicalities concerned her. "That's a long way from here. We've got Johnny to think about, too. He needs medical attention."

"I'm not putting all our faith in a guy who had the virus," Callan said. "I still think Sydney is our best hope. Holsworthy is a big base. They *must* be working on a vaccine."

Dylan leaned forward. "Wagga is closest, though. What if we just went there first, and then worked out our next plan?"

Callan ground his jaw. "Johnny will be dead by then."

Johnny will be dead no matter what, Kristy thought. "How far is Sydney?"

Dylan said, "Holsworthy would have to be four and a half hours. Besides, the guy said it would be overrun soon. Does it make sense to go to a place where there are five million dead?"

"Melbourne will have almost as many. Sydney is a straight run. Almost one road. We stay on the Hume Highway and maybe make a couple of turns. Easy driving; safe."

"And Wagga?"

"An hour, maybe a bit more."

Howard said, "Canberra's two and a half. That's a compromise."

Kristy left the others to decide, and went into the darkened bedroom. A slit of white light around the edge of the curtain gave the space a murky look. She met Johnny's eyes as she sat on the edge of the bed. "Hey." She had known Johnny since she was six or seven, when Callan had been in the fourth grade. They had gotten along, but she had never felt the same brotherly connection as with Greg.

"Hey."

"How are you feeling?" He shifted back and lay up against the wall with a pillow supporting his head, holding his arm out as though it was broken. Kristy wanted to examine the bite for changes, as much for Johnny's welfare, as her knowledge about such things.

"I've been better. Arm's throbbing. Starting to feel achy all over."

She could hear the change in his voice, and the congestion in his nose. "I'm just going to open the curtains, let some light in."

"Is that safe?"

"I expect so." She pulled back the curtains, and Johnny twisted away from the sunlight. When he turned back, Kristy caught her breath. His eyes and nostrils were puffy and red, his face pale, sickly.

"Show me your arm," she said, sitting beside him. Johnny pulled back the sleeve of his shirt, revealing a bloody bandage. She turned his arm by the wrist, examining the location, and slowly unwound the bandage, being careful not to touch the wound.

"How is it?" His voice was shaky.

"It's a bad bite."

"Am … am I gonna turn into one of those … things?"

She considered leaving some hope on the table, but Johnny was a realist, and most patients just wanted the truth.

"I think you're almost certainly infected. All the bites we've seen like this don't end well. Dylan's father had something similar." Kristy put a hand over his. "I'm sorry, Johnny. So sorry."

He stared at the wound, and for a long moment, Kristy thought he might explode. "Hey, shit happens, I get that. Probably payback for all the stuff I did growing up. There's a party for zombies going on somewhere." His eyes were red and glassy. "Callan's probably celebrating."

"No, he's not. He's trying to find the quickest way to get you treatment."

"Well, I can tell you now, I won't be turning into one of them. I'll finish myself off before that happens."

"Don't talk like that." He cupped both hands over his face, and wiped at his wet eyes. Johnny had never cried in front of Kristy, and he wouldn't want the others to see. "I'll tell the guys to give you some time. Anything I can get you?"

He shook his head. "Thanks Kristy."

She gathered herself outside the bedroom, in the dark space in front of the bathroom door, then stepped out of the shadows and into the meals area where the others chatted about something of less importance than Johnny's life. Her failures as a doctor resurfaced. He would surely die, and there was nothing within her powers to do anything about it.

"Someone's coming," Dylan said, standing between the front curtains.

Callan joined him. "It's Eric and his wife." Callan explained his meeting with Eric the previous night to those who hadn't heard.

They made the introductions all around; Eric's wife was named Julie. She wore a green, summery dress revealing pale, fleshy legs. Short hair, cropped for easy maintenance, topped an expression of concern. She kept looking about, stopping at the window leading to the front.

"What are your plans?" Eric asked after formalities were complete. He pulled a cigarette. "Anybody mind?"

"I do," Kristy said. "I'm a doctor, and I've seen those things kill a lot of people."

Eric smiled and stuffed the cigarette back into the packet. "Sure, love. No problem."

Callan outlaid their choices about where to go next.

"You should think about staying here," Eric said. "Holbrook is a small town, and there doesn't appear to be too many zombies left. We got plenty of food, and we haven't even raided the local stores yet."

"One of our friends is ... sick. We need to get him treatment," Kristy said.

"Sorry to hear that. We got a pharmacy just down the road. Still got most of the medicine in there, minus the stuff we took for all the aches and pains you get at our age." He smiled. "But I suspect you might need more than that."

Callan made a pained face. "Yeah. Unfortunately. It means we can't really stay."

They discussed the positives and negatives of all their options. Eric provided sound advice, and along with Howard, it was comforting to have wiser, older heads around to bounce ideas off. Eric was a man who had lived. They discovered he had gone to Vietnam, driven trucks up and down the east coast of Australia for many years, fought devastating bush fires and immense floods. He had countless stories of hardship, mateship, and death. They sat and listened, and the answer to their question seemed a whole lot simpler, in the end. It was agreed by all that they would drive to the Kapooka barracks at Wagga Wagga.

And then it happened. *As it always will,* Kristy thought.

Standing by the window, doing the umpteenth check, Dylan said, "We've got a problem."

Kristy joined him and felt the familiar feeling of dread slither over her. Blue Boy stood at the door, growling.

A male zombie had its head stuck through the half-open window of the Jeep. But it was worse than that. Further down the driveway, hundreds of them gathered at the entrance of the motor inn, working their way north along the main road. They were tall and short, half-eaten, armless, legless, and some were almost headless. "Where are they coming from?"

"I don't understand," Eric said. "We've barely seen any until now. Just the odd group around town."

Julie's expression twisted into anger. "I don't like it, Eric. I told you we shouldn't have left our place."

Callan stood behind the curtain, watching. "Albury," he said in a flat, disbelieving tone. "They've walked from Albury looking for more food."

TWENTY-FOUR

"WE HAVE TO LEAVE," Callan said, turning away from the window. "Let's get our stuff together."

Dylan closed the gap in the curtains. "They're coming down the driveway. We can't go out into that."

Blue Boy barked several times, and Callan called him away from the door. He lifted one of the bags filled with weapons up onto the table with a clunk. He removed a Browning pistol, fast becoming his favorite, and stuck in a full magazine. "We've been in worse."

Kristy said, "But there's more people to consider now, Cal. Sarah and Johnny. Greg still has a bad ankle, and he's nowhere near a hundred percent."

Greg sat forward at the table. "I'm feeling better. I can walk fast, and shoot with both hands."

Callan pulled the curtain aside again. The zombies were staggering down the driveway towards the Jeep, a dozen now, with their shabby clothes and clumsy, desperate mannerisms. "Bugger," he said under his breath. He didn't want to be holed up in these apartments. If they didn't leave today, Johnny would surely be dead by tomorrow.

"Damn you, Eric." Julie's lips were peeled back in disgust. "I never wanted to leave. We were safe there."

Eric placed a gentle hand on her shoulder. "Hush, honey. It's okay." Julie's mouth trembled, and her large, outlined eyes blinked back fear.

How could Callan get them away? He and Dylan could provide cover fire. Howard was capable, although Callan didn't want to rely on him, and he couldn't suffer somebody else getting bitten again. Eric looked like he could handle a stick, despite being in his late sixties. Greg would fight too, even on his death bed.

"Enough of us can shoot a gun," Callan said. "We can make it. That's why we parked the Jeep so close to the door."

Callan left the living room and entered the bedroom, picking through another bag of supplies. Greg joined him. "Can you do this, mate?" Callan asked. Greg nodded, but wobbled, and held out a hand for the bed. His ashen face and red eyes gave Callan little confidence. "Is it the infection, or have you been drinking all night?"

"Does it matter?"

Callan stood up. "Are you fucking serious? We're about to go out and fight for our lives. We need you sharp, not tripping over your feet. I can't be worrying about whether you'll fall down."

"I'll be fine. Aren't I always?"

"Yeah, you have been, but there's always a first."

"Won't happen."

Callan continued sorting guns. "What about Howard?"

"He doesn't look like the fighting type."

"A strong breeze would blow him over." Howard appeared in the doorway. "Can you shoot a gun?" Callan asked, handing Howard a brand new Winchester .30-30.

"I've shot beers cans a couple of times at a friend's property near Echuca. I'm not much of a gun man, to be honest."

"You'll have to learn fast."

"I'll do my best."

Callan smiled. "I know you will."

Zombies were milling around the car and trailer. A tallish man in overalls and a cap played with the corner of the tarpaulin, trying to pull it loose. Several others beat on the side windows, as if somebody was inside that might let them in. Others stood around, feeble-minded, waiting to follow. A broken trail extended down the driveway to the street, where the line continued into town.

It wasn't going to happen, Callan realized. For now, they were stuck there.

TWENTY-FIVE

AT FIVE-THIRTY, THE zombies wandered off. Not just one or two, but all of them. Blue Boy gave three shrill barks, as if sending them on their way.

Dylan was on shift at the window, watching them poke about the trailer, pulling leftover supplies out and scattering them over the gravel. Greg had proposed shooting the ones that were destroying their gear, but the others had judged it too dangerous. As soon as they fired the guns, more would come, and the risk would increase. They were safe while they stayed quiet, and out of sight.

"They're leaving," Dylan said in a loud whisper. Callan, Howard, and Eric joined him.

Eric narrowed his eyes. "Something has distracted them."

"How do you know?"

He shook his head. "They don't leave unless there's a good reason, and certainly not in numbers."

"A mass of them came to my parents' property in Albury," Dylan said. "Hundreds of them. We think they were drawn there."

Howard rubbed his chin. "I saw this kind of behavior a number of times in the hospital. I'd be bailed up in one supply closet or another, and they'd just leave."

"A better offer?" Dylan asked.

"Who knows? But they always came back and usually in a larger group."

"You don't know how long the virus takes to manifest, do you?" Dylan asked.

Howard grimaced. "I do, unfortunately. I had a man with me early on who was bitten. I suppose it's a bit like alcohol, where body size impacts sensitivity, but within thirty-six hours, he had turned."

They stood and watched for another ten minutes, until all the zombies had left the motel parking lot. Even the line along the road had thinned to a trickle. Callan grew edgier, pacing the room, checking weapons. Dylan knew Callan was keen to get moving. Now there was no excuse.

"We need to have that discussion again," Callan said, heading for the other apartments.

It had been hours since the zombies had first appeared, and they had taken rest in the other sections of the three rooms while one or two had stayed watch. Kristy and Sarah were in unit one, with Julie. Johnny hadn't left his bed all day, and Greg had retired to the comfort of his room with a bottle of grog.

Eric had retrieved Julie, and they were standing at the door, ready to make an escape back to their house.

"Take this," Dylan said, handing Eric a fully loaded 9mm semi-automatic pistol with a spare magazine. Eric nodded his thanks.

A cry sounded from the second unit. *Kristy.* Dylan ran through the internal door and swung around to the right in the direction from which he thought the voice came. He ran into Callan running from the other unit. Kristy and Sarah appeared from Johnny's bedroom.

"What is it?" Dylan asked, expecting a feeder to have breached their sanctuary.

"Johnny's gone."

Callan threw a hand to his forehead. "What?" Greg stumbled out of his room holding a bottle of wine by the neck.

Sarah handed Callan a small square piece of paper. "Here. I found this."

Callan read it. *I'm sorry for what I did, Callan. I wish I could take it back. I'm going out there to die on my own so none of you have to be part of it. Don't come after me. I don't deserve any help, and don't waste your time trying to find out if anyone has a cure. Just know I'm sorry I did it. Johnny.* He screwed the note up and threw it on the floor. "I'm going out to find him. He can't be far."

Dylan and the others followed Callan into the third apartment. He searched through one of the bags of weapons on the table. "Is this a good idea, mate?"

"He doesn't want to be found," Kristy said. "Maybe it's better this way, Cal."

Callan scrunched his face in thought. "No. Fuck that." He kept rummaging.

Kristy moved to his side. "It's his choice though. He's probably going to die, and he's ashamed of what he did. He can't face you—"

"Yeah, he slept with my girl behind my back and might never have told me, but that was one fuck up amongst a world of good deeds he did for me."

"And me," Greg said, leaning against the internal door.

"Everybody thinks they know what Johnny is like. But nobody knows the real person. When I was a teenager, I had no money, but Johnny always spared me some. Always. When I got cornered by the cops while joy riding that car in Wodonga, Johnny offered to take the rap for me. Who does that? The guy would have done anything for me." Callan's face tightened into a pinched look. "I know he fucked up. He knows he fucked up. But he doesn't deserve to die like this. You've seen what this virus does, what he'll turn into. I'll blow his brains out myself before I let that happen, I swear it. We can't let him die alone. Everybody deserves a second chance, don't you think?"

Callan argued a compelling case, and Dylan agreed with him. They had all changed in the last few days, some more than others, but without doubt, Callan had changed the most.

"I'll go with you."

Kristy snatched Dylan's hand, squeezing it. "No." He felt the pull of her love, but there were unwritten laws in this new world, obligations to each other to protect and support in times of need. Callan was providing that for Johnny, and now Dylan would provide it for Callan.

Dylan raised his eyebrows as if to say, *what do you want me to do?* Anger flashed across Kristy's face. He took her hand and kissed it. "I'll be okay. We won't be out there long."

Greg hobbled to the table. "I can go. I'm almost better now. I feel—"

"Sorry, mate," Callan said. "Besides, your ankle's still no good. Kristy?"

"You're not ready, Greg. You've had three antibiotics. There's ten in a cycle and you might need two cycles to kill that thing. If you put yourself through too much, you won't get better. You have to rest. That's not me being picky, either, it's a fact. If you don't rest, you won't get better."

Greg swiped at a plastic bottle of water on the table. It thudded onto its side and rolled onto the floor as he left the room without looking back.

"We'll leave with you," Eric said. "Make a break for our house at the same time."

"You sure you wanna stay in Holbrook?"

"You sure you don't?"

"The idea of settling down and staying out of harm's way for a while is appealing, but we need to keep moving. There's no help for us or Johnny here." Eric nodded. Callan turned to Dylan, "We travel light. A handgun, ammo, a knife, and a torch. Let's get our Kevlar on."

They met again in the middle apartment where the others gathered around.

"Start getting our gear together," Callan said to Kristy. "We should leave first thing in the morning, if it's still clear. Keep heading north."

They left out the back door, through the laundry, following the same path Johnny had taken. Blue Boy ran between their legs, and Dylan didn't look back.

TWENTY-SIX

A HOT NORTHERLY WIND blew in their faces as they jogged away from the motel. Callan led them along a paved sideway that turned back towards the front of the building, stopping at every blind corner and crossway, expecting with each step to find the decayed and bloated face of a zombie. He checked often to ensure the others were following—Julie second, Eric third, Dylan bringing up the rear. He was glad Dylan had offered to join him. A comfort and reliability had developed between them. Callan still marveled that the relationship had formed in such a way. He had a suspicion that Dylan knew more about the Johnny and Sherry situation, but he didn't want to know. Callan had reached the understanding that he needed to move on and forgive the past, otherwise it would corrupt the future, and *it* needed every advantage. They reached the curb at the edge of the motel driveway. Not one zombie in sight.

"We're heading that way," Eric said, pointing down the road. He stuck out his hand to Callan, then Dylan. "Good luck boys. We're in Rand Street, number ten, if you need a place to hide."

They watched Eric and Julie trundle down the road and take the first right turn.

The boys jogged north along Albury Street, towards the center of town, ducking down side streets to check for Johnny. The dog's feet tapped along the pavement, easily keeping pace. Callan didn't think Johnny could have gotten far, not only because he didn't have a large head start, but because he was sick, too. Kristy had confirmed the virus had begun to develop, and that his physical abilities would soon deteriorate. It had been more than twenty-four hours, and Howard had confirmed he'd seen a man turn within thirty-six. Callan felt a growing desperation to find Johnny soon, or time would run out.

Eric's comments about the general order of the town were right. As the boys moved northward, they saw most of the buildings were in good condition, untouched by looters or zombies. Holbrook wasn't a big town, perhaps twelve hundred people, with a handful of shops. If the virus had turned half or more into zombies several weeks ago, they may well have left in search of further supply. What worried Callan more were the feeders they had seen walking along the main road earlier. It was feasible that they had walked from Albury in the time since Callan and the others had left.

They cleared the shopping strip and stopped, assessing their location.

"What do you think?" Dylan asked, scanning the street.

"I don't know. He could be anywhere. I guess we just keep walking."

They did so, north until Albury Street finished in a dead end, where they concluded he could not possibly have travelled so far. They turned around, then cut east, following Racecourse Road until it turned into Bath Street, and eventually met up again with Albury Street. The odd car lay on the roadside; the occasional property looked trashed, as though looters or zombies had been poking about, but overall, the place was relatively untouched, and the lack of visible zombies concerned Callan.

The last glow of a hot orange sun had disappeared over the horizon. At a light jog, and with their pistols drawn, they pushed on, up and down the parallel streets of Holbrook, trudging across parklands, peering over backyard fences. They even checked the fringes of the racetrack, a now overgrown circle of withered, yellow grass. Nothing. Were they wasting their time? Callan began to wonder.

He noted the sun sinking lower in the west and grew concerned, picking up their pace as they cut along Bath Street and past the Holbrook show grounds. Callan found an old container on a front lawn and filled it with water for Blue Boy, whose tongue lolled from his mouth. They turned left and went south at the Boral concrete facility, then right onto

Wallace Street and left into Railway Parade. Many of the streets in Holbrook ran parallel, so they could cover the distance by travelling up and down, north to south, and repeating. They ended up in the southeast corner of the town, on Jingellic Road, past the golf course.

"He could be anywhere," Dylan said as they turned down an unnamed dirt road and began the trek northward.

"I know. But seriously, you think he got far, in his condition? Kristy reckons he's getting sicker."

Dylan shrugged. "Sounds like he was pretty determined."

"We have to find him. I can't leave it there, no matter what happens."

"For what it's worth, man, you're showing a lot, the way you've handled it."

Callan grunted. He knew he had changed; the old Callan would have needed blood. He felt a sliver of contentment at that, but there was too much else going on, too much life or death, to care.

As the first layer of darkness discolored their surroundings, they stood outside the empty takeaway shop on Main Street. Blue Boy sat on his haunches as if he were waiting for his owner. Dylan peered in through the dark windows. Callan read the light, trying to determine how much time they had remaining. They walked side by side again, past the remaining shop fronts, and out into the township, when Dylan threw a hand out across Callan's chest. Blue Boy growled.

"Don't move. Stay there, Blue."

Callan froze, scanning the black road and the weatherboard houses on either side of the street, with their snarling gardens and weedy lawns. Their route had followed the winding grey curb, and now they stood on a patch of concrete where kids had scrawled their names before it had set: *Darren and Muzza waz here*. He wondered where Darren and Murray were now. Probably dead. "What is it?"

In a whisper, Dylan said, "Over there, on the other side of the road, near the red car on the front lawn."

Callan looked out across the intersection about forty yards ahead, went left, and found the red car. He was about to ask again when something moved, and he felt the chill of pure terror run up his back.

Two zombies moved with the grace and control of humans, but even from the distance, Callan could perceive their pale skin and tattered clothes. They sat crouched on their haunches, feeding, bobbing their heads in and out of a body, although it wasn't clear whether it was human or a dead zombie.

"Oh, fuck," he whispered. Had he loaded his pistol? He thought so. There was a good distance between them, but still, they moved fast.

"What do we do?"

They had guns, but only a magazine each. Callan expected to have found Johnny already. They could kill these two easily, but if there were more, and they ran out of ammo, all they had were knives. No choice but to avoid engagement, for now. "Walk backward. Slowly. Blue Boy, come."

They did, stepping back as though they were walking on glass, limiting their arm movement and keeping their heads still. The dog turned and trotted after them. The restless northerly wind kicked, filling their ears with a momentary whistle, and carrying their scents towards their enemies. Callan knew what would happen in advance.

The right feeder sat up and turned its head sideways. They had about three seconds. The thing locked its gaze on them.

"Move." Callan turned and ran.

TWENTY-SEVEN

KRISTY SUSPECTED THE QUANTITY of carbohydrates in Sarah's meal had not been enough, and now her blood sugar levels had dropped too low again. She had left extra test strips for her monitor in the Jeep. "I need to get something from the car," Kristy said, double-checking her medical bag where she thought she had placed all of Sarah's diabetic supplies.

Greg stood from his place on the couch. "I'll go."

Howard said, "I can do it, if you like."

Greg waved him back. "All good. I'm feeling a little better."

He was recovering well after four of the ten tablets in the cycle. Kristy had chosen the strongest antibiotic: a short, intense burst over five days. Patients generally felt an improvement after the first day. The redness around the wound had reduced, and Kristy had redressed it earlier, showing Sarah in detail how to perform the task.

"I guess, Greg, if you're feeling up to it. Just make sure it's clear." Greg raised both palms, as if to say, *Sure.*

"Come with me if you like, Howard." A smile cracked the older man's face, and he followed Greg to the door.

Kristy explained what she needed. Greg collected a Winchester rifle and handed it to Howard.

"Know how to shoot one of these?"

Howard chuckled. "Just."

Kristy closed the door behind them and stepped to the window, pulling aside the fabric. Greg peeled back the rest of the tarpaulin, and rifled through the remaining supplies. Howard stood to the side like a policeman, holding the Winchester by the muzzle and resting the stock on the gravel.

Sarah wore a pained expression and had a hand on her belly. "I feel funny."

"Hold on, honey," Kristy said. "They won't be a moment." She thought about just giving Sarah a dose of sugar, but preferred to wait and check her levels. She cursed herself for not bringing in the second box of test strips.

Greg was shifting boxes of supplies from one corner to another, pulling out items of irrelevance and tossing them aside. Kristy tried to recall where she had put them after cleaning up the zombie's mess.

Sarah stood, still holding her stomach, and stumbled towards the kitchen. "I need some juice. My sugar levels are low. I know it."

Kristy left the window and guided Sarah to one of the chairs. From the lifeless refrigerator, she took some warm orange juice and poured a glass. Sarah took it with a trembling hand and gulped it down, emptying the contents, then dropped the glass on the table with a clunk.

A gunshot sounded from the parking area. Kristy felt her insides turn. She ran to the wall beside the window, yanked aside the curtains, and pressed her face against the glass.

A trail of zombies led from the roadway deep into the parking lot. One had almost reached the car, and another lay on the ground with trails of bloody matter from its head. Others were coming, closing in on the fresh sounds and smells.

Howard stood beside the trailer with a firm, wide stance, the rifle pointed at the attackers. He fired again, the shot echoing across the darkening, cloudless sky, and another feeder slumped to the gravel. Greg stepped back out of the trailer, a small box clasped in his hand. On the right side, one of the attackers reached the Jeep, arms extended, hands groping for his flesh.

With his escape cut off, Greg staggered backward and crashed into the trailer. A second reached him, and Greg's expression told Kristy he was in trouble.

Howard shot another in the face at close range, spreading its features in a mess of blood and flesh. It fell forward onto him, and he lost his rifle as he fought to fend it off. Another sensed his weakness and lumbered in from the side, clutching Howard's arm.

How was this happening? The place had been empty five minutes ago. She had asked them to go outside, and now they might get bitten, or die. Kristy debated going out to help, eyeing the remaining guns on the table.

Greg had stumbled free. He pulled a pistol from his belt and fired twice, hitting a feeder in the throat, another between the eyes. Both fell as bloody streamers flew, pasting the gravel in a crooked red line. In two steps he was with Howard, pulling the zombies away by the shoulders and knocking them to the ground. Greg ushered the other man away from the Jeep, the rocky stones crunching as they stumbled towards the motel.

Kristy rushed from the curtains and yanked the handle, swinging the door open. Both men burst through.

"Lock it!" Greg yelled.

Kristy fell on the door, depressed the button, and latched the chain. They were panting, hair disheveled, eyes large and terrified.

"I thought … I was dead." Howard clapped a hand on Greg's shoulder. "Thank you."

Greg nodded, handing Kristy the box of strips. "I thought I heard something at the end of the drive when we went out, but stupidly, I didn't check."

Kristy's heart thundered. She had thought they were dead too. Another lucky escape. What about Callan and Dylan though? They were stuck out there, and the zombies were back. The thought of Dylan getting attacked the way she had just witnessed left her skin cold. "The boys …" But it was all she could manage.

Greg stood at the curtains. "We got our own problems."

A handful of feeders reached the window and banged on it with impatient fists.

"They know we're in here now," Howard said. "They might be slow and bumbling, but they have some sense of purpose and awareness. Don't let them fool you."

Greg tossed the gun onto the table. "We need to leave."

"How are we going to do that?" Kristy asked. They had fought for their lives yesterday, and just escaped. Now, they would have to do it all over again.

"I don't know, but there's more coming."

Sarah sat on the couch, hugging her knees to her chest. Kristy went to her. She squatted and wrapped her arms around the young girl. They would make it out as they always did.

TWENTY-EIGHT

DYLAN, CALLAN, AND BLUE Boy ran around the corner and cut through the long grass of a children's park with a tall slide and two chain swings. It was deja vu for Dylan, no different to running from the swarm of zombies and the type three outside Callan's parents' house when … two days ago? He couldn't be sure.

He followed the black soles of Callan's boots as they beat a path down the road, along the curb, and across dying lawns. Dylan kept glancing back, expecting a type three to be chasing. On the third turn, he slowed with the faint burn of oxygen deficit in his lungs.

"What do you think?" Dylan asked.

"We're fucked. Two of them? Not good."

"Do we head back?"

Callan shook his head. "Uh-uh. You go if you want, but I'm gonna keep looking." He reached down and scratched Blue Boy around the neck. "Good boy. Stay with us, buddy."

Dylan wanted to return to the motel. Leaving Kristy alone, albeit with Greg, worried him. They were in the motel, behind locked doors, and the zombies had disappeared, but whenever they were apart he couldn't help but fear for her. *Love, mate*, Dylan imagined his father saying. *You're in love.*

Callan walked away, and then turned. "You coming, or going back?"

"Coming," Dylan said, swallowing the heartache.

They set off at a jog, watching for followers, the shadows merging with the earth. Dylan sensed they were winding their way back towards the main street, and wondered whether Callan had subconsciously given up.

The road ascended, and as they reached the peak, both were panting. They jogged on though, bumbling through the darkness before reaching the summit of another slope that looked down onto a car parking lot at the edge of the football field. Several vehicles sat parked, including one from which flames leaped out the windows. It provided enough light for them to visualize the scene, and what they saw stunned them into silence.

Dozens of zombies wandered about the area. Most were the slow type, but amongst the group were several type threes. At first, Dylan thought they were killing the slower ones, but then Callan echoed his thoughts, and terror washed over him.

"They're biting them."

Blue Boy raced forward with a deep growl. Callan called him back, and the dog stopped, resting on its rump. They stood transfixed, watching the systematic approach. The more aggressive types were taking a single bite from their inferior siblings. Several lesser types wandered away from the pack, as if they knew to flee, but as they reached the apparent safety of the darkness, the one or more type threes were alerted and efficiently retrieved them before proceeding to inflict their bite.

"I don't …" But Dylan did. Someone had said it in the last few days—he couldn't recall who, and it didn't matter now. The type threes were turning the lesser zombies into the more aggressive types.

"You know what they're doing?"

"Biting them, but … why?"

"They're turning them. Turning the type ones and twos into type threes."

One of them had collapsed. Now, it rose slowly, like a fighter returning from a knockdown, and shook itself off. No longer awkward and ungainly, it gathered a newfound balance and strength. One of its new brothers stood beside it, and Dylan would swear they were communicating.

"You're right," Callan said, giving a humorless scoff. "You're bloody right." Blue Boy growled again. Callan scratched his fur. "It's alright, mate. You don't worry about them."

"We have to leave. Now."

They had witnessed some terrifying things over the last few days, but the thought of a large number of the smarter, aggressive types of zombies lifted Dylan's fear to a new level. If confronted by a pack of them, they didn't stand a chance.

They ran along the edges of the streets, using the ashen path as a guide, swooping on trees for cover, glancing behind them despite the empty blackness. Left, right, straight for a time, then left again, tripping on poorly laid concrete slabs of the curb, and their own undermined actions. Each time Dylan turned his head, breathing heavy, his heartbeat thudding, he expected to hear their powerful footsteps thundering down the road like a surging army.

They hit Albury Street about a hundred yards north of the motel, when they heard moaning from the other side of the road. Dylan knew instantly that it was Johnny. Callan ran hunched over across the street, weapon drawn.

"Johnny?" Callan said in a loud whisper. A small flame appeared from Callan's lighter, and in the shadows beyond, somebody groaned.

It was Johnny, lying in a clump of agapanthus bushes at the edge of an abandoned front yard.

Callan dropped to his knees and held up the lighter. Blue Boy snuck in close and tried to lick Johnny's face. He smiled, pushing the dog away. His appearance had deteriorated significantly. A pale, crusty face, with red circles around his eyes and nose, stared back at them. His teeth were chattering, but a film of sweat glistened on his cheeks and forehead. It reminded Dylan of the old guy they had found on the roadside coming back from the lake.

"Johnny, man, why the fuck did you leave?"

Johnny's teeth chattered. "I … wanted … to die … alone."

Callan winced. "Stupid, man."

Dylan said, "Come back with us. You can't stay out here."

Between the shakes, Johnny smiled and stiffened. "I never liked you before … but I've changed my mind. You're

150

okay." Dylan managed a pained smile. "You were right about things, man. Spot on."

"Don't talk, man," Callan said. "We're gonna carry you back—"

Johnny groaned. "No." He shifted position, drawing his arm into the light, revealing faint purple lines running outward from the bite. "No, Cal, I'm not going ... anywhere."

Dylan had to look away. It was over for Johnny, and it filled him with a deep, unsettling grief. Johnny, the sneaky, hateful, arrogant bastard with whom he had fought and argued endlessly in school. Once upon a time, he might have been cheering, but there was no joy now. Without Johnny, they may not have escaped the lunatics at his parents' house, and Dylan probably would have died at the hospital. He had told Callan the truth, in the end. That was enough.

Callan spun away, grinding out a muffled cry of frustration and helplessness. Darkness filled the spaces.

Johnny chuckled. "Nice to know I'm loved."

"Is there anything we can do, mate?" Dylan asked.

"Mate? You've never called me mate before." Johnny considered the question. "The gun. Leave me with the gun."

Dylan thought about other possibilities. Maybe the strain of virus Johnny had wouldn't turn him into a zombie. Dylan's father had said that not everyone who became sick turned. Some just died.

"There's nothing," Johnny said. "Nothing." His cough was wet and raspy. "I can feel it burning through my blood, getting into my bones. It's killing me, like a super-fast cancer, and I fucking hate it." Callan returned with the flame, lighting their sad faces in equal proportion. "I don't want to feel it anymore." To Dylan, it sounded eerily similar to what his father had said. "Both of you would do the same."

It was difficult to argue. Callan considered this, and the rest of it, as they stood in silence by the lighter flame. Finally, with a grave expression, he slowly stuck out his right hand. Johnny took it. "I won't do it, but I respect your choice." He blinked several times, as if fighting the emotion. "You've been a good mate, even counting the thing with Sherry, and I'll miss you." They shook again, a hard, tight handshake full of friendship and respect. Johnny could only nod, biting his tongue as tears ran down his cheeks. Callan broke the grip, handed the lighter to Dylan and left, calling Blue Boy to his side.

Johnny sobbed, watching the darkness beyond where Callan had disappeared.

"You sure?" Dylan asked. "It doesn't have to be this way."

Johnny gave several quick nods and held out his hand. "Yep. Does."

Dylan slipped the Browning pistol from the back of his pants and handed it over. Johnny took it, flexing his fingers around the grip, and laid it in his lap. "Thank you. And look after him for me. He's one of a kind."

"I'll do my best." It was a strange feeling, standing before somebody whose life was about to end. Death had always been a mystery to Dylan, impossible to comprehend, alive one moment, silent, forever sleeping the next. What did one say? There was no comfort in words; nothing could ease Johnny's ending. But Dylan understood his decision. The alternative was that his friends would have to do it. He deserved their respect. Dylan wasn't sure he would have similar courage.

"You've got guts, I'll give you that. Yesterday, my dad did exactly the same thing. For me to talk about you in the same way as him means a lot."

"Thanks."

Dylan offered his hand, and Johnny shook it. They looked at each other, passing unspoken words, and then Johnny let go. Dylan turned away and staggered off into the darkness with the lighter guiding his way.

He found Callan squatting by a tree along the roadside, an arm around Blue Boy's neck. A roadside bin had been kicked over, its side dented By Callan's boot. Neither men said a word, but Dylan saw Callan's twisted mouth and stiff jaw. They jogged along the road, using the thin veil of moon as a guide. Dylan listened for the sound of a gunshot. He had never expected to feel such sadness for Johnny. Perhaps it was the change over the last few days, or maybe it was that so many had already died, but losing one more, even an old enemy, just wasn't right.

Dylan had forgotten their encounter with the type threes, and now, as they jogged the last few hundred yards back to the hotel, their existence became more acute. They only had one gun.

Finally, Callan broke the silence. "We have to leave in the morning."

"Where?"

"Wagga. It's only an hour or so."

"Not Sydney?"

"Wagga is closer."

Ahead, Dylan saw the dark shape of the motel building high above the bubbling silhouette of the trees. He glanced behind them, jogging backward, straining to peer into the blackness. Nothing was following.

"Oh, fuck," Callan said. "We got trouble." Blue Boy ran forward. "Blue! Get back here." The dog circled and ran back.

Dylan slowed. Thirty yards ahead, an awkward body hobbled out of the motel driveway, followed by a second, then a third. The silent seed of panic took hold of him. The zombies had returned to the motel.

Callan scratched at the stubble on his chin. "Through here." He led him into the property adjoining the motel through a squeaky gate. They crossed a rough front lawn and took a narrow path beside the house. Trees hugging the fence hung down in their faces.

In a moment, they reached a low gate, where Callan told Blue Boy to sit. They climbed over the wire and found themselves in a small backyard surrounded by the boiling shadows of brush on three sides. Callan stepped up to the fence line, dug his way through the growth, and climbed up. The dark oval shape of his head poked up slowly over the top.

Dylan hung back. Without a second gun, their path back to the motel would be more difficult. Callan climbed down and joined him.

"There are heaps of them. I can't see them all, but they're scratching around the gravel. The Jeep is still there."

"Any ideas? I don't have a gun."

Callan peered around the tiny backyard. "You've got your knife. What about if we light a branch full of leaves? Maybe fire keeps them away."

"That's a plan."

They dug deep into the garden, feeling around for any cuttings or broken branches, but without luck. Callan used the small lighter flame, and they found a pile of cut brush in long, bushy stalks. They fashioned together several lengths, enough to burn for a few minutes so Dylan could keep them away.

They made their way back to the street and stood on the footpath, twenty yards from the driveway entrance. Dylan held the brush torch out, but as Callan touched the flame to the first dry leaves, gunfire sounded from the motel.

TWENTY-NINE

EVELYN HAD EXPECTED TO see Alex the following morning, but he didn't show up in the sleeping hall, or at breakfast. In silence, they ate porridge on their own, and had fried eggs on plain bread from a flock of chickens someone was keeping on the base. She gave Jake part of hers, and tried to suppress the hunger pains. Other people floated around, smiling, passing the occasional word, but most conducted business in quiet. The lack of general chatter surprised Evelyn. Kids sat across from each other, eating their breakfast without quip or conversation. When had children ever eaten in silence? It was as though people had been warned not to make too much noise.

A burly woman in white coveralls issued the work detail in their area of the base. Evelyn and Jake received kitchen duties. The woman explained to Evelyn that Jake could work with her for now, but in the longer term, he'd be expected to support himself. Evelyn was horrified, but repressed a response, not wanting to have an argument on their first full day. She planned on speaking to Alex though, hoping he might be able to arrange for Jake to continue working with her.

The day passed by quickly, consumed by toil, a snack, and more labor. Evelyn kept a lookout for Alex–even asked several men who appeared to be part of the outside work detail, but they all just shook their heads and said they hadn't seen him.

"Don't move," Evelyn said. "I need to use the toilet before dinner." Although she was reluctant to leave Jake alone, she felt he would be safe in their sleeping area, in view of the people, but she kept glancing back at him until turning down a corridor that led off to the bathroom.

Afterwards, Evelyn flushed the toilet, and lightly rinsed her hands, before leaving the room without drying them. She scurried down the hallway leading back to the sleeping area, a growing panic in her heart. She thought of Alex, and worse, the other man, Roger, who had disconcerted her the few times they'd met. What if they had taken Jake? She realized it was a ludicrous thought, with no basis.

However, when she reached their beds, Jake wasn't there. Neither were their bags.

Evelyn felt her legs go weak. She stumbled and caught hold of the bed frame, then turned, circling the area, looking for him. Other children were in the vicinity, but all had adults with them, and none were Jake. She blundered away from the sleeping area bemused, looking for a flash of his maroon t-shirt. Maybe he'd gone to the other toilets. She took off towards the bathroom, when an older woman with wrinkles and a twirl of grey hair pinned on her head caught Evelyn by the arm.

"He went that way." She pointed towards the other side of the eating area. "With the tall one; short grey hair, and tattoos."

Oh, God. Roger. "Thank you," Evelyn said, as she rushed away.

"He's bad," the woman called out. "Be careful."

Her heart beat so hard it was almost throbbing. Evelyn passed into the meals area and hurried between the rows of tables and chairs. Nobody moved, but she noticed several people looking her way in silence. Something wasn't right. These people were safe from the outside world–had food, shelter, and security, but they weren't acting like it. Perhaps it was all they had endured, the uncertainty of where life might lead that left them subdued.

She left the food hall and ran along a corridor towards an adjoining building. Puffing, she passed through a large doorway and found rooms branching off both sides of the hallway. Evelyn glanced into each and found empty sleeping quarters. She quickly moved on, wondering whether she was in the wrong place, her terror growing with every step.

She was about to turn back when an elderly man dressed in jeans and a red checked shirt appeared from another room. She asked if he had seen a young boy. He grunted and pointed down the hallway.

Three-quarters of the way along she found them. They were sitting on a bed talking; both backpacks lay on the floor at their feet. Jake didn't look scared, but Roger was sitting too close, and there was a gleam in his eye that sickened Evelyn. Her natural instinct took over. She rushed forward and took Jake by the hand, pulling him away.

"What are you *doing*?" she hissed.

Roger stood, towering over her. "Settle down. I—"

"Don't you ever go *near* my son again!" Roger's face twisted in anger. "Are you alright, Jake?" He nodded. She pulled him back to the doorway.

"What's the problem?" Roger asked. "I took the kid because you're going to be living with me now. These are your new sleeping quarters. I didn't—"

"I don't care. We're fine back in the hall. We don't need any special treatment." It all came out in a rush then, the terror of thinking something had happened to Jake. "Why would we want to live with you, anyway? You don't just take people's children without asking."

He stiffened, and stepped forward, hands in fists by his side. "I can make your lives here comfortable. I'm one of the original founders. You can have whatever you need here with me." Evelyn shivered. "If you want to live on this base, you stay with me. Those're the rules."

Was he serious? She almost expected him to laugh and say it had been a prank. But his eyes were hard and unflinching. Evelyn tried to stand straighter, and lifted her chin. "So you're saying that if we don't live in these quarters with you, we can't stay on the base?"

His face was impassive. "That's right."

Evelyn's shoulders sagged. Part of her wanted to agree to the terms, for the safety of Jake, to avoid zombies, exhaustion, and starvation, but the man had taken him without her consent, and that was indefensible. The minutes she was unsure of his whereabouts had stung her with terror far greater than any zombie. A person's common sense and general decency was on trial when they considered it acceptable to do such a thing. They would take their chances in the open, again.

She tried to smile, but imagined it appeared as though she was in pain. "Okay." He relaxed. She had to ask another question to defer her discomposure. "Have you seen Alex today?"

Roger grunted, and scoffed. "Yeah. I saw him earlier. He's left the base. Decided it wasn't for him after all."

She tried to keep a poker face, not to show the surprise behind the façade, but the comment shocked her. She suspected something bad had happened to Alex, and that they would never see him again. There was cunning and menace in Roger's eyes that chilled her skin.

"Can we have our packs?"

"You're leaving then?" She nodded. He narrowed his eyes, glaring. "Lady," he said. "I'm giving you a chance to live like a queen here. Not many people get that opportunity."

"I don't *want* an opportunity. I just wanted food, a bed, and safety for my son and me."

"And whatta you expect the cost of that is in a world like this?"

Evelyn had no answer. She was about to tell him that, when another man appeared from a doorway ahead. He was of medium height, with a shaved head and a goatee. He approached with a scowl, looking back and forth between Evelyn and Jake.

"What the fuck's going on, Rog?"

"Nothing, Tom. I'm just trying to convince this lady that staying *with me* is her best option."

"Another one who can't appreciate the," he turned, theatrically, emphasizing their surroundings with a wave of his hand, "environment we've created?

"Can we go, Mom? I don't like it here."

"Yes, honey. We're going." But their packs were lost. She turned, conceding their life possessions.

They hurried out of the building across a courtyard, the place empty, as darkness closed in. She thought she knew the way out, past the supply area where they had initially received their bedding allocation. Alex had been with them then, and things had seemed more solid. She wished he were there now, confident the situation wouldn't exist. *They killed him.* That thought wouldn't leave her, driving her aching feet faster across the pavement. She glanced back, expecting to find Roger following, but their trail was empty.

They had nothing except for their clothes. Where would they sleep? What would they eat? They passed the vacant supply room, when a thought struck her.

"Follow me."

Evelyn pushed the door open, her heart thumping again, and entered, expecting a greeting from the attendant that had issued their original supplies. The place was empty of people, but full of provisions that would help them.

"Hurry, Jake. See if you can find a backpack, and some food."

Evelyn found piles of blankets and pillows; items they had been given on their way in. There were tents, torches, ropes, and gas bottles. Jake found a bag, into which he stuffed a torch and several blankets. Evelyn found one too, and filled it with more bedding and several bottles of water from cases stacked in the corner. She stopped to assess their inventory, expecting somebody to come marching into the room with a team of trouble close behind. She kept reminding herself that she wasn't stealing, that they had been unfairly placed in this situation. She added a pack of matches, slung the pack on her back, then picked up a small tent and cradled it under her arm.

"Let's go."

She peered outside the doorway, checking for signs of Roger or anybody else that might expose them. It was clear; most people were probably still eating.

159

They had one more problem though. The gate was manned. They reached it and saw three guards wandering around outside the gatehouse. They couldn't walk out through the main area. Evelyn didn't know what would happen, but she suspected they might be detained.

Instead, they crept along the high perimeter fence until the bush swallowed them up, and they waited for darkness, when they would somehow sneak out past the guards.

THIRTY

ON DARKNESS, KRISTY HAD closed the curtains and lit a candle in the center of each room. They had all hauled bags and supplies from the outside two units to the central section, then piled ammo in boxes on the table and loaded it into the bags. Greg and Howard filled their Winchester rifles with the maximum eight-round capacities. Kristy stuck one of the automatic pistols under her waistband. It felt awkward, but she supposed it was better to have it. This was all done in eerie silence, while the clunking and clanging of the zombies sounded outside. She hoped the Jeep wasn't ruined.

"What about the boys?" Howard asked.

Kristy had tried not to think about them. Did they even have a torch? She didn't think so. They hadn't put much thought into it. But she couldn't contemplate their fate now; she needed to focus and help formulate a plan to evacuate the motel with their supplies and their lives.

"The boys know what they're doing," Kristy said. Greg agreed, but she couldn't match the easiness of her words with similar feelings.

As if reading her mind, Greg said, "Once we get clear, we can drive around looking for them."

Kristy smiled at him, and for the first time in days, he reciprocated. He was a handsome man, and she wished he'd found someone the way she'd found Dylan.

Fists banged on the windows, coaxing them out. Sarah jumped. Howard picked up a rifle from the table and levered the bolt.

"What's the plan?" Kristy asked. "Open the door and start firing?"

Howard shrugged. "That's about the size of it." His thinness was painful, but there was strength in his stance and intensity in his eyes. "I've got nothing to lose. I'll do my very best to get you guys safely to the Jeep."

Kristy frowned. "Don't say that. Your life is as important as the rest of us."

"I don't wanna die yet, but I think I've made my peace, if it comes to that."

Greg tightened his hands around the rifle. "It ain't gonna come to that. We go out back to back, make a pathway for the girls."

They checked and rechecked the parking lot, put out the candles, and mirrored the fear in each other's eyes. Kristy slung a pack onto her back and slipped her arms through the handles. Pain surfaced in her shoulder blades and spine, but there was no other way. They had only brought the essentials into the motel, and most of the weapons and medical supplies they'd be able to return to the Jeep. Some of the clothes would have to remain. She helped Sarah with one of the smaller bags, while Greg and Howard slipped the heaviest packs onto their backs. Kristy picked two up in her left arm, including her medical kit, with Greg's pills and Sarah's diabetes medicine. Her shoulder gave another twinge, but she ignored it and took Sarah by the hand.

They stood in the doorway, listening to the sounds of zombies beating on the car, fighting with each other, and eating. Kristy breathed deeply, trying to quell the thud of her heartbeat. The others looked scared too; Sarah had glassy eyes, Howard wore a grim face, and Greg was psyching himself up with a look of hatred. Had she given him the latest antibiotic? She considered asking, but realized she was just trying to prolong the inevitable.

Greg unhooked the chain, turned the deadbolt, and clasped the handle. "Good luck." Then he turned it and yanked the door open.

At first, Kristy saw a clear pathway to the Jeep. Zombies staggered about in varying forms, but there was a direct line to the driver's door. Then the feeders turned, bumbling towards the motel, drawn to the light and sound and smell of fresh meat. Kristy was about to tell Greg to shut the door and get back inside, that it was too risky, and she didn't want them to die at the hands of these gruesome creatures. And then Greg was outside, screaming as he fired into their mangled, bloated faces. The noise pained her ears and she wanted to throw her hands over them, but Sarah clung on with a death grip, and she had her medical supplies in the other hand.

Howard followed, punching rounds into the horde as they closed in on the motel room. They fell away as bullets clunked off the Jeep.

Kristy went out.

THIRTY-ONE

SHOTS RANG OUT LIKE firecrackers.

Callan touched the lighter to the leaves; the crinkled and curled edges caught alight. "I'm gonna kill every last one of these motherfuckers."

They ran along the street towards the motel, Dylan holding the branch carefully so the movement wouldn't fuel the flames. Part of him wanted to throw the torch aside and run, take his chance on getting to Kristy, but their number frightened him.

They reached the driveway entrance, and the first feeder ambled for them. Blue Boy rushed at it, snarling. The thing swiped at him, and he leaped aside at the final moment.

Dylan poked the flaming branch at its red t-shirt, and a chunk of burning bush broke away, hanging off its clothes like a tuft of wool. It had no idea what was happening. The flames ran up its chest, burning its shirt. It tumbled backward onto the gravel in silence.

Two more came at them with groping hands. Blue Boy ran forward, separating them. Callan used his left shoulder to knock one down, but another replaced it. Dylan waved the burning branch, keeping several at a distance, allowing the two men to run down the middle of the driveway with the dog following.

Ahead, countless zombies milled around the Jeep and trailer. Was Kristy inside? Dylan couldn't see through the mayhem. More gunfire sounded, and Dylan saw two tall figures in the shadows behind the light, moving and firing. Zombies fell, but more poured from the darkness, limping, groping, running into each other.

Blue Boy had gotten too close, and one of the zombies had him by the tail. He yelped, snapping his jaws. Callan brushed aside two feeders trying to bite him and aimed the pistol at the thing that had his dog. The shot cracked and its neck exploded. It fell back, releasing Blue Boy who ran away yipping. Two more came at Callan. He turned the gun on them and fired into each of their faces, knocking them down.

They weren't moving quickly enough. Dylan peered through the chaos again and saw Kristy standing at the driver's door. Zombies reached at her from all sides. She was going to get caught. He tried to scream, but terror stole his voice, and suddenly he lost sight of her.

Dylan waved the burning torch, fanning the flames and catching the clothes of the zombies nearby. The others sensed danger and withdrew as he stumbled through the pack. Fire climbed the shirt of a skinny elderly man, but Dylan had thrust it too hard, and the branch snapped apart.

Ahead, Callan went down on one knee. A zombie fell onto him, and then Dylan was running, screaming at them, waving the torch as the last of the branches fell away, leaving him with a useless, glowing stick.

THIRTY-TWO

WE'RE GOING TO MAKE it, Kristy thought as she reached the driver's door on the other side of the Jeep. She pulled Sarah ahead, let go of her hand, and grabbed for the handle. She expected it to be locked, but the clip sprung and the door swung open, promising safety.

"In." Sarah scrambled up over the driver's seat and into the back. Kristy slung the pack off and tossed it in as she felt a stiff grip on her left shoulder.

Sarah screamed. Kristy threw her left elbow backward and felt the point connect with soft, wet flesh. The hand fell away, and she leapt into the seat, striking her head on the door. Pain jagged through her skull. Another feeder appeared in the doorway with a ghoulish grin and a mouthful of rotten teeth. She swung her leg around, pulled her knee back, and thrust it forward with a grunt. Her attacker spun backward and propelled into a scraggy haired female with hideous lesions over her skin. The first zombie toppled to the driveway, but the woman came at Kristy as she reached out to close the door. Her fingers clasped the handle, but a bony arm clamped around her wrist. Screaming, she shrugged it off, and pulled the door closed with a thud, shaking the car.

From her waistband, Kristy pulled out the pistol and tossed it on the other seat. Where had she put the keys? She scratched around the front console without luck. *Your pocket.* Bloody hands beat on the windows, faces pressed against the glass. She fished the keys out, fumbled for the ignition slot, and jammed it in.

The Jeep whirred into life with a twist of the key. Relief washed over her. "Hold on, sweetie."

Gunshots cracked off around them. Dozens of feeders staggered about in the headlights, some attacking each other, others moving towards the Jeep. She fought the urge to drive forward and run them over. That would solve some of the problems, but create others.

Where were the men? She twisted around to find Greg leaning against the back window in the red glow of brake lights. No sign of Howard though.

Greg slid along the side of the Jeep, pushing them away and firing into their faces. They dropped out of sight, but there were too many, and several avoided the gunfire. He reached the back door and tried to open it, but a zombie tackled him, pinning one arm. He grasped for the handle with his free hand but the thing wouldn't surrender its prize. They wrestled against the passenger door, thumping and clunking against the glass as other zombies reached the fight.

Kristy had to help. She wasn't getting out, afraid she wouldn't make it back, so she took the pistol from the passenger seat and readied it. "Get down on the floor and put your hands over your ears." Sarah did. Kristy lowered her window and leaned out, jamming the gun into the back of the zombie's head.

"Push it out of the way," she yelled to Greg.

He did, and she fired, the thunderous boom ripping through her ears. The force nearly tipped her out of the car. She scrabbled for the window frame, managed to secure her grip, and pushed herself back inside. The zombie had fallen away from the Jeep, but others clamored for Greg.

A gruesome thing, little more than a skeleton in threads, rushed at her. Kristy lifted the pistol and shot it in the throat. It fell, and she leaned out through the opening again, taking aim. But Greg was overcome with zombies. He lay on the ground, swinging his fists as they groped for his hair and pulled at his arms. She would have to get out. She slipped back in through the window and pulled the door lever, when Howard appeared.

Kristy had thought he was dead. Howard came stumbling forward, swinging the rifle like a bat. He struck them across their faces and on top of their skulls, splattering blood and bone over the Jeep. They fell aside, providing Greg a second, and he crawled forward, breaking free of their death grip. Howard met Kristy's eyes but he was too far away, and they were on him, hands around his waist and shoulders. Howard screamed, then stepped back into the crowd, letting them take him.

Kristy's silent screams for Howard went unanswered. Greg reached the car as more hands caught him, but he shrugged them off, yanked the door open and scrambled inside, pulling it shut.

"Drive," Greg said. "He's gone."

THIRTY-THREE

"I'M NOT GOING," JULIE said. "You can leave without me."

A single candle threw a thin hue of orange light from the kitchen. Eric stood in his familiar position at the curtains in the lounge room, watching the last of the straggling zombies shuffle down the road. He had packed the camper van with extra items after visiting the group that afternoon, in hopes that Julie might agree to leave whenever they did.

"I can tell you that Callan and his friends will be on the move. At least if we go now, we can catch them." Twenty minutes ago, he had slipped out the rear door of the house, climbed up on the paling fence, and looked through the darkness across backyards where he had attended barbecues. In the distance, he could hear the zombies congregating around the motel in wait. He'd wanted to go then, but Julie had started crying again.

"There are things out there. You're telling me you want to go out there now, with them all over the street?"

It was a fair question. If they remained in the house, they would probably survive. They'd have each other, enjoy modest eating, a perpetual sense of boredom, but live on, for now. One day in the near future though, chasing beer or cigarettes from the rabble that was once the general store, Eric would trip and break his leg. Waiting patiently at home, Julie would either come looking for him and end up dead, or never summon the courage to do so, thus leaving him to die. Either way, such a scenario highlighted their need to find other people. They were stronger in a group, but he kept reminding himself that not all groups were decent. They might jeopardize their lives now, but the benefits outweighed the risk, a risk Eric believed strongly they should take.

"Yes. It's not too bad at the moment. We can drive through them." What else would help persuade her? "They're good people, Jules—"

"You've only met them for five minutes!"

"I'm a good judge of character. You know that. If they leave Holbrook, we'll miss our chance. Maybe they need our help."

"NO!" She leaped up off the couch. "You're not listening to me. I'm not going out there. I've lost three children to this madness, and I can barely get up in the morning, with that." Her voice began to crack. "You expect me to let you risk your life? I don't give a shit about myself, but I'm not going—" She began to sob. His annoyance had washed away, replaced by pity. Julie lifted her chin. "I'm not going to lose you, too."

Eric's voice softened, pleading. "I won't lie. There's a risk going out there, even in the van, but there's risks staying here, too. I'm convinced if we don't go now, we'll regret it. I've got one of those feelings, like the time we didn't go out in the boat with Ian and Christine, and it ended up sinking."

"I'm so scared, Eric."

"I won't let anything happen to you." He smiled. "Or me."

"If you get bitten, or killed, I'll never forgive you, Eric Norman."

He hugged her tight. "Yes you would."

THIRTY-FOUR

ZOMBIES SWARMED OVER CALLAN, scratching, grabbing, and jostling for position on the rocky ground. Dylan was still too far away. They would tear Callan's arm off before he could reach them. Blue Boy raced in, growling with an intensity Dylan had never heard in a dog, and leaped up against one of them. It tumbled backward, knocking others over in a chaotic stack.

Dylan reached Callan and stuck the burning stick in the face of the first zombie. Its skin hissed and the thing fell away, pawing at its cheeks. There were too many of them, though, climbing, standing, and falling over Callan. Blue Boy took fabric between his teeth and tugged at one of the crawling zombies. Dylan kicked out, grunting and growling, shoving them aside. They turned on him, and before he could think about it, his fists were pumping in and out like horizontal pistons, striking their rubbery faces. Callan scrambled onto all fours as they clutched at his legs. A fat arm reached for his ankle and seized it. Dylan drew his foot back and kicked, the heavy bone from his toes to his ankle striking the zombie's jaw with a bone-splintering crack. He gagged at the pain, but the feeder released Callan and fell flat on its face. Another one reached for Callan, but Blue Boy barged in, pushing the thing back with the top of his head. Dylan reached down and yanked Callan to his feet.

They both staggered away, momentarily free, but there was still a mass of zombies swirling about between them and the Jeep. Callan fired at those close, knocking them down with head shots and opening a pathway. He shoved his way through, pushing others aside, shooting into their eyes, and faces, even their ears. Blue Boy ran barking in a distractive path between their clumsy feet. More swarmed, ending Callan's run. He tried to brush them off, swinging his arms and backtracking, but he stumbled and fell onto the rocky road.

171

Dylan drove them aside with his shoulder, punching when they drew within reach. A skinny, emaciated zombie in green outdoor pants and a shirt, perhaps a council worker, lunged at him. He threw the remaining branch at it, then pushed the thing to the ground, feeling something jab him in the side. *The knife.*

Three feeders had fallen on Callan.

Dylan withdrew the solid handle, spun, and rammed the eight-inch blade into the side of a zombie head. It went deep enough to stick in. He kicked out for leverage and yanked on the handle, drawing it out with a gruesome squelching sound.

With Blue Boy's help, Callan had managed to shove two of the zombies away, but the third—a huge brawler of a man who easily outweighed Callan—had both arms around his waist, and his leering face close to Callan's body. Blue Boy gave a shrill bark and clawed at the big zombie, but it did nothing to stop him biting into the upper part of Callan's back.

Callan grunted, squirming to get free, but the weight and positioning of the feeder had him pinned. Dylan shrugged off loose hands, rushed forward, and stuck the knife through the side of its head. It slumped forward. Dylan dragged it off and retrieved the blade.

Callan climbed to his feet and collected the pistol off the driveway. They staggered on, Dylan waving the knife, Callan shooting at anything that moved.

Callan was bitten. Dylan didn't know if it had broken the skin, and there was no time to ask.

The driveway opened out into the lot. The Jeep and their companions lay ahead, Kristy sitting safe with her hands on the steering wheel. At least that was something. Greg was inside the Jeep, too, but he couldn't see Howard.

From the shadows behind the motel, something moved through the darkness with terrifying speed. It hit one of the feeders and knocked it to the ground.

Callan saw it too. He stopped and raised the gun. Others joined the first—a second, third, and fourth. Callan screamed, "DRIVE!" motioning for Kristy to bring the Jeep and trailer forward.

She did, spewing rocks up from the back wheels. Several zombies stood in front, but she knocked them down and drove over them like they were roadside warning cones. The Jeep leaped up, then crashed down, and a moment later the trailer did the same, its aged frame clattering.

Callan turned and ran. Dylan realized that if the Jeep stopped, the zombies would attack, and they might all die. Their only chance was to outrun it. More type threes had arrived, and their acute sense of smell tuned them to the boys' escape. They moved in unison, sweeping from the parking lot in formation down the driveway.

Dylan followed Callan, driving his legs into the gravel. He glanced back; the Jeep was coming fast now. Kristy had knocked several over, but the remaining type threes ran on undeterred.

They hit the street and ran right in a southward direction, back towards Albury, full of adrenaline, swallowed up by the darkness, Dylan wondering how they were going to get out of this one.

THIRTY-FIVE

YOU'RE NOT BITTEN, CALLAN told himself as they sprinted along Albury Street. It probably wouldn't matter; any second the type threes would catch up and finish them off. His back ached, and the skin around the bite area tingled, but he couldn't be sure if it was genuine, or whether his mind had concluded the inevitable. He could hear the grunts and groans of the type threes chasing them, and the Jeep engine humming along. He thought he had used all thirteen rounds in the magazine, but didn't want to test the theory by stopping to fight in case he was empty.

Ahead, bright light swung from the right side, splashing into their eyes. Callan threw up a hand in front of his eyes. At first, he thought it had to be a car, but the lights were too bright, the engine loud and grumbling. It came straight at them, horn beeping, and they ran to the side of the road.

It was a camper van, the type of long-bodied mobile home used to travel across country. Behind the wheel, Eric slowed the monster, signaling for them. A door opened along the side of one wall, and Julie appeared.

"Quickly, get in."

Callan shoved Dylan towards the opening. He glanced back towards the driveway of the motor inn and saw the taillights of the Jeep and trailer. They were going in the other direction. Some of the zombies were following, but the majority were moving towards them. He glanced the other way, back along the road towards Albury, and saw two yellow headlights in the distance.

"Who's got the dog?" Dylan asked.

Blue Boy. Callan stuck two fingers in his mouth and whistled. A dark shape zipped from between the legs of their attackers and ran for Callan. "Get movin', boy." The dog scampered into the van.

Callan climbed the step and brushed past Julie. He joined Dylan behind the driver and passenger seats as Julie slipped

174

back into the front. Blue Boy pushed against his leg, whimpering. Callan squatted, looping an arm around his neck, and scratched his throat. "I don't know how many times you saved me out there, boy."

"Thank you, Eric," Dylan said, chasing his breath.

"Did you see the car headlights behind?"

Eric looked up into the mirror. "Yes. Unfortunately we can't wait around though." Eric tightened his grip on the big steering wheel and drove the van forward. "Hold on though. We're in for a rocky ride."

Zombies wandered across the width of the road. There must have been seven or eight type threes moving towards them. Eric drove hard, and the engine groaned. The feeders were smart though, stepping easily aside to avoid the vehicle. A medium-sized female with straggling blonde hair ran directly at them, then leapt up and crashed into the windscreen. Callan waited for her to fall off, but she clung on, hands gripping the front edges like talons. Its gruesome face sneered at them, eyes the size of peaches, skin as pale as old bones, and a mouth full of bloody flesh. Blue Boy's ears and tail pricked, and he barked madly at the thing clinging to the glass.

Eric yanked on the wheel and the zombie swung back and forth over the glass. To Callan's surprise, it hung on. Through the wide window over the kitchen sink, more of the type threes ran alongside the van. There was a thud on the outside wall, then another. Callan peered out and saw that two more had latched on.

The camper van picked up speed, chasing the Jeep and trailer at the end of the headlight sweep. Eric swerved across the road again, but still, the zombie retained her grip.

Dylan said, "Jam on the brakes." Eric frowned. "The momentum will throw it forward. It won't be able to stay on."

"Grab onto something," Eric said, and braked hard.

The zombie flew from the windscreen as though falling backward from a plane, and landed with a sickening thud on the road. A clunk sounded from the side of the van, and another hit the bitumen.

Dylan peered out the window over the sink. "The ones on this side are gone, too."

The zombie in the headlights slowly climbed onto one knee.

"Punch it," Callan said.

The engine whirred and the van shot off. The thing wobbled, caught its balance, and came at them. In the final moments though, it darted sideways out of the way and disappeared into the shadows at the edge of the road. Dylan fell against the sink, searching the darkness.

"Gone."

"I'll keep driving until we're far enough away, then signal the Jeep to pull over."

Callan rubbed his temples. It was too much—Johnny, the fight at the motel, and the bite on his back. The dull throb had not abated. He would need Dylan to check it. He was physically and mentally tired. He needed a few days rest from the fighting and death; they all did.

As if reading Callan's mind, Dylan caught his attention and drew him to the back of the van. "Did … it get you?"

He wondered if he should wait and let Kristy examine him. "I don't know. I felt its teeth on my back, but I'm not sure if it drew blood."

"Let me check."

Callan wanted to know, but knowing meant he had to make choices. If he was infected, could he be strong like Johnny? Would he have the courage to leave the group, or the guts to kill himself? He shuddered.

"You'll just worry if you don't know," Dylan said.

"Easy for you to say. I'll fucking worry if I know."

Eric glanced back at them. "You boys alright back there?"

"All good," Dylan said. "Just sorting out a minor issue."

"Minor? Thanks."

"The Kevlar probably stopped it. I had their fingers scratching the shit out of me, but it didn't get through."

"We'll see."

Beneath the pallid glow of a light globe outside the rear bedroom, Callan removed his bike jacket. The white singlet stuck to his body, saturated in sweat. "I'd fight a zombie for a shower." He peeled off the singlet, heart thundering. He didn't know what he would do if it had broken the skin.

Dylan bent to inspect the area. He moved Callan into different positions to catch various angles of light.

"Anything?" Callan asked. Dylan remained silent. "Come on man. Is there a mark, or not?"

"There's a mark, but the skin isn't broken."

"Are you sure? Keep looking. I want you to be certain."

After a moment, Dylan stood. "There's nothing there, man. You're clean. The teeth didn't break the skin." Callan's wide eyes suggested he didn't quite believe him. "Put some fresh clothes on though, you stink."

Callan gave a relieved sigh. "I thought I was gone. I really thought I was bitten."

THIRTY-SIX

KRISTY LOCKED HER TREMBLING hands around the wheel and drove on at a steady sixty miles per hour, willing the Jeep and the camper van away from Holbrook. They were safe for the moment, but who knew what really constituted safety anymore. How long since they'd felt any semblance of safe? Leaving Lake Eucumbene had been the last time. Since finding the old couple at the gas station, a shadow of uneasiness had followed them around.

That final image of Howard letting the zombies take him left a sickening imprint on her mind. Could she have done more? Perhaps she should have garnered the courage to leave the Jeep. She didn't think so, but a part of her felt a sliver of doubt.

They drove for another fifteen minutes, until Kristy felt they were far enough away. She edged the Jeep and trailer onto the side of the road, the headlights revealing wisps of dry grass and weeds along the edges. No zombies in sight.

Kristy clicked the door open and rolled out. Dylan was already halfway towards her. They met with a strong hug. Kristy pulled her head back and they kissed, soft and warm, and she thought, *our lips are made for kissing each other*. The rough stubble on his cheeks and chin scratched her skin, but she would put up with that forever if it meant having him this way, whenever she wanted.

"I thought you were dead," she said.

"I thought you were.*"

"We nearly all were," Callan said. "If it wasn't for Eric, and Julie."

Eric smiled. "Glad to help."

"Where's Howard?" Callan asked.

Greg shook his head. "He didn't make it."

"*Shit*. Poor bugger."

"He gave Greg a chance," Kristy said. "Then took a few with him."

"I don't know if I would have made it," Greg said.

They all let the silence drift. While they hadn't known Howard for long, he was a decent man, and had made a small contribution to the group. Kristy turned to Eric and Julie. "You changed your mind? I thought you were staying in Holbrook?"

Eric spoke, glancing at Julie, who looked annoyed. "We had to make a choice. We knew you guys were moving on. It made sense to be with others, in case something happened to me if I went out alone. What would happen to Julie if I didn't make it back?" Kristy glanced at Dylan. The same thing had happened to his parents. "And those zombies freak me out. We saw that the slow ones disappeared, but those other ones … we decided in the end not to stick around."

"There were headlights coming from Albury as we were leaving," Callan said.

"I saw them in the rear-view mirror," Eric said. "But they disappeared."

Callan looked back the way they had come. "Do we wait? See if they drive this way?"

Kristy started towards the Jeep. "I don't like being out here. We don't know what's hiding in the shadows. We need to leave." The others agreed.

Outside the van, Callan explained that they had found Johnny and said their goodbyes. Greg fell into a deep silence and wandered back to the Jeep to wait for the others. Julie suggested Sarah ride with them, where she could sleep in one of the bunk beds. With some reluctance, Kristy agreed, but it was made easier by Julie's latent motherly nature, which had been absent earlier under the stress of attack.

It was only twenty minutes further to Wagga, and most of the time was spent in thought. It was back to the original four, and Kristy felt strange without Sherry sitting between them. How long had it been since Kristy had watched her walk into the garage? Yesterday. It felt like a week. Dylan lay against the seat with his eyes closed. How he was *really* coping? So much had happened, he couldn't have dealt with it all yet.

They reached Wagga in darkness via Holbrook Road, finding a similar picture to that of Albury upon their return from the lake. Smashed-up cars littered the streets, broken glass spread over the blacktop. There were bodies on the roads, and they saw a few straggling type one zombies feeding on them, but Kristy had expected more of the scrawny scavengers.

"It doesn't look that bad, here," Callan said as they passed a set of shops where steady flames burned behind a broken window. "I expected more zombies in a place this size."

They skirted the central business area, remaining on Glenfield Road as it turned into Pearson Street. There were any number of places they could investigate, but the town was dark, and silent, and Kristy knew Callan had only one place in mind. She shared his desire to feel safe, to close her eyes, and not worry about the next zombie attack.

At the Sturt Highway, they turned left, and followed it onto the Olympic Highway. A mile down the road the bright white lights of the Kapooka army training centre came into view. It was one of the major teaching facilities in the Australian defense force, where all new recruits came for basic training.

"You beauty," Callan said, smiling for what felt like the first time since before Sherry's death. "We'll be safe here." He turned the Jeep and trailer onto the entry road, the headlights revealing a wide white sign topped with a green and gold panel that proclaimed: BLAMEY BARRACKS beside the Australian Army insignia.

Dylan squeezed Kristy's hand and she closed her eyes, lying her head on his shoulder. "I'll be so glad when we're safe again. Really safe."

Callan swung the car left, following the road until a huge grilled gate prevented their way forward. "Safe as a church."

Two men dressed in black clothing stepped out from a gatehouse with machine guns slung over their shoulders. Both were heavily built. One wore a white t-shirt, his arms dark with tattoo ink; the other a baseball cap turned backward.

Kristy felt a dash of unease. "Where are the army guys?"

"Hold the phone," Callan said. "Let's just find out what they have to say." Callan stopped the car and pulled on the handbrake. "Greg, you got me?"

"You bet."

The two boys stepped out of the Jeep and approached the guards. Kristy turned and saw the camper van had stopped fifteen yards behind.

"What do you think?"

Dylan shifted in his seat. "Not sure. Maybe the army doesn't have control of this place anymore."

Kristy unclipped her belt. "I want to hear what they have to say."

She trotted towards the gatehouse, losing the conversation in the distance.

"But we've been through hell," Callan said. "Can't you just let us inside? We'll stay in our cars until we can talk to somebody in the morning. Surely—"

"Sir, I have my orders."

"But where's the military?" Greg asked. "What about Major Bacon? I did some electrical work out here and got to know him pretty well. He'll let us in."

The other man with the baseball cap pushed his palms towards the ground. "Take it easy, folks. We don't want no trouble."

"All we've fucking had is trouble. Four days of it. We've lost parents, friends, and … partners." Callan's face folded with lines of anguish. "Please. Just let us come in. We won't be a problem, I assure you. I absolutely promise."

The men passed a grim look. "Mate, if it were my call, I'd let you in," the first guard said. "But we're grunts. We don't make the rules, and if we don't follow them, we get in trouble. Come back in the morning and you can talk to someone and plead your case then. I'll make sure we pass on a good word about how understanding you've been."

Kristy pressed her eyes closed, unable to believe they were so close, only to be denied. It was so unfair. They were twenty yards from safety, twenty yards from not having to live in constant fear.

"Okay," Callan said. "Okay. We'll do that. Can we park here and wait for the night?"

The man pinched his expression and shook his head. "I'm sorry, but you'll have to park somewhere else, sir."

"Really?" Callan asked.

"They like the entrance clear. We've had … some trouble with people parking here before."

Callan sighed. "Any recommendations?"

The man pointed a thick arm back the way they had come. "Couple of clearings along the roadside in that direction. Just wait there till about seven in the morning, and come back. I won't be here, but tell the next shift you spoke to Simon."

Reluctantly, Callan nodded. "Okay."

The guards disappeared, and the four of them stood before the high gates. The original barrier had been added to: beams, a metal frame, and posts were meshed together, topped with barbed wire.

Eric met them near the Jeep. "No good?" Callan explained. "Well, we have space in the camper. The table folds down into a double bed. We're happy to share."

They found a spot about a mile and a half from the barracks, a strip of gravel off the main road, hidden behind a string of poplar trees. There was a bin, and a single cubicle public toilet. Eric pulled the camper in alongside the Jeep and trailer. Both drivers left their lights on as they all scouted the area looking for zombies. There were none.

"I don't know who's inside that base, but I reckon they've cleaned up Wagga," Eric said. "At least they've done us that favor."

"Do we need to post guards?" Greg asked.

"You and I can sleep in the Jeep," Callan said. "We'll keep an eye and ear out."

Kristy and Dylan would use the fold-out double bed. Dylan made a face when Eric suggested this, and Kristy understood his disappointment.

She touched his hand lightly. "We'll get our chance." She kissed him, and he gave a thin smile.

"I don't think I can keep my eyes open much longer."

"Yeah. I've never wanted sleep more than I do right now." They walked towards the camper van arm in arm.

THIRTY-SEVEN

THEY WAITED IN THE snarled brush at the perimeter of the base until darkness had swept in and blackened the land. Jake had fallen asleep almost immediately in Evelyn's lap. She had watched with growing apprehension as the torch lights bobbed through the surrounding bush and along the road beyond the fence. Arching her back forward, she'd curled her head down, trying to conceal the white of her face in case the yellow glow swung over them. *No doubt looking for us,* she thought. The men had come close, their conversation perceptible, as the snap and crunch of twigs and sticks carried to her. Eventually, they had moved back toward the barracks. Evelyn didn't want to think about what they might do to them if they were found.

On their way out, she had spotted a cut in the fence, but had not been able to sneak through it due to the patrol. After the men departed, she woke Jake and collected their supplies, dropping the tent twice before she discovered a way to handle it all.

"We're just going for a little walk," she told him. The truth was that it might not be little. She had no idea where they were headed, or how far they would get. Her main priority was to escape the base. The rest would hopefully work itself out.

In the dark, Evelyn found the opening in the wire by running her fingers over the fence. She pushed their supplies through first, and strained her back pulling the flap aside for Jake. She talked him through and, with more twisting and puffing, wriggled her ample body beyond.

They crossed the road in the shadows past the barracks entrance and started through the long grass and over the rocky ground. But their progress was slow; Jake was exhausted. They hadn't eaten since lunch—a muesli bar and half an apple each. Evelyn had passed beyond hungry, but she knew Jake would be struggling.

It wasn't long before her legs and feet gave out. The lights of the entrance had grown tiny, and Evelyn thought they were far enough from the road and surrounded by brush to be concealed. They would wake early and start back toward Wagga.

The real concern though was food. Even if they made it back to town, finding ample nourishment was going to be a problem. In her brief foray through the streets prior to being saved by Alex, she had found little. And what was she to do in the morning? Jake couldn't walk all the way back into Wagga on an empty stomach. *In the morning,* she told herself.

The tent was lopsided and struggled to erect properly, but it would suffice. She found a rock and knocked the pegs into the soft earth until she was confident a light wind wouldn't blow it down. They crawled inside, climbed onto and under the thin blankets, ignoring their hunger, and fell asleep on the rocky ground.

The sound of vehicles rolling over the blacktop woke Evelyn. Jake stirred, mumbling as he always did. She pulled a blanket over him and stroked his hair. The glowing hands of her wrist watch read eleven-fifteen. She thought about one of the torches, but would only turn it on in an emergency.

She pulled on her pants, unzipped the door of the tent, and slipped out into the warm air. In another life, such a night would have found her and Cameron swimming through the green light in their backyard pool after Jake had been tucked into bed. Memories surfaced, but she shoved them away for another time. She had become an expert at that lately.

Stretching under a banner of jeweled stars, Evelyn watched two vehicles park in a rest area about half a mile ahead. It looked like an SUV and camper van. Her mind had already begun working on possibilities. This could solve their short-term food problem. She needed to get a closer look though. Could she leave Jake alone? No. Too risky. Evelyn crept forward though, lifting her legs high to avoid tripping on the long grass and fallen branches. She passed the end of the tent and kept going, giving herself another fifteen yards.

It didn't improve her view much, but the two vehicles splashed their headlights into the scrub, giving up some of their secrets. There appeared to be several people from the SUV and one from the camper van, although she suspected more were inside. Attached to the Jeep was a heavily packed trailer. Her eyes widened. Here was their chance. Such an outfit would surely have *some* food. She hated the idea of stealing, but in this world, risking death was the other option.

A croaky voice sounded from behind. "Mommy?"

Evelyn swiveled. "Shhh, baby." She hurried to him. "What are you doing up?"

"It's hot. I'm sweating."

She placed the back of her hand on his forehead. Warm, but not hot. Ever since the outbreak, the mention of 'feeling hot' left Evelyn with a case of the chills.

"It's a warm night."

She turned back to the group parked in the rest area. They'd killed both sets of headlights, but the internal lighting in the SUV was on, and vertical strips of light appeared behind curtains in the windows of the camper van.

"What are you doing out here?"

"Nothing, hon." But an idea popped into her mind. The next hour would be their best chance to steal supplies from the trailer. The group had just stopped, and if they'd been travelling all day, sleep would come fast. Once daylight came, they would be away, possibly inside the high fences of the barracks, and she'd have lost her chance.

"Empty both the packs and bring them with us, Jake. And grab the torch. Be quick."

Evelyn twisted the concept around in her head. They had taken from the abandoned houses in Wagga, but nobody had held claim to that. This was different; they were people's possessions. Evelyn was desperate though, and without sustenance, they might not make it into Wagga. Jake was already thin. Another day or two without eating was dangerous.

They reached the highway and walked at the edge of the blacktop, looking for cars at both sides of the horizon. Evelyn doubted they'd see one, but she had made such mistakes before. After ten minutes, they reached the rest stop. The lights on the camper van had disappeared, and the SUV was a silent dark shadow, except for the tiny green and red dots of the dashboard. Whoever was sleeping in the vehicle was still awake. They would have to sit and wait.

They perched themselves on soft grass along the shoulder of the highway, sitting back to back so they wouldn't fall down. It was something Cameron had taught her from his army days. Before they had Jake, they used to fish on the Murray River at night, sitting the same way on the banks, waiting to catch a big Murray cod. The pain of the memories stung her. She tried not to think of the old days too often. Cameron had been dead eight months, well before the outbreak, and she had worked hard to accept that, but still, fond memories saddened her often.

"Mommy?"

Evelyn gasped as she came awake. She'd fallen asleep. Her watch read 2:15. She rubbed her eyes and peered into the darkness. The silhouettes of both vehicles stood before them.

"Sorry, honey. Did you fall asleep?"

"A little."

"That's okay." She tousled his hair. "Let's move."

It had worked out well. The owners would be asleep. If they were quiet, careful, and not too greedy, they might come out of this with enough food to help them back into

Wagga, and a few days beyond. And the people wouldn't suffer too much. Assuming the trailer contained food.

They walked with slow, cautious steps as they approached. A layer of crushed rock covered the rest area, worn and spread over time by the endless vehicles stopping for a toilet break or quick cup of coffee on their way in, or out of Wagga.

Reaching the trailer, Evelyn felt around the outside for any traps or encumbrances. Perhaps these people had been stolen from before and had taken preventative measures to ensure it didn't happen again. Images of rabbit or bear traps popped into her mind, and suddenly she didn't want Jake getting too close.

In a whisper, she said, "Just stay there a minute," as she circled the trailer, feeling underneath the chassis, scratching about in the dirt around each wheel. There was nothing, of course. Most people were still too trusting. *We didn't meet the likes of those inside the base, or even us*, Evelyn thought. There wasn't quite enough desperation in the world yet. Food remained, water, supplies. Perhaps there weren't enough survivors to use it all, and those alive would have years of rations. She and Jake had only survived this long because of the old bomb shelter at her parents' house. It was coming though. Sooner, or later, they would all run out.

A plastic tarpaulin covered the contents. One knot at a time, she undid the rope looped through the eyelets. Jake stood behind her, looking out for lights on the road, glancing at the SUV and camper van for signs of movement.

Evelyn stepped to the second and third knots, pleased with the progress. The tarpaulin was made of polyester though, and when she turned it back to gain access, it creaked and crinkled. *Thank goodness there's no breeze*, she thought. She took the torch from Jake and placed it on the flap to keep it down.

She wanted to use the light to explore the contents, but wouldn't risk it. Instead, she used her hands to feel the items. Her excitement grew as she realized there was water, tinned food, even several packs of toilet paper. She felt bad taking too much of that, so she only took half a dozen rolls.

They filled their packs, squeezing supplies into every corner until they were bulging. She filled Jake's with the lighter items—crackers, dried apricots, and potato chips, ensuring that hers carried the heavier stuff like bottled water and tinned spaghetti. Guilt washed over her again, and she sent a silent apology to the owners, but there was still plenty in the trailer. She and Jake would be set for several days now, with enough food and water to regroup and think about their future.

Earlier in the night, when Roger had given her the ultimatum, Evelyn had wondered how they were going to survive. But now, her resourcefulness had delivered, and they would manage a little longer until the next challenge presented itself.

They packed the last bag until items spilled out of the top and assembled them on the ground at their feet. She wouldn't bother retying the tarpaulin; they would know soon enough that goods had been stolen.

Evelyn handed the lightest pack to Jake and took the other, feeling the weight tug on her arms.

Light flashed over them, and at first she thought a car had appeared out of the darkness. Then a voice sounded, and she knew that somehow, they'd been sprung.

"Move and I'll shoot you."

THIRTY-EIGHT

AT FIRST, CALLAN HAD struggled to sleep in the restricted confines of the Jeep. They had leaned the front seats back as far as they'd go, but still, his bulky body wouldn't lie well in the bucket. Greg's hulking frame provided more problems, but he seemed to have overcome the issue and was snoring in less than ten minutes.

Finally, Callan drifted, and with it came more of the same dreams he'd experienced in Holbrook. This time, he didn't cry out though. He woke with a start, realizing it had been a dream, and lay there grinding his jaw, a hollow, pitiless feeling swallowing him. He sat up eventually and was considering getting out and walking off the effects when Blue Boy growled.

The dog's nose touched the window, peering out. Callan reached out and soothed the thick fur around his neck, following his gaze. The shadows moved. Callan thought his eyes were playing tricks. They adjusted, and he saw there were two of them, one medium height, the other short, both moving in slow motion. He knew they were going for the trailer. When they reached it, the taller one untied the tarpaulin.

Sneaky bastards. He thought about turning on the headlights to scare the shit out of them, but he wanted the confrontation. He took the pistol and a torch from the center console.

Holding his breath, Callan gently pulled the handle and opened the door. It clicked, sounding like a gunshot in the silence, but their lack of notice told him they had not heard. He slid out, motioning for Blue Boy to stay, and squatted as he moved alongside the Jeep. Their whispers drifted to him, but he couldn't make out the words. He reached the hood, then stood, cocked the gun and walked over the gravel with slow, careful, movements. At seven yards, he stopped and aimed his weapon. "Move and I'll shoot you."

190

The torch threw a yellow cone over the trailer and beyond. There was a dark-haired woman and a young boy. A moment of terror washed over Callan when he thought it was Sherry–or how she had been a few years ago before losing a little weight. This woman looked strikingly similar, except for her thicker, darker hair, and another thought chased the first, jabbing him like a hot poker in the gut. Maybe that's what his and Sherry's son would have looked like?

Callan circled them and stood in front, poking the light into their eyes. "What do you think you're doing?"

The woman froze. The boy dropped his pack and began to cry.

Just a ploy, Callan thought, *worked out beforehand so if they were caught, the victim would offer sympathy.* The woman put down her loot and crouched beside the kid, soothing him.

"That's not gonna work," Callan said.

The woman shot him a dirty look. "Don't be an asshole."

"Lady, you just tried to steal our shit, and I'm the one with the gun. Be fucking nice."

The light in the camper van came on. The woman glared at Callan. "Don't you swear around my son."

Callan laughed. "Don't swear? What's that compared with teaching him to steal?"

Kristy appeared in the doorway, one eye peering out from a sleepy face. "What's going on?" She stepped off, misjudging the ground, and stumbled. "Shit."

"Hang on, no swearing," Callan said. "You might upset the kid." The woman sneered at him. "I caught these two stealing our stuff." Kristy looked from the trailer, to the bags, and finally at the woman and boy.

"Why?"

At first, the woman pressed her lips into a thin line, as though refusing to speak, but Kristy kept her eyebrows raised, waiting for an answer. "We're desperate. We got … kicked out of there." She tipped her head toward the barracks.

Callan made a face. "Come on, that's bullshit. I know your kind. You deceive people. You tell them one thing, and act on another. I've just had a major experience with it."

Kristy looked at them for a long moment. "You were kicked out?"

"Yes. I was told we were no longer welcome. We haven't eaten a proper meal since the day before."

Dylan and Eric appeared from the van.

"Why would they kick you out?" Kristy asked.

The woman thought about this, then pulled her son closer, a tight arm around him. "I … I wouldn't do what they wanted."

Callan was about to ask what she meant, when Kristy shot him a look that told him to keep quiet. Suddenly the woman looked sheepish, embarrassed. He softened his stance, and returned the gun to his waistband.

Greg opened the car door and hopped out, rubbing his eyes. "What the hell is going—" he saw the woman and child. "Who are they?"

"We were just finding out," Callan said.

The woman stood. "My name is Evelyn Burson. This is my son, Jake. We've been inside the barracks since the day before yesterday, until last night. Before that, we were staying in an old bomb shelter at my parents' house in Wagga. We ran out of food, so we came looking for it, and … ended up in there."

"So you're stealing to stay alive?" Kristy asked.

Evelyn nodded. "Our tent is about a half a mile east. We don't have much. You can check it if you like."

"I will," Callan said.

"Cal."

"I sympathize with their story, but they're stealing our shit. It's—"

Eric tilted his head. "Come on, Callan, she's just a mom trying to look after her kid."

Evelyn smiled at Eric, and Callan felt his teeth grind. Why couldn't they see she was no different than Sherry and

Johnny? They had deceived Callan, too. He turned away and walked to the car, where he leaned against the door and watched, suppressing thoughts of Sherry and Johnny.

"You can go," Kristy said.

"Thank you." Evelyn stood and signaled the boy to help return the bags to the trailer. "If you're planning on going inside the barracks, be careful. Some of those men are … untrustworthy."

Eric stepped forward. "Keep the food. Thank you. We'll be careful."

With a grateful smile and her son in tow, the woman turned and disappeared into the brush.

THIRTY-NINE

DYLAN WOKE TO THICK, stuffy heat inside the camper van. He rolled out of the small double bed, rubbing a place in his back where one of the buttons from the cushions had dug into his skin, and went outside.

Callan and Greg stood around the trailer, picking through supplies. Blue Boy lay nearby, chewing on a soft ball. Sunlight from the east washed the land in a soft orange glow. Dylan guessed it was about seven. While the air was still cool, the clear sky and intense orange rays gave the impression it was going to be another scorcher.

Greg popped a tablet into his mouth and swallowed it down with a mouthful of bottled water. Color had returned to his face and, as he slotted the container back into the trailer, Dylan noticed he was no longer favoring his ankle. Greg turned to him and asked, "What do you reckon? Would you have let the woman and her kid go?"

Dylan scoffed. "What else would we have done? Are we a prison? She stole some food. Big deal."

Greg laughed. "Told you."

Callan made a face. "I just meant that she shouldn't have walked away getting to keep the food. It condones what she did."

"Is your conscience still dirty taking food from the gas station at the bottom of the lake?" Greg asked. Callan stuck up his middle finger. "Relax, man. She was just trying to keep her kid fed."

Dylan chewed on crackers and ate a banana before washing it down with a small carton of juice. His stomach was beginning to accept the slimmer choices. Eric appeared with greetings. Dylan decided it was time to wake Kristy.

He stood watching her, immersed in her beauty: the peaceful rise and fall of her shapely chest; the lock of long blonde hair that fell down her cheek; the sharp, perfectly proportioned nose. He was surprised by the length of her eyelashes, their light coloring camouflaged against her skin. *Women would have paid good money for lashes that long*, he thought, and with hindsight, the triviality of such a thing saddened him. She looked calm, and happy, and he hoped her dreams were pleasant. He half-expected her to wake up and catch him, and before she could, he bent and kissed her lips, filling him with soft warmth.

She opened her eyes, then stretched and turned away, smiling. "I must look terrible."

Her modesty was charming. "You look perfect, and I wouldn't swap you for any other person, living or dead."

She rolled over. "Where have you been all of my life?"

"Well," he said, raising both eyebrows, "just down the road, actually." She laughed, beckoning him. It was the moment of normalcy they had both been craving. It might have happened on any Saturday morning in the first months of the relationship.

They kissed again, and the gentleness of her lips surprised him. He suddenly decided that lips were one of his favorite body parts.

The door to the van creaked and Julie entered. "Sorry." She turned to leave.

"No, please don't," Dylan said, pushing back off the bed. He gave Kristy a cheeky smile that she returned. "You'll keep until later."

Those who hadn't eaten devoured a hearty breakfast of baked beans on toast, banana in cereal, and hot instant coffee from the camper van kettle. Kristy monitored Sarah's blood sugar levels, and Greg ate more than he had since leaving the lake. Dylan watched Kristy most of the time and wished it was just him and her, on a camping holiday back in the old world.

Eric filled the camper van with fuel from a Jerry can and inspected the damage to the exterior caused by the zombies: minor scratches and a broken window clip. The Jeep had a shattered indicator light and a handful of dents, which Callan called battle scars.

The Jeep pulled out of the rest stop and the van followed its U-turn. Now in full daylight, the entrance to the barracks greeted them, a wide space of bitumen kept neat and clear. After parking, Dylan joined Callan, Kristy, Greg, and Eric as they strode across twenty yards of blacktop. A two-meter - high chain-link fence ran from the gatehouse into thick bush, disappearing behind overgrown trees.

This time, three men left their watch and approached the convoy.

Callan turned to Eric. "You can do the talking. They might be more willing to listen to a reasonable, middle-aged man." Eric scoffed.

"Gentlemen." Eric stuck out his hand. The lead man wore heavy black boots, green army trousers, and a white singlet top. "We spoke to Simon last night, and he suggested we'd be able to gain entry into the barracks if we came back this morning."

"Sure," Black Boots said. "Just drive up to the gate so we can examine your inventory. Once we make sure it meets the regulations, you're free to enter."

"Regulations?" Callan asked.

"Just a list of basic rules that everybody has to follow."

"Like?"

The man stiffened, glancing at the other men. "No weapons. We confiscate them until you leave. All your food and supplies go into a kitty for everyone to share. Everyone gets a number."

Dylan and Callan exchanged a look. On the back of what the woman had said about being careful, Dylan had a bad feeling.

"And what happens inside? Are we free to do our own thing?"

A second guard stepped forward. Despite the heat, he wore full army greens, including a long sleeve shirt. "Men help with the town clean up, women assist with the running of the barracks. It's all about getting the place operational again, self-supportive, functional. We do detail out in Wagga, clean up the streets. There's plenty of artillery still here."

The first guard couldn't take his eyes off Kristy. Dylan felt uneasy. He'd never been the jealous type, but perhaps it was because he'd never had anything worth being jealous of. "Hey buddy, what are you looking at?" The guard looked away, but as he turned, he mumbled something and laughed. The third man did the same.

Dylan turned his back. "I don't like this."

Callan nodded. "Me neither." He drew them away from the men and they formed a huddle. "Remember what the woman said? *Be careful.*"

"I don't like the way that asshole was eyeing Kristy."

"Well, what are our options?" Eric asked.

"Callan has been pushing for an army facility."

"Yeah, but I'm not sure about this one, though. It doesn't sound too accommodating." Callan glanced back at the men. "We came here to find out if anybody was working on a cure or a vaccine."

Eric said, "I doubt that's going on. I'm not even sure this place is run by the army anymore. These guys don't look like army to me."

The flash of static sounded from a walkie-talkie on one of the guard's belts, and he jogged back to the gatehouse. The clunk and grind of metal sounded, and then the gate rolled back. Moments later, a battered and beaten Toyota SUV groaned its way out of the barracks with four men inside. The front passenger, a big man with tattoos and cropped grey hair, signaled the guards with a nod of his head.

Dylan watched them drive off up the road, thinking *Militia, rather than army personnel.*

"Is the army still running this base? Eric asked.

After a long silence, the second guard said, "The army was wiped out by the virus. We took over and, with the commitment of those inside, we've put the place back in order."

197

"So there's no doctors working here on a vaccine, or cure for the virus."

The guard shook his head. "No."

Callan turned away. "Let's just keep going to Sydney. Try Holsworthy. Surely the army still has control of that."

Dylan wanted to go to Melbourne and find his sister, but such a drive was impractical, at present. "I agree. I don't like the feel of these men, or this place."

"Anybody disagree with that?" Eric asked.

Nobody did.

"Listen," one of the guards said, jogging toward the departing group. "The rules might be a bit tough, but you're safer here than anywhere else. Humans have to work together against the zombies. It's the only way to beat them. You join us here and you'll get safety, food, and a bed. Believe me, in this world that's the best offer you'll get."

Callan glanced at the others. Nobody spoke. "Thanks, but we'll take our chances alone."

FORTY

KLAUS STEPPED AWAY FROM the bench, ignoring the bead of sweat running down his forehead, and lay the beaker on the bench. Work in his protective suit was always hot and stifling. He should have been used to it now, having spent so much time of late stuffed inside it. The last thirty-six hours had been a long stretch, stabilizing and preparing most of the ingredients he had found for a batch of the serum. The interferon was the key component, but he'd used other elements to balance the result carefully. There might have been a small amount of the constituents in one of the other laboratories, but Klaus was treating this lot as though it were his last; taking extra care in the preparation. Lives, no doubt, would depend on it.

He slipped off his heavy boots, stepped out of the airlock and removed his suit, then went directly for the coffee machine, feeling the bite of his caffeine addiction. He'd re-run the serum tests another five times, fearful the initial result was an aberration. It had worked though, and from there, he had set about making a quantity of the drug. How much interferon stocks would he find in the world? There wasn't much left on the base. By Klaus' estimates, it might treat several people for a week, at most, but only trials would quantify this. Now, he needed a subject–preferably one recently infected. None of those they had captured upstairs qualified; the virus was too far progressed. At some point, to prove the serum on humans, he would need to go out into the real world, and to do such, Gallagher was essential.

Klaus was in desperate need of a shower and a decent meal. The dull ache of hunger had almost disappeared, but if he didn't eat properly soon, he'd suffer, as had happened in the past. Returning to the sleeping area was risky, but finding Gallagher posed a bigger problem. They hadn't crossed paths since their altercation. Gallagher's quarters were in the same location, and he hoped the man would be there, drinking his life away. Under normal circumstances, Gallagher was the last person he would turn to for help, but by now, Klaus suspected the admiral was all he had. He needed to find Gallagher and engage him to get out of there.

Klaus finished his coffee, stripped off the remainder of his suit, and went to the doorway. He passed through two heavy glass doors and stepped out into the cool air of the corridor, pausing to ensure none of the infected were nearby. He listened for the sounds of activity, wishing them back to life, but there was nobody left. Perhaps even Gallagher was dead by now, and Klaus would have to battle out in the new world alone.

He snuck along the hallway, stopping inside dark doorways with a pounding heart. He peered around corners, expecting one or more wandering zombies to startle him, but the emptiness filled him with hope. His few forays out of the lab had met with little resistance; his level had not contained any of the infected, but he knew the smarter subjects could traverse stairways. It was still difficult to believe they had managed to escape the containment cells at all.

Klaus stepped into the elevator and pressed the button for level two. He had avoided the area because of the prisoners. During the initial outbreak, staff returning to the site had been sick, and it had taken doctors several days to determine they were infected. With the numbers growing, any unused rooms in the sleeping quarters had been converted into holding cells. But these were people he knew, people that had been his friends. How long since Klaus had actually been up there? A week, maybe more. He often slept in the first aid room near his laboratory. What if some of them had gotten out? He scoffed at this, but the idea chilled his skin.

The elevator doors opened and Klaus stepped out. On his right, a corridor stretched off into the distance. He walked straight along a gloomy hallway with faint lighting. He passed dark rooms with open doors, almost expecting things to jump out of them and attack him. But he knew that unless the infected had escaped, or the more intelligent specimens had changed levels, he was safe. He followed the route, which was as familiar as his own bedroom, and soon reached a sign marked: SECTION A SLEEPING QUARTERS. Klaus slowed as he approached the first doors on his right.

They were dark and silent, and he had no way of knowing if the occupants were still inside. Rick Handley and Shona Cumberland, people he knew well, had been put in some of these rooms. Harris had told him they'd both returned to the site ill after catching the virus on the outside. Klaus had worked closely with both of them for a number of years.

Crouching, he hurried past the closed doors, focused on reaching the end of the corridor. He arrived, slightly out of breath, and looked back, expecting one of them to be following. The hallway was empty. *You're being stupid.*

He turned the corner, the throb of hunger increasing, and stopped suddenly. Furniture, bedding, and bloody clothes had been pulled from rooms and strewn across the floor, feathers and fluffing ripped from gaping tears. Klaus leaned against the wall. No more speculation. They were out. He contemplated making a run for his lab. It was the safest option, and had he considered the question in safer circumstances, he would have surely returned. But now, having proceeded this far and needing Gallagher, Klaus felt he had no choice. If he went back to the lab, the chances of escaping the facility might be forever lost.

"Shit."

Klaus approached a second doorway. A narrow gap cast a streak of light into the corridor. Did he run for it? Hope he'd go unnoticed if one of them was inside the room? *No. That would be stupid*, he thought. He reached the line of the entrance and peered around the doorway. An uneasy feeling pervaded him. It was going to happen. Klaus knew it. *Run. RUN!*

The shadows beyond the edge of the lamplight moved. Fear liquefied his muscles and he stood, staring at the thing standing in the center of the room.

It was of medium height, with chunks of hair dotted across a rotted, bleeding skull. It wore dirty blue jeans that had been shredded in places, and a blue t-shirt covered in dark stains: blood. Bare feet had trekked dirty smudges over the floor. It hunkered over another body lying on the lower bunk.

Holding his breath, Klaus was petrified. If he moved, if it sensed him, he wouldn't survive. It would run him down before he could reach his quarters, and with it, any hope for survival of the human race would disappear. He recalled watching a zombie they had in an observation room, standing for hours at a time in the same position. As much as they revolted him though, they were also fascinating creatures. The science of their existence challenged his thinking, and he was desperate to know more. For now though, Klaus would pass on the opportunity to get closer. He had never wanted to run away so much in his life.

It still hadn't moved, the body too compelling to look away. Klaus calculated his chances. He couldn't run. That would surely alert the thing.

The body on the bed stirred. The thing watching over it moved closer. Spurred by terror, Klaus took his chance, sprinting ahead with tight lips and a weak stomach. When he turned the next corner, Klaus let out a breath, sucking in air. The clang of metal on metal drifted to him from behind. Klaus jumped, let out a cry, and ran on.

FORTY-ONE

WITH THEIR MIDNIGHT FORAY into thievery, Evelyn and Jake slept past dawn. Jake shook her awake as the little green two-man tent crept toward a low oven temperature. Evelyn stirred, remembering the events of the night. They had to get moving. What she wouldn't give for a sleep-in like the old days. When Cameron had been alive, he would often take Jake out for an early bike ride, or to the local skateboard park on the weekend, leaving her to curl up in the bed covers. It was just another tiny thing she missed about him and their old life.

She buried the thought and rolled off the hard earth. They ate crackers, sultanas, and dried apricots. Jake began to revitalize, and Evelyn felt a little more optimistic, although she was keen to get moving.

They rolled up the blankets, stuffed them into the packs, and squeezed the remaining food in alongside. Evelyn took the heaviest, and strapped the other onto Jake's back. They were lucky to still have them. She lodged the tent under her arm, realizing she would need all her might to make it back to Wagga. She was of average height, but had always possessed an uncanny strength, sinewy muscles she could call upon to perform unusual feats of power. Play wrestling with Cameron in bed, he had often been amazed by her ability to push him away. She could swing a pick or shovel with most men, split wood, or use a brush cutter for hours at a time. She had grown up on a rural property with such things, and loved the testing hardship of living on the land.

They had setup camp amongst a bushy area off the main highway, but now the walk back loaded with their supplies stretched before them, and Evelyn saw the look of weariness in Jake's eyes. She opened a packet of potato chips, shrugging off the guilt of thievery, and urged him to eat.

As they cut their way through stout bushes and snarled ground cover, Evelyn thought about the people from whom they had stolen. That was the sort of group she needed to be with; they had sense and kindness. Aside from the muscle-headed guy, the rest had appeared genuine. Others probably would have shot both her and Jake; certainly Roger from the barracks looked as though he'd wanted to hurt her. The other appeal of the group was the protection it afforded, more than the interaction that she craved.

The easy contour of the highway beckoned. Evelyn preferred to stay fifty yards or so back to avoid any interaction. The walk into Wagga along the rough ground and through the dense bush would take them hours, but they had water, and plenty of time.

The soft whir of tires on the highway drifted to Jake first. He turned, and picked out the vehicle. "Someone's coming."

Evelyn felt cold fear squeeze her heart. "Keep walking." She hoped it would be the party they'd met the previous night, but there was only one vehicle, and a familiarity to it that she couldn't place.

It reached a bend and she watched it in her lateral vision. It took the curve as she held her breath, willing it to pass. It was Alex's vehicle, the one in which he had saved them from the zombies. It clattered off the road and into the scrub with a loud bang, aimed right at them.

"Run," she said, suddenly feeling like she could no longer carry the weight of the pack.

Jake took off; he was an excellent runner, could go on for miles, but from her experience the other day, Evelyn knew she wouldn't last long. Jake quickly opened up a gap on her, but stopped when he glanced over his shoulder and found her falling behind.

"Don't stop," she gasped. "Keep going, Jake."

But he waited. When she reached him, he jogged at a slower pace, providing her updates. He was a good kid, thoughtful, kind, and she knew he'd never leave her behind.

Evelyn chanced her own look back, and saw the vehicle ploughing through the brush, swinging left and right, bouncing and hopping as it hit low embankments and avoided fallen trees.

They're going to catch us. She knew it the way she knew the world would never be the same again. These men were savages. She had defied them, stolen the tent and accessories, and now they would hunt them down and tear her apart. The idea of harm befalling Jake spurred Evelyn on. Pain tore through her back, and her lungs gasped for air, but images of Jake in their clutches wouldn't allow her to stop.

"Come on, Mom," he said, desperate to unwind, stretch his legs and let the breeze take him away. He'd escape if it wasn't for her slowing him down, but alone, beyond her death, he wouldn't last long.

She could feel the rumble of the car through the dry, dusty earth. *Close. Don't give up. Make them fight.* Her sneakers, almost worn through the sole, scratched in the dust, fighting on. But the vehicle closed the gap in seconds, until the men pulled the car in front, cutting off their escape.

The car skidded to a halt, dust floating up from the wheels in clouds.

Evelyn baulked, cutting right through a cluster of prickly bushes. Car doors slammed, and the men shouted abuse, promising that if she didn't stop, she'd suffer worse.

She was going to suffocate. No time for air. The lactic acid burned her legs from the inside. Sweat dripped into her eyes, stinging as she blinked it away. Her back became a giant, painful ache, begging her to abandon the pack, but she ran on. If she stopped, they would kill Jake, and employ sexual torture on her before death.

Gunfire cracked. Dust smoked up nearby, and she realized they were only trying to scare her. From the corner of her eye, she spied the road. Maybe luck would be with them and somebody driving along would help. Surely there was some goodwill left in the world? She wondered about the others from whom she had tried to steal.

"The road," she said to Jake in a hoarse whisper. But he ran on. Had he heard? Louder. "The road!"

"Okay."

Evelyn tucked her head down and drove her thighs, arching her back further forward to take the load. The pain was everywhere, stabbing into her spine, legs, arms, and lungs. She had lasted longer than she expected, her will to live, for Jake's safety, divulging a latent strength. They just had to make it to the road.

"Look," Jake said, and suddenly he was streaming ahead, kicking away like an Olympic athlete in the final of a long race. "It's them."

More gunshots sounded, closer this time, severing bushes on their left near Jake's exposed body.

A terrible pain flared in her neck. Sweat blurred her vision. Her stomach turned and she thought she would vomit. She wiped the heel of a clumsy hand in her eyes and saw the black Jeep and the white camper van on the roadside.

She wanted to cry. What were the chances? She didn't care. "Run Jake, run for your life!"

Three of them were standing at the edge of the bush, holding guns. God bless them. Her vision fell on the one who had discovered their thievery. Callan. She didn't care about any of that in the moment.

The final clump of bushes stood in their way. The gunfire had ceased, but in her mind's eye, Evelyn imagined the men lining up Jake in their sights. He jumped over one of the low trees, an impressive feat, and she held her breath waiting for the bullet to strike him down only meters from the others.

He reached the line of men and halted under the shadow of the camper van, hands on hips. Evelyn collapsed into Callan's arms, the pain in her lungs unbearable.

"I got ya," he said. "You're alright now. Take it easy."

She slipped off the pack and he lowered her to the ground. She hunkered on all fours, chasing oxygen, her breath wheezy and hoarse, an unprecedented fire burning through her chest. Was this death? It couldn't be worse.

She heard voices raised further away, softer close by. Her arms trembled and she thought she'd have to stay in that position for an hour, maybe longer. Jake was moving about again, and she felt awash with relief that he was safe. Even if she had a heart attack and died, these people would look after him.

She managed to raise her head and look at the men who had chased them for their lives. Only two of the four had reached the scene. Roger stood before them, wearing jeans and a sleeveless shirt, beside a second man dressed in a green army outfit. Both were puffing heavily.

"Just give her ... over to us," Roger said.

The older, grey-haired man with Callan spoke. "Why? What'd she do that took four men to chase her and the boy?"

The other men arrived. It surprised Evelyn that they had been so far behind. Her breathing had slowed, but her arms were jelly. She climbed to her feet, feeling overwhelming pain, and faced their four pursuers.

"She stole from the barracks. We want our stuff back, and there's got to be punishment."

"Death? Hasn't there been enough?"

In an incredulous voice, Army Man said, "We weren't gonna kill her."

Callan stepped forward. "Then let her go." Evelyn noticed the pistol at his thigh.

Army Man looked at Roger, who considered the request. His jaw flexed. He glanced at the other men.

"We don't want any trouble," Dylan said. "But we're not going to let you take this woman, or her son."

It was then that Evelyn noticed the muzzle of a firearm pointing through a crack in the window of the camper. She felt a sudden flush of enormous gratitude for these people and fought back tears. She was safe; *Jake* was safe. She had betrayed their trust, and still they were standing up for her.

OWEN BAILLIE

"What will it take to call off your men?" Dylan asked.

Roger kept silent, grinding his jaw. Army Man shifted his position. "If she returns our things, we'll leave."

Evelyn knew a good offer. She climbed to her feet, hoping she wouldn't vomit, and grabbed her pack.

Callan smiled. "Don't worry, we'll get some more."

Nodding, Evelyn scooped up Jake's bag and carried it over to the men. She glanced at them all in turn. "I'm sorry I stole it. We had little choice."

Roger took both and lifted them onto his shoulders. The others turned and started back, while Roger held the gaze of each, finishing with Evelyn. A cold shiver touched her skin. He wasn't a man to cross.

Finally, he turned, and with Army Man, walked to the Toyota, while the others started back along the road toward the barracks.

When the men were out of sight, Evelyn said, "Thank you. Thank you all, so much."

A man stepped out of the camper van holding the rifle Evelyn had spotted in the window. "I'm Greg."

She fought back more tears. "Thank you, Greg."

"We'd better get moving," Eric said. "I don't believe they'll let this go."

The men dispersed; Dylan, Greg, and Callan headed for the Jeep, and Eric disappeared into the camper van. Kristy approached Evelyn and Jake. "You look like a similar size to me. You can borrow some of my stuff until we can find some more clothes."

Evelyn wiped sweat from her brow. "Thank you. I'll be saying that a lot, but I really mean it. You people don't owe me anything after what I did to you last night."

"Forget it. We know what survival means. You do what you have to."

Eric reappeared from the camper and turned to Jake. "You can ride in the van with my wife, Julie, and Sarah. She's about your age."

208

A middle-aged woman stood in the doorway, offering a smile and a wave of her hand, inviting them in. She took Jake by the hand. "Come here, darling. Are you hungry? I've got something you might like."

Evelyn let the tears flow as she stood on the dusty earth, watching the men in the old SUV drive out of the rough brush and back onto the highway. They had been dead, she was certain. Talk about luck. She would never question it again, nor would she question the generosity of these strangers.

After a moment, she wiped her eyes and went inside.

FORTY- TWO

CALLAN LED THE CONVOY around the outskirts of Wagga. The two vehicles had pulled up next to each other just before the junction of the Sturt and Olympic Highways. There were two choices about which way to leave town, but where were they actually going? The group in the Jeep agreed staying in Wagga was out. Retribution against Evelyn and Jake seemed obvious. Although they had gotten off to a poor start the previous night, Callan felt sorry for the woman and her son. He understood why they had reverted to stealing, but it was the deception that had touched a fresh nerve in him.

They went along Edward Street, which turned into the Sturt Highway, avoiding most of the city. Callan saw the Wagga Base Hospital through a row of trees and thought that he never wanted to visit a hospital again. Although Kristy had explained that Sarah would never stop needing medication, and sooner or later they would require more.

Wagga was clean and silent. No smashed-up cars, and not one zombie, yet. They saw two SUVs driving along streets off the main road, and Dylan guessed they were crews cleaning up the town. He had to admit that those administering the work detail from the barracks had done an incredible job. It was a fine example of what people could do working together. Part of him wished they had been able to stay and utilize the benefits of the barracks and its management.

Another thought struck him as they drove out of town. The secret he had kept from Greg had been sitting in the back of his mind for the last few days. With all that had gone on—Sherry and Johnny's lies and treachery, he would be the king of hypocrites to retain such information. It was time for him to confess. It had been a mistake to keep the death of Greg's grandparents to himself and to burden Dylan with the knowledge. Callan had learned a lot since then, though.

Sherry's death, and the likely death of his parents, had provided a different perspective on life. The death of Dylan's parents had saddened him, too. Witnessing another suffer the heartache of losing a loved one was difficult to watch. These things had changed him forever.

He fished the note out of his back pocket and laid it in his lap, then glanced at Greg to gauge his mood. He seemed relaxed, one arm on the window, peering out at the passing scenery.

It had been a rough few days for Greg. Callan knew Kristy had concerns about his mindset. The injury, the infection, and the prospect of having the virus had all affected him in some way. There had been times back at Dylan's house when Callan wondered if Greg would get through it. Throw in Kristy's relationship with Dylan, and the guy could be excused for erratic behaviour. Now, Callan was going to deliver the news about his grandparents.

Callan turned down the music. "Greg, I have to tell you something, and you're not going to like it. I'm sorry I didn't tell you earlier, but … I didn't …"

Greg stared at him. "What?"

"Your grandparents died. I knew, but didn't want to tell you."

Uncertainty flashed over Greg's face. He forced half a smile. "You're fucking with me?"

"Jesus man, you think I'd fuck with you over something like this? What sort of an asshole do you take me for?"

"Yeah, okay, but what do you mean they're dead? You found them dead at home, or …"

Callan hesitated. He couldn't stop now. "The house was empty, but they left this note." He handed the piece of paper to Greg.

Callan watched Greg's face change as he digested his grandmother's beautiful words. He clenched his jaw, a trait that typified anger. *It's going to get worse, old mate.* Suddenly he wished he hadn't said anything. Dylan wore a frown of concern.

Greg laid the note on his lap and stared out the windscreen. Luckily, he hadn't been drinking, otherwise it might have made for a more emotional confrontation. "So they were dead when you found them?"

Callan shook his head. "No. At first we thought they'd left. But then we saw them both in the backyard."

"Zombies? Like the things we've been killing for the last three days." Callan nodded. Greg slammed the bottom of his fist against the door. "So they had to suffer through that." The realization fell upon him. "You killed them?"

The emotion of it all returned, and Callan found himself choking up. That was why he hadn't told Greg, because he didn't have the guts to stand before his best mate and justify killing the only real parents he'd ever had. But his head betrayed him, nodding, and he heard himself say, "Yes."

Greg looked away and the note fell to the floor. "You should have told me."

"I know. I was wrong. I'm sorry."

Callan held tight to the wheel, concentrating on the road. He didn't know what else to say. He didn't want to explain what they had seen. Greg understood what being a zombie meant. Callan felt a hand on his shoulder and turned to find Dylan giving him a solemn, but supportive look. Greg lifted a bottle of Scotch from his feet and took several mouthfuls.

They reached the east side of Wagga along Hammond Avenue, the wide, slow-moving Murrumbidgee River glistening in the morning sunlight ahead on their left. Dylan spied the roadblock with his hawk eyes, again.

"Stop." Callan stomped the brakes hard, thrusting them forward. He glanced up to find Eric knew what he was doing, and had kept a good distance behind.

Half a mile ahead, two SUVs blocked the road. "We don't want another confrontation."

"You think they know about what happened?" Dylan asked.

Kristy squinted. "If they had two-way radios, they could."

"Either way, I don't think we can go straight."

"What about that street there? Lawson Street?"

They had nothing else. "It's worth a shot," Callan said, turning the Jeep down the road.

He took the car down Lawson Street at a slow pace. Eric followed. They passed Schiller Street on their left, but then a quarter of a mile from where they had turned they had only a left or right choice. It felt to Callan like they were going the right way.

"Copland Street. Left or right. Shit, I wish I had my GPS."

"Right is back to Wagga," Dylan said. "Go left."

"Greg?"

He shrugged. "Not sure."

At least he was talking, Callan thought. "I say left, too."

He spun the wheel in that direction and headed down Copland Street, past an automotive workshop and a furniture warehouse. They reached Tasman Road, and saw to their left that it met back up with the Sturt Highway in a quarter of a mile. Ahead, a large, cream-colored tin shed proclaimed itself as a business no longer operating.

"I don't think we'd have passed the block yet."

Callan turned the wheel to the right. "I agree."

Tasman Road was an open stretch, the faded blacktop flanked by low gum trees on either side, and beyond, yellow paddocks full of grass that would generate a massive bushfire under the smallest spark.

"We need a left turn," Dylan said.

Luck was with them, and Edison Road beckoned, taking them further away from town. But in a quarter of a mile, their luck ended when another T-intersection appeared. Their options were north, back toward the Sturt Highway, or south.

"South," Callan said, and they all agreed.

The road was lonely amongst the fields of yellow; no buildings, just a mile or two of fencing—loose wire poked through tilted, rotting stumps. A couple of cows swished their tails under gum trees, flies buzzing about their faces in the growing heat.

They reached Inglewood Road, which finally offered the left turn they desired. Callan followed it without asking. The dusty track took them over two miles through country that appeared to be under development. Signs read "WILLOW GROVE HOUSING ESTATE. COMING SOON! House blocks and home packages will be available in late 2014." *No they won't*, Callan thought. He kept glancing at the mirror and peering through the dust clouds to ensure the camper van still followed. Had the blockade drivers noticed their diversion? Did they have other vehicles waiting to pursue people who tried to avoid it?

At the end of Inglewood Road, they took another left on Elizabeth Avenue, the Wagga Royal Australia Air Force (RAAF) base and Wagga Wagga Airport on their right. Callan pulled the car up and peered off into the distance, looking for signs of life.

"It's dead," Kristy said. "Just like everything else."

Dylan turned away. "I'm sure if there was anything of value here, or the place had merit to build a camp, those guys at the army barracks would have used it."

Callan pushed the shift into drive and rolled away.

They reached the Sturt Highway in an outer suburb of Wagga called Forest Hill. There was no sign of the blockade. Greg peered through the Zukon scope. "They're still back there."

Callan turned right and headed for Sydney.

FORTY-THREE

THEY PULLED IN OFF the Hume Highway at Goulburn, having been on the road for almost three hours, taking the exit ramp at thirty-five miles an hour just in case there were any surprises. Kristy sensed that Dylan was disappointed they weren't heading south, to Melbourne, but she also understood the logic of trying the Holsworthy base in Sydney, and failing that, the command center in Canberra.

From Hume Street, they immediately saw the Shell gas station, the bowsers empty, no sign of cars, or more importantly, zombies. Callan pulled the Jeep up under the towering awning where twenty cars could fit, two per bowser. None of the bowsers had been damaged, and all the windows in the shop were intact. The camper van rolled in beside them, Eric offering a salute as he turned off the engine.

They were well out of the town center, close to the highway. If they could limit their Goulburn visit to the gas station, they would keep their risk low.

"Do we need to go into town?" Kristy asked, clicking open the passenger door.

Callan did the same. "Depends what we find here."

Blue Boy barked as he jumped out of the Jeep and raced around in a circle. The boys checked the convenience store for zombies, a wide, glass shop full of candy and savory snacks. The shop was empty, probably too far from town for the zombies to have wandered yet.

They all stretched their legs as Eric and Callan filled the vehicles and replenished their store of Jerry cans. They poked about outside the service station, finding the contents of the ice chest had melted. There were a dozen full propane gas bottles, several of which they promptly slotted into the trailer.

Kristy decided it was the perfect time to eat lunch. They picked from their stores and it was prepared at the kitchen table in the camper van by Julie, who seemed to relish the motherly role. She had been cold, almost unlikable in the beginning, but Kristy supposed, given they were deep in the throes of zombie chaos at the time, it was understandable. Now, under less intense and life-threatening circumstances, Julie's true personality became clearer.

The children ate uncooked Maggi noodles topped heavy with chicken seasoning, while the adults ate crackers with a variation of toppings straight from the camper van refrigerator. Kristy even had some of her favorite tasty cheese, telling their new friends that she was a mouse in a previous life. As they finished eating, Dylan dragged Kristy away from the main group.

"When are we going to get some time alone," Dylan asked, holding both her hands.

She smiled. "You had your chance, mister."

He closed his eyes and shook his head. "I'd take it back now if I could."

Kristy leant against his chest and Dylan hugged her with gentle conviction. She marveled at his tenderness, and was again reminded of the rightness of their relationship.

"I'm trying."

"I know."

Such commitment from her previous partners had always been missing. There was always something else they had to be doing rather than being with her. She understood the problem now. A friend had once told her that the right man would rarely want to be apart, especially in the beginning of the relationship. "I promise we'll get our chance soon." She squeezed his hand as they followed Callan and the others inside.

Kristy smelled the sour milk first. She held her breath, but couldn't avoid the stench of moldy bread, and rotting meat from the failed refrigerators. They took whatever food had value from the shelves, and filled plastic bags from behind the counter with all the bottled water in the fridges. Dylan collected all the medical and personal supplies, and

Kristy gathered up the batteries and replacement motor vehicle accessories: oil, windscreen wipers, fuses, even a 12-volt car battery. They found several maps of the greater Sydney area and Victoria, in case they ever went south to Melbourne.

Sarah and Jake were running around the large space underneath the awning when Kristy came out. Evelyn and Julie were watching, smiles on their faces. It struck Kristy then—despite the weight and hair color difference—the similarity of appearance between Sherry and Evelyn, now showered and wearing some of Kristy's clothes.

Kristy forced a smile. "You look a little like someone … we used to know."

"Oh. Is that good, or bad?" Evelyn laughed. "I hope she wasn't a bitch. Actually, I shouldn't say that, almost everybody has passed now."

Kristy felt her smile crack. She glanced at Callan, who was busy checking the tires. "Yes, she could be a bitch. She was going to be my sister in-law, and she only died two days ago."

Evelyn's face turned red and she put her palm on her chest over her heart. "I'm so sorry. I'm an idiot. I've been known to do that—stick my foot in my mouth."

"It's okay," Kristy said, feeling a pressing sensation in her throat. "We've all lost someone close, right?" Evelyn nodded. "But don't mention it around Callan, okay?"

Evelyn smiled tentatively. "Sure. And thank you. Really. The other night, you went easy on us when you could have been horrible. We were in the wrong, but you showed a kindness I haven't seen since this thing happened."

"I understood why you were doing it."

"It's still shameful, and I'm not proud of it. I suppose though I'd do it again to keep Jake alive." She tousled his hair.

"I think I'd do the same."

They packed the extra supplies where they could find space and climbed back into their vehicles. Kristy wished they could stay longer. She'd had enough of driving.

Barking from inside the shop drew their attention. With the driver's door open, Callan stuck two fingers in his mouth and whistled. "Blue?" More barking. He reached down beside the driver's seat and snatched up a pistol. Dropping the magazine from the chamber, he walked toward the convenience store. Greg followed, holding a rifle.

Kristy watched Greg stride across the concrete. He was barely two days into the antibiotic cycle. He seemed much better though.

Dylan collected his faithful Remington bolt action from the backseat. Kristy put a hand on his arm.

Callan turned back and said, "We got this, Dylan. Have the engine going, Kristy, just in case."

She watched them disappear inside the convenience store, and headed for the driver's seat.

FORTY-FOUR

KLAUS RAN PAST OTHER rooms whose doorways hung partially open. He didn't dare look into those, and he wouldn't stop, despite the burning in his lungs. His shoes thumped against the floor, and he thought about the sound drawing others, but still he kept running. There was a gun in the bottom drawer of the bedside table in his room. He had to reach that. He hadn't fired it before; his mother had presented it to him when he was hired by the military. He told her that the Army had enough weapons, but she'd insisted. Klaus didn't even know the make, only that it was a revolver, and contained a barrel where bullets were loaded.

He took three turns, ran down a long hallway and skidded left, finally reaching his quarters. Four rooms hung off a hallway leading from the main corridor. Klaus had shared the accommodation with several other doctors, one who had been a general practitioner. The man had developed the virus early on after a visit with one of his sons in Sydney. He had returned to the facility with the intent of leaving shortly after, but the infection had quickly gripped him, confining him to his room until Klaus had found him one day with a puddle of vomit beneath his mouth. The virus hadn't quite killed him; asphyxiation had. *He was almost lucky,* Klaus thought, *having not suffered the same horrible post-death symptoms as others.*

The door to his room was open, revealing disheveled, dark blue bed linen atop the mattress. Klaus fell back against the wall. Had he left it like that? He couldn't recall. Much of the last week had been a caffeine-fuelled sleepless daze. A noise sounded from somewhere beyond. Klaus glanced back down the corridor. *There's nobody there.* Part of him didn't want to go inside the room in case there was something hiding behind the door. *Toughen up,* he told himself. He remembered Billy Peters, his best friend as a boy, whose mother used to say to them whenever they scraped their knee or elbows. "Come out back and let me give you a spoonful of cement so you'll harden up." That's what Klaus needed now. A spoonful of cement.

He needed a weapon. A weapon to get a weapon. Sounded absurd. Down the hall were several more rooms. Klaus hurried past the open doorway to the next door, but it was locked. The subsequent room contained useless medical supplies that he didn't think would be suitable against a zombie. He considered trying to break the metal leg off a chair, but in the end decided a small fire extinguisher was his best chance. He unclasped it from the wall, then peered both ways first before stepping back out into the corridor. It was empty. Perhaps the other zombie hadn't seen him after all.

Klaus crept up to and stood aside the doorway holding the extinguisher. *You're ready*, he told himself. It might even be empty. But the fear wouldn't let him move. He stood listening for sounds, watching the corridor ahead. Where was the crazy zombie? The place was silent, eerie, and then it hit him that finding Gallagher might be more difficult than he had anticipated. But what would he do when he found him? Plead for help? Klaus had never been one to ask for help under normal circumstances, let alone after an altercation. In his mind, he could always solve the problem, so why did he need to ask for help?

This was different, he realized. He had devised a serum capable of halting the virus. He didn't know if anybody else had achieved so much. He had to assume they had not, and therefore mankind was relying on him. Alone, Klaus probably wouldn't make it out of Canberra. *Hell*, he thought, *I might not even make it off the base*. While the things Klaus had said about Gallagher's alcoholism were true, Gallagher was also a military man. He had training and experience that could help Klaus. He needed Gallagher if he was ever going to find more interferon supplies. You can't get to step four unless you go through step two.

Do it, now. His mother's voice. Klaus stepped around the edge of the doorway and into the room, lifting the fire extinguisher over his head. It hung there, his arms quivering, as he scanned the room. Empty. The bathroom door was wide open, as he had left it. He shuffled forward, around the end of the bed, peering into the shadows until he was certain it was clear too.

He put the fire extinguisher down and dropped onto the floor beside the bedside table. He snatched the drawer open. No gun. Had he put it somewhere else? Klaus tried to think, checking the doorway for signs of the zombie. Sooner or later they would come this way. He couldn't recall moving the gun, which meant someone had taken it. No gun, and he couldn't lug the extinguisher around.

Klaus left his room and headed along the passageway toward the elevator, watchful of open entranceways. He passed from the living quarters into an administration area filled mostly with closed doors. As he reached another intersection, he heard a noise from behind.

He forced himself to turn around. The zombie who had been standing over the bed, and the one who'd been lying on it, hurried toward him. No question that they were both the aggressive kind. Klaus fell against the wall, his breath cut short. *RUN*, his mind demanded. RUN! He did, finally, but they were within twenty yards and moving fast. He'd have given anything for Gallagher's help at that moment.

As he sped around the corner, he spotted a red alarm button set behind a plastic cover in the center of the wall. They were placed throughout the building in case of an emergency. Klaus stepped across the corridor and slammed the back of his fist against the cover. It smashed open, spilling pieces onto the floor. A modest alarm sounded through the PA system, followed by a female voice. "Emergency situation on level two, location three. All available security personal please attend immediately." The message repeated.

Ahead sat another cluster of offices. Perhaps hiding was his best option; running wasn't his strength, and he knew they would soon catch up. Klaus ran to the first room and pulled on the handle, but it was locked. He scurried to the next, and this time it opened. He burst inside, clunking his knee on the door. The thud reverberated, and he felt certain they would hear. He swung the door shut and closed it quietly, trying to control his breathing. He lay back against the front wall, drawing his knees to his chest, and listened. The emergency call played on through the loudspeaker in the corridor.

It was over, he knew. Their sense of smell was exceptional, and they would track him the way a bloodhound might track game. A bang sounded outside in the hallway. Klaus held his breath. He had nothing to fight them with. If they opened the door, he was dead, and if he died, so might the remaining hope for humanity.

FORTY-FIVE

CALLAN LED THE WAY down the aisle toward where Blue Boy was barking. He cursed himself for not keeping an eye on the dog. Greg walked a step behind, the rifle raised and aimed. Callan had a fleeting image of Greg shooting him in the back. *Payback for not telling me about my grandparents, fucker.* But when he glanced around, Greg was at his side, peering cautiously ahead.

The bark turned into a howl, sending chills up Callan's spine. How many times had that happened over the last few days? "Blue Boy," he whispered. "Come here." A whimper floated to them.

Callan hurried forward, two hands around the pistol, arms extended. A short corridor stretched ahead, at the end of which he saw Blue Boy standing in the doorway of another room, head stiff, ears pricked, teeth bared.

"Blue." The dog didn't move. "*Blue.*"

The dog crept backward. A nauseous terror uncoiled in Callan's belly. Blue had fought dozens of zombies; had run between their legs and teased them with his speed and agility; but now, he was scared.

"Here, boy. Come here."

Blue Boy yelped, then spun around and sprinted down the hallway. He ran through Callan's legs, barking.

A shadow filled the doorway. Callan braced himself; Greg adjusted his aim, wrapping tight hands around the rifle. A zombie appeared in the entrance, causing the skin on Callan's neck to tingle.

Greg said, "Jesus Christ." It had to duck to get through the door. It turned, fists clenched, and glared at them. "Shoot the fucker."

Callan hesitated, lost in its monumental size. It had to be six-foot-eight, and was as wide as two men, with bulging shoulders flanking a thick neck. Blood smeared its lips and cheeks, and it glared them with eyes like coals from the fires at the lake.

"Do it, man."

Callan lifted his gun and fired. The bullet missed the zombie and splintered the door frame, sending wood up in a shower. He fired again, hitting the zombie in the neck and splashing blood over the wall. It fell against the door frame with a thud and went down on one knee, a hand over the wound. The gun roared, but the thing was already moving, striding toward them, blood running down its throat onto a tattered shirt.

Blue Boy barked like a machine gun, flecks of foam spraying from his muzzle. Greg stepped up beside Callan and the rifle cracked, causing a shrill pain in his ear. He fired the pistol again and, with Greg's second shot, they both blew chunks of the zombie's head away at the same time. It collapsed, as though it was a puppet and the strings had been cut.

Blue Boy kept barking, replacing the gunfire with a piercing yap. Callan squatted and wrapped an arm around his neck, trying to quell the trembling. Callan was relieved the dog had not been hurt; there had been a moment when he'd thought otherwise.

Maintaining his aim, Greg stepped over the body and continued on before turning into the room. His voice rang down the hallway. "You better come look at this."

Callan gave Blue Boy a final scratch under the neck, then walked along the corridor with the gun pointing at the dead monster. Blue Boy didn't move. As Callan stepped over the corpse, he expected it to reach up and clutch his ankle.

He reached the doorway and saw Greg's grim expression.

"Oh, fuck."

Lying before them were a dozen or more human bodies spread over the floor. Some lay across others, as if they'd been tossed into the room like sporting equipment.

"Are they dead?" Callan asked.

"I think so."

Nothing could have survived the bloody gashes around their necks. They looked human, freshly killed, but on closer inspection, their pallid complexions and the tell-tale red lines through their skin confirmed their infection.

Callan moved back through the doorway. "What do you think it was doing with them?"

"Dunno. But I don't wanna hang around to find out." Greg turned and walked down the corridor. Callan followed.

FORTY-SIX

GREY, BOILING CLOUDS HAD floated over Goulburn, blocking out the sun and bringing a somber feeling to the day. Intermittent spots of rain tapped on the gas station roof.

"He was changing them all into type threes," Dylan said. "I'd bet money on it."

Callan considered this. "You might be right."

They stood under the awning between the camper van and the Jeep as the boys explained what had occurred. Blue Boy sat patiently beside Callan. He had become Callan's, no doubt, and Dylan felt like he had failed his father, who had fostered the dog before his own death.

Kristy walked over from the Jeep. "Based on what you told us the other night, I think the more aggressive zombies are smart enough to strategize. I mean, I know how that sounds, but, it's as if they are—"

"Building an army?" Dylan asked.

"Exactly. An army of the strongest, smartest, and most aggressive zombies."

Callan rubbed a hand though his hair. "That would be trouble. Seriously *big* trouble."

"So there's a smarter zombie?" Evelyn asked with a hint of skepticism.

Dylan scrunched his nose. "There is. They're a much more aggressive breed. Fast, strong, and intelligent."

"We've faced them a few times, and believe me, if there's more than one of them, you run," Callan said.

Greg shook his head. "I didn't think that big bastard was gonna go down."

"He was a giant. Would have made a good basketballer in his day."

"At the army barracks, I heard some of the people talking about the super zombies. I didn't pay much attention to it."

"They're real," Kristy said.

Eric estimated they had an hour and a half to the Holsworthy army barracks. There was some discussion about whether to proceed directly there, or find a safe place along the highway to rest and wait it out until the following day.

Dylan liked that idea. He was sick of the repeated confrontations. He worried about finding more of the same at Holsworthy. Sydney was enormous, and if Albury were any comparison, there would be millions of dead looking for food. His father's Tasmanian idea had never really left his thoughts. It was a smaller area to control, and maybe the virus had never even reached the island.

As they pulled out of the gas station and chugged back toward the highway, rain fell in thicker drops, splattering the windscreen. Thunder grumbled in the distance, and a flash of light illuminated a pocket of grey clouds. Callan turned the wipers on, which drew dirty streaks across the glass. As they rolled along the entrance ramp onto the Hume Highway, a mob of kangaroos bounded across the road. Callan slowed the Jeep, and they watched a giant buck lead the pack of twenty or so. It was an uncommon sight.

Near Mittagong, they began seeing the occasional abandoned car on the other side of the road, all pointed in a southerly direction. The idea of more congestion and death unnerved Dylan. Driving provided respite; time to consider what they had gone through, and what might lie ahead. He couldn't escape some of the memories, though. His father's proud, dying face flashed into his mind often, and he found himself overcome with emotion. He had been given more time to grieve for his mother, but the wound was still fresh, and raw. Kristy's presence was all that kept him from the insanity of the situation, and he felt he could survive any amount of tragedy as long as he had her.

The rain grew heavier, pounding the roof and saturating the blacktop. Even with the wipers at full speed, the road ahead was barely visible through the spray. Callan slowed the

Jeep to almost fifty and turned the headlights on as the clouds turned darker with menace.

"We should get off the road," Kristy said. "This is getting worse."

Callan switched the headlights to full. "If it doesn't let up soon, we'll have to stop"

It didn't improve. Torrential sheets fell far ahead, sweeping the highway in a curtain of rain. Spray from the back of the Jeep forced Eric to stay back a hundred yards.

On a large hill, just past the Campbelltown turn off, another gas station and service center entrance beckoned. Huge red signs blared at them from behind a wall of trees, camouflaging most of the establishment.

"In here," Greg said.

Callan guided the Jeep off the main highway and up the incline, splashing through pools of water gathered on the uneven road. It straightened before splitting two ways. He took the left fork, then swung around through overhanging bush before the narrow roadway straightened, leading to the gas station. The rain limited their visibility, and by the time they noticed the other cars parked underneath the awning, it was too late.

FORTY-SEVEN

THERE WERE SEVEN VEHICLES: two sedans and five SUVs parked in a way that protected the outer edge of the awning from the weather. The canopy was enormous, even bigger than the one in Goulburn.

"What do I do?" Callan asked, braking hard. He had a bad feeling. It might be Steve Palmer and his crew all over again. He was boxed in, though; the way ahead blocked by the other cars, and Eric's camper van was right behind the trailer. There was little choice. "Lock and load."

"Wait," Kristy said. "There are kids." Two children appeared beside one of the vehicles smiling and waving. "I don't think these people are a threat."

They all climbed out of the Jeep and joined the others from the camper van. Blue Boy ran along at Callan's heel. He felt more confident having the dog with him. An overweight man wearing shorts and a red striped polo shirt stepped out from behind one of the larger SUVs holding a shotgun. Beyond, several more people holding weapons watched.

"How goes it?" the man said in a jolly voice. "That rain's pretty bad. You can hang around here for a bit until it passes, if you like."

Eric, who Callan learned had once been principal of a primary school, stepped forward and offered his hand. The man shook it. "Thanks. We'd appreciate that."

A second man with a head of thick silver hair joined the first, whose name was Samuel, and made himself acquainted. His name was Jacob Taylor, and he had a friendly face. Callan eyed him closely, looking for signs of deception. Their luck so far in making contact with others had been somewhat poor. He explained their intended direction and from where they had travelled so far.

"How goes Albury?" Jacob asked.

"Not too good," Callan said.

229

"Same up north, I'm afraid to say. We started in Coffs Harbour, been collecting folks along the way. Travelled as far down as Wollongong. I'm sorry to say, but Holsworthy is no more." Callan's eyes widened. "Been abandoned. Probably overrun with infected by now."

Dylan asked, "You were there?"

"We checked the place. Thought we might have been able to get some help from the army. We're working our way down to Melbourne, now. Heard there was a laboratory there working on a vaccine."

Dylan perked up. "In Melbourne? Where exactly?"

"We don't know yet. Arty, one of the guys we picked up along the way, is a chemist. He says there are several manufacturing facilities across the city. We're gonna drive down and check them out."

Talk of Melbourne reminded Callan how much Dylan wanted to go south. He knew his sister, Lauren, went to university down there, so he could understand Dylan's desire. If they ever headed to Melbourne, Dylan would be pushing to find her.

Jacob continued. "We've just started setting up for the night. There's twenty or so of us, and we share the shifts to make sure the perimeter is safe, but we think we're probably far enough from any main town to worry. We're stocked up with food, and in truth, it's not difficult to find when we need it. There are plenty of abandoned farms along the way with enough surviving crops to keep us from starving."

"Have you lost many?" Callan asked.

Jacob stiffened. "We've all lost people. Ours were mostly in the beginning, and we haven't lost anyone from this group for over a week."

Callan made a pained face. "We haven't been so lucky of late, but I intend to change that."

The discussion was brief, and all agreed that continuing on in the torrential rain would be a mistake. Hail pounded the roof, washing water over the guttering in thick torrents.

From east to west, the sky had turned the deep grey of wet concrete. It wasn't going anywhere.

Jacob introduced them to some of the others members: his own wife, Monica, along with a handful of male and female adults, and a number of children ranging in ages from four to sixteen. The group seemed about as normal as they could expect. Callan felt better about the inadvertent circumstances.

As the group disbanded, Rebecca, a woman of similar age, took Dylan by the hand and offered to show him the site. He shot a look of surprise at Kristy, who returned a frown as the woman led him away. Kristy couldn't stop looking at them as they passed through the undercover area and then into the shop, the woman explaining all the details of the structure. Callan watched Kristy's face change, knowing she could be the insecure type. "Don't get jealous, sis." She glared at him.

Callan was impressed with the layout. He stood with Greg, Kristy, and Evelyn for a time, observing and discussing things quietly between themselves. It might have been a large site at any camping ground in Australia. Two generators rumbled in the background, and cords snaked over the concrete floor. They had unloaded most of the supplies from the SUVs and stacked them around the central courtyard, then unfurled bedding and spread it over the backs of the vehicles. Several tents had been erected, and numerous people were inflating camping beds. There were four fold-out picnic tables and numerous camping chairs, all parked around several gas-cooking appliances.

Eric and Julie disappeared back into the camper van. Callan wanted to ask Eric about their sleeping arrangements, so he left the others and headed toward the vehicle. Outside the door, he heard them talking in soft tones, and waited, giving them privacy they probably hadn't enjoyed since leaving Holbrook.

"I wish we hadn't left," Julie said, stacking small boxes of food on the kitchen table. "We should have stayed there."

"And been overrun?"

"You don't know that."

"It's likely. Besides, we're helping people. What would have happened if we hadn't come along at that time? These people could have died. You don't want that."

"No. Of course not. It's just that we're old, Eric. We're not made for this kind of thing."

"Look, how often have I let you down since we've been married?" Julie mumbled something. "That's right. So trust me. These are good people. We could do a lot worse. And we couldn't have stayed in Holbrook forever."

They hugged, a warm, loving embrace, the kind of hug Callan had always dreamed of having with Sherry. Despite ample girths, their bodies fit perfectly together, their heights a consummate match so Julie could fit underneath Eric's arms and lay her head on his chest. It was full of a love and affection Callan had never known; might never know, now. Had he really loved Sherry? He thought he had, but had begun to wonder. Maybe he'd been in love with the idea of having a partner who felt the same, someone he could marry, make a home and a family with. Sherry had not been that person, so how could he have loved her?

Sarah appeared at the doorway. She smiled. "Can I go inside?"

Callan broke from his thoughts. "Sure. Sorry." He moved, and Sarah entered. Callan followed, moving toward the rear of the van.

Eric smiled. "Be with you in a moment."

Sarah was thirsty. Julie sat her down and fussed about, finding a clean cup and filling it with cold water from the refrigerator. She took a couple of cookies from a plastic container and handed them over. Sarah smiled and took a bite.

Callan hadn't warmed to Julie yet. Mostly she had complained about their circumstances. Her fear was obvious, but who wasn't scared? She handled the children well though, doting on them, providing things they would otherwise miss out on. She gave them her time, answered their questions, and showed care they might receive from a grandmother in another life. *That was an underrated skill*, Callan thought. She might not be standing outside with a rifle, but she added value to the group.

"How can I help?" Eric asked, handing Callan a cold can of beer. It was a wet day, but the air remained warm, and thirst came easily.

"I just wanted to ask about sleeping arrangements. We've only got the Jeep—fits two, but if you have room for two more …"

Eric clamped a hand on Callan's shoulder. "Happy to help, my friend. We've got room in here to sleep the rest of you."

"Thank you. We appreciate that."

"Let's see if we can settle down for a few hours and enjoy ourselves–I know we're all still carrying a lot of heartache, but … switch off if you can."

"I know what you mean. If I think about it too much …"

They talked of other matters; drank two beers each, shared a bag of potato chips Julie had left for them without a word, and stood beneath the awning, looking out at the blanket of rain sweeping across the countryside. Had the end of the world not been imminent, Callan thought it would have been a most enjoyable time.

"It's funny," Callan said, cracking another beer. He had begun to feel a sweet buzz. "This is nice, but I know I might be dead tomorrow. This might be my last day on earth." He looked at Eric. "If tomorrow was your last day, is there anything you wished you'd done? Any regrets?"

"Not many, but I wished I'd taken more of my own advice."

"How do you mean?"

Eric took a mouthful of beer and looked out at the rain, thinking. "For years, people have radiated toward me for advice. I seem to have a knack for it. And it worked. I've helped people with their jobs, relationships, and other endeavors. People just need someone to believe in them, and mostly they can succeed. But if I'm honest, I took it easy. I could have made more of myself; gotten a better paying job, or had a crack at golf when I got offered the chance–I was pretty good. I wanted *things*, but I never took a chance on myself to get them. I spent years helping improve other lives, encouraging, giving them strength to stretch themselves, to achieve more." He turned to Callan, his eyes glassy. Maybe some of it was the beer talking. "I should have been bolder. I would have been more courageous if I had my time again."

"It's not too late."

He considered this for a long moment. "No. It's not, but I've missed out on many chances." He smiled, and clapped Callan on the shoulder. "What about you, my friend?"

Callan sighed. "Sherry. I should have ditched her a long time ago. I don't think I really loved her. I lusted for her, but love? You don't love a person who does that to you. And you know what? I wanted to try a different life. I love the outdoors–fishing, hunting, just going out bush and living off the land. Sherry hated it. Would never have considered doing it permanently." He let the words drift, listening to the rain on the aluminum roof.

"I know it might seem like you didn't love her, but in time you'll change your opinion. Regardless of what happened, sometimes people aren't meant for each other. The secret to a strong marriage is having similar likes. Sharing your lives is a key part of it all."

"I still can't believe she's gone. Like I said, who knows if tomorrow isn't going to be our last day?"

Eric shrugged. "Yeah, but life has always been like that. Before all of this happened, it wasn't much different. Now the risk is just higher. You can't think about it though. You just have to accept it. I said something the other night, when we met; something I've learned as I've gotten older. You can't live life being scared about what *might* happen. You just enjoy the moments you have, like this." He stuck out his can of beer, and Callan touched it with his own.

"Cheers."

Smiling, Callan took another mouthful of beer, and thought it might be their first decent night since the lake.

FORTY-EIGHT

KLAUS HELD HIS BREATH. He wasn't sure if he could hear them in the corridor, but he imagined they were outside the door, searching for his scent, slowly working their way toward the office.

He peered into the shadows for a weapon. Boxes of papers stood stacked in the corners and on top of and underneath a thick wooden desk, scratched and gouged with use. A tired-looking black fabric chair had been rolled to one side, two boxes of documents loaded on the seat. *Perhaps the drawers hold something I can use*, Klaus thought. He wanted to crawl over and check them, but his fear of alerting the zombies to his presence kept his back against the wall.

Beyond, like background music at a shopping center, the female voice kept informing emergency services of the incident's location. Under normal circumstances, a horde of armed and highly trained personnel would have descended on the scene, but now, all that remained was Gallagher, and Klaus wouldn't have been surprised to find him lying passed out somewhere on one of the lower levels, probably where they stored the booze.

He had to try the drawers. If they contained any kind of weapon, he needed it.

Klaus waited thirty seconds before crawling across the hard tiles. On reaching the desk, he looked up at the windows, certain they would be staring in at him. The space was empty, although if the zombies walked past at that moment, they would discover him.

With a shaking hand, he opened the first drawer. Stationery spilled out. He removed several boxes of staples and rummaged through the deeper section, finding nothing of worth. He closed it, then tried the second and third with the same result. In the fourth, he found an old computer keyboard with a long cord attached. He took this out and gave it a firm practice swing. It was flimsy, and light, but it was better than his fists. He repeated the action, feeling more at ease with his new weapon, until soon he'd made a dozen swings, each with increasing force.

He was about to sit back down when the door crashed open, smashing into boxes stacked against the wall. Klaus screamed. The dark, soulless eyes of the class A zombie glared at him. At its sides, tight fists hung, ready to kill.

He scrambled backward, forgetting the keyboard, and fell against a column of boxes. One tottered and fell, crashing onto him. The thing in the doorway started forward. Klaus spun, looking for somewhere to hide. He reached underneath the desk, grabbed the box of papers, and heaved them out. He scurried forward, pressing himself into the recess. *The keyboard.* Klaus reached out, grabbed the cord, and drew himself back, pulling the item by the long tail. It clattered over the floor to him and he collected it up just as the zombie reached the desk. It growled, swiping at the place where Klaus had been.

This was it, he realized. They had classified the class A aggression levels at three times a fully grown ape at its peak. It would tear Klaus apart. He'd never thought his life would end like this.

The thing squatted, reaching underneath the desk with one groping hand. It skimmed Klaus' knee, and he slammed the keyboard down on its fingers. The hand shot backward with a grunt. But it wasn't giving up. It locked onto Klaus' ankle and, with a mighty pull, yanked him out from beneath the desk.

Klaus struck out again the way an old lady might strike a thief trying to steal her handbag. The keyboard clattered against the zombie's shoulder, but it swiped the frail weapon away with a powerful stroke. Klaus kicked out at it, striking its leg. It was like kicking a tree. The zombie grabbed Klaus by the foot and twisted his ankle. Pain shot through his calf muscle. Klaus screamed as the zombie pulled his foot up toward its mouth.

"NO! NOOO!!"

A loud, ear-splitting noise filled the room. The zombie's head exploded over the desk, spraying Klaus with muck. The thing fell onto its knees, then slumped forward with a thud. Gallagher stood outside the doorway holding a pistol.

Klaus scrambled to his feet, unsure whether he was really still alive. "Thank … you," he managed, panting. His heart thundered. He had either wet himself, or sweat had run down his back to his legs. He didn't care. He was alive.

A flash of movement came down the hallway from the left. Klaus shouted, "Watch—"

But it was too late. The second class A struck Gallagher with the sound of a heavy bag hitting the ground, knocking him down.

Klaus scrambled to his feet, scooping up the keyboard. He realised how futile it was, but ran for them anyway.

They wrestled their way to the wall of boxes. The zombie grunted and growled. Gallagher's face was bright red, twisted into a mask of desperation. He was losing though. The zombie had both hands around Gallagher's throat, while Gallagher had his hands pressed against the face, trying to keep its mouth away from his body.

Klaus raised the keyboard and swung it downward with all his strength. It crashed over the zombie's skull and shattered into pieces. The infected lost its grip and fell aside. Gallagher was fast. Klaus didn't know if he had ceased drinking of late, but he snatched the gun up and stuck it under the zombie's chin.

The noise was like the loudest firecracker Klaus had ever heard, scorching his ears. He turned away as blood and brains painted the wall.

Gallagher pushed the zombie off and it slumped aside. Gore covered his upper body and face. He wiped a shaking hand across his cheeks, clearing most of it. His face twisted in pain when he tried to move. He touched a place on his upper leg, and Klaus saw a bloody mark.

"It bit you?" Klaus asked with incredulity.

Gallagher climbed to his feet, shoulders slumped, and handed Klaus the gun. His dirty, wrinkled clothes looked like they hadn't been changed in weeks. He turned his bloodshot eyes away from Klaus. There were no tears, but his features were grim. "Do it. Finish me, will you?"

Klaus drew back. "I'm not going to kill you."

Gallagher grabbed his arm, showing gritted teeth. "Listen, I've got about thirty-six hours before I turn into one of them. You don't want that, do you?"

Klaus shook off the arm. "Hold on. I've got something that might help."

FORTY-NINE

THE BLANKET OF GREY clouds weren't moving. Rain continued to beat its steady drum on the roof of the gas station. Thunder gathered in the distant sky, and through the surrounding trees the occasional flash of lightning turned heads. The temperature had dropped significantly, bringing pleasant relief from the insipid heat that had plagued the state for much of the summer.

Kristy had simmered while Dylan received a tour of the place from the girl. She had never been the jealous type, but something about the pretty girl unsettled her. She was thinner than Kristy, with long, sandy hair that touched her lower back. Kristy had tried to grow her hair long. What if Dylan liked her? What if he realized Kristy wasn't all that he thought? He'd been exposed to her for so long, perhaps he'd developed feelings for her because she was the only available woman. Eventually, he and the girl had parted, and he'd begun talking with Greg and the other men.

Kristy wandered away, diverting her thoughts. She was impressed with the way Jacob and the others had setup the gas station. They'd used all the vehicles, even directing Callan and Eric to place theirs a certain way so it protected people from the rain and provided an ambience of security. They even managed it so that each vehicle was parked to allow a quick exit from the service station if trouble arose.

There were fold-out chairs and tables, lots of delicious food, and plenty of discussion. One of the men, Stuart, was a butcher, and had processed several cuts of lamb and beef along the way, using a portable freezer to store the meat. As darkness made shadows outside the awning, a portable barbecue appeared, followed by the mouth-watering smell of steak and lamb chops that soon overpowered the fading scent of petrol.

People mingled, and when the others found out Kristy was a doctor, several asked for minor consultation, including one man who had a severely blocked ear canal. Using a large syringe, Kristy managed to dislodge the blockage and relieve his discomfort. From that moment on, she was a hero, and the man proceeded to attend to her every need.

She took the time to sit and speak with Evelyn and Julie, listening to their stories. She sensed there was more to Evelyn's tale involving the men from the barracks, but she was coy, her answers short. Kristy did more listening than talking, which was unusual for her. Julie noticed.

"Is everything okay?" Kristy tried to brush it off but Julie smiled. "I'm a woman, too, and I've been around. I know when something's wrong." They got it out of her eventually.

"It's nothing," Evelyn said. "I've seen the way he looks at you. He's infatuated. He would have gone with her out of courtesy."

Julie put a hand over hers. "Honey, if you've got a man worth having, there will always be women hanging around. If he's the one for you, if he feels the same way, then he'll come running back. I know it's difficult, but you've just got to have some faith in him to do right by you." It was good advice. She had never had any reason to doubt Dylan's feelings. And if he was as wonderful as she thought, she had nothing to worry about. "And for what it's worth, his eyes don't stray far from you very often."

Kristy smiled easily. "Thank you. Both. I feel better."

Jake and Sarah mingled with the other children, who had board games and even a couple of iPads that were charged through the car batteries. They ran and played and acted like children who might have been on holidays at a park with their family. Kristy watched Sarah closely, ensuring she had enough food to meet her energy requirements.

There were toilets, showers, even a small device that washed clothes. Jacob's wife, Monica, guided people around the setup, sending them inside the convenience store for extra supplies, washing bowls, containers, plates and utensils. On the outskirts, several men sat holding weapons, watching the boundaries for unwanted guests.

As Kristy applied some gauze to a cut on a boy's leg, Callan and Dylan appeared. She gave Dylan a sharp look, but was pleased the woman had disappeared. "We've got a lot to learn from these people," Callan said. "They run an incredible setup."

"My head is spinning," Kristy said. "They've got a million things going on at once. Everybody knows their place."

Jacob appeared with several large torch batteries. He handed two to Callan. "We've had a lot of practice."

"How long did it take you guys to get this organized?" Dylan asked.

"We've been at it for a few weeks, but it helps that several of us were in the army, and such experience builds routine and order into your life. It's all about process, and everyone having a job to do." He chuckled. "We've even got a portable oven, and if the weather cools, and we can find a place to settle, we might bake some bread. We won't give up on our old lives, yet."

They sat around on chairs and at tables, in the back of several SUVs, and ate like kings, comparative to what they'd been fed on of late. Kristy had lamb basted with a sweet sauce, and when she was finished, she almost asked Dylan for his yet uneaten piece. He saw her eyeing it, and when she glanced the other way, he slipped it onto her plate.

"No," she said, "you have to eat yours. It's … amazing."

"Cut me off a forkful. That's enough."

She felt stupid for worrying about the other woman. She loved him, really loved him, and his kindness showed he reciprocated.

Greg found some drinking buddies, and soon there was laughter and a stack of empty bottles that would make a public bar proud. Later, after they had eaten and swapped stories of survival as the rain continued to fall around them, Kristy and Dylan snuck away to the Jeep, Kristy having whispered in Callan's ear that he would need to find accommodation in the van. Greg continued drinking with his new mates, but as they walked casually through the array of tables and chairs, he cast a glance their way and spotted them leaving. Begrudging sadness lined his face. Callan had told him of the sleeping arrangements, and although Kristy felt a stab of guilt, she hoped this would fortify Greg's acceptance of the situation.

They stuffed the front seats full of the supplies and lowered the back seats until a long, flat bed beckoned. Kristy laid out a sheet and two pillows, hopeful their bodies would provide the extra warmth. They crawled in and closed the doors, using their phones to guide them. They were away from the kerosene lamps and torchlights of the central area, finally with the privacy they had sought for the last few days.

Dylan crawled in beside her, and sat with his legs crossed. Kristy pulled off her t-shirt. Dylan didn't move. "Hey. What's wrong?" She drew his chin to her with the tip of her finger, feeling a swell of lust. She leaned forward and kissed him softly on the lips. He drew away with a pained expression.

"What is it? Tell me."

He was silent for a long time. She waited. Finally, he spoke. "We've built this up now. I don't just want it to be good for you; I want it to be *great*. I want you to enjoy it, and smile when you remember it tomorrow, and the next day, and every day afterwards." He leaned forward, and stroked her arm. "This might sound crazy, but I … want to marry you one day. I don't know how that's possible now, but I'll find a way, I promise—if that's what you want. Every moment of every day now I think about you and what I'm doing and how that impacts you, and if I'm not doing the right thing by you, then I might as well not be alive … I don't know whether this," he waved his hand around, "situation has magnified my feelings, or whether deep down I've always burned a candle for you. I know I always thought you were an amazing woman; beautiful and smart and intriguing. I guess I just put you out of my mind because you never went out with a guy like me. I know I'm not like Callan or Greg—tough and strong and full of guts, but I'm trying, I really am." His eyes widened earnestly. "I'm going to be, I promise, I'm going to be braver and fight harder and longer. To keep you safe. Always you. Because if you're not with me every day, if you're not driving, eating, drinking, fighting zombies, and sleeping beside me every single night for the rest of my life, I don't want this life. I don't want it."

Tears spilled down her face. She couldn't see him clearly in the light of her phone, but it didn't matter. He was there, beside her. She could smell him, hear his breathing, and she thought, *I never want to be away from that. Ever.* She didn't know whether it was unprecedented joy, or sheer amazement that another human could love her so much. She reached out and stroked his cheek with her fingertips and she thought, *No person has ever loved another the way I love him at this moment.* She opened her mouth to respond, but the words were not enough to convey the deep, intense feelings. She wiped her eyes and looked up. His face was stern, and she realized he meant every word, that he was going to be tougher. It wasn't what she wanted.

"Never mind about anyone else, Dylan. You're perfect. You know my history, the kind of guys I've thought were 'right' before. I think I went through those periods of my life to be here now, to know what I really needed, for the realization that you, Dylan Robert Cameron, are my soul mate. I can't say it the way you can, with your beautiful words and expressions, but the best way I can say it is to say ditto, right back at you, with every kiss and hug and word and feeling you've felt. Just know I feel the same. A hundred, a thousand, a million percent the same. And if you're asking me to marry you, I'd say yes, in a heartbeat, and unless I spend the rest of my life with you, I don't want that life either." She felt unoriginal, as though she had just repeated everything he had said, but the meaning was the same.

Dylan smiled, and Kristy kissed him again, full and loving, tasting his saltiness on his lips, wanting him on her, and in her. This time, he responded, cupping the back of her head and pulling her toward him, and she felt it now, the love of which he had spoken. The kiss went on, and she drifted into a place of the most sensual feeling, oblivious to the world beyond his lips and tongue, concentrating on the tiny sensations rippling through her, the delight and ecstasy, pushing, pulling, rubbing her hands up the base of his neck, cupping his cheeks in her small hands, taking his bottom lips between hers, sucking his tongue.

They came apart, and she felt giddy. She had never kissed like that. Her heart thumped, and her breathing had escalated.

Gathering herself, Kristy guided Dylan to remove the rest of her underwear. In moments they were naked, exploring each other's skin with their hands and mouths. Kristy had a distant thought about who might be walking past, but she didn't care. They were lost in their own world, hungry for desire they could find in nobody else.

Afterward, they lay on the pillows with the sheet pulled up to their waists, their fingers lying loosely together. Kristy felt like her face was going to split.

"Was I crying out?" she asked, giggling.

Dylan laughed, clapping a hand on her leg. "Ah, yes!"

"Well, it was incredibly good."

"Worth the wait?"

"Worth the wait." And it had been. She had expected Dylan to be shy, that she would have to take the lead, but after the initial stages, he had exerted himself and led the way. Bliss filled her in a bubble.

They rolled over and kissed again as the rain thrummed on the gas station roof, loud enough for them to have to raise their voices.

"I love you," he said.

"I love you too."

And Kristy thought, *it can't possibly get any better than this*.

FIFTY

EVELYN WOKE TO THE sound of thunder. It cracked and rolled across the sky and she turned over, pressing her head deeper into the pillow. She and Jake were allocated the fold-down dinner table in the Norman's camper van, and it was surprisingly comfortable. Better than the stretcher she had stolen from the barracks. She waited for the thunder to die away, then reached out for Jake beside her, but the bed was empty.

She sat up and peered into the darkness. A cold hand gripped her heart. "Jake?" she whispered. Thunder rumbled on, and now she heard the rain drumming on the roof. Another noise sounded in the distance, but she couldn't place it.

As her eyes adjusted, she found the murky shapes of the kitchen sink and the door. She pulled the covers back and swung her legs around, thumping her heels onto the floor. She'd left her phone on the table, and fumbled for it, almost knocking it off. She pressed the circle near the base and it glowed, lighting her way. When she opened the door, the wind took hold of it and almost yanked it from her hand.

She squinted, looking for Jake, her heart beating faster. She remembered Eric telling them the toilet had a blockage, and if they needed to use it, they'd have to go outside until it was fixed. Jake usually woke once a night, and while he was probably outside, she still hadn't sighted him.

Evelyn stepped down and pushed the door closed with both hands. The smell enveloped her, a dank, rotten scent the wind had carried to them from some distant place. She supposed it was going to be like that for some time, the cities and towns full of dead bodies. She held the phone out, realizing how pitiful it was in the pitch-black. She searched the shadows for his shape at the edge of the light. Something moved near a length of bushes. Jake.

She ran across the concrete to him, feeling drops of rain blow in on her arms and face. He swung around as he finished his business. The thunder grumbled again.

"Jesus, Jake, what are you doing?"

"Peeing," he said in a croaky voice.

She hugged him, knocking him off balance, and realized she was probably overreacting, but he was her most precious thing in the world, and the last link to Cameron.

She put an arm around him. "Come on, back to bed."

The thunder groaned, cracking the sky with a flash of lightning. It rolled away, leaving a strange noise that caused her to turn her ear toward to the north. Were they voices? No, barking.

"Did you hear that?"

Jake listened. "I can't hear anything, besides the rain."

"Is that a dog?"

They walked back across the concrete to the van. Evelyn peered out from behind the phone, searching the darkness beyond the service center perimeter, down the exit road, toward the highway. She strained her eyes, watching the shadows. The breeze rippled her hair, blowing tendrils across her face and splattering it with raindrops. *Just the wind.* They reached the van, but as she opened the door and guided Jake up the step, the shadows moved.

It was a dog. Barking. She couldn't recall seeing the blue dog when she'd gotten out of bed. Had he run outside?

She put a hand on his back. "Into bed, quickly."

Evelyn walked closely along the side of the van. Behind her, the door clattered in the wind. She paused at the end, holding her breath to avoid the horrible smell that had blown in, and squinted into the squall.

The barking grew louder. Ahead, a zombie materialized out of the blackness, moving along the road in its stilted shuffle, as if someone was chasing it. Evelyn's stomach dropped. It was forty yards away; still plenty of time to kill it before it reached the camp.

Did she wake the others, or grab one of the guns and finish it herself? Another appeared close behind, and a portentous feeling stirred in her. Suddenly she knew there wasn't going to be only two. The shadows moved again. Evelyn gave a soft cry. There wasn't just one or two, but dozens, working their way up the exit road toward the gas station. The dog appeared from the trees, barking at them, its voice suppressed by another bout of thunder.

"HELP! HELP! ZOMBIES! THEY'RE HERE!"

She ran back to the camper van, banging on the aluminum side as she went. The internal light brightened and the door burst open. Callan stood holding a rifle, topless, wearing only a pair of boxer shorts covered by the Australian flag.

"Zombies," Evelyn said. "Hundreds of them, coming up the road."

"From the north or south?"

"North. From Sydney."

Callan leaped down past her. "Grab Jake and stay in the van."

Other shouts sounded, followed by gunshots from the north. Evelyn leaped up into the van as Greg came bumbling toward the door. He brushed past her, mumbling an apology.

"Jake?"

"Here, Mom."

She found him, and he wrapped his thin arms around her waist. He was trembling, or was it her?

"What is it?" Eric asked, appearing from behind the curtain of the main room. He pulled on a blue dressing gown, the top of his grey, thinning hair sticking up like a cockie's crest.

"Zombies," Evelyn said. "Lots of them."

FIFTY-ONE

"THEY'RE ALL OVER THE place," Gallagher said, limping along the hallway toward the stairs. His pace still caused Klaus to walk faster than normal. "I've been fighting them. Spying. Trying to find out what they're up to."

"How the hell did they escape from the cells? They should have been locked in."

Gallagher grimaced. His eyes were deeply bloodshot, his pocked face covered in salt and pepper stubble. Klaus had never seen a military man in such poor condition. Even Harris had kept shaving after the outbreak.

"It's probably my fault. I haven't checked on them for days."

Klaus suppressed an angry reply. Gallagher had saved him. He owed the man a little respite. "Why didn't you just shoot them?"

"The armory is locked. I had a key, but … I misplaced it."

"What about the shooting range?"

Gallagher frowned. "I didn't think of that."

"You must have been hitting the drink hard."

"I could do with one now."

"That's what caused this issue." Gallagher pressed his lips shut. Klaus knew it was a useless discussion. Gallagher would never admit his problem. For him, it had become a way of life Klaus would never understand.

They passed closed doors and turned corners, taking them away from the sleeping quarters. Klaus was surprised there weren't more zombies. "Do you have any ammunition?"

"A handful of bullets. Probably not enough to get us out of here."

"I had a gun, but somebody stole it from my room."

"Could have been anyone. How long since you used it?"

"I've never used it. I haven't looked at it for months." Gallagher shook his head. "What about help? Is there any possibility of—"

"Help's not coming," Gallagher said.

"What do you mean?"

"I've been monitoring the emergency frequencies for the last few weeks. They've all dropped off. There's nobody left."

"Nobody?"

"They're all gone."

"What about the U.S.?"

Gallagher shook his head again. "There are probably a small number, but no semblance of the former government."

"The U.K.? China?"

"We've lost contact with everybody. As far as this facility knows, we are alone. And the last we heard from them, nobody had anything close to answers about how to handle this thing."

They reached the intersection outside the elevators. On their right, the door to the fire escape staircase beckoned. Gallagher had a hand over his wound, and now he pulled it away. Blood stuck to his palm. "I hope you weren't bullshitting when you said you could help."

"I can," Klaus said as they stepped into the elevator. He explained what his work in the lab had achieved, and his theories about the serum. The elevator descended.

"But you haven't done human trials yet?"

"No, but I'm certain it will work."

"I hope you're right. Otherwise, you're on your own." The elevator stopped, and the doors opened. Gallagher dropped the magazine from the automatic pistol, checking the number of remaining rounds. "Did you see any before you left this level?"

"Only noises."

"They'll be there," Gallagher said, stepping through the opening. "They're everywhere."

Klaus followed, terror overshadowing his desire to test the serum on Gallagher. Nothing was proven until he had human results. After that, if Gallagher was right and the zombies had infiltrated every level of the facility, there was only one option: leave. That suited Klaus too. He needed to find an installation where he could produce it in greater quantities.

They followed the turns of the corridor until they reached a more familiar area, rooms full of expensive-looking equipment. Klaus took the lead, using a shortcut through the supplies area, where they reached a sliding door along the side of the preparation room outside the lab.

He was about to swipe himself in when Gallagher grabbed his shoulder.

"Wait." He guided Klaus backward, away from the glass. "Over there."

Klaus felt a cold hand grip his belly. Standing near the entrance of the preparation room were two class A zombies. "Shit." They stepped away from the door, out of sight.

"We might have to give this place a miss. It's too risky."

"No. *No.* I need that serum. It's our only hope." Klaus turned back to the door. "I'm getting into the laboratory to get that serum. You can either help me, or not."

FIFTY-TWO

CALLAN RUBBED SLEEPY EYES and ran toward the end of the van. He'd been in a deep, peaceful sleep; hadn't slept so soundly since the lake. Evelyn's cries had ripped him back to consciousness with a fright and stung him into action. She had to be wrong, though. Jacob had posted lookouts.

Torch lights poked holes in the darkness. Others had reached the fringes and stood firing into the night. BOOM. BOOM. BANG. People screamed. The rain drummed the roof. Thunder grumbled with menace. Nearby, lightning cracked, flashing like a strobe light, adding to the insanity.

He had thought, for the briefest moment, about the possibility of making the service center a more permanent place of residence, just until they had searched the surrounding region. They could access Holsworthy, the greater Sydney area, and even Canberra from there. It had been a thoughtless idea though.

Blue Boy raced up to him, barking and snapping his teeth. Callan was glad to have him by his side. The mutt had been asleep at his feet on the floor of the camper van, but must have sensed the disturbance and left the vehicle. Callan had developed a strong affection for the dog. It was wily, courageous, and possessed a sixth sense knowing when they needed assistance.

He passed the end of the van and stopped. He whistled the dog back to his side, and it circled, obeying the order. Suddenly they were back at Dylan's parents' property, watching the zombies swarm over the paddocks. This was more concentrated though, like a march, or a protest. Beside a tree at the edge of the gas station, the remnants of a man lay on the ground, his body torn to pieces by feeders. Callan assumed he had been one of the sentries. Perhaps he had fallen asleep.

The first zombies had reached the undercover area; dozens more transformed out of the darkness, fixed on their presence. Engines grumbled to life, throwing beams of bright light toward the horde. There were hundreds: men and women, children, the elderly, all bug-eyed and ambling toward the congregation. Some were naked, their pale skin covered in bloody wounds; others wore the clothes they had died in: nighties, pajamas, jackets, suits, and uniforms.

"Problem with your gun?" Greg asked, arriving at Callan's side. He pulled the trigger of the Remington pump-action and the thing roared. A zombie at twenty yards lost a chunk of its head and dropped to the pavement. Greg fired again.

Callan locked onto a female wearing too much eyeliner, with long, ropey black hair. She might have been a Goth, once. The gun boomed, and the thing collapsed. His shooting had improved, and maybe he had reached his father's high expectations. He fired again and knocked another one down as if to confirm.

But there were more than he could count, tramping through the bush, and up the bitumen roadway. He knew they should flee, but the zombies had already reached some of the vehicles and were attacking people who were either unarmed or responding poorly. Callan felt the deep, intense madness crawling over him, an unrivalled hatred of their existence. An obese male wearing a baseball cap attacked a man from Jacob's group trying to open his door. Inside the car, two little girls in nighties and pigtails screamed, one of them banging against the window.

Callan ran between two bowsers and made an awkward jump-kick at the attacker. A muscle in his groin twanged. The zombie lost its grip and fell to the floor. Callan put the barrel into its mouth and pasted the concrete with red and grey fluid.

"Thank you," the man said. Maurice was his name, Callan recalled. His wife had died a week ago, and he had two young daughters to care for.

"Get out of here. Get your girls safe." The man yanked the door open and jumped into the seat. Callan grabbed the top of the door. "Wait. Did you guys have a rendezvous point?"

"No. Just head to Melbourne."

Callan threw the door shut and tapped twice on the roof.

The first zombies reached the camper van and beat against the sides with heavy fists. Beyond them, dozens more continued their clumsy gait up the road. They were going to be overrun. He realized this might make the numbers back at the property in Albury seem small. Eric stood outside the door with his blue dressing gown open, pumping rounds into the nearest feeders, but he couldn't shoot fast enough despite not missing a shot.

Where were Evelyn and Jake? Dylan and Kristy?

Callan shot several hovering outside the van. Two more converged on Eric. He downed one, but the other beat the gun down and grabbed onto his arm. It pulled his bicep to its mouth and tried to bite him. Callan focused his aim, but a shrieking Julie leaped from the van brandishing a broom and struck the thing across the nose. It released Eric, but turned on Julie, striking out at her. She screamed, lost her balance and fell back against the van. Eric tried to maneuver the gun into position, but another feeder fumbled for him. Two more noticed the open door and disappeared inside the van.

Evelyn. Jake. Screams sounded from behind the van where the Jeep and trailer were parked.

Callan was torn between the two options. Then another body bumped him aside, and Greg staggered past. "I've got the Jeep."

Callan ran for the camper van.

FIFTY-THREE

DYLAN HAD BEEN IN a deep, comfortable sleep when he came awake to the sound of gunfire. It took a few moments to register that he was actually awake. Lights outside the Jeep gave off a faint glow, and he saw Kristy, silent, fragile, asleep. Then he realized something was going on beyond the confines of their little world; something terrible, and dangerous.

The face of a zombie appeared at the window, teeth bared, eyes bulging with prospect. It thumped the glass and Dylan flinched. He could hear shouts, gunshots, and the incessant drum of the rain. What the fuck was going on? He fumbled for a torch as Kristy woke.

"What? What's wrong?"

"Zombies. They're back." He pressed the torch button, blinding them with light, and then swung it around and shone it through the side window.

Others turned toward the light, shuffling at the Jeep. Three more had joined the original one, all feverish for their blood.

Dylan speared the torch around the service center and saw chaos. Dozens, maybe even hundreds of zombies sauntered down the road from the north. The camper van blocked out his vision of the entire gas station, but Dylan saw people running, cars driving away at the south end.

Noise sounded from behind the Jeep. Dylan shone the torch through the rear window. Three zombies were ransacking the trailer. Two scratched at the edges of the tarpaulin, while another had buried itself under a flap, the lower half of its body sticking out.

"We gotta move," he said to Kristy. "You drive."

Kristy scrambled for clothes, then climbed over into the driver's seat and took the keys from the center console. The car hummed into life, the front lights bursting yellow cones ahead. "Oh, Jesus. There's hundreds of them."

"Drive."

"What about the others?"

"We'll get them in a moment."

She shoved the gearstick into place and feathered the accelerator. The car edged forward and bumped the legs of two feeders, knocking them back. They turned around and thumped on the front of the Jeep. A large number of zombies had detected their movement and now headed toward the vehicle in a group.

"*Drive*," Dylan said. "Slam it, babe."

The revs soared; the engine screamed. The Jeep bowled them over like pins, crunching the front and side fender. Dylan waited for the sound of bodies underneath the wheels to end. The vehicle finally sped out from behind the camper van, scattering more feeders as they banged and bumped every side of the vehicle. The trailer clattered as it bounced over those left in their wake.

But the northward exit road was blocked. Hundreds of zombies continued toward the service center, drawn by the noise, and lights, and the smell of human flesh. It was like the drawing of them to his parents' property, only on a larger scale.

Gunfire popped and cracked all around. Kristy yanked on the wheel and turned the Jeep back into the service station area. The headlights blasted aside the darkness, revealing unprecedented mayhem. Some of the cars had already left, screeching from the lot. Many remained, their owners fighting off groups of attacking zombies, and now one careened forward and smashed into the left front end of the Jeep, pinning a zombie between them. Both Dylan and Kristy lurched forward.

"Shit." Kristy slammed the gears into reverse and backed away. The zombie collapsed.

The sudden reversal skewed the trailer sideways though, preventing her from moving further. The other car hurtled past, clipping the Jeep's fender and shattering one of the lights.

"Forward," Dylan yelled. "Drive right through the middle of the station."

She crunched the stick into gear. Another gunshot boomed nearby, and the back window shattered. Three more shots cracked off in quick succession. Kristy accelerated and then Greg appeared, running alongside the car.

"Wait!" Dylan screamed. The car slammed to a halt. "It's Greg."

Countless zombies lumbered toward anything that resembled food. A dark-haired male with a scraggy beard bit into a pipe running from one of the bowsers. Three more had found leftover meat from the BBQ and were fighting over it, one with its mouth locked around another's arm. There must have been six or seven climbing over the trailer. Greg fought his way toward the back door, elbowing and kicking them aside. He shot two in the face and they tumbled backward, knocking others to the concrete

"Get in," Dylan yelled, but Greg was in trouble. A fallen zombie had latched onto his leg. "Shoot it," Dylan screamed. Others pushed at the big man, groping for his arms, neck, and face. Greg swung fists and elbows, connecting with their mushy skulls. He turned the gun around and fired, but there was no blast. *Empty.*

Two more zombies fell on him.

Dylan stared at Kristy grimly. "You leave if we're not inside in one minute. Drive away, okay?" She stared back. Where was a gun? There was a pistol in the back, but he didn't have time. He reached down onto the floor and felt around for one of the other weapons. His hand touched the smooth surface of the tomahawk handle. Dylan clasped it, then pushed hard against the door with his shoulder.

"Hurry," Kristy said.

FIFTY-FOUR

"OKAY," GALLAGHER SAID IN a raspy, tired voice. "We do this together though."

Klaus peered through the corner of the glass door and shuddered. The zombies had torn most of the preparation room apart. Tables had been flipped, tossing their contents into piles. Equipment had been ripped from the cupboards and scattered over the floor. Glass lay shattered over the ground and tables as though somebody had smashed a chandelier. "How many bullets do you have?"

"Enough for this. I'm going around to the front entrance. I'll draw their attention, and you'll run into the lab and get what you need to get." Klaus agreed. "Have you got a timer on your watch?" He did. He had multiple uses for it in the lab, timing various processes to measure their changes. "Give me ten minutes." Gallagher paused, then added, "Listen, I'm sorry for being such an ass of late. I haven't handled this situation well."

The admission softened Klaus. "We've all been under stress. It's understandable."

Gallagher left with an exaggerated limp. Klaus wondered how they would endure, even if they escaped the facility. He was no survivalist, and Gallagher, who had admittedly saved Klaus' life, looked broken. But he had no choice. He wasn't ready to die, and he had made a commitment to himself to produce the serum to save lives.

He counted down his watch from three minutes. Twice, Klaus leaned over and looked in through the door. Both zombies were engaged with something in one of the cupboards underneath a bench. That was good. They were distracted, and far enough away to give him the moment he needed to reach the safety of the lab. Beyond that, he would rely on Gallagher to kill them.

As the timer ended, Klaus thumped his fist against the button on the door. The air pressure released, and it slid open. One of the zombies had worked its way along the lengthy stainless steel bench toward the lab. It looked up and glared at him. He froze, instinct telling him to run back the other way. Gallagher appeared in the opening at the front and shouted for Klaus to go.

He did, running to the middle of the first bench, feeling exposed. He feigned left, then right, but the zombie had locked onto his intent, mirroring his movement. It was too fast. Gunfire sounded from the front of the room, and the remaining glassware on the far wall exploded. It caught the attention of Klaus' attacker, providing him a second. Was it enough? While calculations were a big part of his life, instinct told him it was, and he ran for the lab.

FIFTY-FIVE

GREG STUMBLED PAST CALLAN and disappeared behind the van. Callan ran for the doorway and leaped, landing with a thump inside the camper as the screams started. He struck the wet, heavy body of a zombie and almost fell backward out the door. He threw up a knee, striking it in the groin, and shoved the thing in reverse. It hit the fridge and knocked a pot from the sink onto the floor with a clatter.

"Help!" Evelyn screamed.

The second zombie had its hands around Jake's arm, pulling the boy toward it. Standing on the bed, Evelyn threw punches into its head and neck. The feeder struck out at her and she took the fist directly in the face. Her head jerked back, but she did not flinch or turn away. Callan stepped forward and struck the zombie across the skull with the butt of the pistol. It released the boy and turned on Callan, hissing like a cat.

"Get down," Callan said.

Jake dove onto the bed, and Evelyn rolled on top of him.

Callan swung the pistol up and pressed it against the zombie's big, brutish nose. It reached for him, clawing long fingers over his clothes. Callan pressed the trigger, and the zombie's face disintegrated in a mass of pulpy flesh, splattering red over both walls. It collapsed forward at his feet.

Evelyn pointed behind him. "Look out!"

The second monster grabbed his leg at the calf muscle and leaned forward, mouth open. Callan kicked backward, striking it in the head, then stuck the gun downwards and fired through its ear. The zombie dropped into its own bloody mess.

Evelyn sat on the bed staring up at Callan, Jake wrapped in her arms.

"You alright?"

260

Evelyn nodded, rocking Jake. "Thank you." The image of the zombie punching her in the face replayed, and he was struck with admiration.

Sarah sat atop the bunk beds, clinging to her pillow and sobbing. Callan went to her and put a hand out. She let the pillow fall away and hugged him. She felt small, warm and fragile. He squeezed lightly and made a crooning noise, letting her know that he wouldn't let anything happen to her. "Are you okay?" She nodded, taking her pillow and moving back against the wall.

Sporadic shooting continued outside. Julie fell into the doorway, followed by Eric. Callan offered his hand and helped her up the steps.

Eric leapt into the camper. "We gotta move."

Callan said, "You drive, I'll get rid of these." He dragged the bodies to the step and rolled them out the door, his face straining and the muscles in his back pulling taut

"What about the others? Your sister and boyfriend?"

Zombies gathered in groups across the gas station. The fight had been small compared to the one they were about to face. A dozen or more smelled fresh blood and broke away toward the van. If Callan stepped out there was a good chance he wouldn't make it, but he considered it.

Eric peered out the side window. "I can't see anything but zombies. You can't go out into that."

Evelyn pleaded. "Don't."

"Then keep an eye out for them as we leave." Callan felt guilty saying it.

He pulled the door closed and locked it as the hands and fists beat upon the aluminum. *They might tip us over,* he thought. There were enough of them. "Go, Eric. We have to move."

The van rolled out.

FIFTY-SIX

KRISTY WATCHED WITH SICKENING horror as Dylan slid out of the seat and into the worst zombie attack they had experienced. Worse than Holbrook, worse even than the property back in Albury. If she accelerated the Jeep, she could run half a dozen over. The part of her that had been awakened over the past few days wanted to blow their heads apart—for Sherry, and Howard, for Dylan's parents, and probably her own. She was stuck waiting though, at the mercy of fate, and she thought she might throw up.

Dylan hacked at the zombies attacking Greg. One fell away, and he stuck the tomahawk into its neck, ripping the blade out before it hit the ground. Blood soaked the passenger window. He disappeared from her vision, but the weapon rose and fell in a frenzied burst. A flurry of action followed, zombies ambling toward him, arms out, desperate for flesh. Gore splattered the side of the car. She contemplated getting out to help, but finally, Dylan stood, dragging Greg to his feet. He pulled the back door open, then stepped forward and met the next wave with the same furious intensity.

Greg fell through the doorway into the backseat. In a moment, there would be too many for Dylan to fight alone.

"Get in, Dylan!" Kristy screamed.

For a moment, she saw the outcome—Dylan torn apart by a horde of zombies scratching and clawing at his flesh, or she would have to exit the vehicle and drag him free. But she shook it off as he dispatched another, then leaped inside and joined Greg in the back.

"Go!"

Kristy took off, feeling a heavy weight drag on the back of the Jeep. In the rearview mirror, she saw them covering most of the trailer.

"Just go," Dylan said. "They'll fall off."

"What about the others?"

On their left, the camper moved. Kristy accelerated, turning sharply to avoid other cars streaking through the area as zombies slapped desperately on the outside. The van had circled and now followed them along the perimeter of the station in a southerly direction. Several zombies hung on the front of the camper. One leaped up onto Eric's window. He stuck a pistol through the opening and blew its head off, his face cold and stern. The other feeders clinging to the vehicle dropped and rolled underneath, sending the vehicle into a dance. Another wandered in front of the Jeep and Kristy hit it with the corner of the fender, producing a heavy thwack.

"Keep going."

She guided the Jeep and trailer past the last bowser, the camper following, including several other cars that had escaped. They were going to make it. She just hoped Callan was in the van. The green numbers on the dashboard clock read 3:18 a.m.

Rain pelted the windscreen as one remaining headlight guided their way. Passing the last few drifting zombies, Kristy lost control of her anger and swerved to strike a dirty straggler, sending it sprawling into the bushes with a thud.

They hit the highway and drove south in the wrong direction until they reached the first crossover. They switched to the other side of the highway through a layer of rainwater, and continued on south. Callan stuck a hand out of the broken window to indicate he was okay, and with that, Kristy relaxed.

The head and taillights of other cars dotted the long road ahead. Kristy wondered how many had safely escaped, and felt a pang of guilt for those they had left behind. A week ago, she would have fought to save every life. Now, she had come to the realization that in this new world, people would die for the sake of others. It was random, pot luck, and there might be a time when her luck would run out.

Fifteen minutes later, as the rain stopped, the camper van pulled over onto the soggy highway shoulder. Callan stepped out into the shadowy night, and the others joined him, looking back along the roadway for more approaching vehicles. A handful of twin headlights were spread out in the distance.

"You guys okay?" Callan asked. From the camper van, torchlight pried aside the darkness, bouncing toward them. Eric and Evelyn appeared.

"Yeah. We're okay," Kristy said. "You?"

"We're fine. All safe. Somehow."

Evelyn gave a thin smile. "Jake and I have Callan to thank."

Callan said, "We got lucky. Where were the sentries they posted? And why did you guys take so long at the Jeep?"

Kristy started to speak. "Hang—"

"I fell," Greg said. "Had—"

Callan put his hands up. "You fell? Is that because you're pissed again? Fuck, man, you're gonna get yourself killed if you keep drinking that shit all the time."

"Okay, okay," Eric stepped into the middle of the huddle. "Let's just take a moment. It's been a shitty night, no question about it. But we're all here, aren't we?"

"That's not the point," Callan argued. "All it takes is one slip up, one mistake, and we'll end up like Johnny, or …" He turned away.

"You're right," Kristy said. "We have to be more careful. All of us."

Evelyn pressed both hands to her face. "I'm sorry. I should have shut the door after Julie went to help Eric."

Callan turned back. "We just need to be thinking all the time. We drop our guard and we'll die."

A car approached from the north and tooted its horn as it passed. Eric waved, indicating they were alright.

"As for where we go next," Callan continued. "I've been thinking about it, and I think we should head to the base in Canberra."

"What?" Dylan asked. "Canberra? What about Melbourne? I thought the others were all heading down to Melbourne."

"I think the Joint Command Centre is our best chance to find someone who knows what the fuck is going on. If anyone's there, they can help us."

"You know what," Eric said, "maybe it's worth a shot."

Dylan ran a hand through his hair. "Do you know how many dead people there'll be in Canberra? It'll make Albury seem like a picnic. How many army bases are you going to have us check before we realize they're all gone?"

"You think Melbourne's gonna be any better? And what do we do when we get there?"

"We go to Tasmania. Exactly what my old man was planning. It's the most liveable, self-contained place in Australia. We get there, we've got a chance."

"And how the fuck are we gonna get there? Can you fly a plane? Or drive a boat? I'm sick of driving around this fucking place. Tasmania is a long way. What if the base in Canberra is operational? It's too close not to try."

"It'll be just like the barracks in Wagga."

"Aren't you sick of driving?"

"Yeah, I am, but every time we stop, we get into trouble."

"When we find the right place, we'll be able to stop for good."

"Let's put it to a vote," Dylan said. "Hands up for who wants to keep on going to Melbourne?"

Kristy felt a stab of guilt. Either way she would lose: supporting her boyfriend and failing her brother, or viva versa. She raised her hand, along with Dylan, but they were the only two votes for Melbourne.

Eric gave an apologetic look. "I think Canberra is worth a shot."

"Fine," Dylan said, and walked back to the Jeep.

Kristy didn't know whether to stay or go.

Callan said, "I might ride in the van, try and get some sleep, if that's okay, Eric?"

"Sure."

Kristy felt like the group had fractured. "We'll follow you guys then."

On their right, from the south, a vehicle approached, yellow cones broadcasting the wet road in greasy light. They all stopped to watch it, a dark SUV that slowed as it drew opposite.

"Is that one of theirs?" Kristy asked.

It drove on, though. Callan started for the van. "They won't find anything that way."

They parted, and Kristy returned to the Jeep with Greg. Dylan was already in the front seat.

"I'm proud of you for fighting in what you believed in," she said as she pulled the driver's door shut. "You wouldn't have done that a week ago. You would have just kept quiet."

"Maybe." Dylan stared out the window. "Didn't do me much good though."

"Sometimes you have to go with the majority."

"Yeah. Try and get some sleep. It's more than two hours to Canberra. I'll drive for an hour and then we can swap."

This wasn't how Kristy had wanted to end the night. By the time they reached Canberra, it would be morning. She had imagined waking beside Dylan, curled up in his arms, discussing their relationship, and their future. She supposed that ideal had left them now; they might never have it again. At least they were all still alive, and had shared a night that had exceeded her expectations. They had reached a new level of the relationship. In some ways, it was strange, given they had really only been together for less than a week, but their friendship had been building long before that, and she knew it was the basis for any strong association. Besides, in the new world, under life and death scenarios every day, feelings were more intense.

FIFTY-SEVEN

CALLAN HAD ONLY MANAGED an hour of shuteye, despite his build-up of sleep deprivation over the last week. The window over the sink had been smashed during their escape, and they'd taped pieces of cardboard over the hole, but the wind whistled through the cracks. As the first threads of light seeped in through the mess of clouds, he lay on the bottom bunk thinking about what had happened, and what lay ahead. He only got to the first thought—the argument about where to go next, when he felt weight drop onto the end of the bed.

Evelyn smiled. "Hi."

"Hi."

"You're not sleeping?"

"No." He didn't yet know if he could be bothered talking. Sometimes he liked to sift through his thoughts in silence. Sherry had never been one to listen to his problems, probably because she had so many of her own. Occasionally, he would mention something that was bothering him, and she would comment, but mostly, he had learned to internalize them.

"I wanted to say thank you again ... for saving Jake, and me." She laughed a little. "We haven't had someone come to our rescue like that ... in a while."

With the light at her back, it was difficult to perceive her face. He had acknowledged early on, albeit briefly, a similarity to Sherry, but now the silhouette of her hair and the way she sat made him feel it more acutely. It was both pleasant and saddening.

"No big deal."

"What is it?"

"What do you mean?"

"You're looking at me funny." She turned her head and brushed her hair down, briefly highlighting her face. "Have I got something hanging off my nose?"

Callan chuckled. "No." He closed his eyes and then, before he could stop, the words came out. "You look like someone … that's all."

"Oh. Is that good, or bad?"

"Neither. It is what it is." He gave a pained smile. He had to change the subject. "You agreed with me about going to Canberra?"

"I didn't really care, but I felt obligated to support you because you saved us."

Callan liked her honesty. Such had initially drawn him to Sherry, although her frankness had turned out to be mostly pointed. "Fair enough." He wondered what collateral damage she had suffered. "I think it's our best chance of safety and ongoing survival. I'm not prepared to lose anybody else, even if we don't know each other that well, so wherever we go needs careful consideration."

"That's admirable. And yes, I lost my parents."

"I'm sorry to hear that. What about …"

She lifted her hand and looked at her wedding ring. "He died a while before this. Thankfully. Although, if he'd been here …"

"He's lucky he's not. You're not lucky he's not though. I get that."

She hesitated. "You lost someone close, too?"

He nodded. And he would probably lose some more. "Of course. I don't imagine you'd find anyone that hasn't lost someone close."

"How do you deal with it?"

How had he dealt with it? "I don't, really. I'm still numb from Sherry's death. If I stop and think, really think about it, I won't be able to function anymore. Besides, there hasn't been enough downtime. We have to keep going." He rubbed his eyes. "Dylan's in the same boat. He lost his mom and dad within two days. But then I suppose you might be the same. How did you deal with it?"

"I tried to hold it in, but I cried for a long time. In the end, I felt better."

Maybe that was his problem. Maybe he needed to let it all out. He doubted that was possible. He hadn't shed real tears since he was twelve, when his father had accidentally run over his cat in the driveway. It had been sick, dying from kidney disease, but he had tried to hit his father with a cricket bat as tears streamed down his face.

"Anyway, for now, there's no time to grieve. We'll probably all be dead soon, anyway." He swung his feet off the bed.

"That's a bit cynical, isn't it?"

"It's the truth," he said, standing. "And yeah, I've probably become more cynical in the last week."

Evelyn smiled as he walked away.

Eric guided the camper van around the long, arching corners of the Hume. The first light of day appeared over the low, shadowy mountains to the east. Trees and bushes along the roadside grew gnarled and flaky features. The stretch of the headlights slowly retreated back to the Jeep.

"How far from Canberra?" Callan asked. He slumped down in the seat behind Eric.

"'Bout forty minutes."

It couldn't come quickly enough for him. He needed to know if there was anything in Canberra. He was over driving in cars, and vans, over the smell of exhaust fumes and gasoline. He just wanted to stop, and rest, to find a place to call home for more than a few days. He wanted to sit and think about everything that had happened, and work through his own shit. He didn't know how it would turn out on the other side, but he had to deal with it. Evelyn was right, although he wouldn't admit that to her.

FIFTY-EIGHT

THEY REACHED THE OUTSKIRTS of Canberra with the sun a blazing eye in the eastern sky, promising another day of dry, burning heat. Back in her old life, Evelyn would have risen early, packed a swimming bag, and taken Jake to her parents' house, where they would have relaxed on lounges under a shaded awning and swum in the clear waters of the pool for most of the day. At dinnertime, despite her protests, her mother would have insisted they stay, and the four of them would have eaten cold roast chicken, potato salad, and coleslaw out on the deck by the water. And while that would never, ever happen again, the memory was strong and enjoyable, and her heart ached.

Eric explained that they wouldn't actually drive right into Canberra, that the base was nine miles to the east of the city. Still, it was heavily populated, and the signs of a major destructive event were everywhere, even if the main road was clear.

They went right onto the Federal Highway, which would take them around the edge of the city, but a pile-up of trucks and cars had blocked the road, and Eric was forced to turn right into Phillip Avenue.

The streets were full of abandoned vehicles, some smashed beyond repair, others with thin threads of rising smoke. The van weaved in and out of their empty carcasses, glass and plastic popping beneath the tires. The first zombies appeared in fragmented lots: ones and twos, picking through the waste, bottoms sticking out of cars. Individuals wandered in the snarling gardens of empty houses, perhaps the owners, or neighbors, who had once celebrated Christmas around a portable barbecue in the street with their friends.

Evelyn recalled walking away from her parents' house. They had a cat, a beautiful brown Burmese named Elsa, and Evelyn knew she couldn't take it with them. She had filled several large buckets with water, and emptied the remaining dry food into three bowls, placing them in different locations around the property. It had been an emotional affair, knowing she would never again pull into the driveway and meet her mother on the front veranda. She had cleaned the house, putting everything in place as though they might return from vacation in a week, and took only what they needed. The tears had come as she had locked the front door, and hadn't stopped for some hours afterwards.

At one stage, she didn't think Eric's van was going to make it. A similarly large vehicle lay halfway across the street, flanked by an overturned SUV. Eric tried to take the opposite gutter, but another car had smashed into a power pole and knocked it to the ground where it lay, half-suspended at a point where the van couldn't drive over it.

"I'll move it," Callan said. "Greg and Dylan will help me."

"No," Eric said. "Stay inside. I can get us over it."

Evelyn had to admit Callan's bravery. He was tough and strong; manly, her mother would have called him. And handsome. She had not thought about a man in that way since … forever. Since before her husband. She recalled their earlier conversation, the bitterness and baggage he carried. He had a long way to go in getting over that.

The odd zombie picked at the clutter along the street, nothing they hadn't dispatched easily before, but Eric persisted, and eventually the SUV slid along on its roof and the van pushed it aside. The road cleared briefly and sloped upwards to a rise. It grew congested again, narrowing until the camper's flanks scraped along the side of a bus. As they drove a thin gap through the congestion, the rise peaked, and what they saw on the descent turned Evelyn's stomach. Eric stopped the van thirty yards short. She turned Jake away, called Sarah over, and made them sit on the lower bunk facing the other way, reading a book.

A sea of feeding zombies covered the width of the road for a hundred yards ahead. Amongst them, a bus had overturned, or the zombies had turned it over, littering bodies across the bitumen. Two motorbikes lay on their sides, and Evelyn had a flash of understanding as to what might have occurred. Hundreds of them fed on the dead, holding a body part or chunk of flesh, the grisly remains coating their hands and faces in blood. The odd pair or group scrapped and fought over food. The thought of getting past was terrifying. If the mob all decided to attack the van, they'd have no hope.

Eric checked the side mirrors. "It's gonna be a jam going backward."

"You can't," Callan said. "Keep going. Full speed ahead. This thing will run them down."

"Are you mad?" Julie asked. "We can't go through that."

Eric said, "We copped some heavy damage last night. Any more, and we'll begin to lose lights and God knows what else."

Callan wore a tight frown. "We've got no choice." He took a rifle from the bench and stood by the door.

Eric sat there a long moment, watching the scene. "Okay. You're right. I'm just going to ease my way through." Evelyn felt a nervous tension sweep through them. "Hold on, folks."

Julie stood from the front seat and sat at the kitchen table. "This is ridiculous."

Evelyn spoke to Jake. "Grab onto something, hon." He curled his hand around the thin bar atop the bunk that prevented the user from rolling off. She couldn't believe they were going to attempt it.

The hood of the van reached the first zombies. Eric braked, and even so close, they didn't take much notice. They were too busy feeding, or watching others with impassive faces. The occasional dead searched through the carnage for more nourishment. None of the handful at the front noticed as Eric nudged them apart, separating the five directly in their path. A short female struck out at a bald male chewing on a chunk of flesh. He fell onto another, and they both collapsed onto the road. Others moved aside, interested by the commotion. The female dove onto the fallen man, and several more joined her.

The van pushed through slowly, separating the mob. Eric's white knuckles gripped the wheel, and his face was a taut mask of apprehension. Numerous feeders turned on their comrades as though they had been the ones pushing them.

Evelyn saw a ripple of nervous energy pass through the throng, as though at any moment they might turn into a crazed mob. The slope descended, and she found herself adjusting her stance to accommodate the descent. Ahead, the crowd crammed into the van's pathway.

Callan spoke softly. "Keep going."

The vehicle moved into the center of the gathering. The sound of hands and bodies touching the back of the van echoed through the walls like branches on a narrow bush track. Evelyn held her breath, reaching out for Jake. They had about seventy yards to make it to the other side.

Eric guided the van at such a slow pace that it almost helped the zombies aside. "It's working," Julie said in a shaky voice.

"How's the Jeep going?" Eric asked. "We might be provoking them. They might turn on the others."

Callan left the door and hurried to the back window. Evelyn followed.

Several of them were showing interest in the Jeep and trailer, touching the hood and the sides of the vehicle as it slithered past. A tall, lean zombie— Evelyn was unsure if it was a man or a woman—struck the passenger window, causing Kristy to jump. Dylan said something to her, and kept both hands tight on the wheel.

"He's a cool cat," Evelyn said, feeling her heart beat faster.

She had only known these people a day or two, but already she felt a connection. Maybe it was that they had saved her life, or the way Eric and Julie doted over Jake, like his grandparents had once done, or perhaps, it was the man standing beside her. Either way, their safety was important to her.

Evelyn waited for something to happen. More zombies had noticed the black Jeep, and its cargo, clapping on the sides and roof with their clumsy hands. One tried to climb onto the trailer and fell off the back, where it turned slowly onto all fours. Several collapsed onto it, and the thing thrashed beneath their desperate attack. Her stomach folded again.

"So they just eat each other? That's their existence?"

"These types, anyway, as far as we can tell. They eat and eat and when they run out of food they find more. When this shit is gone, they'll move on."

Another zombie climbed onto the trailer. Dylan slowed the Jeep, but it didn't fall off.

"Don't do that," Callan said under his breath.

Others climbed onto the hood and stepped along the side of the vehicle. Suddenly there were five hanging off the body, and three in the trailer.

"*Shit.*" Callan slid open the back window.

"We're just about through," Eric called out.

Dylan took off with a lurch. Three dropped off the car, and one tumbled from the trailer. Two still clung to the windscreen and hood though.

Callan rested the rifle on the window ledge. Kristy's eyes grew large, and Dylan waved his hands, indicating Callan shouldn't take the shot.

"Too late." Callan's right eye squeezed to a slit behind the site.

The throng began to move. More zombies had turned to investigate the movement. Others were attacking the trailer with weak hands and slow feet. The pack was growing restless though, and those in the immediate vicinity were interested.

"Block your ears and step back," Callan said.

Evelyn repeated the message to the others and stood back from the window with both hands cupped over her ears. The rifle jerked in Callan's strong hands, and the blast filled her ears with discomfort.

A zombie crawling over the hood jerked sideways and fell onto the bitumen with a clunk. The others crashed onto it, desperate for its scant remains, and it disappeared beneath the feet of the mob. Callan shot the second feeder hanging off Dylan's window, and the scene repeated. And then they were through, chugging slowly away.

She watched him step back from the window and lay his gun on the bed. He slid the window shut, and the stench receded. *He knows what to do,* she thought. He was a natural leader, taking over when required. *I trust his judgment, the way I trusted Cameron.* She had never thought she would say such a thing again, and in many ways, she suddenly realized, Callan and Cameron were similar. Except Callan was brasher, rougher, less refined. Maybe that's what it took to survive in the new world.

Through the rear window, beyond the Jeep and trailer, several zombies followed them. Another one joined the train in its slow, brainless gait, and then another. She turned away, feeling safer as the van picked up speed.

FIFTY-NINE

KLAUS HAD HALF A room's length on the zombie. He slid over the floor like an ice skater as he reached the end of the bench. His right foot hit the skirting board, realigning his balance, and he ran straight along the glass wall of the laboratory toward the wide air-lock door.

The thing was coming fast, knocking steel benches aside. Wild hands smashed the remaining items onto the floor. More gunfire sounded, and Klaus saw Gallagher wrestling with the other zombie. Each had arms locked around the other, and there was no sign of the gun. *He's dead*, Klaus thought. *I'm going to be alone.*

He reached the door. Surprisingly stiff fingers poked the numbers of his six-digit code into the keypad. The door slid opened with a *kshhhh* sound, and Klaus leaped in. Normally, the door would self-close in three seconds, but he didn't think he had that long. He reached for the red override button on the other wall with painful slowness.

Something knocked his foot, tripping him, and he lost balance, stumbling to the floor. He turned, expecting to find the zombie, but his lab boots glared back at him as though he ought to be more careful next time.

Klaus reached up for the red button, but stopped at the sound of the door closing behind him. Relief washed over him. He would make it, even if Gallagher might not.

A weight dropped on his back. He screamed. Hot breath touched his ear, and a low growl chilled his skin. One arm was pinned, and he was powerless to the strength of its grip on his shoulders as it rammed his head into the hard floor. The airlock beeped a warning, signifying an obstruction was preventing it from closing.

Klaus' free arm swung wildly, and knocked something on the floor. His boots. He'd left them in the airlock earlier. The standard-issue boots were lined with steel as part of the

276

government's tightened occupational health and safety laws. Straining, Klaus reached around and groped for them.

He felt a cold, sharp pain on the back of his neck, and then heat spread through his shoulders. Had he been bitten? *Yes.* Terror flooded him and instinct took over, his hand pawing for the boots. His fingers seized the laces, scratched for the ankle support, and finally he had a firm grip. Klaus swung the boot around, striking the zombie in the side of the head. His aim had been for the ear, knowing they still required balance. The zombie tottered, then fell backward toward the doorway and onto Klaus' left leg.

Klaus realized he was screaming. He had to get inside the safety of the lab. He kicked out with his right leg, the heel of his shoe smashing the zombie's face. It fell backward off his left leg, but immediately roused despite a bloody nose.

With both legs, Klaus drove it backward through the doorway. The glass closed another half foot, but the zombie clutched onto the frame, jamming its upper body in the gap. For the sake of his life, he had to get the zombie out of the doorway. Klaus scrambled on shaky legs, a wave of giddiness threatening to knock him back down. The zombie had moved onto all fours, its face covered in Klaus' own blood. He *had* been bitten. A day ago it would have meant death, but he had the serum as long as he survived this.

The zombie climbed onto its knees. Klaus kicked at its face, but it batted his leg away like a thin tree branch. There was only one way; he would have to shove it backward.

Klaus dove forward, pushing with his scrawny scientist arms, straining until he thought he would burst. It thrashed about, fighting to stand, but he shoved with all his weight. It was too strong though; his feet were sliding backward over the hard floor. Klaus grunted, his thighs straining. He felt the momentum change, but then it turned its head and bit into his wrist, blood spewing from the edges of its mouth.

Klaus screeched and shoved it with his free hand. The thing overbalanced and fell backward, but still had hold of his wrist in its mouth. Klaus went with it. The door closed further, and Klaus stuck a foot backward, blocking its closure. With his other hand, Klaus jammed his thumb into the zombie's right eyeball. It released him and Klaus fell back through the doorway. It hissed shut.

He sat momentarily, staring at the zombie's hideous, angry face, wondering what it was thinking. Finally, he stood, opened the door to the lab, and stepped inside, glancing back to where he had last seen Gallagher. Both he and the second zombie were gone.

SIXTY

THE GROUP DROVE THE final stages to the base down a wide, flat road, with fenced paddocks stretching to the distant hills on either side. It appeared the military had secured most of the land within several miles, probably to restrict people from the base. They pulled up in front of a double gate made of heavy wire and thick steel poles. An empty gatehouse sat to one side like a remnant from an age past. A tall cyclone fence topped with rolled barbed wire ran in both directions as far as they could see. Long grass waved in the breeze, and on it floated the subtle scent of the countryside.

"Let's take a look," Eric said.

Callan opened the side door and they stepped down onto the dust-swept bitumen. The others swung out of the Jeep and joined them. Blue Boy ran straight to Callan, tongue rolling from his mouth. He squatted and scratched the dog behind its ear until it produced a low, pleasurable groaning noise.

Eric shielded his eyes to the glare of the bright, cloudy sky. "Looks empty. These things usually have guards posted, or Jeeps buzzing around. I can't see a vehicle anywhere."

Dylan strolled toward the fence. "Nothing. Not even zombies."

"It certainly doesn't look like anybody is there," Callan said.

What now? Callan wondered. He had insisted they come here, when the rest of Jacob's group had probably gone to Melbourne. He had almost regretted it driving through the sea of zombies. Now they were here, he needed to take the lead and make some decisions. Was this place a fortress? Could they rest up a few days before moving on? Perhaps they should investigate. What were the chances of zombies having penetrated such a strong fence?

"I say we—"

Evelyn pointed toward a narrow strip of building between two tall rooftops. "Look."

A person had appeared from one of the structures and was walking toward them. He moved slowly, and as he drew closer, it was obvious something was wrong. He was limping.

Greg had the gun at his side. "Say the word."

"Wait," Callan said.

At a hundred feet, the man raised his hands, palms facing them, and shouted, "I'm not armed."

He stood about six feet tall, with cropped grey hair, but as he drew closer, they saw his t-shirt and green army pants were covered in blood. Strength rippled through his muscly arms and barrel chest, but his posture and gait told them he had fought to be standing before them now. As he got to within fifteen yards, he spotted Greg's gun, but didn't slow his approach. With a shaky voice, he asked, "Can you help me?" The man gathered himself, taking a deep breath, and wiped blood off his cheek. "There's another man inside the base. A scientist. He's trapped, and I can't get him out alone. There's nobody else."

Callan suddenly felt uneasy, but took a step forward. There was nobody left on the whole base? That sounded absurd. Maybe it was a trap. "Nobody?"

"No. They're all dead."

Eric stepped closer. "What's in there?"

"If you've survived this long, you'll know what's out there. The same things are inside this facility, only worse." He approached the fence. There was more to the limp as his heavy boots clomped over the tarred area behind the gate. His eyes were bloodshot, and there were long, dark bags underneath. It was a more common look for the times, but there was something else he couldn't place. "We had a number of the infected in this facility, including the more aggressive types. But some of them got free. I don't know how we've survived, to be honest. Klaus has been stuck in his lab most of the time. I guess I'm just lucky."

Callan repressed his questions. There was an urgency about the man that belied his skepticism.

Eric asked, "What do you need from us?"

The man curled his fingers around the chain-link fence for support. "I don't care so much about myself, but we need to get him out." He wiped blood from a nick on his forehead. His chiseled jaw flexed, his cheeks pocked with scars from teenage acne. Dylan marveled that he looked tougher up close, but there was also a weariness in his posture.

"He's a scientist, and he's been working on a … serum of some kind, to stop this thing. It might save a life." He seemed to consider what else to say. "I can't leave him in there, and he may be the last hope any of us have got."

Callan said, "A serum—"

"If we can save him, he'll explain it all. The last time I saw him he had just about made it into his laboratory, He'll be safe in there, but the infected are waiting outside for him. I shot one, but ran out of bullets, and it wasn't dead. He was attacked, but I managed to make it inside, to safety. I can't save him on my own though. I need your help—guns, bullets." He squinted, and the last of his energy ran out of his expression. "I've got nothing left, and if I try to make it elsewhere in that facility, I'll die, and so will Klaus."

The notion of a serum of some kind interested Callan. It was part of what they had been seeking. Could it be a trap though? Could he want something from them, other than their help? The thought faded. He wasn't that pessimistic about the human race yet, despite the likes of Steve Palmer. This man had been through a battle. Still, would any of his group be prepared to fight again?

"I'm not sure we can." Callan glanced around at the others. "We've suffered enough casualties. I hear you, and I'm sure we all want to help, but … it's risky." The man nodded, understanding. Callan called the others together with their backs turned to the man. "What do you think?"

Greg shifted in place. "I say we help."

Dylan sighed. "Me too." Maybe they were right. Helping others was the way of the world now; perhaps that was the new currency of life. Dylan continued, "If what the man said is true, there's even greater incentive than saving lives."

"I wouldn't bank on that," Callan said. "He could just be saying that to get our help."

"Either way," Greg argued, "the three of us should go with him and see what it's all about. We can always come back if it's too risky."

"Hang on," Kristy said. "I'm a doctor. Shouldn't I go, in case he needs medical attention?"

Callan shook his head. "Uh-uh. We need you to stay here. You're too important to the group." Kristy opened her mouth to respond, but closed it. She knew Callan was right. A doctor in this world would be a rare thing. Callan turned to Eric. "And as the patriarch, you won't mind staying back here, too?"

Eric smiled. "Sure. We'll have the Jeep and van ready to go."

They gave their decision to the man, and loaded up on guns and ammunition, sticking pistols into their waistbands, loading rounds into the chambers like men who had been fighting for years. Callan supposed their experiences over the last week probably meant more than what most recreational shooters faced over a long period.

Callan called Blue Boy back to the car, but the dog wouldn't move.

"Maybe we should just let him come along?" Greg asked.

"No. He has to stay here." Callan walked back to the dog sitting patiently in the middle of the road. He picked it up in his arms, carried him back to the Jeep, and lowered him through the back window. "Stay here, boy. I don't want anything to happen to you. I'll be back soon." Blue whined, and pressed his ears back. Callan scratched his head once more, then closed the back flap. The dog barked as he walked away.

Kristy and Dylan embraced. This time, Callan didn't turn away, as he had done in past days. He was happy for them. He knew love could be transient, broken apart in seconds. Dylan was a good man, someone Callan would be happy to have as his brother-in law. He glanced at Evelyn, who was watching him with a somber expression, but she gave a faint smile, which Callan reciprocated, then turned away.

"Take care," Kristy said. "Hurry back. If it's too crazy in there, just leave."

They passed through a cut in the wire fence, and as Callan drew close to the man, he smelt a familiar odor. He turned to Greg, who nodded knowingly. Booze. That explained the bloodshot eyes and sallow face. They walked in a line, guns ready, Callan at Gallagher's side.

"What's your name?"

"Gallagher."

"You're in the Army?"

"Navy. Was."

"You don't look so good."

"I don't feel it."

A wide paddock led to a low structure, spread over a thousand square feet. Wispy yellow grass tickled their knees. The place had been neglected of late, but that was no surprise. The world was going to end up a mess of long grass and snarling gardens before men had organized themselves enough to clean it up again.

"So this is like the defense force headquarters?"

"Was."

"How many of you are really left?"

"Just the two of us."

Gallagher led them through a single steel door into a foyer. A passageway straight ahead took them to a more open area with elevators. They climbed in, the three newcomers watchful of their surroundings. Callan waited for zombies to stagger out of doorways from darkened rooms. The silence, in contrast to all they had experienced over the last few days, was eerie. He held the rifle so he could lift and fire it in a heartbeat.

The elevator ride took thirty seconds. Following Gallagher, they stepped out of the carriage and into a hallway. The decor was different on the lower level: clean, new, like a laboratory or a hospital. On the surface, the place was old, beaten, much like the outside, but it was a different world deep beneath the earth.

"Why couldn't you live here?" Callan asked.

"It's overrun. Infested. They're everywhere." Gallagher stopped them at an intersection. "Truth is though, we don't know how many, exactly."

"What is this place? Really?" Dylan asked.

Gallagher considered the question. "It's where the top brass of the Australian Defence force and their families are supposed to go in a crisis. Where they were supposed to be safe."

"So where are they all?"

"Many of them got claustrophobic and left. Others, whose families struggled, took them and headed for the far reaches of the country. Problem was that some guru decided to bring the infected back here for testing. Some of them escaped." He narrowed his eyes. "Are you sure you guys can handle this?"

Callan raised his eyebrows and glanced at the others. "I'm sure."

They walked down a long hallway with doors on both sides. Some led to open, lighted rooms; others were dark and closed. The passage took them through several security doors, down two sets of short stairs, and through a multitude of left and right turns.

"Jesus, don't leave me to find my own way out," Callan said.

Gallagher grunted. "Stay alert. We're getting close."

They made several more turns, then entered a locked door and reached another corridor. Gallagher explained the orientation of the preparation room and the laboratory.

Callan felt the tension rising. He kept expecting a zombie to slither out of a dark doorway and attack.

Gallagher stopped suddenly and put a hand up. He crouched and pointed to the next lot of windows along the corridor. They squatted and shuffled along like ducks until they were beneath the windows, then peered up and over the ledge. Before them was a large, lighted room filled with long stainless steel benches. At the far end, a heavy door led to another room. Two zombies waited outside, one pacing back and forth. They were type threes, as Callan had suspected.

"This is the prep room," Gallagher said. "Klaus is in the lab, which is through the air-lock." They observed for several moments. "What do you think?"

Callan thought they should keep it simple. "We're just gonna walk in there and shoot them both, the way we always do." Greg and Dylan nodded. "Any other ideas?"

"No, but just be careful. These things are super quick and smart."

Greg shuffled to the front with the rifle in firing position and led them to the door. Callan felt a flicker of pride at how far they'd come. Here was a military person enlisting *their* help to rescue somebody. Callan was glad Greg had recovered. He felt stronger with the big man at their side. Greg pumped a round into the rifle chamber, and Callan did the same.

The zombies turned the moment Greg stepped through the doorway. The closest one flew at them, covering the distance in seconds, crashing past the nearest table and spinning it sideways. Greg fired first with a booming report, filling the room with heavy, painful noise. The opening shot took the zombie in the throat, jerking its head backward. As the other guns roared, more holes appeared in its head and torso, sending threads of blood and flesh in all directions. It fell against a long table, smashing its head with a thud and rolling to the floor. The second zombie caught several bullets in the crossfire, but ducked low, using the benches for cover. Bullets pinged off the stainless steel tops. Greg moved forward, exposing himself, and put two shots into its head at close range, splattering the tiles in dirty red matter. The thing slumped to the floor.

Silence rushed in, and clouds of gun smoke hung in the air.

"Dead," Callan said with satisfaction.

Gallagher prodded the first body with his foot. "Don't let that fool you. These bastards are—"

From somewhere, deeper inside the bowels of the facility, came a deep, primal scream. They all froze, listening as it rang out.

"If you had to estimate, how many would you say there are down here?" Dylan asked.

Gallagher coughed, grimacing. "We don't know, really. How many people were down here when the virus started? A hundred. Two. Five? Klaus might be able to tell you more. We captured the class A, and that was the stupidest thing we could have done. Once they escaped, there was no stopping them."

Through the air-lock doors, they saw a man with a long, white lab coat, flowing blonde hair, and thin-rimmed glasses standing in the room beyond. He stepped through the opening into the preparation room with a grim expression.

Gallagher gave a curt nod. "Good to see you're still alive."

Klaus scoffed. "I thought you'd left me for dead."

"I went looking for more ammunition. I thought there might have been some in one of the facility rooms upstairs. Then I saw these guys approaching on one of the CCTV screens. Thankfully, those were still working."

Klaus nodded at the boys. "Thank you, gentlemen."

Callan nodded back. "Gallagher tells us you've been working on some sort of medicine for this thing?"

"Yes," Klaus said. "Speaking of that," he looked at Gallagher, "I need to get some of it into you."

"You're bitten?" Callan asked Gallagher.

He nodded.

286

"We both are," Klaus said. He explained what had happened. "So we will be the first human trials."

Neither Dylan nor Greg seemed concerned. Callan felt uneasy about having two infected men with them. Or was it that Johnny had missed out on the opportunity that these men would receive?

Another long, angry cry sounded from far away. They watched the door, imagining the horrors beyond. Callan didn't want to be there when whatever it was making that noise arrived. "Maybe we should get moving."

"I was just thinking the same thing," Klaus said. "As soon as we administer the drug."

SIXTY-ONE

EVELYN GAZED AROUND THE broad, grassy plains. There were only three tiny white puffs of cloud across the vast expanse of deep blue sky. The heat, which had quelled the previous night, now returned, hotter and more biting than before. She wiped at her brow, feeling a slick of sweat. It wasn't the only place. Her shirt clung to her lower back. What she'd give for a shower, or a swim, and a change of clothes.

She walked back around to the shaded side of the van where it might have been a degree or two cooler. The door hung open, latched to the van wall. Inside, Kristy was testing Sarah's blood sugar levels. Jake sat on the step, chewing on ice cubes. At the kitchen table, Eric perused an unfolded map, and Julie stood at the sink preparing a jug of cordial.

There was a palpable unease amongst them. Eric maintained a vigil through the door and windows. Kristy had gone in and out of the van several times, while Evelyn had volunteered to stand out in the heat and keep watch. Although she had only known them a short time, the risk the men faced going inside the facility left her on edge, too, and she found herself glancing through the fence toward the cluster of buildings often.

She didn't see the cars immediately. They appeared on the horizon as she tied back the loose ends of her brown hair into a ponytail. A blue SUV led a red station wagon. They were coming fast, closing the gap quickly. She felt the urge to run, stung by a sense of foreboding she hadn't felt since attending the barracks.

"We've got company," she called out, and in a second Kristy was at her side, waving the Winchester .30-30. Eric followed with the Remington pump-action. He handed a faded shotgun to Evelyn. "Get inside, Jake. And close the door." The boy scrambled up the steps and disappeared, pulling the door closed.

"Let's just wait until we find out what they want."

"In my experience," Evelyn said, "trouble is coming when two cars are speeding toward you."

The wheels squealed as the vehicles took the arching corners at high speed. Her apprehension increased. They finally slowed as they reached the end of the straight, clipping the edge of the dirt and sending up puffs of dust. At thirty yards, the front vehicle skidded to a halt, stones and gravel ripping under the tires as they left the sealed road. The front and back doors flew open, and men leaped out in dirty army green clothing.

"Oh, Jesus Christ." Kristy dropped the rifle. "We're in deep shit." She took tight hold of the gun, and aimed it at the oncoming man. "It's bloody Steve Palmer."

The man lifted a gun at Kristy. "Well, look at what we have here."

"Who are they?" Evelyn asked. A lump of dread dropped into her gut.

"That's a long and horrible story," Kristy said, her brow furrowed with grim concern. "I can't believe they've tracked us this far."

Two men dressed in jeans and green army jackets followed the one Kristy had called Steve; all had guns drawn and aimed. From the second vehicle, another three men joined them. One had a bad limp. Evelyn didn't know whether to shoot, or run, but her hands began to twitch.

Steve stopped ten yards away. He had a split above his eye, and his nose was bruised. "Payback's a bitch."

"How did you find us?" Kristy asked.

A mocking chuckle turned into a sneer. "We've been following you guys since you ran us off the road in Albury. We found your infected friend with his family in the back of the truck. After he suggested we might be able to join up with your group and told us where you were going, we killed them all." Two of the other men laughed. "We came into Holbrook just as you were leaving. We ended up with half a dozen of those crazy zombies attacking us and we had to

289

find another way through. Then we saw you near Campbelltown, near the gas station that was overrun. You were parked on the other side of the road, but one of our guys was badly hurt so we couldn't stop. We didn't know about the horde of zombies ahead and we got into more trouble there."

"Pity you survived," Kristy said under her breath. She knew it was horrible to think such a thing, but this man was unworthy of any sympathy.

"We caught up in the end though." He glanced around at the others. "Just like I told the boys we would."

"Seriously, Steve, what do you want?" Kristy asked. "Don't you think we've all got enough problems in the world without this shit?"

Steve gritted his teeth. "I wanna run your car into a lamppost." He walked forward until he was within reach. "Then I wanna smash your face with the butt of my gun." He drew it back as if to strike Kristy.

Eric stepped forward. "No need for that."

Steve said, "Ducky?" The third man from the first vehicle fired his gun. Evelyn jumped.

The side of Eric's thigh exploded. He stifled a cry as he fell to one knee, the gun clattering onto the hardtop.

"Not bad, old timer." Julie ran to Eric's side, whimpering. Steve turned to Kristy. "Where are the others?"

Kristy flexed her hand around the rifle. Evelyn thought she was going to shoot. She still had her own gun aimed at Steve, but wasn't sure she had the courage to kill a man under these circumstances, despite what he had done. Eric stood, grimacing. Evelyn felt admiration; there was steel wire in him, just like her father.

A noise sounded from the van. Steve pointed that way, eyebrows raised. "In there?"

Evelyn's body stiffened. She couldn't move. One of the other men with long dark hair and a goatee walked to the van. He opened the door, and Jake and Sarah almost fell out.

Evelyn's stomach grew sickly. She hurried over to the van and stood between Jake and the man.

"Oh, brave, sweetheart," Steve said. "But I promise that if you don't tell me where Callan and the boys are, I'll kill one of those kids. Or both."

Evelyn felt her world sway. She caught her footing and tried to swallow, but her throat was thick and dry. *Don't let him see.* But he poked the gun at Jake, and Evelyn knew she had lost.

She pointed towards the barracks. "In there." She shot a look of apology to Kristy.

"You blokes," Steve said, pointing to two of the men, "stay here and keep watch. Kill them if they try anything."

Chris said, "We'd better hurry, man. This place is gonna get very busy soon."

"It won't take us long."

They disarmed the women, tossing the guns near their vehicles, and then the four remaining men crunched over the gravel toward the gate. Evelyn held her breath. The one they called Duck cocked his rifle and turned in a circle, watching them. He didn't smile or say anything smart, but his eyes narrowed, and he was chewing a toothpick, which made him appear more menacing.

The group slipped through the gap and jogged toward the building. Steve glanced back twice, but soon they had disappeared.

Kristy went to Eric and examined the wound. The bullet had grazed the side of his quadriceps muscle, tearing through his pants and flesh. "You're so lucky. Took a chunk out, but it's a superficial wound. Sarah, can you bring my medical bag from inside the van? I think it's beside the table."

"I'm okay," Eric said, grimacing as he limped around. His red face twisted with pain.

One of the men objected, but Kristy convinced him that she should at least dress the wound. Sarah disappeared inside the van and returned with a long, rectangular fabric bag.

Evelyn had no idea Kristy was a doctor. The woman was impressive: strong, courageous, and intelligent.

Kristy cleaned and dressed the injury, explaining the process and details to Sarah, who watched with grim interest. Evelyn comforted Jake, glancing sideways at the two men. "Stay inside the van. Just keep quiet and out of the way. It's going to be alright, honey."

But would it? Callan, Dylan, and Greg were the three strongest members of the group. If anything happened to them, they would struggle to survive. Evelyn couldn't help but think they wouldn't see their way out of this with everyone intact.

SIXTY-TWO

THEY ALL WATCHED AS Klaus Weinstrem administered the serum into the upper section of Gallagher's forearm. He had done the same to himself earlier, leaving a spot of blood on the surface of his skin where the needle had entered.

"What about the rest of the world?" Callan asked. "Have you had contact with anyone outside of this facility?"

Klaus glanced at Gallagher. "Yes. Not everyone is dead, but the pockets are thin, and most governments have been eradicated. We did have contact with a facility in Melbourne, but that stopped a few days ago. I've put out emergency calls to dozens of facilities in every Australian state and many others throughout the world."

Dylan tuned out. He couldn't stop thinking about how the serum could have saved his father, and Johnny, too. It was ironic. If only they had lasted a little longer. Maybe his father could have made it this far. Certainly Johnny would have. It saddened him. He tuned back in, trying to concentrate on the conversation. Callan had just finished explaining the large group of zombies they had driven through to reach the base.

Klaus adjusted his glasses and scrunched his nose. "The infected are well known for moving in mass formation. We don't know why, but suspect they have some innate mentality like a prairie animal— a buffalo, or bison, the way they migrate, searching for food. It might be scent-related. They have an acute sense of smell. They may 'scent' a new source of food, and go after it as a group. When a source of food is gone though, they'll change direction and chase a fresh supply."

Dylan thought about the bare paddocks and open fields they had passed on the way to the army base. Nothing existed in between to side track the zombies. Was it possible they would wander so far? Could a horde of bumbling undead really move in such a formation, with that sort of coherency? He thought back to the beginning. They had been in a group in the center of Albury on the first night; had chased them along the streets, and eventually attacked the house in a large mass. It was possible. They had seen it.

"So they might conceivably have caught our scents in the vehicles and followed?"

"It's possible. It could also be some sort of 'understanding' between them, especially the smarter ones. We saw some evidence of it in captivity. They seem to know what the others are doing. Perhaps they're communicating without us knowing. They can't talk, of course, but I suspect some form of communication is occurring."

"That would explain how they all converged on my parents' property back in Albury," Dylan said.

"It could just be that they were looking for food," Klaus said. "Their prime objective— at least the lower intelligence specimens—is to feed. Flesh and blood provides their sustenance. They require a constant supply, chasing fresh scents and new sources. Once they get hold of your scent, they either won't let go, or can't, and if there's nothing better, they will follow you."

Dylan turned away. "I'm going back then."

"We can all go," Gallagher said.

Klaus took the container of serum. "I just have to collect more ingredients from one of the other laboratories. It isn't far. As it is, we barely have enough to fight the virus for one person, let alone two."

Voices sounded from the corridor beyond the preparation room.

"Expecting anyone?" Callan asked.

A man wearing jeans and a green army jacket stepped into the entrance holding a rifle. A second man, tall, shaved head, a face cut from granite, followed. Gallagher opened his mouth to answer, when the first man drew the gun into his sight and fired.

They ducked for cover as bullets zinged and pinged off the walls and benches. Dylan pressed his back against one of the benches. He was furthest away, closest to the back right corner of the room. Klaus had tucked himself up into a ball with his hands over his head. Gallagher's gun appeared to be empty, so Callan slid a handgun across the floor to him on the far side of the room. He snatched it up and fired. Greg, closest to Dylan, sprang up from behind the barrier and unloaded the rifle on the strangers. Dylan did the same from around the corner of his bench.

Return fire was sparse, thumping into the heavy glass walls of the laboratory. Who were these people? Had they come from the installation, or were they civilians storming the base? That idea caused a feeling of dread in Dylan. If they had come through the front, perhaps they had passed Kristy and the others. He had to get back to them. There were now two potential risks.

Amidst the sporadic gunfire, he whistled, catching Greg and Callan's attention. They turned, and Dylan pointed at the rear door, then up, toward the surface. Callan nodded and gave him the thumbs up. Dylan poked his head out from beyond the edge of the bench, decided his pathway was clear, and crawled across the hard tiles on all fours to the door without incident.

From the front of the room, a loud clunk sounded, then another, followed by an intense hissing noise. It spurred Dylan on, and he bobbed up, slapping his palm against the green button to open the door. It slid back, and he darted through, looking back over his shoulder at a growing cloud of smoke filling the back half of the room. With the exception of Greg, the others had disappeared. Greg sat crouched behind the bench where Dylan had been, and now rushed across the open floor as gunfire clanged off the walls and benches, striking the walls. The door began to close. Coughing, Greg scampered through as it slid shut.

"Shit. What do we do now?" Dylan asked, pushing on the door. There was no button on the outside, only an odd-shaped keyhole. He didn't want to abandon the others, but he felt a growing pressure to reach the surface, to make sure Kristy was safe.

A thud against the wall from behind drew their attention. The corridor ran a short distance before a four-way intersection. Two zombies shuffled along the passageway toward them.

Greg raised his rifle and shot the front zombie in the neck. It spun around as blood leaped against the wall, knocking the second aside. Dylan fired, sprouting matter from the front of its skull, and it collapsed onto the other. Greg finished the first off with a head shot. Gun smoke drifted around them.

"We can't stay here," Dylan said. "Let's try and go around to the front of the prep room and attack from the other side."

"Good idea."

They reached the intersection and turned right, but came to a sudden halt. Ahead, a string of feeders hitched and bounced slowly toward them, shreds of clothes hanging from their rotting, disfigured bodies.

Dylan walked backward. Greg fired into the pack and put the first one down.

"Forget it, man," Dylan said. "Don't waste your bullets. We'll have to find another way." The feeders kept coming. There were too many to stand and fight. Dylan felt the swell of hatred. He wanted to kill them all, for who they were now, for what they had done, and what they would do. He tried to imagine a time when they wouldn't have to fight for their lives, and couldn't.

They ran back to the intersection and saw more approaching from the darker corridor straight ahead. Dylan turned right, but before he did, glanced left, toward the prep room door, hoping Callan and the others would be escaping the battle. A thick haze of smoke covered the entire window.

The passageway ahead was clear, and they picked up their pace, glancing back at the stragglers who had locked onto their scent. Dylan had no idea how to get back to the prep room, or even reach the surface. He took left and right turns in what he thought was their intended course, but couldn't be sure. His general sense of direction was poor, and Greg didn't challenge the decisions. They passed rooms full of open-plan seating, followed by large offices with lockable doors and corridors dead-ended by heavy doors with thick steel locks. Dylan was surprised at his control over the fear. It kept him moving and his senses tuned, but it wasn't paralyzing as it had once been.

It soon became clear that they weren't going back toward the prep room. The corridor walls were brick, filled periodically by more bulky metal doors. The zombies were lagging far behind, but their grunting and moaning echoed along the hallway. Dylan felt the sting of guilt for leaving the others behind, although he told himself it had not been deliberate. Separation under duress was a natural part of their lives now, it had happened before, and if they survived this, would probably happen again. They all understood the rules.

They made a series of quick turns, finishing in a long corridor, at the end of which stood a stairway.

"That's what we want." Dylan hurried on.

As they drew closer though, Dylan saw that the corridor branched off to the right at the base of the stairwell. In the shadows, bent over an eviscerated body, was a zombie. It drew chunks of flesh to its mouth and savaged them like pig slop.

"Stop," Greg whispered. It hadn't noticed them. He crouched and took aim. He seemed to pause forever. Firing the gun would alert other zombies to their location, but they had to get up those stairs. The zombie stopped eating and slowly looked up, its eyes hidden by shadows.

The gun cracked, and the zombie's mouth exploded, tearing apart its face. It fell forward onto the body and slid onto the floor. Greg led them to it with the weapon pointed. As they reached the base of the stairs, movement sounded from the side corridor. Both men fell back into position, looking down the barrel of their rifles.

The lights went out.

SIXTY-THREE

"I'D LOVE A DRINK," Gallagher said, spluttering, as they crawled through the air-lock into the laboratory. The door slid closed with a hiss, leaving clouds of tear gas behind in the middle room.

Callan hacked out a cough, the gas stinging his throat. He rubbed his eyes with the palms of his hands, pressing hard to remove the noxious substance. He had never encountered tear gas before, but now understood why it was so effective in riots. It rendered sufferers incapable of doing much but fleeing the cloud. They were safe in the laboratory for the moment, but beyond that, who knew.

"That's what got us into this mess." Klaus stumbled toward a sink at the far side of the room. He took a bottle from a shelf and squirted something into his eyes. He handed it to Callan. "Saline." He glanced again at Gallagher. "Or don't you know that?"

The relief was immediate. His eyes felt full, and uncomfortable, but at least the stinging sensation began to pass.

Callan handed the bottle to Gallagher, who rinsed and dried his eyes, then looked out into the hazy room with a solemn expression. "I do. Or did. My ex-wife and I divorced some years ago, and we had no kids, as much as I begged her to start a family. But I had two sisters who live on the Gold Coast, and my parents lived in Brisbane." He smiled in thought. "We had the best family gatherings. I had lots of aunties and uncles, cousins. We were all so close. Had at least two big catch-ups a year." He leaned back against the bench, arms folded. "It's funny, I've always thought it was a rubbish line, but you don't know what you've got until you lose it." He coughed, clearing his throat. It had grown raspier. He turned to Klaus. "You ask why I bother with the drink. I do it so I won't feel anything. So I won't remember as much. When I drink, the memories and guilt wash away."

"What are you guilty about?" Callan asked.

Gallagher took a long time to answer. "The week before all this shit started we had another catch-up. I didn't go. I was working. I knew I should have gone–I could have swapped the shift, but I don't do that sort of thing. I just thought I'd see them all next time. But there's no next time. And I won't be catching up with any of them again."

"I'm sorry," Callan said. Klaus looked away.

"I thought I would handle it better. Hell, I've been trained by the best to handle it better. But when it came to it, I haven't been able to. I dream of them all nearly every night. I'm there though, at the barbecue." He smiled, imagining. "We're laughing and joking, having a drink and something to eat. It's like the best party we ever had." The smile faded. "Then a big sink hole opens up in the ground and they all fall into it. It closes up, and I'm the only one left. They're all gone." His dry eyes had grown redder. "The only time I don't dream is when I drink."

Klaus stood staring at the floor. Callan felt Gallagher's pain. They all had a story to share. "I hope you can get past it," Callan said. "It's a heavy burden to live with, but none of it is your fault."

The gunshots had stopped. He supposed the men couldn't see into the room either, but when the fog cleared, they would be waiting. He'd watched Dylan and Greg escape through the side door, feeling the pull of their departure. He could have followed, but the two military men needed the help.

"Where are these extra supplies?" Callan asked.

"Close." Klaus pointed up. "A level above."

As the tear gas began to clear, Gallagher and Callan stood at the front of the lab behind the bullet-proof glass with their weapons drawn, waiting for signs of the intruders.

Callan joined him. "Where are they?"

"Out there. Somewhere. They could be hiding. Waiting to ambush us."

"But we're trapped. We have nowhere to go but to shoot our way out."

Callan and Gallagher paced, casting frequent glances out into the other room. Klaus gathered laboratory equipment on the bench, rummaging through drawers and in cupboards. By the time only a thin haze of smoke hung around the lighting, there was still no sign of the other men.

"We have to move," Callan said. "My mates are out there, and my sister and friends are up top. I've left them too long already." He turned to Klaus. "You can have five minutes to get your extra supplies, but after that, we're out of here." Klaus nodded.

Callan loaded the rifle and made his remaining ammunition more accessible. Gallagher did the same. He no longer looked as disheveled and beaten as he had on first appearance; perhaps because Callan had seen him fight. But he wondered how much more Gallagher had remaining. Klaus stood behind them, clutching the cooler bag as though millions of lives depended on it. Callan had to give the little scientist credit for that. He understood the importance of what he had created, and was ready to protect it with his life.

The lab door slid back first, followed by the outer door, and they all stepped through into the preparation room. Guns drawn, Gallagher and Callan moved in unison, their attention focused on the doorway where the men had been. Full of nervous energy, Callan kept expecting a head to appear, knowing he would only have a split second to shoot.

Gallagher moved ahead to check the entrance. Callan tightened his grip around the rifle as Gallagher counted down, then swept around the corner and stuck the pistol out in the expected direction. The corridor was empty.

"Doesn't make any sense," Callan said. "They had us. We had nowhere to go."

Klaus adjusted his glasses. "Yes it does. There's an enemy at loose in this facility that poses a greater threat than us. They must have had some kind of interaction. Now let's move."

Klaus led the way, Callan and Gallagher following with their guns aimed and ready. They slowed at an intersection where they could hear distant noises—aggressive calls, and the occasional loud bang—and moved through it to an unlocked red door marked FIRE ESCAPE. They took the concrete stairs up a level without incident.

The corridors changed again. A bumbling type one zombie fell through an entryway in front of them. Callan shot it in the head and it slumped to the floor, the deafening noise echoing down the hallways.

They passed more ominous doorways on both sides of the passageway. Callan expected more feeders, but it wasn't until they had passed a particularly dark room that more type ones spilled out behind them. At the rear, Gallagher face off up close. They clamored for him, a bony grey hand taking hold of his arm. Gallagher shot it in the face. Callan dropped another who reached for Klaus. The scientist took off down the hallway, followed by Callan and Gallagher, leaving several zombies to feed on the fallen.

They quickly added distance. Klaus' lack of athletic prowess soon showed. His long white lab coat and trailing blonde hair flapped behind him, but he couldn't keep up. Gallagher fared better, but his face was red, and sweat glistened on his forehead. Callan slowed, realizing that all his activity of late had developed his fitness. These men had been stuck in this facility for weeks, maybe longer, while Callan and the others had been in the real world, preparing themselves for survival.

The zombies weren't giving up. Others had joined the pilgrimage, trailing the group.

Klaus stopped outside a door marked SUPPLY ROOM. Callan nudged in front of him, pushed it open, and held it for the others as they hurried through. The zombies were closing, lumbering down the hallway like the lead pack in a running race, led by a former medical employee dressed in a white lab coat and wearing a pair of broken glasses.

"SHUT IT!" Klaus screamed, once inside.

Callan stepped into the doorway and fired. Medical Zombie's left cheek exploded in a flash of gore. It faltered, falling to one knee, then slumped to the ground. The others tottered as they ran over it.

Callan meant to fire again, but Gallagher pulled the door shut, clipping the end of the gun and altering his aim. "Jesus, man. I could have killed more."

Gallagher threw his weight at the door, turning his back and pressing his legs into the floor. "The button, press the button!" Klaus punched a red button on the wall and the airlock kicked in, securing the door.

Zombie hands thumped on it, smearing blood and dirt. Faces pressed against the glass, bulging eyeballs rolled, mouths opened and closed, revealing teeth like the rusted pipes of an old house. They were stuck again. More type ones joined the throng, pushing against those at the front for prime position. Callan turned away. "How many rounds do you have?"

Gallagher emptied the pistol's magazine. "Four."

"I've got six." To Klaus, Callan said, "Are there any more here?" Klaus shook his head.

They were in a small room with tall glass cabinets fixed all around. Plastic suits with clear face masks hung from the walls. Beyond, Callan saw a metal door marked with numerous warning signs. Klaus hurried to the door and disappeared into a shadowy room beyond.

Callan topped up rounds in the rifle. "We need to move."

"With that lot waiting outside?"

"I'm not hanging around here. We need to get back to the surface."

When Klaus reappeared, Gallagher said, "He's ready to shoot his way out."

Callan adjusted the rifle. "The type threes are gone."

Klaus looked at the door. "They're smart, though. They're calculating your next move. They're out there hiding, waiting for us. The only advantage we have over them is that they are impatient. They won't wait forever."

"I don't care," Callan said. "My sister and friends are out there. I'm not waiting here, when they might be in trouble."

Klaus turned to Gallagher. "How has he survived this long?"

"I've survived because I'm not afraid to fight when I have to fight. What happens if more type threes arrive? When there's seven or ten of them out there? We can't defeat that many. While we have a window, we need to take it. You can wait here if you like, but give me some of that medicine. You can make some more."

"Is one of you bitten?" Gallagher asked.

"No," Callan averted his eyes. "But we've lost people who were bitten, and if that happens again, we need something for them."

Gallagher sighed. His red cheeks and wary look told Callan he wasn't prepared for what they were about to face, that this life was asking too much of him. "Ten bullets?"

Callan shrugged. "I've faced worse."

A strong vibration passed hidden pipes in the roof, and then the lights cut out. Nobody spoke. Then the emergency lights came on in the hallway outside, bathing the zombie congregation in a soft green glow.

"He's right," Klaus said. "We have to leave. Now."

SIXTY-FOUR

KRISTY HAD NEGOTIATED WITH the gunmen for the group to sit inside the van, arguing that it was easier to keep an eye on their captives by having them in one place. They all sat around the kitchen table, on the bunks, and stood by the sink as the two gunmen patrolled the burning blacktop outside, cursing and spiting, firing off into the distance for their own amusement.

"I've got a plan," Kristy whispered. They'd come too far to let these redneck yobbos stop them. Besides, what was going to happen to them if Steve and Chris overpowered the boys? They'd have no more use for their captives, and they would probably kill them. Perhaps the girls would be exposed to horrible things before that. Kristy wouldn't allow that to happen.

Eric limped closer, his eyes bright and wide. "What is it?"

The two men had swept the van for firearms, confiscating two guns Eric had in storage, but they had not checked the Jeep.

"I need Sarah's help." The girl looked up from the bed, eyebrows raised in anticipation. She'd been quiet mostly, talkative in patches when she and Kristy were alone. She had helped patch up Eric's leg, and Kristy was pleased with both her interest and her development in the basics of first aid.

"Will you help me, sweetheart?"

"Do I get to hold a gun?"

Kristy glanced at Julie and Evelyn, who were both frowning. Kristy supposed it had something to do with losing her father. "No. I'll take care of that part. I don't want you to pick up a gun, Sarah. They're dangerous. Understand?"

She nodded, but looked down, disappointed. "My dad told me I needed to be brave. He said that one day I might have to do things I wouldn't like, but if it saved my life, or the life of other people that I loved, then it was okay. God wouldn't punish me. I'd still go to Heaven."

"Your dad was a very smart man," Julie said. "He's one hundred percent right. God would never punish such a lovely little girl." Sarah smiled, and Julie stroked her golden hair.

Kristy continued. "You're going to fake a hypoglycaemic attack. We're going to pretend your blood sugar levels are low. They won't know the difference, and I'll tell them I need something from the Jeep. I'll grab one of the guns and …"

Evelyn frowned. "That's risky. For you."

"It's a bigger risk not to do anything. We'll die, otherwise. Some of these men have tried to kill us before. I know what they're capable of."

"I don't like it," Julie said. "We shouldn't cause any trouble. You can't be sure they're going to kill us." The woman had opened up to them all, but Kristy saw her weaknesses exposed when circumstances dictated them to be strong. She repressed the urge to tell Julie about the realities of the world now. At least Eric had adapted.

Eric put a hand on Julie's arm. "She's right, hon. I've seen these types of men before. They have no morals." He looked to Kristy. "What's the plan?"

She explained it, refining points as she went. Sarah would fake unconsciousness on the kitchen floor. Kristy would take one of the men to the car, where, while looking for medical supplies, she'd use one of the guns to shoot the bastard.

"It's madness," Julie said. "What's to stop them shooting us?"

"Unless someone can come up with a better idea, I don't see we have a choice."

Kristy set them up in position. Sarah lay on the floor near the kitchen table. "Close your eyes, sweetie, and don't answer any questions unless I say it's time to wake up, okay?"

306

Kristy stood in the doorway and called out for help. One of the men came toward the van. Kristy dropped off the step and started for the Jeep. The man put a heavy hand out and barred her pathway. "Please, I need my supplies, I'm a doctor." She worried her thumping heart would give her away.

Looking into the van, the man gripped his gun and raised the muzzle slightly. "What's the problem?"

"Sarah's diabetic and her blood sugar levels are low. I need to get her glucagon pen from my medical kit."

"Stay there." He walked to the entrance and examined Sarah from outside. After thirty seconds, he returned. "My brother was a diabetic. We used to just give him a cup of orange juice, or some lollies."

She felt her breath catch. "She's unconscious. I can't give anything by mouth. The pen is all that works under these circumstances." He studied her, up and down, pausing at certain parts, his mind drifting from the topic. "Please. It won't take a moment."

Finally, he waved his gun at the other man. "Find out if she's faking." Kristy began moving to the van. "Uh-uh. You stay where you are."

She was about to protest, but his square jaw stiffened. If she pushed it, he'd thwart the plan altogether. They were in the hands of lady luck for now.

The burly man was inside for almost two minutes. Kristy squirmed in silence, switching from one foot to the other, considering actions that might expedite the situation, but she refused to jeopardize the opportunity. When he came out of the van, he nodded to the other man, who began walking toward the Jeep.

"Come on."

Kristy's heart kicked up a gear. Despite the heat, he pulled a cigarette from a crumpled pack in his shirt pocket and lit it. Kristy followed, watching the way he held his gun. She would need to be ready. But what was she going to do, kill him? Shooting a zombie was one thing, but this man was alive, and uninfected. If it came to her life, or his own, could she shoot him dead?

She eyed the Jeep on approach, looking for Blue Boy. The dog had been silent since the men had arrived. When she opened the door, Blue Boy might leap out, and the men would kill him the moment they saw him. Suddenly the idea seemed flawed.

The man stopped two yards from the Jeep and pulled the smoke out between his thumb and forefinger. "You've got thirty seconds."

Kristy peered through the glass. Blue Boy lay curled up in the corner, asleep. She pressed the button to open the flap in the rear door, placing her body between the man and the contents. Blue Boy lifted his head. Kristy reached out and scratched the soft fur between his ears. He rose, but she pushed him down until he fell back into position.

Hiding throughout the clothes and supplies was a number of pistols, two rifles, and several fresh 9mm cartridges. She drew one of the cartridges to herself.

"Twenty seconds."

A moment later, Kristy felt a hand slide over her hip. She froze, suppressing the urge to knock him away. Blue Boy looked up, ears pricked. She made a face, trying to convey for him to stay put. Perhaps she could use it to her advantage.

The man gave a slimy smile. "You're cute."

She forced a giggle, removed her hand from the clothes bag, and picked up a semi-automatic pistol, dropping out the magazine. Empty. He was closer now, right behind her, and she stuck out her ass a little more to distract him. She carefully slotted a full cartridge into the pistol, muffling the sound with a towel.

This was it. She was going to have to kill him. The alternative was clear; she would take a beating, might even be raped and probably killed. The others would fare no better. *That* made her stomach turn. *Do this*.

She took the gun in two hands. "Got it." Kristy felt his weight move away as she pushed back. She turned and swung the pistol around to line him up.

He was fast though, swiping out at the weapon with his left hand. Blue Boy barked, leaping from the back of the Jeep. Kristy fired, creating a booming crack, but the man's hand touched the muzzle and displaced her aim. He came at her, swinging a meaty fist. Blue Boy leapt up at him, growling, and cut his attack short. Kristy lowered the gun and poked it into his big gut, then pulled the trigger.

The blast knocked him backward. He stumbled away, both hands pressed to a spreading red patch in the middle of his stomach. He fell onto his knees with a clunk, and rolled, scooping up his rifle with a grunt and pointing it at Kristy. Blue Boy attacked again, taking the man's forearm between his teeth and giving a ferocious shake of his head. The gun boomed and Blue Boy fell aside, whimpering.

A cry from the van drew Kristy's attention. She glanced up and saw Evelyn lying in the doorway wrestling with the other man. Eric lay motionless on the ground to the right.

The man came again, pulling the gun around in her direction. He was going to shoot her. In her mind's eye, she saw the gun explode. Blue Boy raced in from the side nipping at his arm. He swung an elbow that cracked into Blue Boy's snout, knocking the dog aside, but it gave Kristy a moment. She stepped forward with the pistol held out, pulled her aim into line, and squeezed. The top of the man's head exploded. His face twisted into an expression of disbelief, and then he fell back. His gun clattered onto the blacktop.

Screaming. From the van. Kristy froze. Evelyn had fallen onto the road outside the doorway. The man straddled her chest, ignoring her fists beating against his arms, stomach, and neck. He slammed a magazine into a pistol, cocked it, and stuck the barrel against Evelyn's head.

Barking, Blue Boy scurried across the bitumen toward them, but he wasn't going to make it. Neither was Kristy.

The gunman's finger rested on the trigger. Jake would lose his mother, and the world would sink a little deeper into hell.

A shot cracked, rolling across the sky. The man paused, upright, then fell forward and rolled off to the side. Growling, Blue Boy reached them as the man hit the ground. At the rear, standing with the gun pointed, was Sarah.

Kristy ran. She reached Evelyn just as she pushed the man's legs off her own. Sarah stood with the pistol still aimed, tears running down her face.

"Are you hurt?" Kristy asked Evelyn as she reached her. Evelyn shook her head. Kristy put out a hand, which she took, and drew herself upright.

Still sobbing, Sarah lowered the gun. Eric climbed to his feet, a savage gash across his cheek. The gunman had forgotten about a twelve-year-old girl. Sarah dropped the pistol and ran to Kristy. She took her and pulled her thin body close, stroking her hair, cursing a world where a young girl had to kill to save lives.

Kristy kissed the top of her head. "You did good, kiddo. Real good."

SIXTY-FIVE

DYLAN FELT PANIC TAKE hold the moment the lights cut out. There was something around the corner—he thought he knew what it was; he could hear the footsteps, even smell it. His skin crawled in expectation, waiting for something to happen.

Elsewhere, possibly on another level, gunfire sounded, and they knew the others were engaged in battle. They could probably find their way back to them based on those sounds, but they had a more immediate problem. He poked the gun into the darkness, pointing it in what he felt was the right direction. Then the green emergency signs came on.

The dark shape of something ducked back behind the wall, but it was close enough to prevent them climbing the stairs.

"What the fuck was that?" Dylan asked in a weak voice. A cold hand touched the back of his neck. He had a loaded gun, but still wanted to run.

Greg took a moment. "I don't know, but if you see it, shoot." The soft green lighting above their heads was poor and did nothing for the shadows beside the stairwell. "How much ammo you got?"

"A handful. You?"

"Same." Dylan watched the corner, hearing Greg stick rounds into the rifle. "That's it. Four left."

"What's it doing?" Dylan asked. "Why isn't it attacking?"

"I don't know. These fuckers are smart."

Dylan wanted to ask why Greg wasn't attacking. The big man had not shirked a challenge yet, but this seemed different. There was something creepy about this one. Dylan heard Greg taking steps backward. "What are you doing?"

"Just giving ourselves a little space."

"We gotta kill this thing," Dylan said, following. "Kristy is up those stairs. You know how much that means to the both of us."

"I want it to come out, come after us. I'm not going up those stairs or around that corner. It might be a trap."

The clatter and bang of movement sounded from behind. Both boys turned. It was difficult to see down the long stretch, but far away, shadows moved beneath one of the faint green emergency lights.

A noise from the stairs made them both jump. Dylan twisted back around, realizing their mistake, but it was too late. The thing hiding behind the wall came rushing around the corner like a charging bull, bulky and fast. It crashed into Greg, knocking him to the ground.

In the dim light, Dylan poked the rifle forward, but they rolled on the floor, moving too quickly for him to acquire a clear shot. The zombie made a low keening noise as Greg pinned its arms. It thrashed, growling, and they spun, reversing roles. "Shoot the fucker in the head!" Greg screamed.

The headshot was too risky though. Dylan jabbed the rifle into the zombie's back and fired. It shrieked, the blast knocking it aside. Greg snatched for his gun and crawled away, but the zombie was quick, tackling him back to the ground. Dylan skirted the fight, aiming for another shot, but he saw from the corner of his eye a number of zombies running along the corridor toward them with the poise and aggression of the crazy type.

The stairs were right there, Kristy a minute or two beyond. His legs threatened to betray him. *Don't be an asshole.* He could never do it to Greg. He held firm, locking his feet in place, and fired a shot into the gloom. One of them stumbled, then gathered its balance and kept coming. How long did they have? How many rounds were left? He estimated fifteen seconds and knew that without Greg he couldn't take three of them alone.

Greg and the zombie had rolled to Dylan's feet. Both had their arms stretched, one trying to draw his opponent closer, the other trying to push his away. Dylan placed the barrel onto the stringy-haired skull. It bobbed and ducked, swirling about, but he followed it.

"Shoot it!" Greg screamed in a muffled voice.

At the last moment, the zombie turned to Dylan. He was ready though, gun pointed at its face. He fired, hitting it between the eyes, spraying chunks of blood and flesh on both sides of the corridor. It fell forward onto the floor with a thud.

Greg scooped up his gun and climbed to his feet, panting. Dylan thought about running again, scampering for the stairs and dragging Greg with him, but the memory of his father's last moments flashed through his mind. *Make me proud.* Was he doing that by running away? They had taken his mother and father, and now wanted him and his friends. He would not stand for it.

Dylan stood beside Greg, pumping the trigger and yanking on the bolt to reload. Bullets flew and the guns boomed. One of the zombie's heads exploded like a watermelon. The others took body shots, ribbons of blood exploding from their heads and tattered clothes until there was one left, which Greg dropped with a single, deadly shot.

Silence rushed in. The green light fought its way through a haze of gun smoke. Dylan's ears rang and he wondered how much longer his hearing would survive. They staggered toward the stairs, Greg leading, and Dylan thought finally they would make it.

"I'm out of bullets," Greg said. "You got any?"

"At least one, I think."

The metal handrail beckoned, and as Dylan reached out for it, he noticed movement in his peripheral vision. Something struck him hard from the side with a thwack. He grunted, losing a rush of air, and went sprawling, his gun clattering to the floor. Greg fell too, but managed to land on the bottom of the stairs.

Two type threes glared at them.

Dylan scuttled backward like a crab, snatching an empty space for the gun. A chunk of flesh was missing from the cheek of one, and it crawled toward him, revealing bloody teeth that could chew through tin. Dylan kicked out like a child, swishing air. Where was his gun? He took his eyes off the zombie and saw a dark object about two feet away. He reached for it, and felt his assailant's hot breath on his face as it clambered onto him. He twisted, reaching the gun, clutching it with stiff fingers and rolled, trying to get the barrel around into the monster's face.

Gunfire sounded from the stairs. A thought struck him; *Greg has no bullets.* Dylan realized with horror that he was grasping Greg's empty gun.

He swung the tip and around and jabbed the zombie in the face. It shook a scraggy head, hissing. Dylan drove his knee upwards, striking it in the groin and dislodging its position. It provided him the moment he needed to slither away.

Another gunshot boomed. Kneeling over Dylan, the zombie crashed onto him. He rolled, scratching for breath, and managed to crawl away on all fours toward the stairs, the grunt of the type three behind him.

Greg had ascended the stairs. Dylan reached the first step, but stumbled and fell forward, smashing his nose on the metal edge. Pain filled his face. He gritted his teeth and squeezed his eyes shut. A hand latched onto his ankle, dragging him back. He groped for purchase, but the slick step gave him nothing, and he slid backward. He looked up and saw Greg turn, one hand holding the door open. Terror struck Dylan's heart.

Greg was safe, and free. He could leave Dylan behind, weaponless, standing little chance of defeating the zombie in hand to hand combat. *He'll leave me,* Dylan thought. *I've been a threat all along. I stole the girl he loves. He's been waiting for it, now here it is, and nobody will ever know.* It was an unfair thought though. Greg had saved his life multiple times, placing his own at risk.

The zombie took hold of Dylan's other leg and drew him further away from the stairs. Dylan kicked out, but the feeder jumped on him, knocking the breath from his lungs, and its weight foiled any movement. The thing scratched and clawed at Dylan's torso, trying to turn him over. He threw his fists backward, striking air, and the thing twisted his elbow sideways, spearing pain through Dylan's arm. He screamed. His shoulder gave way and his hand slumped to the floor. The zombie yanked the collar of Dylan's jacket back and leaned down. Dylan knew what was going to happen before it did. He had nothing left with which to fight it though. He smelled its warm, fetid breath, and heard the low grunt. The zombie bit into the soft flesh of his lower neck.

A loud clapping noise sounded as Greg connected the heavy wooden stock of the Remington with the zombie's head. It tumbled sideways off Dylan and slammed against the wall.

Greg yanked Dylan to his feet. He stumbled, thought he was going to fall, but regained his balance. They dashed up the stairs, where Greg opened the door and ushered Dylan through. On the other side, he looked back. The zombie had climbed to its feet, a dark, brooding spread over its face. Greg slammed the door, and they ran.

"Jesus, man, I thought you were gone," Greg said. "When I looked around, it was on you."

"Why didn't you shoot the fucking thing?"

"The gun's empty." Greg offered the rifle, his eyes wide with disbelief. "Did it get you?"

It had bitten him. Blood seeped down the back of his t-shirt. A tingling pain spread in a patch around the bite, and seemed to be getting worse. But he couldn't tell Greg. If he told him, then Kristy would find out, and that would change everything. *It's already changed, you fool.* He needed a moment to think what he might do. He would talk to the scientist first, and find out what could be done. "No. The Kevlar saved me."

Behind them, the door crashed into the wall and the zombie roared.

SIXTY-SIX

KLAUS JABBED THE GREEN button so hard his finger hurt. Callan pulled the door open, and Gallagher stepped into the entrance with the gun extended. The zombies pressed in, reaching for them, their fingers and hands opening and closing like claws. Gallagher shot the closest one through the eye, sending a chunk of blood and muck flying from the rear of its head. It fell back into the group. Most of them stepped over it, but one of the stragglers decided a dead zombie was a better bet and fell onto its knees to feed.

The stench of rotting flesh and death hit them in a wave. Klaus stumbled back from the door. Callan stepped in front of him, firing fast as they groped and grabbed at his arms, all close headshots. They crumpled to the floor as blood flew, coating his arms and legs in straggly ribbons.

Gallagher did the same, risking his life for the easy shot. Callan wondered if he was less concerned having already been bitten. But it worked, and the feeders kept falling with little resistance until only a pile of bloody, broken carcasses lay on the floor.

Klaus couldn't look, but Gallagher picked out several that he had known. He led the way with Klaus between them, the soft green glow of the emergency signage every twenty steps lighting their way. Callan fed the last few rounds into the rifle and handed Gallagher another magazine for the Browning pistol.

"We've got nothing left," Callan said. "If we get into another fight, we won't be able to shoot our way out."

Klaus tipped his head. "There's another place nearby. Just one level up."

"The shooting range," Gallagher said, as if finally working out a puzzle that had eluded him.

Klaus sneered, as if reading his mind. "You've been drunk most of the time."

"There's a small ammunition bank where certain personnel can go and fire off a few rounds. I … should have thought of it."

They ran on, down the hallway, right, straight, then left again. They heard the savage roars of the zombies, and they chilled Callan's skin. The entire facility was overrun, a hive of zombies on every level. It was a frightening thought when one really considered it. He was still alive though, and they might just make it out of there, after all. They had a scientist who had formulated a serum that could at least hold off the disease. It gave him hope.

Klaus led the way between blank walls and dark, soulless windows. Callan wouldn't look. He thought that if they ran quickly enough, they might outrun anything lurking behind a doorway. Klaus took them up a level via the fire stairs, and they entered a quiet foyer bathed in green light.

They reached the shooting range within a minute. It had five targets, and a room off the rear that contained a number of large steel cupboards secured against the wall. From a table in the corner, Gallagher used a heavy fire extinguisher to break the lock. It hit the floor with a dense clunk. He unloaded several rifles, a shotgun, and two handguns onto one of the tables with several boxes of rounds. "Take your pick."

Callan replaced his empty rifle with one of the army-issue versions that looked like it could do some serious damage.

"That's an F88 Austeyr, standard issue for the Army." Gallagher took a second. "Thirty rounds in the magazine, but just be careful you don't let loose and fire them all in the first ten seconds."

Callan also took a 9mm pistol along with several thirteen-round magazines. Gallagher did the same. Klaus stood back, refusing to take anything.

"I'm not touching one of those things. I can barely lift my arm. Besides, if you two are dead and I have to use a gun …"

"I think there's some heavier stuff in these other cupboards," Gallagher said, moving to a second cabinet. "Probably some grenades and other explosive devices."

Callan shook his head. "Forget it. I'll blow myself up. This is enough, anyway, and I don't want to waste any more time." He thought about Eric, Kristy, and Evelyn. Suddenly he regretted leaving them alone. "Take us to the surface."

Gallagher led them back down a long corridor at a slow jog. Klaus ran in the middle, and Callan brought up the rear. The distant gunfire had stopped. He hoped Greg and Dylan had returned safely to the surface. Turning the next corner, an armed man in a green military outfit stepped from behind an overturned stack of electrical equipment and fired. Bullets chewed holes in the wall behind them. Gallagher pushed Klaus to the ground and threw his body over him. Instinctively, Callan turned his aim toward the gunman and pulled the trigger.

The gun jolted, cracking off shots in a rapid blast. Bullets peppered the man's chest and throat beneath his facemask, knocking him back against the wall. He paused; his legs crumpled, and he fell into a heap. Callan approached. It was probably one of the men who had attacked the preparation room. A hitching, gurgling sound came from the body. Callan kept his gun aimed, but the man wasn't in any state to fight back. Bloody holes made an odd pattern across his torso. The body gave a final hitch and then lay still.

The mask had been displaced, and Callan felt his breath catch. He knew that face. "Jesus, it's Chris."

"You know him?" Gallagher asked.

"Yes. We …" His thoughts drifted away. Steve, Chris, and their crew had tried to kill Callan and his friends numerous times. They were a shining example of how people's morals could crumble when the world fell apart. Why were they there? Perhaps they had come seeking help from the army and government, like Callan and his group. If Chris was around, it meant Steve was probably there, too.

He pulled the mask off and saw Chris' eyes staring up at the roof, forever frozen. Despite their differences, Callan felt a hint of sadness.

"Let's keep moving," Gallagher said.

They climbed another level via the fire stairs and met with screaming gunfire. Ahead, at an intersection, they saw a group of humans engaged with zombies in another passageway. They pulled back until they could peer out from the safety of another passageway.

"How do we get out of here?" Callan asked.

Gallagher tipped his head forward. "That's it. There is no other way."

SIXTY-SEVEN

EVEN WITH AN INJURED leg, Eric insisted on dragging the bodies away from the van, even if it was only thirty yards. Upon his return, he fell into the soft seating behind the kitchen table, sweating, his face red, mouth hanging open, and gulped down a large cup of water. The others had resumed their places inside the van, except for Evelyn, who stood poker-faced outside holding the rifle, keeping watch.

Kristy had murdered a person unaffected by the virus, and she didn't feel a scrap of remorse. Her acceptance of killing the man, regardless of the reasons, had been easy. It hit her then, as they sat in the stifling van waiting for the boys, that she had changed as a person; she would never again be the woman battling self-belief, or guilt over the loss of life.

Trying her best to ignore the predicament, Julie fixed a tinned fruit platter and some dry biscuits. The kids ate well, but the adults only picked. They coerced Evelyn inside, and she reluctantly sat at the table while Julie drummed up a jug of cordial with a handful of ice cubes. Eric took a half bottle of bourbon from a high cupboard, offering it to the adults before pouring himself a long glass. The kids returned to the bunk beds and read worn books Eric had stashed in one of the drawers. Blue Boy sat on the floor near the driver's seat drinking from a plastic container of water.

They had to close the van door to try and keep the flies out. Jake and Sarah had killed most of them with a lime-green fly swatter Julie had in a drawer. Eric turned the engine on to fill the room with cold air.

Evelyn swallowed the last of Julie's appetizers. "How much longer do you think they might be?"

"I've read a little about this place," Eric said. "Rumor has it that it runs deep—a hundred levels down, with the ability to house thousands of people for months after any sort of catastrophic event."

"Then why wouldn't they let us in?" Julie asked. "We've suffered as much as anybody else."

"I think it's overrun with zombies." Kristy's stomach turned. She didn't want to foretell a bad result, but she had learned to accept the realities of their new life. "And if they haven't returned in another hour or two, what do we do then?"

"Why can't we just wait here?" Evelyn asked.

"I liked that service station," Sarah said, watching them from the top bunk. "Before the zombies attacked. It was nice. Like it used to be when my family went on holidays, when my mum and dad were alive."

Evelyn took the plate to the sink. "Tell us, Eric, or Julie, how did you end up with this camper van?"

Surprisingly, Julie answered. "It was Eric who wanted it. He had this grand idea of us becoming grey nomads, travelling around Australia and visiting all the places we'd promised ourselves to one day see, but never taken the time. I wasn't too keen on it, but once I saw what he did with this thing …" She looked around, as though seeing the inside for the first time. "You know when he purchased this, it was little more than a shell? Parts of it were rotting. It had no fridge, no stove, no bed." She chuckled. "I actually thought he'd gone crazy. But when I saw what he'd done with it … I was so proud of him." Eric leaned forward and gave her a kiss on the cheek.

They went on, discussing their options back and forth, the possibilities of finding a safe haven, and where that might be. They all had differing opinions, and Kristy realized choosing a direction or a destination was going to be a challenge when everybody thought they should be going a different way. Kristy left the table to do a quick check on her medical inventory. After treating Eric's lucky leg wound, she had diminished key supplies. They would need to find a hospital or pharmacy that hadn't been cleaned out or infested with zombies.

A bump sounded from outside.

Eric stood from the table, grimacing. "What was that?" He took a rifle from behind the driver's seat.

Kristy stood. "Wait, Eric." It came again, louder, and repeated, as though somebody was striking the Jeep.

"Don't go out there." Kristy started for him. She intended to hold him back if that's what it took.

He turned, eyes wide, teeth gritted. "Stay here, all of you."

Julie cried out. "Wait, Eric. Listen—"

Eric opened the door, stepped out, and slammed it shut.

Kristy went to the door and pushed, but he must have been leaning back on it.

A gun shot cut through the air outside.

"Eric?" Julie called, dropping a plate into the sink.

Blue Boy bolted for the door, barking. Kristy stepped away toward the front of the van and snatched the Winchester off the driver's seat. She hurried back and pushed the door. This time, it swung open. The dog leaped from the top step, and Kristy did the same, waving the rifle about.

The sight stole her breath.

A group of zombies had wandered down the road. A cluster congregated around the bodies Eric had dragged to the roadside. Kristy counted seven outside the van. Eric had lost the gun, and it lay on the ground near the door. He'd fallen onto his bad knee, defending himself with his forearms held high above his head. Blue Boy ran straight for him.

"Blue! Wait!" Kristy screamed. "Evelyn, the gun."

Kristy shot the closest zombie in the face. It fell back and knocked another over. She fired again and blew a hole in the chest of the second, coating a stringy-haired old man in overalls and a checked shirt with gore. Once, she would have felt her stomach rise; now, she turned the gun on Overalls and blasted a hole in his leering face.

Evelyn landed at her side with the other rifle. She pumped and fired, pumped and fired, locking Kristy's attention momentarily as the weapon screamed its roaring tune. The girl could shoot, cutting down stragglers as they reached the van.

It hit Kristy like a jolting realization as she followed the trail up the sloping road and saw hundreds of zombies wandering down the bitumen and grassy edges toward them. As some arrived, they fell onto their fallen comrades, tearing into their flesh. *They followed us all the way here,* she thought. It was as amazing as it was frightening.

Worse though, Eric was overcome. He lay on the road, fighting off a growing pack. Blue Boy ran around the fringes, jaws snapping, snarling and yapping, but without getting caught, he couldn't get close.

How was this happening? Seven had turned into fourteen, fourteen into twenty-eight, drawn by the gunfire and the sweet smell of new victims. Kristy ran through the army, knocking others aside. She reached Eric as he began to scream. She put the gun at the neck of the first one and jammed the trigger. Its head exploded and it slumped forward. But they were everywhere. Hands groped her arms and neck. They pushed and bumped her, grabbing for her yellow hair. She spun, looking for Evelyn. There must have been thirty or so outside the van, with more pouring down the hill. Kristy yanked the rifle up and shot another in the head. It fell onto the road with a clunk, and others fought over it. She fired again, but this time, she heard only a click. Ammo. She needed more. Where was it? The trailer.

They had covered the Jeep and trailer like a swarm of flies on a week-long-dead animal. Supplies had been torn from their boxes, clothes and camping gear strewn across the road. Somewhere under the mob was the ammo, forever gone.

She broken free of their clawing hands, but had moved away from Eric. More than a dozen had gathered around him. Tears of frustration sprang to her eyes. It was so unfair. She screamed and swung the rifle, whacking the stock into their heads. They flinched, hardly recognizing the pain. Some turned away, while others attacked, tempted by her smell.

Blue Boy ran in and out of their legs, snarling, snapping, attempting to avert them from Eric. But he knew not to bite them, or get caught, and his attacks were mostly ineffective. "Away, Blue!" she screamed. "Get back." He scuttled free of a groping hand, but circled and ran back toward another. She wondered how he would survive.

"Kristy!" Evelyn screamed. Kristy turned as a hand latched onto her arm. She could barely see Evelyn over by the door. "We gotta go."

Eric. What about Eric? They couldn't leave him. Evelyn had run out of bullets, too. She was using the gun to ram their horrid faces, clearing a thin path to the van. She latched onto the door handle and pulled, smacking the screen into a zombie's head. "KRISTY!"

This was her chance. But the doctor in her, the element of her being that saved lives, and the man that she would rescue, tugged her in the other direction. She had not heard a sound from Eric. No whimper, or scream, no cry for help. Was he dead already? Yes, he had to be. The zombies were on their knees around him, sounds worse than a nightmare coming from his direction. Her heart bled, knowing they could not save him now.

She wondered if Dylan and the others were still alive. Even if they were, they could never escape the horde. They were finished. All of them. She might as well lie down and let them take her. If Dylan was dead, that would be the only solution—

She felt herself wrenched toward the van. She stumbled, then gained her footing and saw Evelyn pulling her shirt. Zombies clawed at them. Evelyn's left fist darted out twice like an attacking snake, rocking the heads of two zombies back. She slung her elbows and parted their way. Kristy had never seen a woman fight like that. Evelyn wrenched the door open and flung Kristy into Julie's arms, and then it was dark, and the door was shut, and they were safe, for the moment.

"Where's Eric?" Julie screamed. "ERIC?"

Evelyn hurried toward the front, panting. "I'm sorry."

Julie's face pinched. She tried to speak, but her lips trembled. She stepped to the door. Kristy grabbed her, wrapping her arms around Julie's thick waist.

"We can't leave him there!" Kristy said nothing. Julie squirmed, slamming her fists down onto Kristy's arms, but she knew if she let go, Julie would be dead too.

The van rumbled to life, rocking them as Evelyn accelerated. Bodies and limbs thumped against the exterior. Kristy guided Julie away from the door and into a seat, feeling warm tears on her arm. Julie wailed. Kristy sat beside her, and suddenly Julie got up and ran for the door again. This time, Sarah stepped in front of her, catching the railing for balance. Kristy leaped up and took her by the arm.

"You'll die too, if you go out there."

"I don't care," Julie blubbered. She knocked Kristy's hand away. "This is all your fault! You *stupid* people. You caused this." Spittle flew from her lips. "We would have been safe at home." She staggered past, through the kitchen, and fell onto the bed, howling.

Kristy thought of Blue Boy, too, whom they had left behind, and a pang of guilt struck her. Evelyn accelerated through the zombies; some of them stepped aside, but others remained and ended up beneath the wheels. The van bumped and bashed a path, and soon they were clear, safe. Out the rear window, they swarmed toward the base, heavy congestion at the place where Eric had fallen.

He was a devastating loss. He had been a paternal light for them, a caring, generous man, someone to ask questions of and bounce ideas off of. He had forged a post in the group they couldn't easily replace. It felt like losing a grandparent who has always given sensible, pragmatic advice.

Kristy should have wept, but the tears had run dry, stolen by their circumstances and the deaths of those before, more than her body was capable of grieving. Her thoughts turned to the boys, especially Dylan. If they were lucky and brave enough to escape the base, they would find a congregation of zombies, and nothing to save them this time.

SIXTY-EIGHT

AS THEY STOOD BEHIND the wall deciding how to negotiate past the firefight, Klaus saw the shuffling throng of infected approach from behind. There weren't just a handful either, but dozens, jostling and bumping each other for first access to the humans.

"They've trapped us in." Klaus sounded complimentary. "They've rounded us up like sheep."

"Fuck." It was all Callan could think to say.

Gallagher rubbed his temples. His eyes looked redder now. Callan wondered how bad he looked. "We're going to use our ammo up pretty fast at this rate."

Callan swallowed a dry throat. Their options were limited. They had enemies on both sides: the humans who had attacked them near the lab, probably Steve Palmer, and more zombies, who would chase them until the end of time. Either way, they were facing gunfire and a high potential for death. A feeling of hopelessness swept over him. Had they had come this far, fought through so much, only to end up like this? He closed his eyes and rubbed the bridge of his nose, suddenly feeling tired and weary.

"You're going to have to shoot your way through," Klaus said.

"Huh?" Callan dropped his hands.

"I'm not going to die here. I've got a serum that will stop people from turning into these things, and it might even be the basis for a vaccine, or cure. I'm not giving up on it. Get me out of here. *Now*."

Callan almost laughed, but it pressed a button, and he felt a sense of urgency. "Alright. Hold on." If he had learned one thing over the last week, it was that there was only one way to go. "We go out firing then. Straight ahead?"

"No other way," Gallagher said.

They turned the corner, Gallagher and Callan leading the way, their rifles pointed ahead. Only one human remained standing amongst a group of zombies, including one of the type threes. Several noticed their approach and broke away. Callan took aim and shot them with deadly accuracy. They crumpled to the floor.

"We got company," Gallagher shouted, firing at the zombies attacking from behind.

Callan dispatched two more as he reached the fight, leaving the type three engaged in a desperate wrestle with the remaining human. The man turned as dirty hands locked around his throat, revealing a face Callan never thought he'd see again: Steve Palmer. They crashed backward into him, the shock leaving Callan unprepared. He stumbled to the floor, striking his cheek on the cold tiles.

Gunfire sounded from behind, and the type three hit the ground beside him with half its head missing. Callan rolled, his vision swaying, but still clutching the gun. Strong hands grabbed his waist and pulled him down, and then Steve crawled over him, striking a knee into his back and knocking the breath from his lungs. The rifle clattered forward. Steve wanted the gun. Callan twisted and swung his elbow back, striking Steve in the face. The weight on him relaxed. He bucked; Steve tipped off, and Callan scrambled forward, breaking free, stretching for the rifle. His fingers found the butt, tightened around the hard plastic, and he wondered if anything had ever felt so good. He snatched the weapon around as Steve took a fistful of his hair and yanked his head backward. Pain exploded, and Callan screamed. He swung the rifle around and struck Steve in the side of the head. He grunted, then rocked back, and Callan prodded the rifle into his face. In that split second, he saw the look of a man who has gone insane: blank, soulless eyes, brimming with death. Callan pressed the trigger, but Steve shifted at the last moment, and the shot scratched past his ear, blowing the tip off in a weak spray of bloody flesh. Steve howled and smashed the gun away in a fit of rage. He straddled Callan's waist, reaching for his throat. Callan struck his left fist in a wide, looping punch, clipping Steve's jaw and knocking his head aside. He followed it with another, bone crunching under the force. It felt like the best punch he'd ever made. Steve fell forward and Callan shoved him off, but soon realized his mistake.

Callan rolled onto his knees as Steve scooped up the gun, rearranging his hands with trick speed. If he stopped, Steve would have him, so he did all he could think in the moment and leaped forward, intent on tackling Steve to the floor.

Steve's upper chest exploded. He fell back against the wall with a mask of pain etched on his face, and clunked his head on the bricks. He faltered, eyes wide and disbelieving, before collapsing to the floor. Callan staggered away, gasping for breath, Gallagher maintaining the pistol on Steve. Behind him lay a spread of dead zombies.

Callan picked up the army rifle and stood over Steve, scrutinizing him for signs of life. At first he thought Steve was dead. The darkness hid the soft rise and fall of his chest, but then he stirred, grimacing. It was a strange feeling, watching a man who had tried so hard to hurt them in such a vulnerable position. It would be a clean finish; just pull the trigger. He drew the muzzle around to Steve's head. He had it in him. He did. He'd killed for less this last week. Steve and his friends had tried time and again to hurt Callan and his group. They had let them go once before—twice, if you counted the car accident. Callan thought that had been the end of them. But he had to assume they had hunted the group down, had tracked them to the army base with the intent to extract revenge and kill them all.

Steve turned onto his side, groaning. His movement revealed a dark mark on the back of his neck. Callan crouched, and although it was gloomy, he was certain it was a bite. If Steve lived now, even if he was infected, Callan knew how irony worked. As crazy as it sounded, he would come after them, and they would suffer. He couldn't walk away from this knowing—even with a marginal chance—that Steve might return.

Callan lifted the gun, gritting his teeth. He hated this man. Hated him as much as any human could hate another. He placed his finger against the trigger, imagining himself pressing down. He recalled Steve's attempts to kill his sister back at Dylan's property; their attack on the car as they left Albury. Now this. Who knew what had happened up on the surface? His grip tightened, and he applied more pressure to the trigger. Irony. The gun barked and the bullet struck the back of Steve's head. Callan turned, looking at the others, but they were facing the other way.

"Thank you," Callan said, surprised at the pile of bodies. "How the—"

Gallagher gave a thin smile. "Lucky."

He led them to the elevator lobby, where steel doors awaited. Poking the torch around revealed a blood-streaked floor and other carnage. Metal on metal clanged somewhere far behind them.

They rode the carriage to the surface, steadying themselves on the railing. Callan felt a weight on his shoulders, and he tried not to think about what had just happened. He hoped Dylan and Greg had made it to the top, and that Kristy and the others were safe.

When the lift clunked to a halt, they all readied their weapons. The doors slid open, revealing a long, gloomy corridor leading all the way to the foyer. A short jog led them back to the entrance, where Callan let out a long, relieved breath. "I never thought we'd make this."

Gallagher agreed. "You and me both."

The foyer was a large space, with a wide front desk and several couches that had been turned over. Barricades had been placed over the windows. They lined up at the door, and Gallagher put a hand on the lever. He looked back at them, as if waiting for approval. Callan nodded.

Gallagher pulled down on the handle and swung the door open, then froze. Klaus ran into him, and Callan did the same. Ahead, hundreds of zombies had gathered in the tarred parking area outside the building entrance.

Callan's mouth hung open. Where was the van? He searched the space, confirming it was gone. The Jeep and trailer were still there though, crawling with dozens of feeders. The doors were open—one had been torn off, hanging by a thread of metal. Zombies were hanging out the windows and crawling through the interior. They stood on the roof, others the hood, the clunking sound of bending metal heard through the grumbling horde. The contents lay scattered about like discarded rubbish. Some were eating it, others were throwing it. Two other vehicles, presumably those of Steve Palmer and his crew, had suffered the same fate.

Callan didn't know where to go. Had the others left through necessity, or given up on them? The weapons they had weren't going to be nearly enough. Even if they had all the guns in the facility, there wasn't enough people to shoot them.

Klaus shook his head. "Remarkable. Was this the number you saw further back in town?" Callan nodded. "It's exactly as we suspected. They work together in a large formation and just wipe things out."

"They're all type ones," Callan said.

"It doesn't matter. Today or tomorrow, next week, or next month, the more aggressive type will find them." Callan slipped past and out into the light.

"What are you doing?" Klaus asked.

"We can't stand here all day."

"What are you going to do?" Gallagher asked.

Callan considered this, as though he hadn't thought much about it. "We shoot a path between them."

The others followed, letting the door close. Callan glanced back, wondering again about Dylan and Greg. Either they had escaped with the girls, or were still inside the building.

The closest zombie noticed Callan and shuffled over. Teeth gritted, he shot it in the face, the crack of the F88

Austyr rifle rolling across the blue sky. It crumpled into a heap. *That was it then*, Callan thought. *We're on. Again.*

Muffled shouts sounded from inside the building. The door clattered open, and Callan drew his gun around, ready to shoot dead whatever had escaped from the facility.

SIXTY-NINE

BREATHE. DYLAN TRIED NOT to think about the repercussions of what had just occurred, but it was impossible. He pulled his collar high around his neck as they ran. *You're bitten. Bitten.* His neck throbbed where the zombie had tasted his flesh, and the realization washed over him that within twenty-four hours, he might be dead. Although the scientist had developed the serum, he'd mentioned the limited supply, and two of them were ahead in the queue.

Dylan kept slowing for Greg, who, despite his earlier efforts, had been overcome by a heavy cough and a gasping wheeze. The image of Greg holding onto the door kept resurfacing in Dylan's mind. Had he planned to leave Dylan behind? Part of him wanted to ask the big guy what he'd been thinking. Although he had come back for him, Dylan couldn't help wondering whether Greg's hesitation had allowed time for the bite, and might ultimately cost him his life. It was too much to think about under current circumstances.

Behind them, they could hear the clunk and clatter of the type three chasing. Without ammunition, they couldn't fight. They had to run. Run toward the surface, where Kristy was still alive. At least, that's what Dylan told himself. He couldn't keep going on any other thought. He had to find out.

But they were close. They ran the last few corridors, taking turns following signs labelled EXIT. It was brighter near the surface, aided by more emergency lights. In the foyer, dark shadows beckoned beyond the murky shape of a reception desk and overturned couches. They heard the distant echo of a crash from behind one of the other doors leading to a different section of the base.

Greg pushed the door open and light flooded in, forcing their eyes to slits. They jumped through the door, daylight their savior.

Two guns pointed their way.

"Jesus Christ," Callan said. "You're lucky you didn't get a fucking bullet."

Dylan's heart skipped. Beyond Callan and the others stood a sea of zombies. *Kristy.* He stumbled forward, searching the mass. "Where are they?"

"They've gone."

"Gone?" He searched the bodies on the ground, hoping she wouldn't be one of them. "Where?"

Callan took him by the shoulders and dragged him back closer to the building. "Hey?" Dylan blinked. "They've driven off, mate. They probably had no choice."

Dylan looked past Callan. The horde was fifteen yards away, a thriving, squirming throng whose numbers were too high to count. They had trashed the Jeep and continued their attempts to extract pieces of it from both inside and out. It made sense that if the van had stuck around, a similar result would have ensued. "Yeah. Right. Okay. What now then?"

"We fight." Callan handed a heavy black pistol to Dylan. "There are thirteen rounds in it." He passed Dylan a second magazine. "Plus this. That should keep you going. We make a path though these fuckers, then run, okay?"

Gallagher handed Greg his pistol, and they all spread apart in a wide line, except for Klaus, who stood at the rear looking like a terrified school kid lost amongst a yard fight. The cooler bag hung over his shoulder on a strap, and he had one arm curled protectively around it.

The guns cracked and zombies at the fringes of the group slumped to the ground, streamers of blood and brains covering the remaining. Some were distracted by the fallen; others continued their march toward the attackers. Dylan missed his first shot, wishing he had his trusty bolt-action, but the second took off the head of a council worker in brown, blood-soaked overalls. The guns continued singing their thunderous tunes, and a thin dent in the crowd had formed, but to see Kristy again, they would need to down many more. Wherever they made a kill, others stumbled into place, preventing sizeable progress.

The door behind them clattered open. Dylan turned to find the type three that had chased them, honing in on him with the glare of the devil. Time froze. He saw every detail of its head: the rotting skin of its balding forehead, the wispy tendrils of hair, and its slatted, burning eyes. It was the eyes that scared Dylan the most. They contained an anger he couldn't conceive, a license for death and destruction of which he wanted no part. His arm stretched out and he fired, envisioning the bullet's trajectory with deadly precision.

The zombie's right eye exploded in a puff of blood, and it fell onto the road with a clap and a random spray of blood. Dylan dropped the cartridge from the pistol. One round left. He slammed the magazine back in and fished the spare out of his pocket. No bullet would he waste.

"Dylan—"

Another zombie appeared in the doorway; a bony Asian with blazing red eyes contrasting black hair. Dylan drew the pistol around and fired, hitting it in the throat. It toppled backward through the entrance and into the shadows. Dylan flushed with pride at his improvement with the pistol. He dropped the empty cartridge to the ground and jammed in the fresh one.

Dead zombies lay scattered about, but hundreds remained, feeding on the dead, fighting amongst themselves, and driving them closer to the building. Dylan fired, aiming for their heads, and left a trail ten deep into the throng, yet he had run dry of bullets again. The others joined at the edge of the building. Their objective to make a path had failed.

"We have to go back inside, get some more ammo," Gallagher said. "I'm empty."

"Me too."

Movement flashed in the doorway. Blocking the entrance was a type three dressed in combat fatigues. The approaching horde stopped.

"Oh, shit," Callan said.

Eyes blazing, it started for them.

SEVENTY

EVELYN WATCHED THE SCENE outside the base from the driver's seat of the camper van. Beside her as the front passenger, Kristy sat, biting her nails. Last week, she might have berated Kristy for such a bad habit. Such things no longer mattered. With a pair of binoculars Eric had kept in one of the compartments above the kitchen sink, they had watched the boys reach the entrance of the building and face off against the edges of the horde. But now, the zombies had driven them back toward the building, leaving them nowhere to go. Kristy had said it all. "The girls have the chance to save the day."

Evelyn flexed her hands around the steering wheel. She was ready. She could do it. She wasn't driving them all to their death.

"You're not driving us to our death," Kristy said as if reading her mind. Evelyn nodded. "We have a choice whether we do this or not. You have a choice whether you drive this van or not." Kristy had a loaded rifle lying across her lap, and another on the floor.

"We can do it."

"We will do it."

"I wish I was as strong as you."

"You are. You're incredibly strong. You just don't know it. Besides, if you'd seen me three days ago, you would have laughed."

Evelyn didn't think she *could* laugh. Her guts had liquefied. She wanted to take Jake under her arm and run the other way. What if they overturned the van? What if she crashed? It was madness. Crazy. She'd gone bat shit. But their friends, which she now felt comfortable calling them, needed help.

"Don't think about what might happen," Kristy said.

"Are you reading my mind?"

"We're thinking the same things. It's logical. I know the idea of doing it is insane, but I'm not leaving any of them behind. Sometimes, we just have to be brave and bold, but I know you know that."

Evelyn turned back to the others. "Stay down, Jake. Hold on tight." Julie sat at the table, her head buried in her arms, Sarah beside her, offering comfort. Evelyn turned to Kristy again. "I don't know if I can. Is it really going to help? I mean, look at it. What hope have they got?"

"Please. We need your help to do this. Without you driving, they will all die."

Evelyn took a couple of deep, sharp breaths. "Okay. Let's do it."

"Go fast," Kristy said. "Don't slow down. Just run them over. If they're inside, beep the horn as we approach the building, and park as close to the entrance as possible." Evelyn nodded. "You can do this. You're strong and capable."

She punched the van into gear and rolled it away. "Hold on, everyone." Her bowels and bladder felt strange, as though she might lose control at any moment.

The van moved down the slope and reached the fringes of the horde, losing sight of the army building through the density of bodies. Only a handful of zombies noticed their approach though.

"Floor it," Kristy said.

Evelyn pressed her foot down and the engine revved, throwing her back into the seat.

The first zombie in line peered at them with an impassive expression. The fender struck it with a clunk, and it disappeared under the van. A louder clunk sounded from beneath, followed by drumming noises, as others struck the sides and disappeared. The van kicked and jumped, and Kristy held tight to the handhold above the passenger window. Some of the zombies slow-stepped aside, but Evelyn adjusted her line trying to mow more down. In the back, Sarah screamed, and when she glanced around, Jake had covered his ears.

But the zombies weren't the only problem. The gate was closed, a wide, chain-link thing constructed from thick bars, glaring back at them with an impenetrable air.

"Smash through it," Kristy said. "Just ram it right through the middle." Evelyn's eyes widened, her mouth formed an "O". "You got any better ideas?"

"HOLD ON," Evelyn screamed. She glanced back and saw Jake still sitting with his hands clamped over his ears. "YOU FUCKING HOLD ONTO SOMETHING, JAKE ALEXANDER!" Sarah grabbed hold of him, slid off the top bunk, and pulled him into the bench seating around the table. Julie threw an arm around them both and clung onto the wooden top. Jake's face twisted with terror, and he began to cry.

Evelyn pressed the accelerator to the floor. More zombies clunked against the front of the van, spinning away like pins in a bowling alley, but they were peripheral now, her focus on the metal barrier impeding their way. She held her breath as they closed in.

The sound when the van struck the center of the gate was thunderous. Evelyn was thrown forward, then wrenched back and tossed forward again. For a moment, she thought they weren't going to make it, but then a loud pop sounded and the two adjoining posts caved in, dragging the gates out of their fitting. Wire twisted around the front of the van, sending sparks up in a clash of metal. Evelyn kept her foot on the gas, mowing down zombies as the attached fence swept them aside.

She glanced back, expecting to find the others strewn about the van, but they were sitting upright at the table, seemingly well, although holding on with grim death.

They were in the thick of the horde now. Most of the zombies had passed through the slit in the fence, into the zone just outside the building.

"Left," Kristy shouted. Evelyn turned the wheel and saw a gap in the crowd. The van thundered off the road and through the dirt, away from the building. There were fewer feeders here, and Evelyn guided the van around the edges. "Go right." Kristy pointed. "There."

"That close? We'll get swamped!"

"Go," Kristy shouted. "Over there, right up close."

Evelyn yanked on the wheel and the van rolled hard to one side, bringing the army building into view. She took them closer, to where the conflict was heavier, and eased the van to a stop. It appeared the men were out of ammunition, as several of them were using rifles as baseball bats. She found Callan standing before a mean zombie near the doorway. Kristy slid the passenger window open and took aim. The rifle noise was deafening inside the camper van.

Zombies crowded the front end, milling around Evelyn's window. She had left it open, and one of them stuck a hand through, groping for her flesh. Sarah screamed. Evelyn reached down for the Winchester rifle as the zombie tried to climb through. She scooped it up and jabbed the barrel into its face. It crashed back and knocked another sprawling.

Kristy fired again, and then the side door crashed open, smashing into the bench. Evelyn was about to scream for somebody to shut it when she saw the blood-red eyes of the scariest zombie she could ever imagine standing in the doorway.

SEVENTY-ONE

CALLAN WAS CERTAIN THEY wouldn't survive this time. The blazing-eyed zombie started for them, fists clenched at its side. Where had he seen that before?

The men all backpedalled toward the mob, nobody keen to engage the type three without proper ammunition. Callan stood closest, and the thing had locked onto his presence, sizing him up with a menacing glare. He could see its mind working and without taking his eyes off it, Callan turned the rifle around to use as his now familiar baseball bat. To his surprise though, it walked to the side and around the group before disappearing into the crowd.

Callan shuddered. "Keep an eye on it," certain it hadn't finished with them.

But the crowd was upon them again. Greg and Gallagher swung their weapons, drawing blood in sprays. Chasing the type three's position, Callan felt the crunch of several bodies and went sprawling onto the bitumen. He pushed onto his hands and found an obese, grey-haired man holding a zombie arm leering over him. It lifted the weapon and swung hard at Callan's head.

He threw up an arm and turned away. The weapon crashed against his elbow, splattering blood and gore, and then the zombie fell forward onto him. He tried to shove the old man off, but its dead, heavy weight made it impossible. He twisted himself, but his arm got caught underneath its monstrous gut. He was going to die. He saw it as plainly as a person sees an impending car accident they cannot stop. The thing leaned into him, took hold of his arm, and pressed its face close to his.

The ground vibrated, followed by a number of thudding noises.

They lay locked in a grapple, neither combatant winning. Dylan thought his face would explode. He was able to see up close its flaking, degenerated skin, the yellowing, bloodshot eyes, and a cracked and swollen tongue streaked with flesh. He wanted to vomit. Screeching, he drove the zombie backward, pushing its head as far as his arms would reach.

Gunfire sounded; the flat crack of a rifle, and the wet sound of ripping flesh. Part of the feeder's head disappeared, and then Callan's arm was free. He pushed harder, and the big zombie shifted, but it was the heaviest weight Callan had felt. He slid his legs out and then it was off, and he couldn't believe he was still alive.

Climbing to his feet, Callan saw the van first, then Kristy poking a rifle out the passenger-side window. She shot two more zombies nearby, and Callan felt a swell of gratitude and pride. They had a chance now; slim, but existent. Moments ago, he had almost given up, had been close to accepting they wouldn't make it off the base.

Bodies lay around him like a vision from a war. Before he could locate his gun, hands scratched at his neck and clamped around his throat. He stepped aside, swinging his elbows, driving his body forward. A woman with grey skin bumped his shoulder, knocking him off balance. He tried to duck and step back, but tripped on the foot of the obese man Kristy had shot.

Callan fell onto his ass, pain shooting up his spine. Both zombies dove for him, but he scuttled backward on his palms like a crab, kicking his leather boots at their heads. One of them, just a kid in a previous life, scrambled for his leg, revealing teeth that would tear Callan apart. He stopped and jabbed a fist into its face, rocking its head backward.

There was more gunfire. The side of Kid Zombie's head exploded, and he toppled over. On hands and knees, the woman rushed at Callan, scrabbling for a piece of him. She kneed him in the testicles and crawled up over his chest like a big spider, the stench of her breath causing him to gag. She locked her hand around his neck, and he beat at it with weakened fists, wondering if this might be the end.

A savage, high-pitched bark sounded from a distance, followed by growling that drew closer rapidly. *Blue Boy*. The dog barked again and leaped up onto the zombie's back with a thump. The feeder squirmed, but the dog held on and bit down onto its flank, blood squirting over its furry face.

"No, Blue!"

Callan shoved the zombie away and scampered clear. The thing collapsed, smacking its face on the bitumen. Callan's breath came in gasps; his muscles felt like cement bags. He reached down for Blue Boy, but the dog scurried away to attack others. He felt a stab of terror; the dog had bitten into the zombie, drawing blood.

A clear space had opened around Callan. Zombies were attacking the van, pushing and pulling on the mirrors and window trims; anything onto which they could hook their dirty, rotten fingers. They climbed up the sides, crawled underneath, and pulled on the door handle.

Kristy had disappeared from her window. Gallagher and Klaus were nearby, Klaus still holding the cooler bag, while Greg and Dylan had separately fought their way closer to the vehicle. Callan scooped up a rifle from the road and swung it around. He backed up to Gallagher and struck feeders across the skull, knocking them aside to make a path. *Blue Boy.* He had to find his dog. He scanned the battle, looking for the familiar flash of blue and white.

The zombies near the van moved aside, shuffling and pushing each other clear of some unseen entity. The type three stepped out from between the bodies and blocked their passage to escape. Callan felt his gut swirl.

The side door of the camper crashed open. Kristy stood in the doorway holding a Winchester rifle, her eyes burning with anger. The zombie turned to her.

"No, Kristy!"

She leaped out onto the road and sighted the feeder. Callan ran.

"KRISTY!"

He saw it happen in his mind's eye; saw the gun whisper a soft click having run dry of bullets as the zombie closed in.

It would tear her throat out, and he would never look into those sparkling blue eyes again.

The zombie shoved two feeders aside and sprinted at Kristy. Another bumbler, in its haste to avoid the wrath, fell into its path. The type three paused to break its neck and threw it aside like a dirty rag. Callan held his breath. She was on her own. It drew within three feet, closing fast, when Kristy casually raised the rifle. It cracked like nearby thunder, and the rear of the zombie's head blew backward over the bitumen. It sank to the road, the remains of its skull clunking dully on the blacktop.

Callan reached his sister, feeling an overwhelming relief, his throat choked with emotion. He squashed her to his chest just to make sure she was real.

She gave a pained smile, guiding him away. "I'm okay. But let's get inside."

"No," Callan said. "I have to find Blue."

Klaus and Gallagher bumped past him and went into the van, followed by Dylan and Greg, both covered in an obscene amount of blood. Kristy stepped in, holding the door for him.

Callan stuck thumb and forefinger into his mouth and blew hard, producing a shrill whistle. The sounds of a bark floated up through the mob. Callan stepped up into the van and held the door. He peered out at the scene: a sea of blood, limbs torn from bodies, zombies staggering around eating and fighting, drinking and killing. Then a flash of blue appeared beneath, limping its way through the mayhem. Callan couldn't breathe. *He's bitten.* Hands groped, and bodies fell, desperate for their final prize. And then he was through, barking when he saw Callan. He flew up the step and into the van. Callan pulled the door shut, shouting for Evelyn to get them out of there.

SEVENTY-TWO

SCREAMING. YELLING. BARKING, ALONG with the clamorous sound of zombies beating against the sides of the camper van. Blue Boy lay shaking on the floor behind the front seats. Callan pointed one of the gunmen's discarded pistols at Klaus. Dylan and the others peered out the windows as the van rolled slowly up the hill and away from the massacre. Zombies staggered along the grassy edges toward the army base the group had just left behind. Evelyn held the wheel tight, glancing at the rearview mirror. Dylan held his breath, the details of the bite on his neck like a bad dream.

"Do it. Now," Callan said.

"There's only enough for one more—"

"I don't give a fuck." The gun waved about. "You either inject that dog with the serum, or I'll shoot you and get my sister to do it."

Blue was bitten, a large crimson wound on his back flank. Callan was on the edge, almost crazed. Dylan understood that. He could read the pain on Callan's face; see in his actions that he loved the dog already. They had all developed a soft spot for it. Could Dylan take its chance away by telling them *he* was bitten? Would they seek to make more of the serum for the dog? They would for him. He knew the scientist had plans to produce more. If he told Callan *he* was infected, what would happen?

But he couldn't do it. Not now. The dog looked up at Dylan with sad eyes. *Do you know what's happened, Blue?* It was difficult to watch. Dylan turned away. He would tell them later. He would calm down; Callan would calm down, and they would discuss it rationally. Dylan knew he should say something, but he couldn't form the words. What if Callan chose the dog?

"You don't understand," Klaus said.

"No, *you* don't understand. If it wasn't for that dog, I wouldn't be here, and if I'm not here, neither are you." Klaus looked back, his face full of pleading. "I am not going to let that dog die."

Klaus put up his hands, as if conceding. "Alright. I'll do it. But you need to understand that the dog might react badly to the serum. That's out of my control."

"So be it. But he's not going to turn into one of them."

"It may not even work. Hell, he may not even be infected. He might have broken the skin and drawn blood, but it doesn't mean he's infected."

Klaus swung the bag off his shoulder and opened the container. Dylan's heartbeat increased. He still had a chance. Part of him wanted to tell them, but he'd never be able to look at Blue Boy again, and when the dog died, Dylan wouldn't be able to live with himself. Callan would resent him forever.

Klaus loaded a syringe, tapped the plastic case, and gave a gentle squirt. "Are you *sure*? How many animals have you found ill? It's plausible they don't even get this virus. We could wait and see if the dog shows any signs of infection—"

"No. Do it. Please."

Dylan's palms were sweating. *This is what desperate people feel like,* he thought. What would Kristy say? It wasn't what she'd say aloud, but she'd treat him differently. It wouldn't be the same between them, and after the previous night, he wasn't prepared to concede that yet. She wouldn't go near him once she found out.

Besides, maybe the scientist was just being pessimistic. Surely they'd be able to acquire more of the serum? Once he told them, it would be their priority.

Callan cuddled the dog, talking in soft tones. Klaus parted his fur, found an appropriate place, and injected the drug. Blue Boy's ears pinned back.

Klaus stood. "Whatever happens to him is on you."

"I know."

Klaus closed the cold pack and went to the kitchen table.

Dylan turned away, the small consolation for the dog lost in a sea of worry about his future.

SEVENTY-THREE

KRISTY FELL INTO THE passenger seat beside Evelyn. Tears welled in the other woman's eyes as she guided the van along the winding road back toward town. Kristy reached across and put a hand on her shoulder. "Thank you." Evelyn nodded, wiping wet cheeks with the back of her arm. They had made it, or at least, most of them. Eric's death was a huge loss, perhaps the sacrifice for Dylan, Callan, and Greg's survival. She would take it, although she knew how it sounded; harsh, and uncaring. Julie lay sobbing on the back bed. The thought of Julie's heartache caused a lump in Kristy's throat she had to fight to keep down.

Callan still held Blue Boy. It was as though the dog had expended all its energy and needed rest. "Thanks for coming back. I wouldn't have blamed you if you hadn't." Kristy returned a thin, sad smile. He dropped his head and whispered, "I can't believe Eric's gone. He was … a great bloke … I'll miss him."

"It happened so quickly. We were inside, and he went out–I told him not to go, but he wouldn't stop–he was courageous, or stupid. But if he hadn't done that, it might have turned out different for all of us."

Callan put his face in his hands and rubbed his eyes. Streaks of blood covered his fingers, and there were spots on his face. "Poor bugger. At least he had a chance to change something."

"What do you mean?"

"Nothing. Just conversation we had." He stood, knees popping. "Ah, shit, it never gets any easier, does it?" He drew the container of water closer to the dog, who gulped it down, washing the splashes of blood from its mouth.

"We were lucky not to lose more," Kristy said. "Lucky more of us didn't end up like Blue."

"Klaus took a hit." Callan paused, seeming to consider. "He's bitten. The other guy, Gallagher, too."

349

Kristy's stomach dropped. "What?"

Callan held up a hand. "Gallagher wasn't bullshitting. The stuff Klaus pumped into Blue Boy is supposed to fight the development of the virus. Doesn't cure it, but stops it getting any worse. He's using it on both of them now."

"Wow." Kristy couldn't help but feel skeptical. "That's incredible. Are you sure though?"

"I saw Blue bite into that feeder. If they don't turn into zombies in the next day or so, we know it works."

The base, and the congregation of the dead, had become a speck in the side mirror. The road flattened out, skirted by paddocks of knee-high yellow grass and flaccid wire fences.

"Where are we going?" Evelyn asked.

Callan rubbed his eyes and turned to face the others. "It's a group decision. I think we should still try Sydney, but … I'm open to discussion."

Kristy waited for Dylan to speak up. He'd been arguing to go south for days. His sister was there, and his father had considered Tasmania their best option, but he sat at the table staring out the side window, impassive, almost apathetic. *Strange,* Kristy thought. Perhaps he was exhausted from the army base. Upon his safe return, they had only briefly spoken, until Callan had taken the scientist hostage.

Finally, Klaus said, "Melbourne." He shifted in his seat, turning to face them. Ahead, the road turned in a sweeping arc, with more dry fields on both sides and several cows hunkering down under the shade of a gum tree. No zombies. "You go on up toward Sydney, but don't expect to come back."

Callan shot back. "Why?"

Klaus grimaced. "Sydney has four million people. Let's say twenty percent of them have turned into zombies. We'll be driving into eight hundred thousand dead people searching for food. These things move in waves. Just take a moment to imagine the kind of wave that might come from that many dead."

"We tried to go to Sydney," Greg said. Callan made a face. "It didn't work."

Klaus continued. "I need to get to Melbourne. The Commonwealth Serum Laboratories are down there. CSL made all the vaccines for influenza. They do all sorts of serums."

"Could they have a vaccine?" Callan asked.

"It's doubtful, but they will have the laboratories and equipment I need to keep developing my formula. I only have a small amount at the moment. And with the two of us–three—bitten, it won't last long."

Callan considered it for a long moment. "I guess it's Melbourne, then."

Kristy put a hand on Callan's shoulder as she passed, and sat beside Dylan. He looked deep in thought, probably still thinking about his father. She reached out and touched his arm. He gave a pained smile. Sending the boys into the army base had been a huge risk. What had happened down there?

She placed her hand over his. It was cold. "You okay?" He opened his mouth to say something, but closed it. Kristy sat forward. "What? What is it?"

"I'm just tired. Beaten." He put an arm around her. "So many times today I thought I was dead. I shouldn't have survived."

She squeezed him back. "I'm glad you did."

Dylan was safe; Callan too, but it felt empty without Eric. They hung their heads and rubbed their tired faces. It had been another long and difficult twenty-four hours. Kristy tried to recall the last full day they hadn't suffered a casualty. Would they ever have a twenty-four hour period where they didn't have to run or fight for their lives? Survival. That was their objective now. Ten of them had survived. Three were bitten, but with the help of the scientist's serum, they might be able to—what? Hold off the virus? Until when? It was only a matter of time for all of them.

They had a little food and water, but no ammunition or clothes. Luckily, Sarah had all her medicines. It was almost a case of déjà vu. They were leaving another town, beaten to the edge of their existence, low on supplies, and tired to their bones.

This is our life now, she thought. *Survival.* At least she still had Dylan, Callan, and the others. She pulled her medical kit out from behind the seat, wondering what would happen if she died. There would be nobody to take care of them.

"Sarah," she said. 'Come and help me."

Having another person trained in basic first aid might one day save a life. Might even save hers, if it ever came to that.

THE END

AUTHOR'S NOTE

Thank you for making it to the end of Book Two. I hope you enjoyed it as much as Book One, although in truth, I hope you liked it a little better. This book was more difficult to write than the first. I still don't know why; sometimes when writing you get into a rhythm and the words pile up, but this time it seemed my rhythm kept breaking, and I couldn't get going until well into the process. I should probably apologize to my wife and children during this period for being a bit grumpy!

The reviews I received for Book One were amazing. I loved reading them all, good and bad, and would be so grateful if you were able to leave one for Book Two (or Book One if you haven't yet), on Amazon. Reviews help readers make decisions about buying books, and often are the only proof that people are reading them, especially for indie authors like me.

I'm currently working on the third book, although I won't be making any silly predictions about the timing of this one. I will say that Melbourne awaits, and so too some new characters, as well as reconnecting with old ones.

In some forums, I have detailed that there are nine books planned in this series, and that after Book Three I will be switching to a different location to follow several groups of survivors for the following three books. This is still the plan, and by the time we reach Book Seven there will be a multitude of survivors from both groups to cheer for that will converge into the one location. I know this is not standard and some people might hate leaving this group after Book Three (for a little while), but I assure you, those we will join in another location will be compelling, and the final three books will be all the more engrossing.

If you want to get an automatic e-mail when the third book is released, or receive the occasional exclusive short story, or giveaways relating to the series, **http://eepurl.com/FU2cH.** Your e-mail address will never be shared and you can unsubscribe easily at any time.

Also, feel free to friend me on Facebook, like the Invasion of the Dead page on Facebook, or follow me on Twitter.

Again, I'd love to hear what you thought about the story, good or bad. You can e-mail me at **owen.baillie@bigpond.com**. I received lots of feedback via e-mail on Book One and had a fabulous time reading and corresponding with people. Seeing a new e-mail in my inbox from a reader is always fantastic. Thank you to those who took the time.

Thanks for reading,

Owen
Melbourne, Australia, July 2014.

Printed in Great Britain
by Amazon